What others are saying…

"In Heart of a Bowman, Jil Koller takes readers into a fantastical, multi-tiered world of flying ships, pirates, love, honor, betrayal, and stones of truth. Settle in with a blanket and hot drink because once you find yourself deep in the realms of the Vertical Horizon, you won't want to leave. Not until the last secret is revealed and the outcome of every battle—of wits or of bows and arrows—has been determined."
>—*Sara Davison*, Award-winning author of
>*Lost Down Dee* and *Driven*

"Jil Koller hits a perfect bull's-eye in this stunning fantasy debut featuring a pair of archers who alone can save their kingdom; a sweet, slow-burn romance; a fascinating, original, and beautifully imagined world; a colorful cast of characters (including pirates!); and vegetarian dragons. Heart of a Bowman captured my heart from start to finish, and I'm so excited to find out what happens next!"
>—*J. J. Fischer*, award-winning author of *The Nightingale Trilogy*,
>*The Soul Mark Duology*, and the *Painted Wind Series*

"Romantic tension and a fantasy world of lighter-than-air craft, invading armies, and elite bowmen highlight Koller's debut. Readers of both genres will enjoy this extraordinary world and blend of unique characters. Great start to a new intriguing trilogy!"
>—*Bradley Caffee*, author of *The Chase Runner Series*, *Captive*, and
>*The Keeper Series*

"Jil Koller delivers a piercingly perfect fantasy in her debut novel *Heart of a Bowman*. Relatable characters are combined with fantastic worldbuilding to take readers on an adventure grounded in eternal truths. From sailing ships to airships, traversing the towering Teirdoms of the vertical realms captured my imagination. A very satisfying read, indeed!"
>—*Heather L.L. FitzGerald*, Author of the award-winning series
>*The Tethered World Chronicles*

"Heart of a Bowman is an amazing adventure story set in a truly unique fantasy world. Cunning pirates, magnificent airships, dangerous dragons—Jil Koller takes you on a wildly imaginative ride where the action doesn't stop!"

—*Amy C. Williams*, Author and coach

Vertical Horizon: Heart of a Bowman

Vertical Horizon: Heart of a Bowman

By

Jil Koller

Dedication

To Linc, Chip, Pips, and Tay.
The code is for you. Never give up.
In all things, trust the truth.

.The Spire.

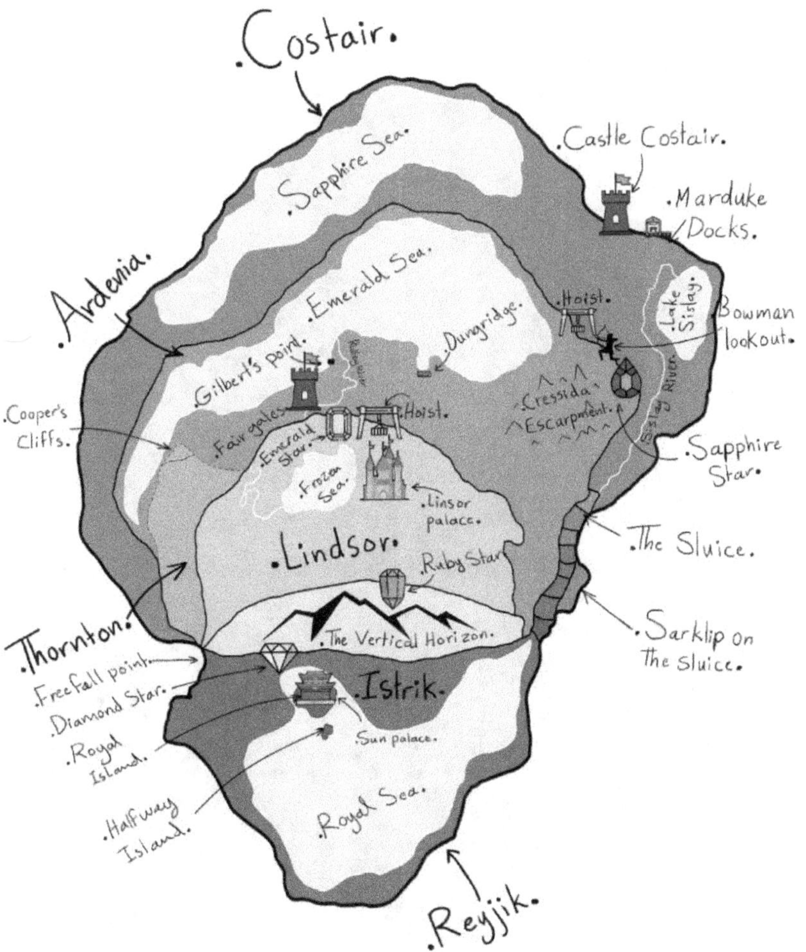

.Costair.
.Castle Costair.
.Marduke Docks.
.Sapphire Sea.
Ardevia.
.Emerald Sea.
.Lake Sislay.
.Hoist.
Bowman lookout.
.Dungridge.
.Gilbert's point.
.Cooper's Cliffs.
.Cressida Escarpment.
.Fair gale.
.Hoist.
.Emerald Star.
.Frozen Sea.
.Sapphire Star.
.Linsor palace.
.Lindsor.
.The Sluice.
.Ruby Star.
.Sarklip on the Sluice.
.Thornton.
.The Vertical Horizon.
.Freefall point.
.Diamond Star.
.Istrik.
.Royal Island.
.Sun palace.
.Halfway Island.
.Royal Sea.
.Reyjik.

Author's Note

This story began when a few simple sparks of wonder caught fire in my heart. I was inspired by the codes of chivalry of old, and the honorable knights that upheld them despite the cost. I am humbled by individuals who persevere under great trial, no matter the cost. I also wondered what would happen if two exceptionally independent people faced an utterly hopeless situation that demanded they work together. What if they were matched in strength of character and fortitude? What if they were equally dedicated to their moral code, faithful to their duty, but their duties were completely at odds? What if I threw in a pirate, opposite in every way yet compelled by his own code and sense of honor?

I wrote Colt, Tess, and Deacon's story first and then envisioned the vertical world in which they lived. A place where commodities were hoisted, not shipped. A world where elevation dictated climate and four different biomes—arctic, temperate, tropical, and desert—relied on each other for survival. Where pirates could fly, exploiting vulnerabilities in a vertically integrated world. A place where four magical truth stones must work together to restrain evil and maintain peace. What if one were stolen?

I conducted a great deal of research to complete the story with accuracy. I bought and trained with a longbow, so I would understand the weight, feel, and strength required to fire it. I studied naval terminology, medieval weaponry, and rock climbing. I went for many long walks with my brilliant son, a military history enthusiast, who would talk through countless strategies and scenarios, and I loved every moment.

But why, why all the late nights, typing cross-legged on my couch? Why the huge sacrifice of time and thought? Why all the work, and rewrites, and revisions? It's so simple, really. I love young people, and I love Jesus. I wanted to write a story in which self-sacrifice was the only answer. Where truth and valor were honored. So much of the messaging kids receive today centers around ensuring they get what they want, no matter the consequences or how it affects others. Colt's and Tess's choices fly in the face of that self-centered line of thought— they follow a code that places others first and themselves last. What could be achieved if that were the case? What would happen to a ship full of selfish pirates swept up in the cause? More than anything else, I wanted to give my kids a story that echoed the gospel and championed self-sacrifice.

Thank you so much for sharing Colt, Tess, and Deacon's journey with me. Thanks for sailing on *The Girl* and staving off war. If you enjoy *Heart of a Bowman*, please leave a review on Goodreads and Amazon—it makes all the difference. Their story is far from over. It gets much worse before there's a chance it can get better. Please watch for *Heart of a Spy,* and *Heart of a Warrior,* releasing in the months to come.

For updates, sneak peeks, and the inside scoop, visit my website, jilkoller.com, and subscribe to my newsletter. You can also follow me on Instagram @jil.koller or find me on Facebook, Tik Tok, or YouTube.

From the bottom of my heart, thank you for reading my story. You've made my dream come true. Blessings, Jil ☺

Chapter One

The Tarragon

Colt

EVERYTHING IS OFF! GERHERT PLANNED TO remove the guard, let the royal court, the delegation, his king go unprotected? For what? Ambiance? It was lunacy, complete madness. Even Colt's hair felt wrong, loose of the Bowman-issue leather thong that usually kept it tightly tied. A day off? Blast Gerhert. Colt hadn't allowed himself the luxury of an entire day off in… he couldn't remember a time. Certainly not since descending to his post in the seaward tier. Even before the Bowman Corps, before the regulars, even as a child there were the thorn fields. He pulled at his sleeve, but it didn't help.

This is ridiculous, I'm going back to the castle to review the sluice roster. Colt adjusted the rapier in his scabbard and stepped clear of the market stall

A young woman strode into his path, and he pulled up short to avoid crashing into her. What was she staring at? Something in the Ardenian merchant's booth had transfixed her.

Colt melded into the shadows behind the bamber post. She obviously hadn't noticed him, but he couldn't seem to look away.

The woman, little more than a girl, was dressed in common clothes, but there was nothing common about her. Her d'orite hair was braided to one side, like intricate hammered filigree that flowed into waves rippling down her back. She stood tall, almost regal, and, while he studied her profile, a lump formed in his throat. Whoever she was, the girl was absolutely beautiful. Her bright eyes locked on something hanging on the back wall of the cluttered shack.

He followed her gaze. Thin beams of light filtered through the sparse thatch, refracting off an emerald hanging on a small wooden peg.

Leaning her hips against the counter, the young woman rose to her toes and reached a slender arm to the dangling stone.

Instinctively, he stepped forward and retrieved the small green jewel strung on a thick d'orite chain.

The girl jerked back her hand and shifted to face him.

Colt stood mesmerized by the wide eyes that met his, emeralds themselves. After a few seconds, she broke from his stare to examine the supposed *truth stone* swaying between them. Her eyes narrowed, and a mischievous grin crossed her lips.

Say something, Hawthorne, quick, and make it something intelligent! "I'm certain it's a fake. The emerald's no more a genuine Ardenian truth stone than the d'orite is mined here in Costair, but if my lady wants to see for herself?" He bowed dramatically and offered her the necklace.

Crossing her arms, her gaze passed over the stone and fixated again on the back wall of the shop. "I was reaching for the leather strap, not the trinket."

Snapping his head back to the wooden peg, he noticed the worn leather strap. Heat crept up his neck. The lump in his throat swelled and he reached out again, this time being careful of how his sleeve pulled away from his wrist. Would she notice what lay beneath? He snatched the leather strap and was about to place it in her waiting hand when he recognized the large, embossed leather oval secured with bladespar rivets at the midpoint between the bladespar fastener at either end. Turning the oval over he read the deeply embossed cursive script:

Serve king and tier with all thy strength.

Show compassion and mercy with all thy heart.

Protect the weak and help the helpless.

Do everything with courage, honesty, and selflessness.

In all things trust the truth.

His breathing shallowed. The Bowman Code. He held an original Bowman quiver strap issued to the inaugural Bowman Corps, one of only twenty such straps in existence. He'd only ever heard of them, never seen, let alone touched one.

"May I?" Her slender fingers gently grasped the dry deerskin.

Colt barely resisted the urge to hold fast. His stomach twisted when she took it from him. "It's Bowman."

"I know." She didn't bother to look up while she dismissed him, only passed her index finger over the worn words of the code, a softness sweeping over her face.

Colt's chest tightened. "It's a quiver strap."

The girl rubbed the bladespar buckles between her thumb and fore finger. "I know."

He couldn't take any more. He had always longed for an original code strap. Why hadn't he noticed it first? It was rightfully hers to purchase. He couldn't, wouldn't deny that, but he just had to know. "How much?" His voice cracked when he addressed the stall owner, and a wave of heat crashed over his chest and face.

Her eyes darted to his, and she stepped back a pace, clutching the strap to her chest.

The stall-keeper rose from the crate where he'd been sitting, watching them. "Thirty spar."

Colt nearly choked. Thirty spar? Seriously?

The girl didn't even bat one of her long, thick lashes. She produced a small, jeweled coin purse and quickly retrieved six shiny five-spar coins, then placed them on the man's outstretched palm.

His thick fingers flipped and then fisted them in one quick motion. A wide smile cracked a thousand deep wrinkles on his broad face. No doubt he'd just earned his entire day's wage, and it wasn't even past-peak.

Colt's hand darted to the back of his neck, and he pressed hard on the long, raised scar. He stole a glance at the girl, but she was examining her treasure again. *You can't afford even a quarter of the price she paid, Hawthorne. Let it go!*

A thundering crash sounded, followed by a piercing screech. They both whirled around.

Leaping into the narrow street, he searched for the source. A second screech, desperate and pained. Screams from villagers. People ran from the stall at the end of market-street. The thatched roof and its support posts lay broken on the granite cobblestone. Colt strode forward three steps. He halted. There, thrashing frantically beneath the debris, flapped the slick-skinned wing of a tarragon. *No!*

Three villagers ran past him.

A man crashed into his chest.

He peered over the man's shoulder at the sight of a large adult male tarragon, sleek, thin, and smoke gray clambering to its feet smack dab in the middle of the market. His heart lodged in his throat.

The man bounced off his torso and stumbled backwards.

Reaching out, Colt grabbed the man's thick arm when a flash of d'orite streaked past him, headed for the screeching beast.

The girl from the Ardenian stall. She ran at full speed toward the dragon.

Colt threw the man to his right and took up pursuit.

The girl was fast and closed the distance to the tarragon too quickly.

He yelled a command with every ounce of authority he could summon. "Stop!" Tarragons were misunderstood as vicious and unpredictable. Still, those claws were razor sharp, capable of clinging to the massive rock they all shared, and could rip her to shreds. What was she even doing? Why didn't she run to safety like everyone else?

She skidded to a halt but didn't look back, her focus seemed to be as captured by the dragon now as it had been by the strap earlier.

The tarragon reared up on its hind legs.

Colt had never seen a tarragon rear like that before.

The girl didn't even flinch.

The tarragon turned its big doe eyes on him. A pang of nostalgia rippled through him. He assessed the dilapidated market stall and the cul-de-sac laying in ruins.

To his right, an archer took up position behind an overturned cart. The young man's stance showed his inexperience, but he could still do damage with his recurve bow.

Two other men, woodcutters, slowly approached from the left, large bladespar axes gripped tightly in white knuckles.

Colt forced a casual tone and nodded to the men. "Easy, lads!"

Would they heed his command without the uniform? Costairs typically didn't take kindly to orders from civilians, particularly one who looked Reyjik, which, given his mixed blood, he did.

The larger man swung the ax in a tight arc. "I'll be takin' it easy when its head leaves its slick neck and not a moment before, seaward boy!"

Nope, he didn't take kindly to the order at all.

Calm, clear, and determined, the young woman's voice rose over the agonized wails. "You'll drop that ax immediately is what you'll do. You're scaring him!"

Colt whirled around.

She stood in front of the tarragon, waving a hand dismissively behind her back as though warning away anyone who might be thinking of approaching. She held her other hand out to the beast and inched toward it.

He scowled. What did she think she was doing? He stalked toward her. Despite his efforts to sound calm and in control, panic thickened his voice. "Get back! Now!" He glanced to the right.

The archer had squared up and taken aim.

"Stand down!" Colt gritted out the words, pointing to the man and then dropping his hand in a decisive command to drop the bow. Couldn't he see the girl? This man was obviously an amateur. How did he think he could shoot the tarragon with her in his path like that?

The girl's words dripped with indignation. "I will not stand down. You stand down!" Her back still to him, she inched closer.

"I wasn't talking to you." Colt edged toward her. "Regardless, same order. Stand down and get behind me, now!"

The girl didn't look back or acknowledge his command in any way while she continued toward the beast.

Every muscle in Colt's body tensed when the tarragon fixed its pale green eyes on her.

The men to his left raised their axes again, and he caught the movement in his peripheral vision when the archer hefted the bow higher.

Abandoning caution, Colt strode after her, advancing within reach of her right arm.

The girl spun around. "He's tangled. He flew too low, and the tanning nets were set out to dry on the roof. He must have caught one and crashed. Now he can't get free." Her eyes flashed with resolve and defiance, and she held his stare a moment before glancing to the left and then the right.

Was she taking in the threats from both sides?

She took two quick steps backward and stretched her arms wide to shield the tarragon. Her retreat had taken her within striking distance of fang or claw.

Colt's heart pounded. He shot a glance over her shoulder at the beast. She was right. Its left wing and foot were held tight by new leather netting, leaving it with no hope of breaking free. Doubtless the other men had come to the same conclusion and figured the dragon would be easy pickins, like shooting barrels off a loaded hoist. He flung a hand into the air and yelled "Stand down all three of you!"

He'd issued the order so loudly the girl jumped.

All three men hesitated.

Now was his chance. In one easy movement, Colt drew his Bowman dagger from its deerskin sheath, brandished his rapier, and took aim.

"No!" The girl's cry was desperate, and she lunged toward him.

Throwing the dagger first, he freed his hand to grab her arm and use her own momentum to spin her to the cobblestone. He then hurtled his rapier toward the beast.

The dagger found its mark, slicing through the netting looped around the midpoint of the tangled wing. The rapier cut free the leather tangling its left foot.

Shaking free of the net, the tarragon sprang skyward, stretched its wings, and took flight.

An ax clattered to the stone street just beyond the stall, followed by a second ax thudding into the scattered thatch. Arcing high in the sky, an arrow disappeared beyond the rooftops.

The tarragon was already out of range, swooping low again, no doubt feeding on the insects for which it migrated each spring.

Relief rolled through Colt, cut short by a wave of heat. All three men had defied his order! But the girl—he whirled around to face her.

Already on her feet, she brushed the dirt from her soiled skirt. She spat the words at him, her face mottled and red. "I had it under control! What were you thinking?"

Seriously? She was angry with him? Colt walked over to the wreckage, dug out his dagger, and shoved it into the sheath. "I was thinking I would free the tarragon and save your life at the same time."

The girl planted both hands on her hips and continued her tirade like he hadn't even spoken. Her voice trembled, although from fear or anger he couldn't tell. "And those three followed your lead, whether you liked it or not. What if they hadn't missed?"

Her words stung. Used to men obeying his orders without question, Colt hadn't considered those three townspeople might interpret his throws as a call to fire. He kicked his sword to his hand with his right toe, catching it easily. His own fingers trembled slightly. Was it lingering fear over how close she'd come to injury or anger that no one had heeded his commands? "I've no idea what you planned to accomplish, but from where I was standing, in one fell swoop you made yourself a perfect target for two axes, a quiver full of arrows, and eight razor-sharp claws. If I had trained in foolishness for my entire life, I couldn't have managed such an exceptionally stupid move."

Her eyes narrowed to slits. "The All-Father created tarragons just like the rest of us, you know. They are His creatures too, and they're only animals." She flung her accusations the way he had flung his sword and dagger. "They're not evil!" Her faced flushed deep pink. "I suppose you think what you did was brave? Seems pretty cowardly to me to throw from such a safe distance. I guess, from where you were standing, it didn't particularly matter to you whether your weapons went through the net or through the heart. Either way it would be a win for the big, brave hero!"

Every word cleaved like a blade. Coward? He clenched his jaw. "I never miss, my lady. Even with you making yourself a royal nuisance, you might have noticed that I managed two perfect shots." Not wishing to hear her response, he strode past her. He'd only walked a few paces when his boot scuffed against something, and he paused.

Under his toe, lay the Bowman quiver strap. Stooping, he clasped the strap, pausing a moment to read the faded words he'd committed to memory even before he could read. He rose slowly. How curious it proved so valuable to her. Stranger still, she would risk herself without hesitation for a tarragon. He pivoted and turned to the confounding girl. Silently, he held out the strap.

"Keep it!" Shoving away his hand, she stormed past him and headed down the street, not bothering to look back.

Colt's heart cleaved again, but he couldn't begin to understand why.

Chapter Two

The Challenge

Tess

TESS TRIED IN VAIN TO TAKE a deep breath, something made impossible by her corset. Her introduction would come next, and Costair's Royal family and every other eye in the ballroom would fix on her, scrutinize her the way they had her older sister. She hated being a princess sometimes. Most times. Maybe all the time. In contrast, Sasha lived for the attention, her smile fixed perfectly on her poised face.

"Your Majesty, may I now present Lady Tess of Ardenia, my lady-in-waiting." Sasha's voice rang sweet and sincere.

Tess blinked. *Lady Tess? Lady-in-waiting? What?* Her right foot slid forward, and she dipped gracefully, touching the toe of her left shoe to the floor behind her. *Wait, do you curtsy differently as a lady-in-waiting?* Tess lowered herself as far as she could without losing her balance, and then slowly resumed her full height. Nausea swept over her. Everyone still watched her. Had she done it wrong? *A lady-in-waiting—seriously, Sasha?*

The ballroom glowed warm and rich in the waning past-peak light. D'orite shadows danced on the walls. Though every courtier stood perfectly still, the thick breeze caused the candle flames to flicker and fold throughout the room, creating a silent silhouette waltz.

King Salmon of Costair began his formal welcome address and Sasha's warm, bare shoulder pressed against Tess's. "That curtsy was a bit much." She whispered out of the side of her mouth, her lips remaining almost perfectly still in that sweet royal facade she had mastered.

Tess fought back a smile. She wouldn't give her the satisfaction.

Sasha elbowed her ever so slightly. "Please, Tessy. I need a Bowman."

I need a Bowman. Really? Sasha hadn't tried to exploit Tess's fascination with the King's Bowman since she was little. Strangely, the smile won, spreading across Tess's lips. Sasha saw it, nodded ever so slightly, and the game was afoot.

A few minutes later, Tess studied the elaborate tapestry hung behind the head table. Each tier of the Spire, displayed in the most vibrant colors, sat one on top of the next. Depictions of the flora, fauna, and ore native to the four tiers were intricately woven in Reyjik silk. Tess's gaze rested on the brilliant emerald beams emanating from her home cliffs, her heart swelling.

Stretching to her eye level, the three foot-tall-tiered cake sitting in the center of the long table mirrored the tapestry almost exactly, the icing of each tier matching the color of the respective truth stone. How strange to think their Spire must appear a giant wedding cake, stretching out of the Endless Sea, and at that very moment, she stood on the sapphire icing of Costair, her home tier sitting perfectly horizontal, hundreds of yards skyward.

A pinch made her wince.

Sasha released her grip on Tess's forearm, plucked the strawberry from her fingers, and popped it into her mouth. "The colors make it look kitsch. I've already told him the wedding cake will be white, all white, no tacky political tribute."

Sasha, you are unequivocally the most spoiled brat in the Realm.

Grabbing her hand, Sasha led Tess past the lavish buffet, piled high with first fruits, to the huge granite column built into the south wall of the ballroom.

They circumvented the column until it stood directly between them and the head table where Prince Durbink sat sipping his soup. The breeze from the open window overlooking the south terrace brought a welcomed respite from the stuffy air of the crowded room.

Sasha turned on her heels and nudged her against the stone support. She spoke just above a whisper. "I'm a spoiled brat, I know, but I brought you down here to figure out Durbink. You can do that better as a servant, you know, speak with his personal staff. They'll be more honest about his character with a maid than with my younger sister."

Honest? Was Sasha being serious right now? Tess whispered in kind. "And the fact that you just lied to the king of an imperial tierdom, not to mention your future father-in-law, didn't give you pause." Tess studied her older sister's placid expression. "You committed treason, Sash. Yet you call me reckless."

Sasha brushed the long, curled tresses draping over the front of her left shoulder to her back. "I am not consenting to descend to this tropical tier and subjecting my hair to this constant humidity if he is a rogue, Tessy. Look at my curls. They're frizzy."

Tess struggled to keep the corners of her mouth from curling.

"Besides, all you've ever wanted is to be a King's Bowman. Consider this a Bowman mission, all the questions and intrigue, subtly interrogating his staff. You'll love all that so much more than hours of conversations at court. If there is the slightest question of character, skeleton from his past, I need to know, Tessy. I need something worth a veto." Sasha reached out and straightened the green lace trim at the neckline of Tess's silk bodice. "Emerald always looked best on you. You've got until we ascend." Slipping her fingertips along the column, she circled to the other side, no doubt returning to the head table.

Exhaling, Tess leaned against the granite that towered behind her, the cool stone damp with condensation, slid against her bare shoulders. Some things couldn't be bought, and no matter how rich or privileged, no one could escape Costair's humid climate, not even the royal family in their grandest ballroom. She sighed. Now what?

A male voice came from her left. "I'm not sure *frizzy hair* will stand up as an adequate defense during your inquisition."

Tess whirled.

Standing outside on the terrace, his face framed by the open window, stood the young man from the market. "I mean, I'm sure you're aware that conspiring to investigate the crown prince without his consent breaks the Sacramance Accord, right?"

He propped his chin on his hand, his forearm resting on the high windowsill, a sly smirk just touching his lips. His dark hair now caught up in a ponytail at the nape of his neck, he cleaned up remarkably well. He looked foreign, somehow, which she hadn't noticed in the market. His complexion was not as fair as that of Costair nationals. He was undeniably handsome. And those eyes. What was someone of his station doing here? He wore white, maybe he was a waiter.

Tess pushed off the column and stood at attention. "Where did you come from?" Her stomach twisted. She tried to hold an even tone and failed. "How long were you standing there?"

"Long enough…Tessy." The smile spread across his face. He drummed his fingers on the sill, never breaking her stare, looking like the tarragon tasting the tull-fly, and he winked.

Her cheeks blazed hot, and warmth creeped up her neck and rested across the bridge of her nose. Did he know she'd been falsely introduced? Likely not, or he wouldn't be calling her Tessy. His grin told her he enjoyed the fact she was blushing.

She raised her chin ever so slightly. "If your prince is a man of honor, he has nothing to worry about. If he's not, I'll find out." She pivoted on her heels, turning to follow Sasha.

"Got some Bowman counterintelligence tricks up your sleeves, do you? Wait, you don't have any sleeves." His voice held laughter.

She shot a look over her shoulder, but the window was empty. She sprang to the sill and stretching on tiptoes scanned the terrace, nothing. Of course, he had to have the last word.

* * *

Two hours later, Tess's toe tapped nervously under the wide emerald skirt while she again stood in front of Prince Durbink, King Salmon, and every courtier in Costair. "Yes, Your Highness, by the Emerald Star, I can outshoot any of your men." She tried again for a deep breath to no avail. "Unless, of course, you retain a King's Bowman in your service."

King Salmon laughed outright, but Prince Durbink looked her over, a smile dancing behind his eyes. The ladies whispered and the lords chuckled before silence swept the room.

Durbink straightened to his full height and rested his hand on his dress sword, tucking the other into his richly brocaded jacket. "We swear by the Sapphire Star down here, Lady Tess. Besides, what if I do retain a Bowman of the Realm at my humble castle?"

Tess bit her lower lip. *Now what? Honestly, Sasha, did you really need to dig your heels in over the equality of women in combat?*

Sasha didn't hold fast to any political views, feminist or otherwise. Now, as usual, she'd made an impetuous claim, leaving Tess with a mess to clean up.

She flexed her shoulders back ever so slightly. "Well, Your Highness, if you have a King's Bowman, I suppose we'd shoot a draw." There. She'd spoken the truth, at least.

The stringed quartet had stopped playing, and a restless silence fell over the room. Oh, the court must love this.

She scanned the crowd. Were they leaning closer, waiting to see how this argument would play out?

Everyone's eyes were focused on Durbink, waiting.

Durbink cleared his throat. His eyes flickered with amusement.

Was he patronizing her? He did appear to be stifling a smile. She glanced at Sasha.

Her sister met her eyes—finally—and mouthed the word sorry with a wince. Clearly realizing she had left Tess to make good on her claims of feminine grandeur.

A smile spread wide across the young prince's face. "Captain? Captain Colt Hawthorne, are you here somewhere?" He stood on tiptoes to peer over the crowd of guests. "Don't know how I have so much trouble sighting you when you always seem to be the tallest man in the room. But then, I guess that is the way of a man with your talents, isn't it?"

The crown laughed, proving to Tess the king's son was well liked by his courtiers. She joined the prince in scanning the crowd, despite not knowing whom she was looking for. She found herself staring into a very familiar pair of deep brown eyes. Her stomach clenched. No, not him.

He emerged from nowhere. She hadn't seen him since he'd eavesdropped on Sasha's marching orders, not at dinner or during this exchange with the prince, until now. Tess forced herself to hold his gaze. Was this the captain? No, he was a peasant, wasn't he? He'd seemed a peasant in the market. Although he had wielded those weapons with uncommon skill. How had that not alerted her to the fact he might be more than he appeared?

A smile lit his face, and he winked at her before turning to face the prince.

Blast that wink.

Puffing out his chest, he saluted. "Present and accounted for, Your Highness."

When he stopped next to her, Tess took in everything from his hair to his boots. He stood at least six inches taller than her brother Frederick, maybe six-foot-four, with a lean strong build. He didn't appear to be from Costair at all. He wore an Ardenian military dress uniform with an enormous longbow slung across his back. The four emerald stripes on his shoulder indicated he was a captain in the select corps, a Bowman of the Realm.

Tess's heart ached. What she wouldn't give to wear that uniform. How in the Realm had this young man earned the rank of captain so soon? He must be good. That's why he acted so cocky. Tess's corset cinched her chest like a vise. Why was the air so thick? And why had she felt the need to mention the Bowmen at all?

The man simply stood there, all casual and grinning.

Durbink released the hilt of his dress sword and pantomimed an archer drawing a bow. "Well, Captain, what say you? Are you man enough to shoot a match of three arrows against this lovely young lady?"

The Bowman rolled his right shoulder, the bow on his back shifting by degrees. "Well, Your Highness, I hate to disappoint, but I don't compete against girls. Wouldn't be fair."

The statement was met with nods of approval and knowing looks of agreement among the partygoers.

Edging toward Tess ever so slightly, the captain spoke out of the corner of his mouth, low and quiet. "Take the out, my lady. I'm the best archer in the corps and have no desire to prove that against you tonight."

A spark of anger flared deep within Tess while the morning's events flashed through her mind. Gritting her teeth, she leaned toward him. Her lips remained almost perfectly still in the sweet royal smile she had mastered over years of practice. "Or maybe you're afraid of being shown up by a girl in front of the entire court." She recalled his dagger throw, one in a million, and her stomach pinched.

The Bowman inhaled sharply. The corners of his eyes wrinkled, and a smirk curled the corner of his mouth.

She took a step forward. "I am sure the captain is concerned for my dignity, Your Highness. Compassion is a mark of the Bowmen, after all, so I will answer for him. The princess and I are committed now, come what may. The captain need not bear the burden of our reckless claim. Three arrows indeed and may the best archer win." She curtsied to the prince and gave a shallow bow to the captain.

His eyes grew wide, and then his grin spread to them, making them dance when he bowed in reply.

Durbink's mouth gaped.

Was he caught off guard by her confidence?

Whatever the reason, he recovered quickly and stood at attention. "Well then, let's have it, shall we? Why not a battle of wits between the sexes, while we're at it?"

Had Prince Durbink just doubled down? Was he not satisfied to simply put his future bride in her proper place? Did he need to cement her there for time immemorial? What better way to do that than to have one of his men best a girl in an area where men and women held common ground, that of intellect? Durbink no doubt figured his Bowman had already won the shooting match. Was Durbink banking on the reputation of Bowman brilliance?

Under no circumstance could Tess back down now. She forced cheer into her voice.

"A battle of wits. Why not?"

"Wonderful." The prince waved a hand over the crowd. "Ladies first. . . Tess, was it?"

Please, Durbink, you know my name. She faked a sweet smile.

The prince inclined his head toward the longbow slung over the captain's shoulder.

The young man frowned when his eyes passed over her slight frame.

How had she fared in his assessment? She was tall for a girl, five feet, seven-and-a-half inches, and thin. No doubt he questioned her strength.

His eyes met hers, but the smirk had vanished, replaced by concern. The Bowman pulled the bow from his shoulder and held it out to her.

Filled with nervous determination, she reached out and clasped the captain's bow, grazing the emerald with her pinky as he refused to release the handgrip and she was forced to grasp above it. His knuckles tightened white. "Can you even draw on a bow this size?"

The anger smoldering deep within fanned into flame. Did he know he insulted her? As though gray powder were sprinkled over that fire, shame set her fury ablaze. No, she had never made full draw, on any longbow, and that failure almost crushed her. "I'll do whatever's required, Captain."

The small emerald set into the oiled yew wood of the bow began to glow. A bright green light emanated from the stone, confirming the truth of her statement. Just as quickly as it came, it vanished.

Tess's heart ached again. What she wouldn't give to own a Bowman longbow, set with her very own truth stone to aid in her duty to the Realm, to her father, to the All-Father. The chance to actually do something meaningful with her life.

Staring at the stone, wild-eyed, his mouth gapped open. After a moment, he snapped it shut and pursed his lips. He shifted from one foot to the other and rubbed his chin before withdrawing three arrows from the quiver slung across his back and holding them out to her. "You didn't answer the question, my lady. Can you make a full draw?"

Tess frowned. Her resolve hardened. She needed to best him. She snatched the arrows from his hand. "The right question, Captain, is can I make a full draw wearing a corset?" She faked a smile and then, grasping his bow, placed two arrows on the floor at her feet. She faced the head table, empty now, dropped to one knee and nocked the first arrow in one graceful movement. "Pray tell, what shall it be, Your Highness, a question of arithmetic, logic, a riddle?" She was a huntress. Nothing could break her focus. No matter what the prince said next, she would best him. She would best them both.

The crowd parted, from either side of the table leaving a clear view to the elaborately decorated wall behind.

Durbink took a long look at the lavish scene. He must be choosing her target.

She committed the vignette to memory, serving tables piled high with the best of Costair's groves, an ice sculpture, and tapestries stretched to the ceilings.

"Well… let me see now, Lady Tess. Oh yes, I have it. A riddle indeed." His royal highness played the part well. Of course, the prince had figured out his move before he'd suggested the battle of wits. Tess struggled not to roll her eyes.

Durbink swept his hand across the room. "I will share the riddle, you may have time to consider it, and then you may show your answer by shooting it."

The crowd erupted around her. She saw Lords place bets and overheard the lady standing closest question if the idea was safe.

The prince held up a hand and the room fell silent. "Then Captain Hawthorne will be given a riddle of equal difficulty and the same amount of time, let's say two minutes, before he shoots his answer. If you both answer correctly, our winner will be determined by the accuracy of your shots, the best of three."

The crowd cheered a second time before everyone went quiet. Wives released their hold on their husband's arms, as if the implications of the result of the competition had set in. Tess nodded her agreement of the rules, fixing her eyes on the prince.

Durbink took a dramatic breath. "Within the storm, a place of calm, and truly a window to the soul—"

She fired.

Midway through the last half of the riddle, the first arrow found its mark. Directly in the eye of a peacock woven into the largest tapestry hanging above the head table. Immediately after the hit of the first arrow, she let a second and third arrow fly.

The second arrow tip filled the eye of a woven unicorn, and then the third arrow shattered the icy surface of the eye of a tarragon ice sculpture. This last arrow vibrated for a moment, and then fell free, clattering on the tile floor at the prince's feet.

Yes! Perfect! All three perfect shots. She thought her heart might burst. Her chest heaved with the effort and speed of the shots, desperately trying to afford the deep breath for which she longed. Her corset dug into her flesh. Still, she had done it. Don't gloat, Tess, don't even look at the Bowman. Eyes front.

The men and women in the room gasped in unison.

The prince jerked his head, his eyes huge. He whipped around to study the arrows lodged in his tapestry and the wall behind. Then his attention shifted from them to the ice sculpture that rested on the table only three feet from him, and his mouth dropped open.

She kept her tone innocent. "The eye. That is the correct answer, is it not, Your Highness?"

The bow moved in her hand, and she looked down to see the Bowman gently tugging it from her grasp. His eyes softer, somehow, he nodded to her and, in a movement so smooth and so fast it seemed surreal, he placed an arrow in the left eye of each creature, three perfect shots in mere seconds.

A startled gasp rose from the crowd again.

This time, the third arrow shot through the icy tarragon's head, clear to the midshaft, forcing the sculpture backwards and off the table where it crashed to the floor.

The dragon's outstretched wings cracked with the impact, and one slid into the toe of Durbink's dress boot. The prince let out a loud yelp.

The captain grabbed Tess's hand and held it high in the air. "Well, I believe she was right about the riddle and about the draw, Your Highness."

Her heart pounded.

His hands felt rough and warm and strong.

"My lords, my ladies, I give you Lady Tess of Ardenia, who has the heart of a Bowman!" The room erupted into cheers.

The applause echoed in her ears and her hand pulsed in his grip. Why did he need to rub in the fact that she couldn't make full draw with a longbow? He hadn't waited for Durbink to pose a second riddle, so how could he be so sure he would have known the solution? Of course, the captain could shoot better; they both knew that. He was a blasted Bowman, for Realm's sake. She would trade her royal title in a stone's flash for the chance to train with the Bowmen.

The captain finally lowered her hand and gazed down at her. His eyes sparked with mischief again, mischief and kindness. And that smile.

I need to get out of here. She tugged her hand free, curtsied, and slipped into the crowd.

Chapter Three

The Lookout

Colt

COLT'S FOREHEAD WRINKLED. SHE WAS JUST standing by this very window. Where had she gone? A movement in the courtyard below caught his eye. Was that her?

Yes, Tess strode across the black stone square.

He cringed when he recalled the moments after their match. Why had he grabbed her hand like that? He placed both hands on the sill and leaned close to watch her, his breath fogging the pane of glass with each exhalation. Was she heading for the vineyards? Why would she leave the party?

The tarragon had recently arrived in the bi-annual migration, and she'd seen one in the market, so why would she want to walk in the vineyards? The morning's encounter haunted him. The girl had shown remarkable courage. Too much courage.

Blast General Gerhert's slack attitude towards security! Not a single guard had been posted in the courtyard. No one to ask Tess who she was or where she was going. No doubt she liked it that way. Colt rubbed both hands against the top of his head and then pressed down hard.

A smile spread across his face when Tess stepped barefoot onto the dark earth of the orchard edging the courtyard. Gathering her dress in one hand and clutching her shoes in the other, she strolled into the trees. What kind of a lady-in-waiting didn't wear stockings?

A girl shouldn't go walking through the vineyards so late at night without an escort, and something about Tess compelled him to ensure her safety. He pushed off the sill with both hands and pivoted on his heel. He'd trade the stuffy ballroom for the orchards any day. The west servant's stairs called to him, and he strode toward the narrow exit without a single reservation. Silhouetted by the orange glow of the torchlight, a tall figure stepped into the narrow entrance—General Gerhert.

Colt nodded and stepped to the left, skirting the general.

Gerhert's ash eyes bore into him and the general planted his foot directly in his path.

Stopping, he regarded the aging man. Even in the warm light, Gerhert's skin looked gray, translucent even. Was he ill? What in the Realm was he doing? "Excuse me, General, but I need to pass." Colt clutched his belt buckle and raised his chin.

Gerhert firmly clasped his shoulder. A foreign, guttural sound emanated from deep within his chest and he cleared his throat. "Why in the Realm would you want to leave the gala, Captain?"

Their ongoing disagreement of the last two weeks boiled inside him. Colt was done measuring his words. "I don't want to leave the gala, but your insistence on removing all security for tonight requires it."

Gerhert narrowed his eyes, confusion flashing across his face. He mustn't have noticed Tess leave only moments before.

"That's right. A young lady just left, and with every security guard and man-at-arms loafing in their barracks, no one has prevented her from entering the orchards. She's not safe out there alone."

Gerhert's eyes widened. He stole a glance over his shoulder and down the stairs.

Colt flexed his shoulders. "You cited diplomacy to the king, but negligence is more fitting, General. How a rational man could advise removing all military presence from an inter-tieral event was sound practice is beyond all logic." A wave of satisfaction washed over him. "With the Ardenian delegation, not to mention every noble family in Costair present tonight, we should have doubled, even tripled our regular complement of guards, not given them the day off."

Gerhert's gray nose and ears flushed a deep red. He clenched his teeth. "As I explained to King Salmon, we didn't want to frighten Durbink's future bride with soldiers at every door. They would think we had a security problem down here. Thanks to you, Captain, nothing could be further from the truth."

This type of double-talk had swayed the king to give the guards the night off. He stepped right and attempted to push past the general, not bothering to look him in his cold, gray eyes.

He startled when Gerhert's hand landed on his forearm. He stopped dead in his tracks. The general stared intently at his wrist, like a viper waiting to strike. "I guess a Thornton boy like yourself would be incapable of enjoying the finer things. I suppose you personify the old adage—you can pluck the thorns from the boy, but you can't pluck the boy from the thorns."

Colt clenched both fists until his fingers hurt. Gerhert had seen his scars and instantly he'd come to an assumption—that he was only another poor farmer who couldn't hack it with nobility.

Twisting his arm, he yanked down, breaking Gerhert's hold. "Someone needs to do your duty if you won't, General." Springing left and clear of the seething man, he took the staircase down two steps at a time.

Upon reaching the cobblestones, he breathed deeply. The fresh air extinguished the bubbling rage that had threatened to overflow. He'd pay for his remarks to Gerhert. As an Ardenian Bowman, Colt didn't answer to the general, but Gerhert would find a way to make him pay— he was sure of it.

He inhaled deeply again. The air was much cooler out here than inside, though much warmer than spring in Ardenia. Indeed, in this mild vineyard, buds were already spouting.

Dark shadows dove and swooped over the groves. Tarragon. Colt's heart beat fast at the thought of the morning's incident, of the dragon rearing on its hind legs before the girl. Why hadn't Tess been afraid? Of course, he hadn't been either, but he'd had the unique experience of having a tarragon as a childhood pet.

Trotting to the place Tess had entered the orchard, he peered down the narrow row she had taken. She lingered at a the end of the line of trees, stooping to pick up fallen blossoms. She rose and began to jog and then run, ignoring the dragon-like creatures hunting flies above the treetops. Where was she going? Should he call to her?

Colt jogged behind her at a steady pace. He could overtake her, but his curiosity forced him to stay back. How far would she run? Would anything prove interesting enough to cause her to stop?

She'd taken an overgrown path that had obviously fallen out of use a while ago. The dank smell of peat flooded his senses. He examined the fruit trees that surrounded him. They hadn't been pruned or weeded yet this growing season. He shook his head. Costairs weren't known for their industrious work ethic. What did his drill sergeant used to say? *It takes three Costairs to carry a shovel and two more to carry the wine for all five.*

This row of vineyard bottomed out at the towering cliff marking the tier border.

Tess stopped walking, tilted her head back and scanned skyward.

A strange sense of panic swept over Colt. She wouldn't. He edged silently closer, his heart pounding while she examined the worn parallel tracks running straight up the limestone cliff comprising the foundation of their native tier of Ardenia.

She stepped back, looked up, and then stood perfectly still for over a minute.

He could practically see the wheels turning in her mind. Had she glimpsed the ladder? She cocked her head to the side and stepped closer.

He glanced skyward. Though the moonlight had proven adequate for her journey thus far, maybe the light shone too poorly for her to make out what lay above the tracks. She stepped to the right and then center and then left. He knew exactly what she experienced—something appearing to cling to the cliff and then, as the angle changed, it vanished. A strange feeling swept over him as he remembered the first time he stood where Tess now gazed upwards.

The music from the gala played faintly in the distance, and her inspection of the secret Bowman lookout lasted the entire length of Costair's tieral waltz, "The Sapphire Sislay".

Had she seen it? He felt an inexplicable sense of victory, pride even, building in his bones.

She reached for the rope, tied to a bladespar spike jutting out from the rock just up and over from the worn track markings, and that pride erupted in a sudden surge of excitement. Had she actually discovered a secret Bowman lookout site? *That's impossible!* Something stirred deep within his heart.

Pulling on the rope, a wooden ladder dropped from above, and she jumped. She traced the sides of the ladder that had worn the markings up and down the rock twice. Yes, she'd figured it out.

Colt looked away, heat flushing through him while she unhooked the skirt of her dress from the silk bodice and corset and untied the hooped petticoat under it. As soon as she was free, she left her shoes and skirt neatly folded under a nearby vine and hoisted herself up to the first rung, climbing in her bloomers.

He edged closer still, almost directly under the ladder, watching as she climbed. Flattening himself to the cliff, he held his breath as she paused twice and surveyed the rolling farmland that stretched to the precipice. She ascended the seventy-five yards straight skyward with remarkable speed and disappeared into the hatch entrance of the small scaffolding that comprised the structure, bolted to the face of Costair's sheer cliff.

Closing his eyes, he pictured the diagrams inside the lookout. They detailed every aspect of trade hoisted in the vertically integrated spire they called home. Down to the last resource, they listed each tier's mining efforts and agricultural products, but none of it classified information. Nothing she couldn't learn from a close study of Spire economics.

Had a civilian ever discovered a Bowman lookout on their own? He couldn't recall an incident. The secret towers usually went totally unnoticed. Their platform sat high above the tier by design. The ladder and walled wooden platform were painted to exactly match the cliff to which they clung. How had she have even known where to look?

Climbing the ladder without a sound, the tips of his fingers, calloused from years of drawing a bowstring, padded against the rough wooden rungs. He hadn't been up here since taking over the post six months earlier, and the Lindsor pine felt soft and damp. The wooden ladder required attention. Upon reaching the open hatch, he remained two rungs below the floorboards, where he could just see Tess.

She knelt on the wooden floor in front of the wall where the diagrams hung, her slender finger resting on the diagram of Reyjik, his mother's exotic hometier. She flattened her hand against the parchment cross section, her delicate fingers stretching over the tier responsible for so much of his pain and alienation.

What did she think of Reyjik? Was she like everyone else? Would she subtly dismiss him the way Ardenians always did? He frowned. Why did her opinion matter so much?

He shifted his weight, and the rung cracked so loudly he thought his heart would stop. Blast! Blast! That rung hadn't looked rotten. Was there any chance she hadn't heard the crack?

He took a deep breath and poked his head and torso through the hole in the floor. He blinked at the sight of Tess, barefoot, wearing only her silk dress bodice with white bloomers. "Hello." He barely managed the greeting. Although he'd known she had shed most of her bulky garments, he still hadn't been prepared for the sight of her this close. She was alarmingly pretty.

"Did you follow me, Captain?" Her tone dripped with accusation. The girl stepped back from the window, dropping her hands from the frame. She'd covered the distance to the only other obvious exit in mere moments. Was she considering climbing out of it?

Nerves gripped him. "You know, there's an easier way onto the observation deck." Hauling himself into the lookout, he rose to his full height. With the pull of a lever, he opened a narrow door in the wall. The diagrams had been perfectly cut to accommodate this door. Her eyes grew wide when he stepped past her onto a narrow walkway that wrapped around the entire platform.

Her focus fixed on the supply crane. "Is this how you get down when you're in a hurry?" She patted the wooden crate held by two thick ropes that looped around the oversized pulleys.

He chuckled. "Not unless you want to get down in a considerable hurry. The crane can only hold a hundred pounds of weight safely. It's only for raising supplies."

Passing the crane, they stepped onto the narrow catwalk wrapping around the entire lookout.

Tess's mouth dropped open. "Oh my stars, the orchards stretch right to the precipice. And the shimmer in the distance, is that the Sislay River? Can we see all the way to the Sislay? You must be able to see seven or eight miles!"

"Twelve on a clear day. With a spyglass… well, let's just say that no one will sneak up on the castle with a Bowman at this post." He puffed his chest ever so slightly. "There's a ladder leading from the roof to a ledge about fifty yards skyward. The ledge runs to the hoist track."

She swiveled and stared toward the looming cliffs. "Look at the hoist, and the ferrite veins, and the kimberlites." Her hands flew to her chest. "Is that the Sapphire Star? It glimmers in the moonlight." She raised her left hand to cover her eyes and then raised her right hand to her forehead. Her right index finger pointing straight skyward, she dropped her hand, in one graceful movement, tracing a slow fall to her waist. The Sign of the Great Decent.

Colt tilted his head. "Do you believe in the Freefall?" He clamped his mouth shut. Why in the Realm would he ask her that? He had never before questioned anyone about their beliefs. *Seriously Hawthorne?*

Sabat day lessons flashed through Colt's mind. Falsely accused, the Fallman was pushed off Freefall precipice, but Colt hadn't visited their shrine since his father died.

She didn't turn to look at him, she just stared out over the orchards. "You don't, Captain?"

Great. Now what would he say? "I don't know. I mean, I'm from Thornton. We border the Freefall, and the Ardenian shrine is only two thousand yards from the edge of my village."

"So?" She didn't break her focus from a large female tarragon diving over the trees.

The thunderous beating of her wings carried on the breeze and struck a chord deep in his heart. "So, I guess I grew up with it all." He tensed both shoulders when he considered the Fallman paying for the transgressions of the people of each tier as he fell to Gehenna. "How could a rational person believe the Sacreds' claim—a brilliant light, the Fallman reborn, ascended from the mist three days later? Costairs, Ardenians, and Lindsites all swore it shone the color of *their* tier's truth stone. Of course they did. People see what they want to see." He relaxed slightly. "I watched hundreds of people pass through our town every year, all with the same goal. To ask the All-Father to take care of their problems. I guess I try to take care of my own problems." The knot in his stomach unraveled a little.

She turned to face him. "When I go to the shrine, I never ask for anything. I go to say thank you."

"Say thank you for what?" The words tumbled out of his mouth before he could stop himself.

She smiled. "For making all people equal. For loving each tier the same. For giving me the faith to believe and saving me."

He searched the bright, sea-green eyes. Oh yes, she definitely believed in the Freefall, the All-Father, and the Great Descent, all of it. Before he could respond, Tess spoke again. "You're a Bowman, Captain. You do know your code was based on the Sacreds, right?" She smirked a little.

"Of course I know that. I like the Sacreds. I love the code." He shrugged. "I joined the corps because of the code. But I guess I figure it's my job so save the Realm, not to blindly hope someone else will do it for me." Blast, that sounded rude.

Still, she only nodded, as though she understood. "What about the emerald star, or any of the star stones for that matter?" Turning, she gazed up at the cliffs again, leaning way back, her arms resting on the railing. Wasn't she concerned they were seventy-five yards above the orchard floor?

"What about them, my lady?" He needed to stall. He had no idea what to say about the sacred truth stones. Kings led by their counsel and men swore oaths in their name. But magical?

"Don't play coy, Captain, you know exactly what I'm getting at. You serve a tier where the very king you've sworn to follow and protect annually consults the emerald star on matters of truth. Every Bowman receives a sacred stone. Your very weapon is set with an emerald at great cost to the king, purely to help you discern truth. Do you not believe in the power of the Emerald Star?"

His mouth had gone dry. Did he believe? "I've heard there is a stone that reads your emotional state, well, your body temperature really. It even changes color with your temperature—slightly. That stone isn't regarded as magical, it's only the make-up of the stone, the elements or structure, a trick, really."

Tightening her jaw, she shifted her attention back to the orchards.

"Don't you find it strange that everything is so perfectly balanced?" She swept her hand from the railing, skyward toward the Vertical Horizon. "The mining, the agriculture. Each tier must trade with the others to survive and thrive." Her slender arm pointed to the frothy waterfalls descending seaward from Ardenia along the distant cliff. "Lindsor's spring melt waters our wheat, and our sea-over irrigates Costair's orchards." She clasped both hands to her chest. "How do you explain a land where those resources were placed so perfectly and exclusively in each tier, forcing us to share and trade and depend on each other?" Her ears grew pink. Passion shone in her eyes, and her breathing became labored.

How could he answer her without sounding condescending? Did she believe the All-Father had created the Spire? "Tess, these rocks settled eons ago. When they did, ore and gems stratified, depending on their density. Are you familiar with the concept of an element's density?" He tried to keep a straight face.

"Don't you dare do that, Captain." Tess stiffened. "I could write a thesis on density. Actually, I might be staring straight at a prime specimen where dense is concerned." She held a perfect deadpan.

Gasping, he pressed a hand to his chest, feigning a deep wound to his ego.

She didn't crack.

He lowered his hand to the railing. "All right, maybe there is something to it all, but you need to understand when I look at that perfect balance of resources you referred to, I see all the ways people try to exploit, extort, and twist it to their personal benefit." He unfastened the top button of his collar and rolled his right shoulder again. "I literally have to defend that very balance with my life because people are greedy and selfish and would sooner see it all toppled than to simply work hard and apply themselves. Why don't the stones or the magic do anything about the nature of men?"

She bit her lower lip. "They do just that, Captain. The four stones, working in unison, restrain our selfish nature. They encourage truth and honesty and discourage deceit and selfish ambition." She closed her eyes. "Remove truth and foundations crumble. Fear unrestrained, all men will stumble."

Colt couldn't help himself. "Well, the Sacreds say that, but it's never been tested. There they sit, inlaid into the very foundations of our tiers, as they have for generations. I mean, we are told they provide this invisible shield against the worst aspects of human nature, but. we don't know what society would be like without them, do we, my lady?"

Opening her eyes, she drew in a long, slow breath. "No, we don't, a kindness I hope never changes. I'm sure we can agree on that, Captain."

A strange feeling swept over him, reminding him of how he felt as a boy, when his father would take him to the shrine. "Yes, we can agree on that, my lady." He wiped the sweat from his brow. How could he change the subject? "So, tell me, how in the Realm did you see the tower?"

"Apparently, I have the heart of a Bowman." Tess straightened and placed her hands on her hips. "I mean, not a Bowman's aim, or skill, but his heart, at least."

Colt's stomach pinched. "I meant it as a compliment. You shoot amazingly well for a girl." As soon as the words passed his lips, he felt their effect.

Her back arched, her jaw tightened, pink tinged her cheeks, and her eyes narrowed.

Replaying the things he'd said that morning, regret washed over him.

"This *girl* matched your skill in there, without the two years of training at the Bowman Academy."

Blast, she was angry. He hadn't meant to insult her. Likely he should have left off *for a girl*, since she shot better than most men he knew.

Turning away from him, she gazed out over the tier, her arms crossed in front of her chest. What could he do to fix this?

"Your aim is amazing, to be sure, but you never actually answered my question before, if you could make full draw. I suppose the ice sculpture answered for you. You would have knocked it off the table if you could draw all the way. I might be able to help you with that." He leaned over the railing, trying to catch her eye.

Inhaling sharply, her hands tightened around the wooden rail. "I believe I was the one who actually passed the test, Captain, you only over hoisted on my answer."

Over hoisted? Colt's entire body grew warm. As if he needed her help to figure out a riddle. His hands were tight, cramping, and he glanced down at his fingers, gripping the railing so tightly the knuckles had gone white.

She pivoted, leaning back against the railing, her gaze resting on Ardenia's precipice looming overhead. "Come now, Captain, how can we even be sure you would have had a chance to shoot at something? What if you didn't solve the riddle Durbink planned to pose to you?"

What? She actually thought she had bested him in wits. Did she believe he had merely matched her shooting to avoid receiving a different riddle? Didn't she understand his concession to the draw for what it was, kindness? Did she think him simple?

"I am a King's Bowman, my lady. I assure you there isn't a problem in the Realm I can't think my way out of."

Turning to him, her gaze rested on his rank designation. She strolled past him to the other end of the of the catwalk. She had assessed him and come to a conclusion. What was it?

"Yes, Captain, it must be nice to be a man. We girls can never aspire to such heights of intellect, valor, and excellence."

Colt scowled. Was she being serious? Did she think they handed the Bowman uniform to just any man? Years of study, training, work, tenacity, and great sacrifice had yielded this uniform. How could she attribute the achievement of his rank and standing to simple manhood? His Reyjik heritage made it all the harder, nigh impossible.

He narrowed his eyes. Wait, was it his race? Was she like everyone else? Did she identify him as Reyjik and look no further? Why? His mother's people were valued trade partners, brilliant, hardworking, and honorable. Why in the Realm was everyone so blind to that? He let out a sigh of defeat.

This lady-in-waiting, whoever she was, proved unworthy of a

response. Drowning in disappointment, he turned back to the tarragon roosting in the cliffs above. Maybe he liked the creatures so much because, like him, they knew what it was to be misunderstood.

He shot at glance at Tess. She stared out at the cliffs as though avoiding looking in his direction. His chest tightened at the slight. He followed her gaze. The huge limestone wall stretched into the night sky. Three wispy waterfalls cascaded to the orchards below.

A tarragon swooped past the lookout. Tess jumped and clasped both hands over her heart. She leaned out over the railing, tracking its path.

The huge reptile glided above the orchard, skimming the treetops. With a wingspan of twelve feet, its shadowy form was easily distinguished against the white blossoms.

Compelled by an inexplicable need to ensure her well-being, Colt repressed the sting of Tess's dismissal and strode to her side. "You all right?" He leaned on the railing and peered at another tarragon walking on all fours between the vines. Its wings bumped the closest trees, knocking loose blossoms that rained down on its head and back. Then, all at once, as if startled by the petals on its skin, it shook itself, like a dog shaking after a swim. Colt chuckled.

Tess cleared her throat. "Don't believe everything people say about them. Just because we don't understand them, doesn't mean they're truly vicious."

He sighed deeply, utterly defeated by her misjudgment. He wanted nothing more than to justify himself. Instead, he found he couldn't speak, totally unable to tear his gaze from the pretty girl.

Seeming to drink in a long look of the breathtaking view, she pivoted on her heel to face him. "I need to get back to the castle and the princess." Just then a blossom petal carried on the breeze landed on her foot.

Tess glanced down at her feet and drew in a quick breath. Her pale skin flushed and then turned a deep crimson. She peered up at him, eyes wide.

Barely restraining the urge to laugh, he bit the inside of his cheek. Had she forgotten she wore only her bloomers, her feet bare and dirty?

Finally, he had the upper hand. He could make a crack about her attire—a dozen different quips ran through his mind—but when she bit her lower lip and crossed her arms over her torso, he felt an aching deep inside. How could he ease her embarrassment?

He opened his mouth to assure her there was no need for her to worry. Before he could utter the words, the piercing boom of a cannon shattered the awkward silence. Whirling toward the castle, he strained to see what had happened, but the darkness and the glare of the distant torchlight made it difficult.

Tess grasped his arm. "Is it part of the celebrations?"

A second cannon fired, and smoke billowed over the west wall.

"That's no celebration." He ran to the door of the lookout and ducked inside. Two spyglasses hung on the hook by the door like protocol dictated. Snatching both, he returned to the railing and, after handing one to Tess, scanned the castle intently, homing in on movement by the northernmost wall.

His breathing shallowed. An enemy force infiltrated the castle at multiple points. Soldiers marched in every direction in coordinated columns.

Tess gasped. "Captain, do you see that? In front of the north wall? Are those soldiers?"

"Yes, and there are more surrounding the men's barracks in the southern quarter." Another cannon shot rang out, and more smoke rose, this time to the east of the castle.

"Are they shooting at the walls?" Her voice was tinged with panic, and she spun toward him. "What's going on?"

He held fast to the spyglass, surveying the unfolding disaster. "A company of fifty men has surrounded the barracks. At least one hundred more have secured the courtyard you crossed, and I can make out at least that many more walking the tops of the walls and guarding the main gate." He redirected his spyglass farther south. "There is also a battalion close to five hundred on the plains to the south, maybe more. They are taking up a defensive position and forming battle lines."

She grabbed his arm just above the elbow. "What are you saying? Are they attacking the castle right now? Who are they? Where are Costair's troops?"

Lowering the spyglass, he shifted to face her, disbelief wracking his mind over what he was about to relay. "I can't tell who they are. I don't see any of our soldiers in play." He tried for a deep breath and failed. "It looks like they have locked our men-at-arms and mounted knights in their barracks without opposition." He thought to the men he'd trained, a lump forming in his throat. "That's hundreds of men simply neutralized. They have secured the ballroom's outer doors and the main gate and formed a strategic position on the open plains to the south, the only way the castle can be accessed." He swallowed hard. "They're not attacking the castle. They have taken it."

Chapter Four

The Onslaught

Tess

TESS STOOD FROZEN, WATCHING COLT. *WHO has taken the castle?*

His head jerked. "I need to secure the hoist. Whatever, whoever this is, they cannot be allowed to breach Ardenia!"

He sprang from the railing and then stopped dead.

A noise reverberated off the cliffs above them. What was that? Voices?

Colt spun around, grabbed Tess's wrist, and pulled her down to her knees on the platform next to him.

Her heart began to pound.

Closing his eyes, he lowered his ear to the boards. "I hear men shouting."

She heard them again and nodded her confirmation, a tightness gripping her heart.

Rising, he crept to the hatch inside the small building. Lying on his stomach, he peered over the opening.

Her bare arm brushed against his elbow as she positioned herself next to him on her stomach and peered over the edge of the hatch.

There, on the orchard floor beneath the lookout, stood two soldiers.

Tess grasped his shoulder, but he did not shift his attention from the men more than seventy-five yards below.

A muffled yell echoed off the ceiling of the lookout.

He raised his index finger to his lips and inched forward.

"There is absolutely nothing here. I don't care what that gray-skinned coot says. If there was some kind of fort out here, I would see it." The words, dripping in frustration, were spoken in Reyjik.

Goosebumps rose on Tess's arms as the tongue of her childhood carried skyward.

A second voice shouted, thick with indignation. "Well, it's supposed to be impossible to spot. This is the exact location the general gave me. Look again."

The first man scoffed. "Well, do you see a phantom tower? We probably got the instructions wrong. Let's retrace our steps and count the rows from the main service path again."

The men turned and stalked toward the orchards.

She studied them through the narrow window in the floor. They both carried curved sabers.

Colt tracked them with his eyes until they disappeared from view then he edged back from the hatch and sat up.

Mimicking his every movement, she sat up, her eyes locked with his. "They said they'd retrace their steps. I came down the main service path. Captain, they'll be back in mere minutes."

Colt rose and strode to the cupboards lining the back wall. "Yes, and I'll be ready for them."

She knelt on the wooden floor, watching the Bowman. Still holding the spyglass in one hand, her other trembled.

Opening a cupboard built into the back wall, he retrieved a grey rucksack. He slid open a deep drawer and began placing items on the rough wooden counter, all without making a sound.

Sasha. She must save Sasha! Tess sprang from the hut and ran to the crane. The rough wood of the railing scratched against her bare feet while she climbed up to reach the davit arms. The thick ropes rubbed her soft hands warm when she attempted to pull them free of the Bowman knot that secured the crane in the skyward position.

"What do you think you're doing?" Colt's ragged whisper hissed out through the small door.

She kept working at the ropes. "What do you mean, what am I doing? I'm readying the crane. We don't have enough time to climb down the ladder, they'll be back any moment, and we'd be totally exposed." His words from earlier flashed through her mind. "I don't care what the weight capacity is. You Bowmen always over-do everything. I'm sure there's tolerance for one trip." Her fingers were already growing fatigued as she pulled at the stiff ropes. Blasted Bowman knots!

"Absolutely not, my lady. I'm going, but you're staying here. I'll neutralize this threat and retract the ladder. No one will be able to reach you, and you'll have supplies for weeks. I'll send someone for you when it's safe."

Giving up on the knots, Tess sprang from the railing and ran inside the lookout. "What? Are you being serious? You are not leaving me here, Captain!" Blood pounded through her veins. She'd always been left behind, by everyone.

He didn't even bother to look at her as he silently latched a cupboard door closed. "These groves could be crawling with enemy troops, just like those two. We can't confirm the actual size of their force. They could be branched out in a flanking formation. I have no idea what I am walking into out there. I will travel quickly and silently, and even then, I may not make it through their pickets. You're staying here, my lady. This is the safest option we have." He sounded so certain while he placed three specialized arrow tips on the counter, dismissing her request.

Heat crawled up her neck. She forced her tone to stay even and unnervingly quiet. "Listen closely, Captain." Finally, he looked up. "There is no version of this argument where I stay here. I am coming with you. I am fast, and I am silent. I shoot straight. I never miss. I do not choke under pressure, and I will not hide in safety. I will ensure the King of the Realm learns of this act of aggression against his kin. And I will face any ensuing dangers, come what may. I will see this through with or without you. Do not dismiss me again."

The Bowman's brown eyes locked on hers.

Desperate to help her sister, she held his stare, not daring to breathe. She could reveal her identity. If he knew she was a princess royal, Colt would be obligated to bring her to Castle Fairgates, the Bowman's code demanded that, but something deep inside told her not to. What was he thinking? She didn't recognize the eyes that stared back. They were cold, calculating.

Colt appeared to be weighing her words, and, after a moment, reached a verdict. He said nothing but turned and opened a narrow cupboard in the wall behind him, one that stretched from the floor to the low ceiling. After retrieving a longbow and a quiver, he handed both to her without a word.

She grabbed them, not wanting the young captain to notice her trembling hands. Relief flooded through her. She would go with him. She would help Sasha.

The Bowman stuffed the items he had arranged into a rucksack, added two ration packs, and tied it shut before striding to the crane. Holding the two ropes tight with his gloved left hand, he nodded for her to climb in the wooden crate.

Another cannon boom sounded, and she flinched.

"You can stay here, my lady. It'll be safe."

Tess shook her head and hoisted herself over the side and into the crate.

Setting one foot in, he remained in a standing position, the other foot swinging free to maintain his balance. In one easy movement he loosened the knot, making sure to clutch the rope tight with a gloved hand. "Ready?"

Giving a quick nod, she held onto the sides of the crate so tightly her fingers strained.

He released his grip and they dropped.

Her stomach leapt into her throat. The damp air rushed past her face and the orchard floor hurtled towards her.

Speaking above the humming sound of the rope rushing through his semi-closed grip, he questioned her. "You understood the soldier, even though he spoke Reyjik?"

"Yes." She looked up at him, but his focus remained on the ground below.

He jerked his chin seaward. "Get ready."

No sooner had he given the warning than they hit the dirt below with a thud. They'd barely landed before he swung the longbow from his shoulder and nocked an arrow.

Tess reached for her own bow, oiled brown yew wood, sleek and beautiful, a full foot shorter than the Bowman's but huge just the same. The thought stopped her short. *My own bow.* Hours of practice alone in the woods—would she truly be able to use it when it mattered?

Sasha! She needed to get to Sasha.

His strong grip clutched her at the elbow. "Hide under that row of trees and don't come out until I'm done." He nodded to a line of peach trees that hadn't been pruned or weeded yet this spring. The overgrowth would provide sufficient coverage even in daylight.

Slipping under the tree where she'd hidden her clothing, he retrieved her shoes. She then ducked to the trees he had indicated and laced them as quickly as possible.

Colt took up position behind another line of trees directly across from the camouflaged ladder. He left his bow strung but placed it by his feet in the uncut grass next to his quiver. What was he doing?

Voices echoed off the cliffs. There must be more than two men.

"I bet you one hundred spar you don't find a thing!" The voice sounded young, carefree, jovial even.

"I bet I find it first try." Confidence rang in the second one's words.

Tess hadn't heard conversational Reyjik in years, not since MaryLee.

Droplets of dew forming on the leaves trickled down her shoulders and goose bumps rose on her arms.

Four Reyjik men strode right past where Colt lay in wait and stood facing the cliffs. Four not two. What would the Bowman do?

She crept backwards out of the low hollow, strung her bow, and began to nock an arrow. Four to one were bad odds, even for a Bowman. The clash of bladespar on ferrite pierced the silence. Colt! She whirled around the end of the row and raised the fletching to her cheek. She gasped.

He wielded two Bowman batons. Two feet long, an inch and a half in diameter, they flashed in the moonlight as he fought two men at once. One soldier already lay motionless at his feet. Sparks spat from each clash of metal.

He drove the batons down with such force, the swordsmen couldn't withstand the blows. Her heart pounded in her chest. How could he be that strong?

Within moments he had knocked a ferrite saber from one man's grasp, and he turned his attention to the second, pounding down on the blade held in a defensive position until the soldier crumpled. The last man stood directly behind him, raising his saber with two hands, seconds from delivering a killing stroke.

Tess reacted without thinking. She stepped clear of the trees, sighted the man's sword, and dre w back as far as she could.

Colt delivered the final blow to the fallen man's sword, and in one seamless movement, spun around and smashed a backhand blow to the last man's knees with such force he dropped like a hoist.

At that exact moment Tess released her arrow, and the bladespar tip clattered into the man's sword, knocking it from his hands. The sword flew into the darkness. She watched the man track it, instead of watching Colt, like he should have been. Before the sword hit the ground the follow-up blow crashed down from Colt's second baton.

Her heart pounded, and she gasped for air, her ribcage straining against the corset.

Rising to his full height, he glanced at the orchard floor and then raised his eyes to meet her gaze.

She lost her breath completely, frozen somehow.

He then stooped to the nearest man and began examining his uniform.

Sprinting to the scene of combat, she took stock.

All four motionless men were armed with long ferrite sabers, each a lethal weapon.

Colt had already stowed his batons in deerskin loops on either thigh.

Moonlight glinted off one of the ferrite blades. "Why didn't you use your bow? They fought to kill."

"I can't question dead men." He rifled through pockets and checked their satchels. "Why didn't you stay hidden like I ordered?" He stopped his search, his eyes burning through hers.

She lowered her bow. "The odds changed."

His lips formed a thin hard line, but he said nothing.

She flicked the feathered fletching with her thumb. "Who are they?"

"That's what I am going to find out." Colt strode to the rucksack he'd left beside his bow and knelt in the damp grass.

Hurrying to his side, she kept her arrow tip trained on the circle of unconscious men, but stood so that she could simultaneously watch what he was doing.

He retrieved a small deer hide med-fold. Upon opening, it revealed four narrow vials of clear liquid, and the Bowman exhaled sharply.

She studied the vials. "What's wrong?"

"This kit only has scopolamine, no smelling salts. And I can't wait for them to wake up. It could be hours, I hit them hard. We need to move now." He rose and then paused. "Still, scopolamine could prove helpful." Sliding one vial from its sleeve, he uncorked it and walked to the man he'd fought last. Bending over, he poured a few drops of the liquid into his mouth and then held his lips shut until the man swallowed.

"What are you doing? Isn't scopolamine a truth serum? What good will it do if they're unconscious?"

He repeated the same treatment to the two men she'd watched him simultaneously render senseless. "It isn't exactly a truth serum, although it can be used to acquire the truth, and it also causes short term memory loss. I'll wager these men won't remember our fight, or even how they got here when they wake." He rose and stepped over the fourth man but didn't administer the serum.

"What about him?"

"I clipped him from behind to kick things off. He has no idea what hit him." He returned to his gear, and after retrieving his bow, quiver, and the rucksack from the damp earth, took off running toward the castle.

Tess sprang after him, her quiver hung low on her back, rubbing against her bodice as she kept pace. The mist had begun to settle on the grove, and it condensed on everything metal, including the buckle of her quiver. A tiny droplet ran down the bare small of her back, and though the air still hung thick and warm, again, goosebumps rose on her bare arms.

The groves lay quieter now. The cannon fire had stopped, replaced by shouted orders from the wall down to the open plain lying south of the huge granite castle.

Colt stopped, held his hand up in a fist, and then ducked into a row of peach trees.

She followed immediately.

Using the trees as cover, he rose to his full height and surveyed the castle with his spyglass.

Stretching on tiptoes, she peered over the tops of the small trees.

What appeared to be an entire regiment of soldiers made camp on the plain, the light linen of their tents glowing silver in the moonlight, dappled with the infrequent orange glow of campfires.

Campfires? They were cooking dinner, making camp. They weren't worried about a counterattack. They weren't taking up true defensive positions. They didn't even face the castle, as if the soldiers inside posed no threat whatsoever. What in the Realm was happening?

"Captain, they aren't even concerned about the Costair garrison inside the castle. They are bedding down for the night." A branch caught in her hair when she leaned to the right, trying to peer around Colt's broad shoulders. Pulling back, she tugged the loop of hair free. It fell loose to her face.

Crouching low to the ground again, he squatted under the fruit trees.

She lowered herself as well, the soft velvety leaves brushing against her face on the way down. "They aren't worried about a counterattack from Costair. They seem totally confident of their victory."

"Yes." Narrowing his eyes, he clenched his jaw before vaulting to his feet and surveying the cliffs in the opposite direction.

"Who are they, Captain?" She waited, the dark, rich soil squishing under her deer hide heels, the scent of peach blossoms wafting past.

The Bowman squatted again and then sighed deeply. "They're Reyjik." Closing his eyes, his brow creased in pain.

Fear coursed through her body. "I know the men at the lookout spoke Reyjik, but that doesn't mean… Reyjik, no. That's not possible. They are a part of Sacramance, one of our greatest trade partners. They would never do this. They would never threaten the balance of the Realm." What was happening? Were the Reyjik attacking? Did this mean war?

The Bowman sighed again. "The uniforms, the army issued gear, their troop deployment, all of it confirms they're Reyjik. I can take you back to the lookout and leave you there, my lady. That offer still stands."

Tess gritted her teeth. "No. I am going with you to the castle. I'm getting Sasha out."

His eyes flashed open. "No one is going in there. The entire castle has been overrun and locked down. I am going skyward to inform the king at Fairgates to raise a counterattack. You can come with me or stay in the safety of the lookout."

Tess's stomach roiled and she pressed a palm to it. What about her sister and the delegation? What about the Costair nobility? "But you're a Bowman. You're supposed to save them, not run. Bowmen aren't cowards. Bowmen stand and fight!" Her whole body trembled, as she hissed the words.

Rocking back to his heels, the captain narrowed his eyes while he stared down at her. Pain flashed across his face. "I'm no coward, my lady, but I'm not a fool either. I am only one man, and I can't help our people by getting caught or killed in a suicide mission trying to storm that castle by myself. I have confirmed the identity of the enemy and assessed their strategic position. Now I need to get skyward, raise the hoist, and bring that information to King Lucius. I ascend to Ardenia immediately. The only question is whether or not I do it alone."

Nausea swept over her. Of course, he was right. What could two people do against an entire army, already dug in and fortified? Nothing. Their only play was to get to her father. She nodded, unable to meet his eyes. Bushes separated as he pushed through, doubling back the way they had come.

When Tess exited the row of trees, a deafening boom filled the air. The ground shook and she fell forward as if a blast of wind had shoved her into the dark soil of the path ahead. Then a storm of dirt, sticks, and leaves rained down over her. She gasped for air, her lungs desperate to fill again.

The captain threw himself over her trembling body just as a second explosion erupted to their right. Shielding her from the falling debris, he bore the brunt of the concussive force of the explosion.

"Stay down! They always come in threes!" he yelled above the ringing in her ears.

She clung to his wrist with her right hand, still desperate to catch a real breath. Blast her stupid corset.

A third shell hit to the left of their position.

Colt yelled out in pain and his entire body spasmed. Still, even before the storm of sticks and stones had finished falling, the Bowman sprang up and tugged Tess to her feet. Holding tightly to her wrist, he pulled her down the debris-laden path that led to the cliffs.

"The Reyjik shell in teams of three. We have about a minute before they reload and launch a second volley. We need to clear the grove and their range as best we can." His words seemed distant over the ringing in her ears, but the message hit home all the same.

She yanked free of his grasp and sprinted behind him. He ran fast, a true athlete, but she wouldn't slow him down.

Colt's palms slammed into the cliff face, and he doubled over, catching his breath.

She collapsed on the ground beside him. "Were they shooting at us, Captain? Did they see us?" Her mind raced at harrowing speed.

"I don't think so. I suspect they are clearing the grove to remove cover from an attacking force. The trees between the castle and the hoist could conceal an invading army from Ardenia. It's standard practice." His voice was calm and even. He had already recovered from the run, his breathing normal.

"But how? How could they do that so quickly? We left only an hour ago. How could they gain such advantage in an hour, and with no opposition, no fight? How is this even happening?"

He slung his bow over his shoulder, leaving it strung. "The sluice gate."

Rubbing her forehead with her fist, she tried to comprehend everything that was going on. "The official sluice gate? They just sailed in and attacked?" She rose to her knees and then staggered to her feet as Colt began jogging along the side of the cliff. She scrambled to catch up to him.

"They must have. The Reyjik don't have hoist access to the Realm. Their tier begins on the leeward side of the cliff and wraps around to the Freefall."

"Shouldn't you have known about the impending attack? Was there no intelligence, any indication of this threat?" The words tumbled out before she considered their consequences.

Skidding to a stop, he adjusted the rucksack on his back. He didn't turn to address her—he didn't need to. His tone was so sharp it could have cleaved bladespar. "No!"

She hadn't meant to accuse him of incompetence. He began running again, his pace even faster than before.

Clearly, he was angry, but she didn't care. She was angry too, and she wanted answers. "They must have disembarked at the Marduke docks. A march at double time would cover the distance to the castle in less than half an hour. But where were the guards? There should be a garrison stationed at Marduke to prevent such a thing, no?" Tess crawled over a log in her path and hurried to catch up to the captain. "Even if the garrison at the docks had been overwhelmed, they could have at least raised a warning. Wait, we embarked at the hoist docks and disembarked at Marduke only this morning and there were no guards. How could that be?"

The captain didn't stop running, only called a single name over his shoulder. "Gerhert."

She frowned. Gerhert? The general?

"General Gerhert must have arranged it all. He insisted the military presence be stripped to almost nothing. Then he ordered the garrison at Marduke to stand down, for their officers to dress for the banquet and all others to take a day's leave. His officers are unarmed and under siege in the ballroom, and his troops are locked in the barracks. He planned this to the minute. No wonder he tried to stop me from leaving the ballroom. He handed the Reyjik Costair with absolutely zero resistance."

Jogging behind him, her mind raced. "But why? Why would the Reyjik do it?"

He shook his head. "I don't understand it. It's all so fragile, so delicate, so interdependent. If King Lucius loses Reyjik's grey powder, Ardenia's bladespar industry grinds to a halt within the year. We need it to blast and smelt. He can't risk that to defend Costair's borders. He likes the wine and the d'orite, but they aren't critical to his economy."

Her fist clenched tight. "King Lucius will answer. They have his delegation, his daughter, trust me, he will answer!"

"Yes, he must, mustn't he? But why would they do it? Why would Reyjik attack? There has been peace for generations. It just doesn't make any sense. Something is very wrong, Lady Tess. There is a piece that does not fit." He stopped and turned towards her, so abruptly she slammed into his chest and looked up at him in surprise when he grasped her arms to steady her.

"I'm going to figure it all out, learn exactly what is behind all this. I will get that information to King Lucius and save the Realm. Once we reach Ardenian soil, I will leave you in the safest place possible, so you don't slow me down. Are we clear?" His eyes grew as cold as bladespar itself.

Tess raised her chin and met his gaze steadily. "I have already said my piece, Captain. I will see this through with or without you. As for slowing you down, you can trust me when I say that won't happen."

Despite everything, his eyes flicked with the slightest flash of mischief. "Right, right, you're fast, you shoot straight, and you never choke under pressure. I guess the only real question is, can you do all that in a corset?"

Chapter Five

The Assent

Colt

COLT STOPPED, RECOGNIZING THE TELL-TALE crevice others would overlook. He ran his left hand along the cliff at exactly shoulder height, his arm aching. The shrapnel from the shelling had done a number on his upper arm. A searing pain ran from his shoulder down to his elbow, but he didn't have time to worry about it. He shook his head and refocused on his fingertips as they searched each depression. He couldn't find it. Though Colt's callouses rendered his touch less sensitive, he had never before failed to detect the Bowman's crest carved into a cliff face.

His mind leapt back to the academy where candidates had to successfully identify the signature crest blindfolded, in case they needed to find it in the dark. Colt had wondered whether such an occasion would ever arise, and here he stood, only two years later, depending on that very skill. The limestone felt cool, rough, and damp. Condensation from the mist collected at this time of night, making the smooth stone even slipperier. When his thumb dipped into a groove and then hit a sharp, curved ridge, he stopped walking and lowered the rucksack. Raising his other index finger to meet his thumb, he found the thin outline of a longbow and the pointy crown within. That was it. They were in the right spot.

Tess stopped beside him, breathing hard and deservedly so, as they had jogged for two hours straight. He was impressed with her stamina.

"Why are we stopping? What are we doing? Why didn't we take the main hoist?" She whispered these questions on tiptoes, scanning the east, north, and west. Was she checking for Reyjik? She had good instincts.

"We don't have the manpower to raise it, even without a load. This is a secret Bowman ascent site. We'll ascend here and use the counterweight to raise the hoist. After locking it skyward, we'll make our way to Fairgates."

Her eye widened. "A secret Bowman ascent site?" Her gaze followed the cliff face until it gave way to the star-filled sky above.

Dropping to his knees, he untied the rucksack. Darkness shrouded them amongst the neglected peach trees that edged the cliff. He felt inside the bag, his fingers passing over the familiar items. Every one of his senses was on edge. The wind whistled through the branches of the short trees. Tess breathed lightly next to him as his own heartbeat thudded. His stomach felt rock hard, tense, and tight, something he vaguely recalled experiencing before, but when?

The memory struck like the Reyjik mortar attack earlier, and he slowed his search through the backpack. War. Colt had felt exactly like this during his time in the archer trench with his father. Ten years ago, to the month, he had knelt beside his father, loading and reloading his arrow basket. He'd experienced the same hypersensitivity to sounds and movement he did now, the same feeling of his stomach being wrenched tight by a vise.

Benjamin Hawthorne lay dead and buried at the base of Shepherd's Pass. Helpless to do anything for the brave farmer, Colt had watched his father fall.

He inhaled sharply when his fingers brushed the cool bladespar of the first pulley in the line of three and the rough rope that fit snugly in its channel. After pulling it free from the sack, he removed his quiver and attached the lead line to the grappling arrow with a Bowman knot he had practiced hundreds of times during training. Rising to his feet, he met Tess's gaze, her eyes wide and shining in the starlight. She was studying his every move. He nocked the arrow, aligned his naval to the crest carved into the cliff, raised his bow to a trajectory of seventy-five degrees, and let fly. The arrow hurtled into the darkness, and Colt lost sight of it. The unmistakable sound of bladespar cleaving stone, like a miner's pick driving into the ground, marked the shot a success.

Tess pressed her hands together in front of her, her eyes dancing.

Colt immediately set to work stringing the line of three interlocking pulleys and ratcheting them into position. He then attached the deer hide harness with a lock knot. Everything was ready.

"How much do you weigh, my lady?" He studied her in her bloomers—it couldn't be much.

"Pardon me?" Her eyes grew wider still as she placed both hands on her hips.

"It's simple math. I've pegged you at one hundred twenty pounds, and I'm one ninety. The hoist holds a maximum of three hundred pounds. It does have a margin of tolerance, but I need to know if it will hold." He tied off every buckle as a failsafe, waiting for her confirmation.

"One hundred and twenty is correct, Captain." She peered up at the cliff. "But surely you didn't shoot that arrow to the precipice? Your rope is only a hundred yards long at best."

A smile crossed his lips. He unbuttoned his white and green dress jacket, stuffed it into the rucksack, and pulled out the long cloak. He didn't look forward to climbing in the cloak since he already felt warm, but his training had taken hold. It was Bowman protocol to ascend in the camouflage cloak, regardless of season. He tied Tess's bow to his quiver alongside his own, shifted the rucksack to his hip, where he would be able to retrieve items when required, and then finally stepped into the foot sling. Buckling the waist belt tight, he checked all straps a final time.

"You'll need to hold on tight. I would buckle you into the harness, but I need its stability, so I don't lose my balance as I hoist us up." He held the sling for his second foot out to Tess.

She examined it a moment before planting her foot squarely in the deer hide cradle. She wrapped her fingers around his arm, and he winced. Tess pulled back her hand and examined it. Blood. "Oh my goodness, Captain, you were hurt in the blast. You were hit." Her eyes locked on his arm, and she stepped back. Squinting in concentration, her brow furrowed as she held the tear in his shirt open to examine the wound. Her fingers were slender and dexterous, and Colt couldn't tear his gaze from them as she gently widened the hole so he could see.

"It's not that deep. I can climb with it." He tried to sound strong and convincing, but she ignored him. Pursing her lips, she stared past him for a moment. "I can stitch it. I know how."

He shook his head. "We don't have time now."

Her eyes filled with concern. "Let me bandage it then—that won't take long."

Lost in the eyes that seemed to shine a brilliant green in the moonlight, Colt nodded.

She immediately reached for the small side pocket of his rucksack where he had stowed his Bowman knife. Had she watched and remembered that he put it there? Opening the hinged blade, she cut a two-inch-wide strip off the bottom of his shirt.

"Sorry, I don't really have much shirt to spare." He laughed, and she joined in, which, thankfully, eased a little of the intensity between them. After she had cut the strip in two pieces and folded a pad from one, she placed it over the wound. She then reached for his free hand and grabbed his fingertips. Moving them to the pad she applied pressure, and he instantly caught on to her intention. He held the pad in place for her as she wrapped the bandage around his arm and secured it. Her fingertips were smooth on her left hand, but her right hand boasted callouses, same as his. She must practice shooting often. She carefully tied off the bandage and adjusted it and then nodded her approval.

Tess grasped his forearms. "Thank you for shielding me back in the orchard. I'm so sorry you were hurt."

Her sincerity caught him off guard. *Nod, Colt. Nod and get on with it.* He nodded and held out the sling once more. Stepping in, this time making sure to avoid his wound, she looked skyward.

* * *

Tess's heart pounded so hard in her chest it threatened to burst. She had never been this close to a man who wasn't her relative. Where should she hold? She hesitated.

"Lock your wrists around my waist, like a Bowman's handshake." Colt pulled sharply on the rope, testing the strength of its anchor.

She reached around both sides of his torso. His dress shirt, woven of fine Reyjik linen, brushed silky smooth against the underside of her forearms. She knew the Bowman's handshake. They greeted each other with the same locking grip used for hauling each other to safety, literally committing to muscle memory the hold that could save their lives. She secured her grip around her wrists as he'd instructed and straightened.

Colt was staring down at her. Before she could react to his intense gaze, he took a deep breath and then turned his attention skyward. In one fluid movement, he reached for the rope and pulled down with his right hand, and then his left. They lifted off the ground and the harness squeaked as it found its weight-bearing resting place on Colt's hips.

A queasy feeling filled her stomach—not vertigo or fear but nervous excitement. She loved the feeling of dangling over the ground. Peering around Colt's chest, she surveyed the tier that stretched out before her. The castle perched at the edge of the northwest precipice, glowing peacefully in the moonlight. The mist blew in from the Endless Sea, and thick fingers of white cloud reached over the warm land. In only a few moments, Colt had hoisted them more than twenty yards. A bead of perspiration trickled down his cheek. His biceps contracted and relaxed as he hauled them farther skyward. Didn't his arms ache? Didn't his wound hurt?

"Captain, what if you get tired before we reach wherever we"re going? What if your arms cramp or fatigue? What keeps us from plummeting?" She looked up at his chiseled jaw.

A smile spread across his face. "Bowman resolve, my lady."

Tess would have laughed were it not for the danger of the situation. His injured arm worried her. Bowman or not, his strength had limits. And yet, something about Colt—the same overconfidence that proved infuriating—made her feel safe.

For a split second, Tess felt the way she did when she read about the Fallman in the Sacreds. A thousand years had passed since the Fallman was falsely accused and forced off Freefall precipice. Since that time, each tier had built their shrines along the narrow slivers of land that edged the Freefall. Tess shivered at the thought. Only one place in the entire continent could claim the geological conditions of Freefall Point. Just the thought of him plummeting uninterrupted from the vertical horizon down to the Endless Sea, passing only yards from each tier as he dropped, sent a bolt of lightning through her whole body.

Prophesied in the Sacreds, the Great Descent of the Fallman fulfilled all striving of men. Three days after the betrayal, when a bright light, an emerald star, was seen rising past each tier, the prophecies came to life. The Sacreds told that the savior would rise and that he would pass each tier, blessing the people of each tierality with redemption as he did, saving them from Gehenna. It didn't matter if you were a Lindsite or Costairs, Reyjik or Ardenian, man or woman, old or young, miner or monarch. If you believed, all were the same in the eyes of the All-Father. Flooded with that feeling of safety again, Tess couldn't help but smile. Why did hanging in certain danger with this cocky, know-it-all Bowman make her feel safe?

The higher they rose, the farther Tess could see, even as the mist obscured places below at an alarming rate. The thick fog consumed the very landscape itself. It billowed and swirled and surrounded the black walls of the castle, with its enormous inner courtyard glowing from the torchlight reflecting off the inner walls, giving the impression of a stout black dragon with fire brewing in its belly. The mist enveloped the dark shadows she assumed were the ships that had brought the invading army and crept forward through the orchards that stretched to the base of the cliffs they were ascending.

They stopped climbing. Tess snapped her head up to check Colt's condition. He stared down at her. "You know you should be more afraid, right?"

She shrugged. "Are you tired? Do you need a break? How is your arm? Can I help you?"

His eyes sparkled as he jerked his head to the cliff face. "No, we're here." Effortlessly, he pinched both ropes tight with his left hand and reached for the rung of a bladespar ladder secured to the limestone cliff to Colt's right by lag bolts at two-yard intervals. Colt shifted his weight, wedged his knee against the stone, and then pushed gently backwards to afford her the space to climb up the ladder on her own.

Slipping her free foot onto the nearest rung, she slowly loosened her grip around Colt's back. *Breathe, Tess.* She inhaled deeply before clasping the same rung Colt held fast. He smiled at her and nodded skyward. As smoothly as possible, she reached for the next rung with her free hand and then removed her foot from the sling, climbing up as carefully as she could.

Should she keep going? Was she to stop? The captain hadn't given any further instructions. Tess pulled herself a few inches higher, stopping when something pressed against the top of her head. She stepped down a rung and looked skyward to see Colt's arrow stuck into the cliff just above her. Dead set in the very middle of the ladder's two uprights, the arrow stuck straight out of the rock, a rope attached near its anchor point. How had he possibly made that shot in the waning light?

"That was some shot, Captain."

Colt gave her a sly smile as he climbed another rung. The ladder, just wide enough for one person, required that she edge to the right so he could slide up beside her. "Want me to climb down a few rungs and give you some room?" She dared look down to the tier below. Mist had overtaken the ground, hiding the rich, dark soil with an ethereal white, wispy froth.

"No, I need you here to set your tether." He went straight to work, untying his rucksack and then, with one hand still gripping the ladder, he retrieved a foot-long clamp from a small side pouch. He attached the clamp to his belt and then to the rung directly in front of his waist. Leaning back, clearly trusting the clamp to hold him to the towering cliff, he was seemingly oblivious to the treacherous drop below. Every movement was smooth and easy. His hands were steady and his focus intense. He felt at home up here, that was clear.

He searched in the sack until he found what he was looking for, obvious by the hint of a smile that passed his lips. Producing a small prybar, he leveraged the anchor tip free from the rock, unscrewed this specialized arrow tip and replaced it in his sack, the shaft in his quiver. Tess instinctively reached for the rope with her left hand and held it for the Bowman. When he finished disassembling the arrow, he set to coiling the long rope and replacing it in the sack as well.

Reaching into the front flap of the sack, he produced a length of rope maybe three yards long. He had mentioned a tether. Was this it? How would it all work?

"You don't have a Bowman belt, so I'll need to tie this around your waist. I'll lock-knot the other end to my belt, and I'll have you in case you slip." Their eyes met again. His were serious and certain.

"But you'll just be holding on yourself. With your injury, if I fall, won't that jarring force rip you from the ladder? I'm sure you won't slip or make a mistake and lose your footing. You're obviously trained for all this. Wouldn't it be better, for the sake of the Realm, if we climbed separately? I can't jeopardize your mission. What's to keep you on the ladder?"

Colt repressed a smile. She could see him struggling to restrain it with his jaw muscles. "Bowman resolve, my lady." He then attempted to loop the rope behind her back, but her right hand shot out instinctively, stopping him. His eyes flashed to hers.

"I can't let you risk falling if I slip. There's too much at stake. The Realm is at stake. I will climb separately!" She would have stamped her foot for emphasis under different circumstances.

Colt only shook his head and tried to slip the rope around her back again, which was totally illogical. Why wouldn't he listen? If he knew who she was, that she was his princess, he would be forced to listen. "If this is chivalry, Captain, it is totally misplaced. Under the circumstances, I am a liability."

He paused. "Are you saying you don't think you can make it to the top? Are you telling me you aren't strong enough to make this climb?" The hint of a smile curled the corners of his mouth.

A spark of anger flared deep within her. "Of course not. I can make any climb you can!"

The smile spread across his lips, and he resumed his work, sliding the rope around her and finishing with an intricate knot. Tess gripped the rung until her fingers ached, not because she had lost the argument, but because Colt had bested her by using her own pride to his advantage. *Infuriating.* Her cheeks burned, and she couldn't look him in the eye. He ignored her, tying a second lock knot to his own belt and pulling on both to test they were secure.

Despite her irritation, Tess couldn't help but be awed by the surety of his movements. Could he do this blindfolded?

"All right, my lady. You climb up, and I'll follow. Go slow and steady and try not to tense your arms. Your grip and forearms will tire far faster than your legs, so keep them relaxed, and remember that I am right behind you. If you need a break, let me know and I can help you."

Tess desperately wanted to protest this last statement but bit her tongue. She turned and complied, attempting to follow his advice.

They climbed on indefinitely, and just as he'd described, her arms ached. Her fingers cramped and her shoulders strained, but her forearms screamed in pain. How far had they climbed? How much farther to the precipice? Her muscles cried out in agony, and yet, she must persevere. She took a deep breath. No, she needed to stop for a moment. She slipped her arm under the bladespar rung, cold now from the increased elevation. Locking her elbow, she hung on, allowing her forearms a brief respite. The captain's injured arm, how it must ache! She twisted to look below her.

Her eyes widened. No longer able to see the ground, she had no way to gauge their height. The mist had overtaken the entire tier of Costair and drifted steadily towards them. The wind had picked up and the smell of rain hung in the air. A cool breeze swept over them from above—a downdraft originating skyward of their location in Ardenia.

This current of cool plummeting air blew the mist off the cliff face, creating a column clear of haze up and down the limestone. A sudden flash of light illuminated the rock, followed by a loud clap of thunder. Tess jumped. The deep, jarring sound struck right to the center of her being. She felt exposed, vulnerable, and … free.

She gazed out at the storm. The mist, kept at bay by the cool air, swirled and twisted a few yards beyond them. Lightning flashed again, and Tess screamed. In the brief light, a huge, dark shadow had been silhouetted against the mist only thirty yards from where they stood. What could that be? She snapped her head down to Colt.

He must have heard her scream, as he had scrambled to her side before the thunder sounded.

"What's wrong? Are you afraid of storms? I won't let you fall, Tess, I promise." He spoke over the sound of the rushing wind and the distant rain edging towards them.

"No, no, I love storms, but there's something in the mist. In the cloud right there. It looked like a giant, floating shield. Right there."

She jerked her head to where she had seen the ominous shadow. Colt followed her gaze. Lightning flashed again, and Tess saw the massive shape once more.

Colt grabbed her arm and slid her to the center of the ladder facing out from the cliff and her elbow still hooked around the rung as an anchor. Then he stepped on either side of her feet and held onto the two vertical side supports. Pulling himself close, he pressed them both against the ladder, shielding Tess with his body. She stared directly into Colt's throat. He stood so close, breathing hard.

Shifting ever so slightly, she peered around him, into the cloud where she had last seen the shadow.

The mist parted to reveal a huge blimpoon, made of massive, seamed strips of white fabric, floating slowly towards them. Mist Raiders. Tess's heartrate quickened instantly. "Is that a lighter-than-air ship?" She tore her gaze from the large balloon and looked into Colt's eyes, inches from hers. He nodded as he watched it. Bladespar itself couldn't match the sharpness in his stare. Was he scared?

"They'll see us here. There's no mist to hide us—they will see us and shoot us." She whispered the words directly into his ear.

He shook his head decisively. "No, my cloak will camouflage us. It's painted with the exact pattern of this strata of stone and ore. We'll blend right in, and they'll be distracted by the storm. People see what they expect to see, and they won't expect us up here, I promise."

She shifted her gaze to the airship, fully visible now.

"What do you see, my lady? Can you describe it?"

She took a deep breath. "Under the blimpoon, what appears to be a sea-raiders' ship swings suspended from bladespar cables. Two great fins stretch off the port and starboard sides, no doubt angled to catch the wind. There are cannons mounted just above the fins and there is a crew." Another flash of lightning illuminated the scene with razor-sharp resolution. "It's named *The Dancing Girl*. What is it doing here? Is it part of the invasion? Why would it be out in the storm?" She gazed up at the man who stood as the only line of defense between her and the cannons mounted to the deck of the schooner.

He met her stare. "Until six months ago, it was a merchant ship from Ardenia. In the last half-year, it's been responsible for at least three dozen acts of piracy—literally the most notorious sea-raider of late. My counterparts skyward are having a hard time catching it in the act. It moors at Dungridge. Obviously, the pirates have modified it with a lighter-than-air blimpoon. I imagine they're here for the next hoistment."

"But the hoist is closed for the night. How can they carry out a raid in this storm?"

"The storm blew in suddenly. They were probably glad for that thick mist that preceded it and took a chance. This might be a reconnaissance mission. If they have recently retrofitted that ship to be airworthy, they probably want to test it." He spoke coolly and evenly. How could he be so confident? Colt tightened his grip on either side of her hands. "Do they show any signs of sighting us?"

Tess glanced over his shoulder to check on the progress of the mist raider. It had floated past them and veered closer to the cliffs. It would soon reach the section of cliff the hoist ascended day after day. He craned his neck to check for himself. Resting her head against the ladder rung, she watched through the narrow gap between the cliff and Colt's profile. A gust of wind swept by them, catching the ship. The vessel blew too close to the cliff, the starboard fin caught in the downdraft, and the entire airship was hurtled down and back into the mist in one circular motion. As suddenly as it appeared, it vanished into the storm.

Sighing deeply, his body relaxed against her. "They'll need to trouble shoot that downdraft before they attempt a raid in daylight." His jaw unclenched, replaced by a smirk.

Tess touched the material at his shoulder. "That's some cloak, Captain."

"Yeah, and it reverses so the inside matches the cliffs of Ardenia. It's protocol to wear it when ascending. My chief used to tell us it would only be a matter of time before it saved our life."

"Saved both our lives. Quick thinking, using it to cover both of us like that." His cheeks tinged pink, setting off a flock of butterflies in her stomach. With a new surge of energy, she turned to face the cliff and climbed skyward again, but after only four rungs, the rope pulled tight against her waist. She looked down to see the Bowman holding a ladder rung in the crook of his right elbow the way she had and gently shaking his left arm.

Rain pelted the back of her body, and the bladespar rungs grew slippery. She climbed down, tucking in beside him on the narrow ladder. Her forearms ached, so she could only imagine the pain he felt in his wounded arm. She locked her left elbow and reached out to stop his arm from shaking.

His smile appeared forced. "It's all right, just going a bit numb. Don't worry, I'm fine."

Grabbing his wrist, she lifted his arm to the side. Lightning flashed again, followed by an immediate clap of thunder. The storm had consumed them, the ladder, and the entire cliff.

"Can you hold it steady?" Colt squinted, biting his lower lip. His left hand and forearm shuddered uncontrollably. Tess lowered his hand to the ladder rung and rested her fingers on his forearm. "It's in spasm, you need to rest it."

He nodded, closed his eyes, and breathed deeply. Then he hooked the injured elbow through the rung, freeing his good arm. His left arm still trembled involuntarily, but as soon as his right arm was free, he began untying the rope at her waist.

She frowned. "What are you doing?"

"I'm the liability right now." He focused on the complicated knot and somehow managed to loosen it with one hand. Lightning flashed and more thunder rumbled.

"Absolutely not. If you wouldn't cut me loose earlier, why in the Realm is this logical now?" She might have jerked out of his reach, but given their precarious position, that could send both of them plummeting to their deaths.

He only smiled, a genuine smile this time, and kept to his work, undoing the knot in only seconds. Then he replaced the tether and nodded skyward for her to resume climbing.

She scowled at him. "This is literally the definition of a double standard, you know that, right?"

"Yep." He nodded skyward again.

"You're infuriating, Captain!" As she spoke the words, the heat of the flame that burned inside did something it hadn't before—it melted a tiny sliver of her heart.

It was clearly useless to argue with him. With a sigh, she reached for the rung above her. She climbed on and on, constantly needing to stop and wipe the rain from her eyes, using the pauses to check on the Bowman, who climbed steadily below her.

Her forearms screamed. How could they burn like that? How was Colt managing? She checked on him again. He clung to the cliff more than seven rungs seaward of her, farther than he'd yet lagged behind. His forehead rested on the rock while his left arm dangled limp at his side. Her breathing grew shallow. Would he make it? Before she could call down, ask him how he was, he suddenly began climbing, nearly sprinting skyward. Tess scrambled to match his pace, desperate not to impede his progress. Suddenly, her head struck something hard above her. The impact shuddered through her entire body, and she looked up. A bladespar grating, supported by thick girders. Barbed metal coiled on either side of her, forming an impenetrable barrier to the tier above. They had reached the infamous Ardenian bladespar barricade.

Colt settled in next to her. He reached into a small pocket on the side of his pack and pulled the clamp out. After securing himself to the ladder at his waist, he used only his right hand to undo a wooden toggle from the leather loop on his pack, and then from the pocket he produced the legendary Bowman crest. Light filled the sky as a fork of lightning cut its way through the mist to the ground below. The crest flashed silver and emerald with the brilliant display.

He raised his hand to the bladespar grate, placed the carved crest into a like-carved receptacle, and turned it sharply to the right. Tess's heart swelled. She had learned more about the Bowmen in one evening than in her entire life. How she longed to be one of them.

"Can you help me push it open? It's heavy, and I'm not sure I can manage with one arm."

She turned to him in surprise. There was no hint of bravado in his voice, no smirk on his face. She nodded, and together they forced the heavy bladespar hatch up and open.

It swung on its huge hinge and banged loudly as it slammed down onto the section of grate beside it. Relief swept over her entire body. Tess was exhausted, wet, cold, and her muscles ached. Would she have lasted another yard? Could she have managed any of this on her own? Did *she* have Bowman resolve? The young captain obviously brimmed over with it. She longed to know the answer.

Chapter Six

The Hoist

Colt

THE LOADED RUCKSACK SHIFTED ON COLT'S back as he jogged to the main hoist with Tess keeping pace. The cool air bit at his cheeks, damp with sweat, but he was glad for the crisp air of Ardenia. It had been over six months since he'd set foot in his home tier, and even under the circumstances, it brought a small measure of relief. Upon arriving at the vertical link between the two tiers, Colt made straight for the counterweight. He unfastened the safety chain and disengaged the impact clamp. Stepping onto the weight itself, he reached for the massive lever.

Tess jogged to his side. She gasped, slightly, recovering from the run. Dripping wet, she examined the huge plumbite block at his feet. Her eyes shifted to the dangling safety chain and then the lever. She let out a long even exhalation. "So, what do you need, Captain?"

A strange sensation rushed through him. Did nothing daunt her? "This isn't going to be easy. We're going to release the counterweight and ride it down. The hoist will rise in direct proportion to our descent. When we meet in the middle, we'll need to jump off the weight to the hoist platform and ride it up. I've set the clamp to disengage on impact with the ground, so when the counterweight reaches Costair soil, the cable will snap free, and the hoist will immediately plummet again. That means that we need to simultaneously engage both breaking levers to lock it skyward before it falls."

She nodded slowly. "If you don't set the clamp to disengage, the hoist will still be connected to the counterweight and they will be able to use its cable to lower it back seaward from Costair, right?"

"That's right."

She nodded again. "We need to ride it up so that we are braced and ready to throw the two levers as soon as the weight hits the ground, and we reach the docking site?"

"Yes." She was remarkably intuitive.

"How much force does it take to lock out the brakes?" She bit her lower lip.

He swallowed hard. "A lot. You'll need to brace your shoulder against it and push with the weight of your entire body." A sick feeling flooded through him. She wasn't strong enough.

Like she could read his mind, a smirk curled her upper lip. "Don't worry, Bowman, I'll get it done, you can be sure of that. Somehow, I'll manage." She stepped off the loading dock and onto the plumbite block to his left, grasping the cable with both hands.

He took a deep breath and forced the lever down with all his strength. As soon as it hit the midpoint in its arcing motion, a loud metallic clang sounded their release. They fell quickly, nothing close to a freefall, but fast all the same. Timing the jump to the ascending hoist platform would be trickier than he thought. Blast. "I'm sorry, but this is going to be hard." He yelled over the noise of the rain and the thunder and the cool air rushing past his face.

She looked up at him, a wide smile on her face. "We'll make it." Her eyes held concern, but mixed with her fear, he saw wonder.

Tearing his attention from the girl, he focused on the hoist. It just breached a layer of mist and was visible, climbing fast and furious. They needed to jump early, probably much earlier than his mind would deem necessary—early was their only play, late wasn't an option. His ears popped and he forced a yawn to stretch his jaw.

Tess did the same thing at the very same moment.

He placed his hand on the small of her back, it was bare. Her skin was cool and smooth. He pressed firmly, guiding her to the edge of the plummeting counterweight.

She released her grasp of the cable and held both hands out to steady herself, ready for the impact of the landing.

"On three…three, two, one, jump." He didn't need to push her. She jumped without hesitation at exactly the same time he jumped. Colt dove to the left, slamming into the wooden planks and rolling onto his injured arm.

Tess dove to the right, rolled and rode the momentum perfectly to a standing position. She reached out and grasped the railing, steadying herself a moment, before a wide smile broke across her face. "You okay?" She nodded to his arm.

No, he wasn't okay. His arm screamed in pain. "Sure." He rose and walked to her side.

She still held the railing for support, clutching it tightly with both hands.

He looked skyward and checked on their progress, squinting to shield his eyes against the rain. They'd ascended farther than he expected in the mere moments since their jump. He sprang to the west lever and pointed for her to get into position. Sidestepping to the thick bladespar handle, she set her shoulder against it, just as he'd described. She placed her feet far enough back that her body leaned into the lever at almost a seventy-degree angle. Nodding her readiness, she stole a glance skyward, closed her eyes and made the sign of descent.

This was it. Colt couldn't misjudge the timing. As soon as he felt the hoist stop, he needed to throw the lever and lock it out. Could she mange the same? There wasn't any time for doubts, the docking platform hurtled towards them only yards away.

A jarring force so strong it nearly knocked Colt over, indicated the weight had slammed into the ground. Colt shoved the lever forward with all his might and almost instantly, felt the tremor of the west gear lock into place somewhere beneath the floorboards. Tess?

The girl pushed at a forty-five-degree angle to the lever, her toes flexed and every muscle tensed, showing the definition in her arms. Would it prove enough? She screamed "help!" the cry desperate.

Colt leapt to her side, grasped the bladespar bar just below her hands, and swung underneath it, pulling down with every ounce of strength. The lock-out engaged, producing the most satisfying clang as it did. He slumped to the platform, his arm spasming in pain.

Tess slid down the lever, hanging from the midpoint with both hands until she released and fell to the floor. She lay flat on her back, her chest heaving as she let the rain pelt her face.

They had done it. The hoist was now inert, and Ardenia was secure.

"I am so sorry I couldn't do it. You saved us, Captain." Shame dripped form the apology, but she didn't open her eyes.

"You managed to hold until I got there. You managed, just like you said you would." Truly, it had been just enough, exactly what they needed.

Colt pushed himself to his feet and leapt from the large platform. He strode inside the hoistment office. The border checkpoint was dark, but he remedied that by lighting a tiny oil lamp. Sliding back the oak chair, he sat at the main operator's desk and retrieved parchment and a graphite stick from his kit. His right hand trembled, though not as violently as the left, which still spasmed, and he concentrated hard, attempting to steady it.

Tess placed her hand on his. "Let me, Captain." She gently took the graphite stick from his fingers. Wiping her wet hands against a canvas sack, she breathed deeply. Did she appreciate the cool air of home? She held up the stick. "What would you like me to write?"

Leaning back in the oak chair, he considered the question. "By order of the King's Bowmen, the hoist is not to descend to Costair under any circumstance, save the order of Colonel Merriweather or King Lucius. Signed, Captain Colt Hawthorne." She scrolled the note in the most elegant cursive Colt had ever seen, as though the tip of the graphite stick ice skated over the frozen lake of parchment. Where in the Realm did she learn to write like that?

"The hoistmen may not understand cursive writing, my lady. Could you recopy it in standard print?"

Blushing, she shook her head, as if she should have thought of that. She quickly flipped over the paper and rewrote the message in neat, even printing, equally beautiful.

Colt searched his Rucksack for his wax block and held it over the lantern. Three large drips of wax landed squarely at the bottom of the note. Where had he put his crest? He felt his left pocket, where he always kept it, but the crest wasn't there. Of course not. With his left arm injured, he wouldn't have used it to stow the vital piece of Bowman identification, but what had he done with it?

"Your crest is in the right breast pocket of your cloak, Captain."

He snapped to attention. How did she know what he needed? Clearly, she had noted where he had placed it after unlocking the hatch. Who *was* this girl?

"Here, let me get it." Before Colt could protest, she reached forward and unbuttoned his cloak breast pocket, retrieving the crest.

He nodded towards the cooling wax. "You want to do the honors?" A smile crept up the corners of her mouth, and she pursed her lips. Was she attempting to feign a serious expression? Regardless, she firmly pressed the Bowman crest into the wax, authenticating the order.

He pushed out from the desk and strode to the main hoist winch. Rain pelted his face as soon as he left the cover of the office overhang. He reached for his rucksack, and his arm began to spasm again. *Blast, concentrate Hawthrone.* As he fumbled with the largest compartment, Tess gently lifted it off his shoulder. He hadn't even noticed she'd followed him out.

She unfastened the deerskin buckle and raised her eyes to meet his. "What do you need, Captain, the rope?"

"Yes, we need to tie off the hoist itself just in case." Colt cut a length of rope and tied off the central cable, again allowing Tess to seal the knot with wax and his Bowman crest. He shielded her from the rain by holding up his cloak.

Once the wax was set, they both ran back to the office. Just inside he stopped and examined Tess a moment. She was soaked through to the skin, shivering, and her lips were blue. He started to pull the cloak off over his head but stopped short when his left arm spasmed. He took a deep breath, pushed through the pain, and then tried again.

This time Tess reached out and helped, standing on her tiptoes to gently tug the cloak free.

He hated feeling so useless.

As soon as the cloak cleared his left arm, she handed it back to him. He opened it, raised it awkwardly, and lowered it over her head.

Her wide eyes met his as she emerged from the neck hole. "No, Captain, your arm needs to stay warm and dry, your muscle is in trauma." When she reached for the hem of the cloak and started to lift it, he gently grabbed her wrist with his right hand.

"Sorry, Tess, but I am pretty sure providing a lady with your cloak in a rainstorm is written into the Bowman Code somewhere."

She smiled but grew serious when her gaze dropped to his wound. Without saying anything, she twisted her hand. When he released her wrist, she clasped his, turned, and pulled him inside and back to the chair. Then she pushed him down onto it.

"What are you doing? I don't have time to rest. We need to cover at least another mile tonight."

"Not until I stitch that wound." Tess perched on the edge of the office desk and opened the main compartment of the rucksack.

"The med case is in the left side pocket with the toggle."

She located the deerskin med case and began prepping to work on his arm. He watched her in the lamplight as she worked, sterilizing the needle in the flame of the lantern and threading it on the first try. Whoever this girl was, she was beautiful. Her d'orite hair glistened like the first glow of dawn and still pinned in elaborate curls low at the back of her head, set off her big eyes that looked like cuper patinaed to a rich blue-green. Her features were perfect, and her skin shone in the low light. Her smile could set an entire room aglow, though he'd seen it only once, before he had managed to insult her.

Tess bit her lip and held up the needle and thread. "I'm sorry. This will hurt."

Nodding his acknowledgement of the warning, he braced himself as she approached his arm. It did hurt. The wound was raw and vulnerable, and the needle pricks only intensified that pain, but he wouldn't show her that. "So, Lady Tess, who are you, and where did you learn to shoot like that?"

She tensed immediately and stopped tying off her current stitch. When she shot him a worried look, he raised his right hand, palm up. "What? Obviously you've been trained in shooting, and quite a few other things, for that matter."

Tess swallowed and returned her focus to her work. "Says who?"

She refused to look at him now. Had he struck a nerve? Why would she care if he knew how she'd learned to shoot? "Says me."

"Are you an expert in the accomplishments of ladies of court, Captain?"

Colt pursed his lips. Why was she dodging his questions? "I am an expert in most things, my lady."

Her jaw tightened, her breathing quickened, and her cheeks tinged with pink. Why did he have to sound cocky?

"Well, apparently there isn't a problem in the realm that you can't think your way out of, so you shouldn't have any trouble figuring out this one." She sat up straight, examined her stitching, and then trimmed the last thread with the sharp surgical knife. She reached for his shirt and without warning used the same knife to cut a fresh, two-inch bandage from the hem of it. After wrapping the wound, she gently tied it off with her nimble fingers. Why did her touch feel so soft, so good, even next to his throbbing wound? *Focus, Hawthorne.*

Colt rose and extended his hand to help her to her feet.

Ignoring it, she rose without help, walking past him and out of the office.

He turned and followed her, and all at once it stopped raining. They both looked up in wonder. The sky cleared above them, and the stars looked low enough to touch. The weather on the sea-surrounded spire could change in a moment. Storms blew in without warning and, after dumping their load, clouds crested the vertical horizon and drifted off over Reyjik.

He exhaled deeply, his breath fogging and frosting on the night air. How could early spring in Ardenia be so significantly colder than Costair? He understood the concept of elevation and the effect it had on the climate of the tiers, but to experience such a drastic change over a mere thousand yards was so very different than understanding a theory.

Tess exhaled as well and then she closed her eyes and breathed in deeply. They needed to put at least another mile behind them before stopping for the night. Would she make it? He set off at an easy pace, and she scrambled after him without a word.

They jogged for twenty minutes, until Colt stopped short of a small creek. He edged down the bank carefully and then reached back to help Tess do the same, but when he turned, she already stood beside him. "We'll camp here and get a few hours' rest, but at dawn we move again."

Before he finished speaking, Tess sat on the ground and unlaced her shoes. She then walked gingerly to the bank and waded into the cold creek.

Colt pitched a large woolen blanket over a rope he had strung between two trees. His arm ached, but the tremors had subsided. The stitching helped, even mentally. Knowing the wound was closed and bound made him feel strong and whole again somehow.

The rope hung a mere two feet above the ground but taut, and it served nicely as the main support for a tent. Colt unrolled the second blanket inside and joined Tess at the water's edge.

"How are your feet?" He felt sorry for her. His dress uniform shoes weren't ideal, but her heals must have proven torture at this point. She simply shook her head and yawned, clearly exhausted. Colt nodded at the makeshift campsite. "I've set up a small tent for you there. You can sleep a few hours. I'll sleep out front."

Tess nodded and walked slowly out of the creek, making her way straight to the tent. Only a matter of minutes after he laid down, he heard her faint call.

"Captain, are you still awake?"

"Yes." Colt sat up and leaned closer.

"I'm freezing."

Colt pressed his lips together. What could he do about that? The rain had soaked any available wood, so a fire wasn't possible. He had been well trained and knew exactly what two soldiers would do in this situation. Swallowing hard, he crawled into the tent.

"I can sleep here beside you, which will help keep you warm." The rucksack sat next to the bed, and he shifted it in front of the opening to block the door and keep the heat inside. "The woolen blanket will trap our combined body heat, and you'll be warm soon, I promise."

Tess stiffened as he edged in beside her, but she said nothing, only lay quietly. Was she holding her breath? A minute passed, and still she said nothing. Was she angry? "Lady Tess, I am sorry. I'm only trying to..."

The quietest whistle cut short the apology. Tess breathed deeply, so deeply that she let out a slight snoring sound at every second exhalation. She had fallen asleep instantly, no doubt exhausted from the climb.

Colt decided the whistle was the most adorable sound he had ever heard. Listening to her deep, even breaths, he drifted off to sleep.

Chapter Seven

The Coast

Tess

TESS STRETCHED HER ARMS STRAIGHT ABOVE her head and pointed her toes as hard as she could. It felt good. She had only been allowed a few hours' sleep, but they had been solid, which surprised her. When she opened her eyes, she found herself staring directly at the captain's shirt buttons. Where were they? She felt the warmth of his right arm against her shoulders and back, her body snugged tightly up to his side, and her head resting on his chest. She froze, holding her breath. Was he still asleep? Could she slide out of his embrace without waking him?

"Good morning. Did you sleep all right?" The Bowman spoke softly. Blast. Of course he had woken first.

Tess nodded. She had never woken up next to someone else before. What did one say in such a situation? A terrible thought crossed her mind. "I didn't snore, did I? Or drool. Did I drool?" She rose to her elbows, her finger darting to the edge of her mouth to check for moisture. "You see, I've never slept with a man before, and I have no idea if I do either of those things."

He smiled broadly, a sly, mischievous smile.

Tess frowned. What was so funny? Warmth flooded her cheeks as she realized what she had just admitted. An honest admission the captain had clearly enjoyed.

She scrambled backwards, putting as much distance between them as she could in the cramped space. "Oh, please. Of course I'm still a maid, Captain. You have a girl in every village, I suppose. The handsome young Bowman comes to town and the girls swoon, fighting for your company. Not me. All the wooing and compliments and long, meaningful looks in the realm couldn't entice me, not a chance. But I thank you nonetheless for the comfort. I was warm enough to sleep last night, and the rest has allowed me the spunk to feel thoroughly annoyed right now." She sat up quickly, forgetting the low rope, and bounced her forehead off the taut support above her. "Blast." That hurt! She rubbed her head.

Colt laughed. He actually laughed at her!

She flipped over, kicked the rucksack out the end of the tent, and crawled into the open. "I am wearing this cloak from now on." Her cheeks burned, and she knew the crimson color they showed all too well. Desperate to hide them, she stomped over to her shoes and busied herself with scraping the mud from their soles. The cold morning air bit against her fingers and cheeks, a drastic difference from Costair the evening before or the tent moments ago. She inhaled, wincing as the sharp air stung the inside of her nose.

The captain emerged from the other side of the tent and immediately began untying the rope that held up the crosspiece, keeping his eye on his work. "More of a whistle, my lady." He glanced over at her, finally, as he wound the rope around his palm and elbow.

"Pardon me?" A whistle? What did that mean?

"You don't really snore. It's more of a whistle, or a whinny, like that of a young filly enjoying her oats." Not bothering to look down at what he was doing, he watched her, no doubt to see her reaction.

Her cheeks had cooled, but they flared again now at his teasing. Not wanting to give him the satisfaction of seeing them, she turned her back to him and headed for the river. Dropping her shoes, she picked her way carefully to the water's edge. She wanted to numb her aching feet with the cold water as she had the night before, but first, she needed to pray. She'd meant to pray the night before, but she must have fallen asleep as soon as she laid down, for she had no memory past telling the captain she was cold. She knelt at the edge of the creek and prayed to the All-Father for her sister and every hostage in Costair. Above every other tieral effort, He could help. She asked for guidance for Colt. Not sure what he believed, somehow, the young captain was key to saving their tiermen.

"My lady?" Colt's voice broke the stillness as he approached. She appreciated the warning call, as she suddenly felt self-conscious, kneeling to pray. Would he think she was childish? She clambered to her feet and quickly stepped into the river.

Colt reached the bank and settled on a large rock. "I'm sorry for interrupting you, Lady Tess." He sounded so weary.

She turned to contemplate him.

His brow was furrowed, his jaw tight. His face betrayed the burden he carried. Did he feel responsible for the very security of the Realm? She felt for him. He might be arrogant, but she couldn't deny his call to duty, and her presence only made carrying it out more difficult. If he knew her secret, it would be an even heavier load. But they were heading back to Castle Fairgates where she couldn't hide her identity, so she'd be honest with the young captain. She would tell him of her royal lineage. He hadn't left her in the lookout, she owed him that.

"Lady Tess." He clasped his hands between his knees.

"Just Tess," she corrected gently. "*Lady* is not my proper title, Captain. Actually, I have something I need to tell you before we go any further." Her hands shook and she stepped out of the cold water and took a seat beside him on a low, flat rock.

"Go ahead, ladies first. But when you've told me, I need to speak quickly. My destination has changed."

Her heartrate quickened. "Changed how?" She hugged her knees to her chest.

He unclasped his hands and drove his fingers through his hair. "I simply don't know enough to properly advise the king right now. Nothing makes sense about the attack, and I can't reason out the motivations of Reyjik. I need to see everything at once—Costair, the sluice, Ardenia's waters and borders—and I don't have time to recon in the conventional way. I require a bird's-eye view, a lighter than airship, so I must head east to the coast. I have a friend who works aboard a merchant vessel that docks at Dungridge, and he might be able to get me aboard a raider's ship that's sympathetic to tieral security... if he'll help."

Tess frowned. Who was this friend? "Are you sure you are willing to risk employing a mist raider's ship? The raiders hate the Bowmen!"

"I hate the smugglers. They undermine the entire economy. It's my duty to bring them to justice, but I have no choice. We need information and we need it quickly. This is the only way." The captain stopped and drew in a breath. "I won't take you to Dungridge, of course. We can swing north to a King's Couriers post in Lampton. A courier can deliver you to Castle Fairgates. You'll be safe in his charge until you get there."

Heat rushed into her chest. "I'm not going to Fairgates. I'm coming with you to Dungridge. I want to help. I told you I would see this through."

"Absolutely not. Dungridge is a hive of thieves. The King's Courier will deliver you to safety."

"Like a parcel, I suppose?" She jumped off the rock and planted both fists on her hips.

Colt rose too, his jaw set. "Sure, if he has to, like a parcel."

"What if you need my help?"

"Need your help? Please. I'm a Bowman, Tess. I don't need your help."

"I suppose you locked the hoist by yourself, stitched yourself last night, Captain—with your toes, was it? Most impressive." She waved her right hand in the direction of his wounded arm to make the point.

"My arm is fine now." He straightened, towering over her.

"It's fine because I stitched it." She straightened, nearly standing on her tiptoes to try and bridge the gap between them, to no avail. What if he didn't relent? What if he insisted on sending her away? He needed her help—she could feel it in the deepest part of her heart. She couldn't leave him.

She could pull rank, yes. She could tell him of her true identity, and he would have to obey her orders. Bowman were sworn to obey the royal family in all matters. No, then he would be duty bound to return her to the safety of her father at Fairgates. He needed to do exactly what he'd described, and he didn't have time to babysit her and take her to her father. She couldn't stand in the way of his reconnaissance. The Realm needed him.

"It's my tier, Captain. Those are my people too, my princess. I should be in that ballroom, but I'm not, am I? I'm out here with you, the one person who can do something about all this, and I *am* going to help. I need to help. The All-Father blessed me with freedom, and I will not waste it on the selfishness of personal security." The urge to stamp her foot like she'd wanted to on the ladder gripped her, but she needed him to believe that she was mature enough to stand at his side, to fight with him, so she forced herself to stand still and wait, keeping her gaze locked with his.

For what felt like an eternity, he stared back. Finally, his shoulders relaxed slightly. "Fine. But you will do everything I say, understood?"

Relief swept through her entire body, and she rolled from her tiptoes to her heels. "Understood. Thank you." She reached out and gently placed her hand on his forearm. "How is your arm this morning?"

He jerked his arm away. "I told you, it's fine." Then he turned on his heel and stormed past her, grabbing his rucksack on the way through the campsite. Without looking back, he called over his shoulder, his tone sharp. "What was it you needed to tell me?"

Tess swallowed hard. He had already begun walking east to the edge of the woods. She thought quickly as she fumbled with her laces.

"Just that I would need new shoes, if possible."

"We'll get you some better ones at Dungridge. Clothes too. But we move now. If we keep last night's pace, we'll arrive at the port just after sunset."

Tess's stomach roiled at the thought of jogging at the pace of the night before for hours again today. *How did wanting to go for a simple run, barefoot in the woods, land me in blisters?*

Chapter Eight

The Draw

Colt

Colt unpacked the ration kit and laid the small package open on a flat rock. The cliffs of Ardenia formed a massive wall to the south, stretching straight up to the tier of Lindsor. Sunshine bathed the Realm until past-peak, but after midday the looming spire's shadow only grew. Much of Colt's waking hours were spent in the shadow of the peak, so he insisted on rising before dawn every day, not wanting to waste a moment of the golden light. His mother had described sunsets to him, and he longed to see one with his own eyes. Sunsets were a daily occurrence in Reyjik, but the Realm heard of them only in the stories of travelers.

Calling to Tess, he insisted she choose from the dehydrated kits first. They had made good time after he remedied her footwear, and they rested midway up the Cressida Escarpment. From their perch, they overlooked a wide, forested valley, dappled with green as leaves began to bud, reminding him how quickly the spring transformed the countryside. The yellow-green buds clashed against the blue-green ore veins of the patinaed cuper that webbed through the slate cliffs.

Tess sat on the rock and hung her legs over the edge of the small ledge. They backed the precipice to the north and faced inland to the tier in the south. Before opening her food, she looked to the Emerald Star. She raised her left hand to cover her eyes and then placed her right hand to her forehead, gracefully dropping it to her navel—the sign of the Great Descent.

He hung his legs over the ledge beside hers, his eyes tracking a vein of ferrite that breached the surface of the slate escarpment, rusted to a dark orange. Reaching out, she traced the same flaking ore with her fingertip.

"That's some arrowhead, Captain, the way it cleaved the limestone last night. What is it? Bladespar?" She reached for his canteen. "May I?"

He unscrewed it and handed it to her. "Yep, pure bladespar. Strongest stuff in the Realm. It's changed everything."

"Yes, it has." Her forehead creased and she traced the ferrite vein again, rubbing some rusty powder between her fingers. She hadn't opened the sack of nuts yet.

"What? What's wrong?" He tore off a piece of venison jerky with his back teeth.

She closed her eyes. "I'm sure you don't really want to hear what I think."

He laughed. "Why don't you let me decide that?"

But she only looked at him, sadness flashing across her eyes.

"What, Tess. Tell me, honestly, I want to know."

She sighed. "The bladespar. The new industry and invention, all of it toted as a salvation for Ardenia's economy, but it's wrong." Her green eyes locked with his.

"What do you mean, wrong?" How could she say that? "Discovering graphite, inventing bladespar, it's made Ardenia rich and powerful. Our tools are superior, our weapons second to none, and everyone wants it. We make a killing. It's so valuable, the entire Spire uses it as currency for Realm's sake. How can you say that's wrong?"

She sat at attention. "It's wrong because we don't share. We don't even trade fairly. We hold a complete monopoly on every aspect of bladespar manufacturing. I know for a fact that Lindsor, Costair, and Reyjik have sent delegations requesting raw bladespar so they might invent to best suit their agricultural needs and mining efforts. The king has denied every request and only offers generic tools in limited quantities at extreme costs."

Colt's chest tightened. His arm throbbed. "Well, you can't be suggesting we give it away." He braced his left arm below the elbow on his knee, hoping she wouldn't notice.

"No, I'm not saying we should give it away, but we could set a fair price. We could trade it and let our fellow tiers apply it to their specific needs. We both know just how dramatically it can change industry." Her right hand darted to the back of her neck, and she began twisting a loose strand of hair around her index finger. "When I think about Costairs trying to farm without it, or Lindsites trying to mine—or even the Reyjik. We all depend on their cloth, and we have something that would make textile production much more efficient, and yet we hoard it." Her brow furrowed. "Well, what do you think, Captain?"

He hadn't thought about it. He appreciated every single bladespar tool and weapon issued in the corps but had never considered life in other tiers. Even in Costair, he'd boarded in the palace barracks and hadn't bothered to take stock of what life was like without bladespar. He reached for the canteen and sipped to stall. "I think that we are making the most of our resources. I mean, we have it. We figured out how to refine it, right?"

Her eyes narrowed. "Wrong. The All-Father placed each resource evenly. For generations there has been at least a semblance of balance. Now He's blessed us with bladespar, all of it–the raw ore, the genius to refine it and the wisdom to apply it, to invent. I am sure, right to the core of my very heart, that we are to share that. He's trusted this amazing gift to us, so we can't hoard it. Every principle in the Sacreds tells me our monopoly is wrong." She bit her lower lip.

He didn't know how to respond.

She shifted to face him. "Think about it. If you were a father and you had four children, and you sent them all off to school one morning, middle-meals in hand..." She paused, her eyes searching his.

He nodded. "Go on."

"Well, let's say that come past peak, the oldest child found four biscuits in his pail, what should he think? Should he assume that his mother and father love him more, and have therefore blessed him better than his siblings?" She paused again.

Nodding, he encouraged her to continue.

"Or should he get up and find his three brothers and give them each a biscuit?" Her hand darted back to the loose strands of hair, and she began twisting again.

What could he say? "Do you really think it's that simple?"

"I think… I think that our greed has consequences."

"Consequences, what kind of consequences?"

"The piracy. We didn't have the mist raiders before the monopoly."

Something like the butt of a spear virtually knocked the wind out of Colt. It was Bowman duty to quell the mist raider scourge, but her entire premise undermined that service. How could she accuse her own tier, her own king of causing the piracy? "The raiding could have come with invention. I mean, before bladespar, we couldn't fabricate the cables, or the burners required for lighter than aircraft. The piracy could be a crime of opportunity, not a consequence of Ardenia's monopoly."

As the sun crested the vertical horizon, a last halo of light silhouetted the peak and then everything dimmed.

She exhaled long and even. "You make a strong point. No doubt motivation and opportunity go hand in glove, Captain. But my heart still aches for our leadership. I just wish the king would trust the All-Father's ways, and allow fair trade, even to share. With the gift, comes great responsibility, a test, as it were. I fear, because of greed, we are failing." She looked out over the shaded forest. "You approve of our policy, then?"

Did he approve? Her argument struck at something deep. A poor, half-blood, thorn farmer, how different life would be if everyone thought like Tess? Like the Sacreds? His chest felt tight again. "I think it's my duty is to defend the policy, not make it, my lady." A cop out to be sure. He cleared his throat. "Right now, I have to defend against something entirely unexpected."

She pursed her lips, her brow wrinkling in concentration. "I wonder if something has happened in Reyjik. Is it possible something has happened to their Diamond Star, and that's why they would do this, jeopardize everything with an attack? I mean, what they've done is so selfish."

His stomach twisted. Was that a slight against his mother's tierality? Was Tess reminding him of his place like everyone else?

They sat in silence in the shadow of the vertical horizon, until Tess tore open the small packet of roasted nuts. "So, we travel another few miles on the south side, then crest the ridge and we should be in sight of the sea, right?" She sprinkled a few nuts onto her palm.

"That's right." Colt raised his canteen to his lips and sipped the water sparingly, leaving some for her. "Can you explain to me how a lady of your station knows this area so well?" He used his sleeve to swipe a drop of water from his lip. Would she evade that question as she had done all the others he had asked her that day? She definitely had a secret, but he had decided not to attempt to figure out what it was. Consumed with the Reyjik and their motivations and means, he didn't have the luxury of unraveling this girl's story. He would simply enjoy asking her pointed questions and watching her attempt to field them. Would he eventually exhaust her repertoire of vague responses? More likely she would trust him before that happened, as she seemed to have an endless cache of ideas.

"Can you explain to me how I might make a full draw on this longbow?" She sprang up, lifted his bow gracefully from the rock where he had lain it down, and then readied the quiver of arrows he had given her the night before. She stood looking at him, clearly waiting for him to respond.

Colt rose quickly, not ready for the unusual request and not sure how to advise her.

Tess frowned. "It is possible, is it not? I mean, I can't be expected to simply accept that it's impossible for me to make full draw." She placed her free hand on her hip.

"Can't you?" He crossed his arms. He knew many men twice her size who had never made full draw on a longbow.

Her eyes narrowed in determination. "No, I can't. I mean, I won't. I won't accept it. Not yet, anyway. Let's think about this. I know I lack the strength for it, but even Bowmen must find their strength compromised at times, no? Tell me, what would you do now that you're injured? How would you compensate to still make a full draw?"

"I can still draw with this injury."

She sighed dramatically. "Well, let's say you couldn't, but you had to. What would you do?"

"Well, let me see. What would I do?" He rubbed his chin, teasing her now.

Sheer delight shone in her eyes, making her face luminescent, and he found himself unable to deny her request. "Draw back as far as you can."

When she complied, she strained against the force of the sprung yew wood. Colt had an idea. "Wait." Gently, he tugged the bow from her hand and handed her the one he had given her from the supplies in the lookout. "Mine is a monster. Custom made. This one is the standard and has more give. The draw weight is about half. Try it and see if it makes a difference." Again, she drew, and this time she pulled back to almost full draw. "Well, that was at least three quarters right there. You should be happy. That shot would carry around two hundred yards."

Her brow furrowed as she released the string. "I don't want to fire it two-hundred yards. I want to fire it three hundred and forty yards, like you shoot. Now please, is there anything I can do to improve my technique?"

Colt sighed. "Draw again?" Circling her this time, he examined everything she did as she drew back the bowstring.

"Couldn't we just get you a smaller bow?" Picking up a small stone, he hurled it into the narrow treeline.

She shook her head. "I don't want a smaller bow. I want to be able to fire this bow. What if I'm in battle? What if I come across the bow of a fallen archer and then I see you. You're about to be slashed from behind by an enemy swordsman, but you haven't seen him, and you are three hundred forty yards away, and your only hope is that I shoot this bow at full draw and place an arrow right between his eyes." She finished out of breath, shaking the bow a little as though to emphasize her points.

"I would think you'd do nothing and let me get slashed, my lady, as you clearly find me infuriating."

She burst out laughing. A genuine laugh. Why did that make him feel so good?

"I am going to shoot him between the eyes, I said!" She stomped her foot playfully.

"Between his eyes? What's wrong with his heart, Lady Tess? You know, central body mass. Or something more ladylike? Perhaps the arm that holds the sword?" Colt teased again. She allowed him this, but she wouldn't be deterred from her quest.

"All right." He stood in front of her and bent his knees so he they stood eye to eye. He cocked his head to the side playfully and met her gaze. "I will need to get closer, my lady." He felt compelled to warn her. Tess got nervous any time that he got close to her, absolutely skittish. It didn't offend him. Indeed, it was the appropriate response for a well-bred girl her age. She nodded her consent.

"Okay, so stand firm on your feet. Now place a little more weight on your front foot." When he touched her right leg lightly with the tips of his fingers, Tess obeyed instantly. "Good. Now, when you've drawn these last few times, you were only using the muscle here in the back of your shoulder." He moved his hand to the spot on her shoulder so she would understand.

"My rear deltoid." She identified it immediately. How would she know such an obscure fact?

"Yes, that's exactly what it's called. It's not a large muscle at all. In fact, it is only a small part of the muscle group I use to draw." He stretched his back and rolled his shoulder. "I was a lot smaller when I began my training as an archer, and I couldn't draw right either."

She sighed, and he frowned. "Sorry. That wasn't a critique. You draw amazingly well, for a girl." She cringed again, and he couldn't help but laugh. "Just let me show you." Colt touched the back part of her shoulder. She tensed slightly as he ran the pads of his fingers all the way down to her side, but he carried on.

"This is your trapezius muscle. It is much bigger than the little deltoid muscle you are using at the top of your shoulder. And this is your latissimus dorsi." He slid his hand to indicate where the other large muscle met along her lower back and side. Her muscles tightened again, but she did seem keenly focused. "See, I don't draw like you, with my arm. I couldn't when I was a kid. I would never have managed. Actually, I don't even know how you manage as well as you do with that technique… sheer willpower, I imagine." He lifted his arm. "I raise my arm like this, in a high arc, elbow up. That forces me to stretch out the latissimus as I nock my arrow and then I pull with the full contraction of both muscles in my back, maybe all the muscles in my back. The deltoid just helps to steady my arm as I sight my target."

Colt smiled to himself. That was a very good explanation, far better than he had ever received in his military service or at the Bowman's Academy. Maybe that innate depth of understanding explained why he was such a dead shot.

Tess cleared her throat, and he glanced down to see his hand still resting on her back. Heat crawled up his neck as he pulled it away.

She broke the awkward silence. "So, you're telling me to draw with my back, not with my arm?"

"Yes, that's it. Message received." He rolled his back and left shoulder again, attempting to loosen the sore muscle.

Tess stepped forward and simultaneously applied everything he had just taught her. She planted her feet, shifted her weight forward, nocked the arrow—making sure to do so with a high arc, her elbow raised—and she then pulled back decisively with all the effort her slight back could muster, to the great achievement of drawing the bow completely. She gasped and then released the arrow. It flew high and true, arcing beautifully.

Colt let out a primeval howl in celebration.

"Did you see that, Captain?"

He laughed as she asked him three more times. Colt assured her he had seen it. He couldn't wipe the smile off his face as she began to trust what had just transpired.

Tess jumped down from the ledge and ran at full speed in the direction the arrow had flown.

He threw his arms in the air. "Where are you going?"

"I want that arrow. I'm going to keep it forever!" she yelled over her shoulder as she ran.

He couldn't help but laugh. "How will you ever find it?"

"It will be stuck in the dirt, or a tree, at three hundred forty yards!" She hollered back triumphantly.

Colt shook his head in wonder at the strange girl. "You've got five minutes and then I'm leaving." For some reason, he needed the last word. Propping a shoulder against a large rock of, he waited for her. In a little less than five minutes, she emerged from the woods, still running. At the look on her face, he shoved away from the rock and strode to the edge of the ledge. "What is it, Reyjik?" His heartrate quickened as he scanned the treeline.

Tess didn't answer, only kept running at a blinding pace, clearly focused on covering the distance between the treeline and the rock ridge where he stood. Out of the woods behind her crashed an enormous brown bear. Although it only appeared to be running at half its top speed, it was a terrifying sight. Instinctively, he grabbed his bow and quiver and nocked an arrow. Lining up the bear, he began to draw.

"No!" Tess shouted. "Don't shoot her!"

Colt hesitated. "What? Why not?" He tracked the bear with the tip of the nocked arrow, ready to draw and let fly.

"Please don't, Colt. I can make it to the ridge. Drop that and pull me up!"

Colt analyzed Tess's chances, keeping the bear in his sights. She could make it if she didn't trip and the bear didn't increase its speed. As she drew closer, he began to mutter curses under his breath. He wanted desperately to end this threat. A bear that size would be tough. He might need to bury three or four arrows in its chest before felling it.

She'd almost reached the ledge, but the bear had nearly closed the distance to a point too close to allow for the number of arrows needed to down it. "Ahhhhh!" He let out a cry of frustration.

"Colt, please. Drop the bow and grab me!" She had nearly reached the ledge and had slowed and lifted her hand. Although it went against everything in him, Colt finally dropped the bow and reached for her. She grasped his fingers and jumped, somehow finding a foothold in the sheer wall to launch herself up as he yanked her onto the safety of the ridge. They both crashed to the ground and lay sprawled on the rock.

Tess's chest heaved. After a moment, she rolled onto her side. "Thank you!" she gasped. "Thank you for not shooting her."

The bear growled and roared up at them. It stood on its hind legs and smashed its front paws into the rock wall only twelve inches from where they lay. Tess sat up, crawled over to the pack, and retrieved something from the open rucksack. She tossed it over her shoulder blindly, a dramatic gesture to show she did not care where it landed. Colt followed the package and watched as it smacked down directly beside the furious bear. She'd thrown a ration pack. Tess crawled back to the edge of the ridge and smiled at him. He glanced back and forth between the food and the girl who grinned triumphantly beside him.

"What? She hasn't eaten all winter and she's starving." She shrugged. "Truly, Colt, thank you for not shooting her."

"Why, why couldn't... why would you... How do you know it's a girl?"

Tess took her index finger and gently pushed his chin until he stared in the direction of the treeline again. His mouth dropped open as two tiny bear cubs scampered out of the woods and into the sunshine of the clear ridge.

"If you had downed her, you would have killed all three of them." Tess's eyes locked on the cubs. The two little bears answered their mother's call, skidding and scampering over to where she tore at their rations. The bear seemed totally indifferent to her audience. She only cared about giving the strange treat to her cubs.

He observed in disbelief for several minutes. Then he turned to study the girl next to him. She still watched the young family with the utmost delight. Only then did it occur to him that in her panic she had called him *Colt*. Not *Captain*, but his actual name. And she'd done it three times. Did she realize she had? His face warmed a little. Why did it matter so much?

Something in her hand caught his eye and he glanced down. The arrow. She had found it! He reached over and wiggled it to get her attention.

Pure mischief danced in her eyes when they met his. "It was sticking out of a tree at three hundred and forty yards. At three hundred forty-five yards there may have been a family of foraging bears."

Chapter Nine

The Seaport

Tess

DUNGRIDGE LOOKED EXACTLY HOW TESS HAD imagined—crooked, cluttered, and brown. The wooden buildings soared three or even four stories in places, as if competing with the towering masts that lined the harbor. Every structure on the coast side of the city was comprised of wood—the huge dock that mirrored the shoreline, the slips that stretched out into the sea, and the shacks that edged the wide timber roadway. The inland buildings were made of stone. Shops, taverns, inns and houses, stood side by side, all made of cut brown stone.

The city smelled of rotting wood, of men, and of the sea. Loud and raucous and full of people everywhere. People strolled down the huge dock. People ducked in and out of shops. People stood in the street and talked, laughed, fought, and whispered. Children played Crumble-stumble-turn-and-burn in a nearby alley, shrieking as they crashed to the stone street in unison. So different from her life at Castle Fairgates where people only ever cared about etiquette, propriety, station, and prestige.

Colt led her into a small cobbler's shop and waved his hand past a small rack of women's boots.

Slipping her foot into the first pair that seemed her size, total relief flooded through her. "These are perfect."

Striding to the counter, he placed his rucksack down and searched it with both hands.

The old cobbler looked them both over more than once and it made Tess nervous. Dressed primarily in a Bowman's cloak that covered only down to her calves, her hair still pinned in an impressive but disintegrating updo, not to mention the longbow she carried over her shoulder, she looked a disaster.

Colt looked odd in his own right. He wore a Bowman's dress uniform, soiled and torn in places, with his bow slung across his back alongside the military rucksack.

The cobbler didn't seem to know what to make of them, but he became most obliging when Colt produced his Bowman-issued purse and withdrew two bladespar coins.

"Thought you might tries to slip me cuper with hands like that, Bowman. Isn't that what you Thornton boys use skyward these days? Or maybe you'd tries to barter with a small sack of gray powder, seein' as you also look to be a seaward boy. But since yous payin' in bonefide spars, I'd be much obliged to git you some new boots as well. All the raiders wears 'em. Pirate Prince owns two pairs, and he bought 'em right here." The cobbler flipped the coins in his hand and flashed a toothless grin.

Colt straightened instantly, pulling back his hands and plunging them into his pockets. His brow pinched together.

Tess frowned. What had the man meant about Colt's hands? And what did he mean that Colt looked to be a *seaward boy*?

Leaning close, he spoken to the man quietly, while Tess busied herself with her laces. He then strode over to her and nodded in the direction of the main street outside. "And now for some new clothes, I think. The cobbler told me of a reasonable place around the corner." The captain offered his arm, and Tess took it gladly.

They had both noticed she received less attention in the seaport when she was on the arm of the tall soldier, and she skipped steps to keep pace with him. She tried to catch a glimpse of his hand, but he tucked it into his dress coat lapel.

They passed a series of makeshift carts selling all manner of food, weapons, and trinkets. When they passed a cart selling swords, knives, and crossbows—a small pennant bearing the pirate crest attached to the cart's crossbeam fluttering in the breeze, Colt only cleared his throat and quickened his pace. She doubted that the man behind the rough wooden counter possessed the proper arms license as issued by the king's registry. Shocked that this man would break the king's law so openly, she stared at the assortment of blades strewn across his display. Then Colt gave her arm a sharp tug, and she skidded forward, only to be greeted by something even more intriguing.

A wiry, middle-aged man with a long red beard sat behind a small cart. Dozens of necklaces hung in the open pass-through and a truth stone dangled on each chain. At least, that was what the sign claimed: *Genuine Truth Stones, three spars each.*

Slipping her arm out of Colt's hold, she stopped in front of the cart to examine the gems.

Well past peak, the sky grew a pinkish gray, and people began lighting the lanterns that hung outside the many shops and taverns. The cart owner lit one as they stood there and hung it on the vertical upright of his pass-through. "Would the pretty girl like to test the power of the stones?"

Colt had continued walking a few paces after she'd let him go and now stood at a distance, watching them. His eyes gleamed as he walked slowly behind the cart.

She fixed her attention on the scruffy man who had addressed her. "These are genuine truth stones, sir?"

The man placed his hands in his pockets, his eyes wide. "The little missy can read!" He rocked from his heels to his toes. "Of course they're real, missy, but you are most welcome to test them for yourself." He waved his hand across the front of the pass-through, just under the row of dangling necklaces, and then stroked his long beard.

Narrowing her eyes, she pursed her lips.

Colt stood two yards behind the cart arms crossed in front of his chest. He rolled his eyes, but she ignored him, not wanting to laugh and insult the man who waited on her.

Finally, she curtsied and stretched out her hand below one of the necklaces. "What do you suggest, sir? Do I simply say something true and then wave my hand the way you did?"

He bowed, leaned against the vertical upright, and gestured for her to do just that.

Repressing a smile, she thought for a moment, before announcing, "Captain Hawthorne is the most skeptical man in the Realm." She spoke slowly and clearly as she waved her hand beneath the pendants. To her amazement, every single stone shone, one after the other, as she passed her hand beneath it. From the corner of her eye, she discerned the source of the light, a small hand mirror concealed in the man's palm, focusing the lantern light onto the stones. The light was magnified and directed perfectly to mimic the effect of an actual truth stone. Impressed, she made sure not to let on that she had seen the trick.

Colt stepped forward, reached around the man, and snatched the mirror from his grasp before the man even noticed his presence. He then held the mirror to the waning daylight, dramatically inspecting it.

The seller held up both hands. "Wot, wot. I'm so sorry, Bowman. I's only trying to give the missy a bit of fun. You did see her eyes light up, didn't cha? She loved it. Just a bit of local charm to tells her friends about is all, Bowman. I wasn't gonna take her spars under false pretences, sir. Never, not me, sir, I promise." The man spluttered and bowed at least four times as he made excuses.

Colt glared at the man who refused to meet his eyes, only stared down at his feet.

Tess covered her mouth with her hand to hide her smile.

Colt shook his head before walking around the cart to join her. He offered his arm, and she took it.

"You're very good with that mirror, sir, and it was fun, thank you," she called over her shoulder.

Glancing down at her, his eyebrows arched.

"What? He *was* good with the mirror," she whispered.

Colt rolled his eyes again before blindly tossing the mirror over his shoulder, back to the cart.

The clothier, located on the ground floor of a low stone building on the west side of town, boasted shelves filled floor to ceiling with used clothing. A surprising selection of gentlemen's jackets, pants, and shirts as well as dresses and even formal gowns for ladies greeted them. Tess could not help but indulge her curiosity.

"Please, sir, tell me how you acquired such a wonderful selection of clothing."

The grizzled old shopkeeper startled, gasped, and straightened in his chair, which sat positioned in the very center of the room. Had he been sleeping? His eyes were wide open, yet how could he startle like that if he was awake? Could he sleep with his eyes wide open?

"Wot! Wot now?" The old man ran a hand over his wrinkled face. Tess flashed a look at Colt, who was clearly having a hard time not laughing. They had been in the store for several minutes, inspecting the merchandise, all the while thinking the shopkeeper was awake.

"I am so sorry to wake you, sir. I only wondered how you came by such a lovely selection of fine clothing."

The shopkeeper leaned forward in his upholstered armchair, laughed a most unsettling laugh, and examined them like a king from his throne. "Are you two trying to have a laugh at the expense of ol' Ebeneezer?" His sailor's drawl was thick enough to spread on toast..

"No, sir." She clasped her hands to her chest, reminded of the way she'd often been scolded by her tutor as a child. "I've never been here before, and I … we were remarking on the great selection of fine clothing."

The old man leaned so far forward he risked falling to the floor. Teetering on the edge of the worn chair, he stared at her as though trying to decide what to make of her. He then turned to Colt. "She for real?" He jerked a thumb in Tess's direction.

Colt smiled. "Quiet real, sir, and she needs a proper dress. One for a lady of good station if you have it." He winked at Tess.

The old man leaned forward even farther and then, just as it seemed he would fall, he used the momentum to his advantage and rose to his feet. He shuffled to the back of the store and returned a minute later carrying a beautiful sea-green dress.

"S'pose you'll need a corset and petticoat?" Not bothering to wait for a reply, he shuffled away again and then returned clutching both items.

"Oh, she has a corset." Colt added the petticoat to his bundle.

Catching his eye, she shook her head to indicate she did not. When Colt raised an eyebrow, she explained, her cheeks warm, "I tossed it this morning."

Colt shifted his attention back to Old Ebeneezer. "We'll take all three, thank you. And I will need a gentleman's jacket and trousers, please, and a clean shirt." He half-turned to contemplate her before calling after the shopkeeper again. "Good sir, could you also find us clothing for a boy, say, twelve years of age or so?"

The man grunted his acknowledgement and returned shortly with a bundle of men's clothing. Old Ebeneezer then took a long, hard look at Colt. "You know, Bowman, I have an Ardenian regulars' uniform that would fit cha. Got cases of 'em. Don't think I have any Bowman uniforms though. Those are hard to come by. Raiders don't usually get the drop on you Bowman."

Was that awe in his voice? Tess glanced at the gown in her hand. Wait, did he say that *raiders don't get the drop on Bowman*? Who *did* raiders get the drop on then? the people who were once wearing these clothes?

Colt thanked Ebeneezer but settled on the civilian clothing. As Ebeneezer tallied up the total purchase, she dared to ask her question once more. "Sir, truly, where do you source your merchandise?" She used the sweetest tone she could.

The shopkeeper looked up at her and smiled widely, revealing that over half his teeth were missing. "Sorry, young miss, I don't mean to seems cryptic. I just thought folks all knows where I gets my clothes." She nodded, encouraging him to continue, as Colt paid the total the old man had written on a scrap of paper.

As old Ebeneezer counted the bladespar coins, he continued, "See, that there's the Pirate Prince, as they call him." He stopped counting long enough to tap a wanted poster hanging on the wall behind his counter. It outlined a bounty on the *Pirate Prince* and boasted a poor rendering of his face. Still, the man gazed at it with pride, as if it were a baby portrait. "Wells, he started out working here before he got all high and mighty on the seas or in the air. Just three years back, he came to Dungridge. Anyways, I guess he just took a shining to Ol' Ebeneezer, thankful for the work I gave him and all. Cuz when he's done his raidin', he lets me go through the trunks and strip the bodies. As long as I make him a fair offer, I can sell all the finery I can handle."

Colt's jaw tightened and he drew in a sharp breath. He shot a glance at the front exit and then at the stairs that led to the basement.

The old man tied the bundle of clothes with a piece of twine and handed it to him. "Don't get many ladies in here though, not real ones anyhows. You could be royalty with that fancy ways you talk, little miss." He took Tess's hand and brought it to his lips.

Stunned at what the man had just confessed, she allowed him to kiss her hand. After a moment, Colt grasped her wrist and tugged her away before leading her out of the store.

As soon as they were outside, she whirled toward him. "Did you hear that? Dead bodies. He strips them off dead bodies!"

Colt's firm grip on her hand sent a clear message—something had changed. He pulled her across the storefront and down the alley that ran beside the stone shop. Then he positioned her so his broad shoulders blocked her from the mouth of the alley. Worry and concentration wrinkled his brow as he stared at the stone above her head.

"What's wrong, Captain?" She whispered the words, as his manner seemed to call for it.

He took a deep breath. "It's gotten worse, my lady. I shouldn't have brought you here."

A circle of children entered the mouth of the alley, joining hands, they began to sing. "Forbidden is hidden, crumble makes you stumble, turn and burn, for the star so far."

Tess refocussed on the Bowman. "What has? What's worse?"

He shifted his attention from the young voices and stared at the stone block wall. "The raiders, Tess. The entire port embraces them. It's blatant, flagrant. I came to Dungridge looking for him a year ago, and at least everyone feigned a certain respect for me as a Bowman. They didn't flaunt their allegiance to pirates. But now, it's as if their admiration of those lowlife criminals has been left unchecked. They use wanted posters like fine art. They brag about the raiders' generosity. They use pirate patronage as an endorsement. The entire port is compromised. It's not safe for you."

He lowered his gaze to her face, finally. Pain and regret shimmered in his eyes.

Tess shook her head. "I believe this could be a good thing."

"Pardon me?" He let go of her hand and rested his hands on his hips, studying her.

"You said you needed a lighter than airship, since you needed to run an aerial reconnaissance of the Reyjik force in Costair and confirm Ardenia's security and didn't have time to do that in the traditional way. And that we needed to get word to the king at Fairgates as soon as possible, right?"

"Right." He said the word slowly, as if wondering where she was going with this.

"Well, if this port openly embraces the mist raiders, then we should have a much easier time finding one to help us. They won't be afraid, trying to conceal who they are. Maybe their blatant disregard for authority and lack of concern over your rank and standing as a Bowman will save us time and effort. We won't need to play games."

Colt crossed his arms over his chest. "You might be right, it will make things easier, and I have no problem walking into the heart of a town of blatant criminals, longbow in tow, flaunting who I am. It's your presence that complicates everything. If this port unabashedly supports raiders, then I can't guarantee your safety. I can't count on the better nature of men here, not the way I could in a respectable town. They've given way to—even celebrate—a total disregard for the king's law. They steal from their own tiermen." Colt uncrossed his arms and drove his fingers through his hair. "There's only one of me, Tess. One bow isn't enough against a town of pirates if they get the notion to misbehave."

She tilted her head. "I'm not concerned about myself. The people here are kind in their own way. Maybe they don't see themselves as totally depraved like you do."

Colt slammed a palm against the stone wall. "If you knew how many raiders Bowmen have shot from the sky, you'd understand how much danger we're in. And the last six months have been the worst of it, worse than anyone can remember. I have read reports from all over the Realm—defiance to the king's law, duplicity, greed, theft, and deception of all kinds is rising."

"We can't give up, there's too much at stake. There's no point trying to conceal our identities. You'd look like a soldier with or without that uniform and the bow slung across your shoulders."

He pushed away from the wall. "And you'd look like a princess."

Her heart seized in her chest. A smirk had crossed his face, but was he only teasing? *Breathe, Tess, just breathe.* She forced a smile. If he knew who she was, it would ruin everything.

She reached for his longbow and slid it from his shoulder. He narrowed his eyes but allowed it. She closed her hand around the deer-hide lacing of the handgrip and passed her thumb over the smooth gemstone. Then she turned the bow a-hundred-and-eighty degrees so the small, inlaid emerald faced the young Bowman.

"We must try, Captain. We need the help of the raiders for the good of the Realm. That's the goal, and it outweighs my personal safety every time." Tess didn't need to see the emerald's glow to know she spoke the truth; she read it in the eyes of the skeptical man who faced her.

Chapter Ten

The Connection

Colt

COLT CHECKED FOR NUMBERS ON THE wooden buildings that lined the east side of the town. When he reached back for her hand, she offered it willingly. Warmth shot up his arm with her touch. He tried to ignore the sensation but couldn't help peering back at her just the same. She ran a hand over the dress, no doubt searching for evidence someone had died wearing it.

He pulled her onto a raised part of the boardwalk leading to an inn named The Wayward Squall. "Don't worry, my lady. I'm sure most of the clothes in that shop came from stolen luggage, not off a body." Colt winked at her, but Tess only shivered as she followed him inside a four-story wooden tower that looked like a series of shacks piled one on top of the other.

The innkeeper smiled wide. "That's it. You've got the last two rooms." Whatever the clothier lacked in teeth, this man more than made up for. "They are both at the very top of the staircase there." He motioned to the ramshackle boards that doubled back on themselves as they snaked up the side of the building.

Tess smiled as she surveyed the ridiculous room and makeshift desk, her captivation written across her face. Colt understood her reaction. The inn felt like a giant fort he and Deacon would have constructed in the woods outside Thornton.

"Um, Captain?" She tugged on the sleeve of his soiled uniform. "Do you think it would be possible to have a bath drawn at this establishment?" She nodded to a silverite platter sitting on the counter. He leaned forward to examine his appearance alongside hers. The reflection showed that his face was covered with grit and sweat, while hers boasted three dark smudges of dirt on her forehead and cheeks.

"Probably a good idea." He sniffed his underarm for dramatic effect. "Good sir, could you please draw a bath for the lady. I will use it after her. And I will still pay you in full for drawing two baths, my good fellow." Colt held up two fingers to drive home the offer.

The innkeeper hopped forward to take Colt's bladespar. "The bath is on the floor right below yours." He nodded again towards the rickety stairs. "You'll see it as you go past. I drew a bath no more than an hour ago for a fella. Said he'd be back in ten minutes and that he'd pay me then. Not seen hide nor hair of him. Probably passed out drunk at The Crow's Nest by now. Anyhows, I can heat up the water with a couple kettles, and she should be ready in a few minutes." The innkeeper seemed quite pleased that his earlier effort would not go to waste, and even more pleased that he'd offered to pay him double on top.

He placed another bladespar coin on the counter.

The distinctive sound caught the innkeeper's attention, and he turned to Colt, placing both hands on the worn wood and facing him head on. "What's on your mind, Bowman?" The innkeeper's jovial tone had changed to one much more serious. Sliding his own hands on the counter, he leaned in slightly. "I need to make sure the lady and I are secure here for the night. I'll pay handsomely for your discretion. No need to be telling folks you have a Bowman in residence. Agreed?"

The innkeeper stared down at the coin and then back up at him. His faced betrayed nothing. He was good, a natural negotiator.

Reaching into his purse, Colt placed a second coin on the counter.

The innkeeper showed all his teeth. "No need at all, Bowman." He slapped his thick hand down on the wood and slid the coins off the counter and into his other waiting hand. "I'll be right up with yer hot water."

He was as satisfied as he could be, considering he was surrounded by a town of potentially hostile raiders.

They made their way across the small foyer toward the decrepit staircase. When Tess stepped on the first plank, he grasped her arm. "Maybe I should go first."

She frowned. Already he knew that look—she hated any suggestion that she wasn't up to a task, that she needed to be protected. Still, she was his responsibility, and he *would* keep her safe. If anything happened to her... *Blast. Focus, Colt!*

To his relief, she didn't lash out, only bowed playfully and gestured for him to go ahead. She did grab the bundle of clothes from his hand and slung it over her shoulder. Had she done that to free up his right hand? To allow him to grab onto the greenish cuper pipe being used as a banister?

"I don't care how athletic you are, Captain. Your mother could be a mountain goat, and you'd still need to hold the banister to keep from falling!"

He shook his head but couldn't help laughing as he clutched the metal bar and started up. When they reached the third floor, he stopped to investigate the bathing room.

Tess peered around him to inspect the small room with unbelievably crooked floors. In the center, a large, oval wooden barrel sat three quarters of the way full with what appeared to be clean water. The bathing room had three doors leading into it—one that came up from the second floor, one that led to the fourth floor, and one that led to the two rooms on the third floor. The only problem was, no doors hung in the openings. Hinges remained nailed to the frames, but the actual door panels had been removed.

For privacy, a folded Reyjik panel had been set up around the barrel. Made from three separate bamber frames joined together with rusty hinges, the screen looked ancient. The panels themselves were made of blue fabric and donned a classic Reyjik wilderness landscape.

He sent her a sideways glance. She couldn't possibly bathe here by herself, totally unprotected. From the look on her face, the same thought had settled in her mind.

"I can sit on the other side of the screen and, um, make sure no one comes in?" He rubbed his chin and adjusted the rucksack.

She shook her head. "Thank you, but you go ahead. I'll just wash my face."

The innkeeper came through the door, struggling to manage the weight of the hot kettle he carried in each hand. Colt dropped his bow and rucksack and took the kettle from his right hand, and they each added the steaming water to the tub.

"There you go, lassie. Finest bath in all Dungridge. The Pirate Prince himself comes 'ere for a bath when he's not out pirating!" The innkeeper flashed that wide, toothy smile.

Repressing a groan, he pressed down hard on his head with both hands. Perfect. He'd chosen a pirate hot spot for them to stay at. The man dropped two large bath sheets on the wooden bench against the wall before turning and heading down the twisted steps.

Tess curtsied as he took his leave. Then she stood staring wistfully at the water, her fingers twisting the loose hair at the nape of her neck.

"If you really want to take a bath, my lady, you can. I will make sure no one disturbs you."

She bit her lip, but the appeal of the hot water was clearly too strong. After a moment, she nodded. "All right. I believe I will."

"Fine." Colt strode around the screen and sat cross-legged facing the door, his back to the tub. "I will sit right here and keep my eyes on the stairs." Waiting a few moments, he cocked his head to the screen. Was she moving? He couldn't hear anything. Glancing over his shoulder, just to check, he could make out her silhouette. She stood completely still beside the tub. Then all at once she began to undress. Colt whipped his head back to the stairs. At least she trusted him enough for this, and that meant something.

Water sloshed as she stepped into the tub. "Is it warm enough, my lady?"

No answer. "My lady?" He spoke louder, still no reply. "Tess!" he nearly yelled her name. Had something happened?

"Yes, yes, I'm fine. Sorry, Captain. I just... I like to swim, and it's been a while with the winter and all, so I ducked my head beneath the water for a moment."

Although his heart still pounded, he had to smile at the idea of her trying to swim in that small barrel. A thought occurred to him, and he reached for the rucksack he'd set against the wall and rummaged through it. "Do you want soap?" Colt tried to sound casual again.

"You have soap? Did that cost extra?"

He laughed. "No, I had it in my kit. Look up, it's coming over."

He tossed the soap blindly over the screen, visualizing the location of the tub and hoping it would land in the middle. When he heard the splash, he grinned. "How did I do?"

"Dead center, as usual." He had to laugh again. Apparently, she was still impressed with his shot from the night before. Water sloshed and what sounded like tiny bladespar coins hit the rough, wooden floor.

"What's that?"

"My hair pins."

Right. Of course. He took a deep breath. "Tell me something about yourself, Tess. I mean, you're obviously keeping a secret, which is fine, but I'm sure there's something you can tell me."

The water went still. He glanced over his shoulder to see her head just above the rim of the barrel. She faced him, he could tell from her shadow.

"Oh, come on, Tess. I'm trained in interrogation. I've been asking you the most benign questions for two days now. You should see yourself dance around the answers. I don't mind that you don't trust me completely—it's actually cute to watch—but give me something. Something of no consequence, even."

Silence. However, she stared at him through the screen. Were it transparent, they'd be peering into each other's eyes only two feet apart. It seemed surreal. Then her shadow disappeared, and the water sloshed. She'd slipped under the surface. Colt turned back to the stairs, contemplating her resolve. A full minute passed before she broke the surface again. In another minute, she appeared at the edge of the screen, wrapped from shoulders to toes in the large bath sheet.

She smiled shyly. "Your turn, Captain. I'll sit and watch while you bathe." The words had barely left her mouth before she clutched the bath sheet to her throat, red creeping across her cheeks. "I mean, not that I will watch you while you bathe, of course. I only meant that I would watch the doors."

He burst out laughing. "I did know that was what you meant."

"Good." The horror faded from her face, replaced by a sheepish grin. Still chuckling, Colt stood and skirted her, giving her a wide berth as he slipped behind the bamber-framed screen. He undressed, stepped into the warm water, then sat, pulling his knees to his chest so he could fit into the barrel. The water felt warm and soothing, and he let out a quiet sigh of appreciation.

Tess sat with her back to the tub as he had done. Although, like him, she wouldn't see anything if she turned around now that he was safely in the high-sided tub, she didn't turn around. "Tell me about your friend, Captain." She spoke quietly. "I mean, you have said that you were friends as children and that he now sails out of this port but tell me about him. What's his name? What's he like? When did you last see each other?"

Colt splashed a little water onto his chest. Should he play her game and refuse to answer? Perhaps he could demand she tell him something first—fair was fair, after all. He sighed. "His name is Deacon Thornby." He sank a little lower in the tub, allowing the warm water to drain away the tension that had tightened his muscles since the first boom of cannon fire the day before. "We lived in the same village growing up, and our fathers were friends."

"Thornton?"

Colt blinked. How had she remembered that name when he had only mentioned it once, when they'd talked about the All-Father?

"Yes, Thornton. I suppose you know all about it?" He had to tease her. This game of cat and mouse surrounding her knowledge had gone on since they'd met. Now that he had her by the tail, he couldn't pass up the opportunity.

She let out a long, dramatic sigh. "Fine. I admit nothing, one way or the other, regarding your prior insinuation of my secrecy, but I will tell you something about myself." He waited, not wanting to seem too eager, until she waved a hand through the air. "It may sound crazy, but I have tamed a Tarragon. Up until a year ago, it waylaid each spring and autumn on the castle roof, and I would feed it."

Colt shot straight up in the barrel, his heart pounding. "Pardon me?"

"It's true. You don't believe me? I'll swear it on the emerald star and the flash of confirmation will blind you."

"No, sorry. It's just…"

"Just what? That everyone says they can't be tamed? That they're truly wild and dangerous? Superstitious nonsense!"

"No, it's only that I've tamed one too." When she didn't respond, he rested his head against the edge of the barrel. "When I was a boy, I was standing on the shore of our lake fishing, and I saw one, a juvenile, shot from the sky over the Lindsor precipice. The Lindsite got it in the wing, and it fell straight down into the water. I swam over and found it knocked senseless and bleeding, a crossbow bolt lodged in his right wing. I carried him home, removed the bolt, and stitched and bandaged his wound. As I was finishing, he woke up and thrashed around something fierce. You should have seen my mom's face! She stayed with Deac's parents until it recovered. He was wild, but eventually he began to trust me."

"When was this?" Her voice sounded shaky.

"I was ten. It happened right after the war, shortly after my dad died. I'm sure that's the only reason my mom indulged me, like she thought nursing him would help with some of the sadness, you know?"

After a moment of silence, she asked, "Captain, how old are you?"

"I'm twenty, why?" A long pause. Colt finished washing and stood up.

As he reached for his bath sheet, she said, "Because I am about to turn eighteen, and I found my tarragon when I was eight, so ten years ago, same as you. It was wounded, shot in the right wing, and the wound had been stitched."

Colt froze. Something like lightning tremored through his entire body, from his chest to his toes. Distracted, he tied the towel around his waist and came out from behind the screen. He needed to see her.

She was still sitting on the ground, wrapped in the towel, but she stood as soon as she saw him. Goose bumps covered her arms. When he looked into her eyes, something passed between them—a connection.

Tess rubbed her arms. "It landed on the castle roof. I sit on the roof of the castle by the east cannon all the time and watch the sea. The tarragon dropped out of the sky, and he was exhausted. He was so weak that he didn't spook when I approached, and he let me pet him and feed him. He stayed a full week, and then he flew seaward."

Lost in her green eyes, he couldn't explain what he felt, only that he had never felt it before.

"I've always thought I had tamed him, but I guess it was you." She lowered her gaze to the rough wooden floor.

No idea what to say, he only stood there staring at her. Finally, she looked up and her gaze landed on his bare chest. Crimson flooded her cheeks, and she glanced away.

Blast, he hadn't even remembered he was shirtless. "Why don't you go upstairs? I'll tidy up around the barrel and come up in a few minutes."

When Tess nodded, he stepped clear of the path to the door. She sprinted up the stairs, stumbling twice on the uneven boards. The old hinges squeaked as she swung open her narrow door and then closed it tight behind her.

Chapter Eleven

The Prince

Tess

TESS STARED DOWN AT THE BUNDLE of boy's clothing that Colt had bought for her, piled beside the new dress and corset. The trousers would be more comfortable for the task ahead, but for this evening Tess needed to don the gown.

A sound caught her ear. Singing, no, whistling. She pressed the side of her head to the wall. Was that Colt, whistling quietly on the other side? "Captain?"

The whistling stopped, replaced with footsteps. "You all right, Tess?"

"You might want to switch floors, considering I just heard you whistling through the walls. I wouldn't want to keep you up all night with my… *whinny*. That's how you described it, right?"

He laughed, which sent warmth flowing through her chest. When he spoke again, the words were clearer, as though he'd leaned closer to the wall. "You asked me about Deacon, and I never answered. I didn't mean to be evasive, I was only teasing you. Do you still want to know about him?"

She couldn't help but smile. He might be cocky, but she couldn't deny the captain's kindness. "You mentioned you both grew up in Thornton, which is on the half-tier seaward of Lindsor, no? Long, cold winters." She grabbed the corset from the pile and began loosening it.

"Yeah, the winters were brutally cold, but the summers were great. Deac and I did everything together. My father taught us to hunt and survive off the land. His father taught us to fish and swim. His dad was a sailor until he got married. When the war with Lindsor broke out, both our fathers served. We went to help, as archer caddies. Deac's father came home… mine didn't."

Her chest tightened, and she stopped tying the bow in her corset lacing. "I am so sorry." The words caught in her throat.

"It's okay. Lots of kids lose their parents. You lost your mother, didn't you?"

She swallowed hard. "Yes. She died delivering me. I never knew her. You were ten?" She hoped the captain wouldn't ask her any more questions about her family.

"Yes. I remember everything about him. He was a giant of a man, so strong, and then he was gone, you know? I took care of my mum, and Deacon's father helped when he could until he passed. She stays with Deac's mum now. My mother is, well, she's foreign, and Deac's parents were worried for how she'd get on alone."

She stepped into her petticoat. "Foreign? Where is she from, Lindsor?"

"Lindsor? Are you being serious, Tess?"

He sounded shocked. Why? Thornton's half-tier was just as close to Lindsor as to Ardenia. They were literally neighbours. "If not Lindsor, then Costair?" Maybe that was why he'd taken the post in the seaward tier.

"No, not Costair. Sorry, I thought you would have realized I'm half Reyjik."

Tess stopped dead. Half Reyjik? The hair on her arms raised. Of course. He shared the same dark hair and eyes and darker skin as MaryLee, her nurse and surrogate mother. How had she not seen it before? "I guess I didn't, not until now."

"Well, you'd be the first to miss it. If my mother wasn't so well loved, and my father not a formidable fighter, I would have had a real tough go in Thornton. As it stands, the military has proven tricky at times."

Her heart wrenched. Did he push himself as hard as he did to compensate for the bigotry of others? Was that why he acted so cocky all the time, because he believed he needed to continually prove himself worthy of his uniform?

He cleared his throat. "Anyway, Deac and I enlisted in the regulars at fifteen, as soon as they would take us. We wanted to see Ardenia. We wanted to earn money and respect and then strike out into the world. Deacon hated being poor and had big plans to make sure he never was. We had no idea what we were in for. The basic training was brutal. Deac and I took turns throwing up after runs and marches. But we got strong, fast. We did well—very well. We began to stand out, you know? We excelled in the service and were selected as Bowman candidates. That's when everything changed."

She stepped into the dress and pulled the lacing tight. It fit her perfectly. Styled off the shoulder—which had been popular in high fashion a few years previously—it showed off her neck and perfect posture. "What changed? Deacon?"

"No." A thudding sound suggested he was tapping his fingers against the wall as though contemplating how much to share. "No, Deacon didn't change–that was the problem. See, the service was one thing. Deac could get along fine with the regulars. Discipline was slack, and he was so funny. The men loved him and his practical jokes and pranks. The things we did! But when we were selected for the King's Bowman, that meant living up to a higher standard. The moral code was nonnegotiable, and the discipline rigid. They weren't training us to march and shoot anymore, they were training us to think, to make decisions… no, they were training us to make the *right* decisions. No matter what it cost us, no matter how complicated, they demanded the very best from us. I loved it. I *loved* it, Tess! I thrived."

Tess held her breath, wishing she could see his face.

"Deacon drowned under it all. He hated the duty and the discipline and the morality. He lasted six months—four of them for my sake—before he quit. He wanted me to quit with him, for us to do what we had always said—to see Ardenia and have fun and live by our own rules, but I couldn't quit. I just couldn't. I was good at it, you know? I was really good at it, and I want to make a difference. I want to serve my tier. I want to protect the trade balance. I love the code." Colt went quite for a few seconds before adding, so softly she barely caught it, "He never forgave me."

Should she ask what happened? She didn't dare. Combing through her d'orite hair, she separated it into three large sections and braided them. Still, he didn't speak. Wanting to give him time, she took the pins she had removed in the bath and re-pinned the braids low to the left side of her head, all the time waiting and listening.

"I let him down, Tess." A sliding sound, as though he'd pressed his back to the wall and was lowering himself to the floor. "His family took me in, like a son. He struggled with the rules and rigidity, and I saw that, but I wanted to be the best and I let him flounder. He would have gone to Gehenna and back for me, but by the time I did something to help him, it was too late–he had already made up his mind to leave." Guilt dripped from his words.

She laced her new boots. "What happened to him? Where did he go?"

"He came here. Every month I send a letter, and he's written back twice. Once, a few weeks after getting here, he wrote to say he was all right and that he had a job in a shop. Then he wrote again to let me know he had joined a merchant crew."

Finished with one boot, she crouched to do up the other. "How do you know we'll be able to find him, that he's not up the coast somewhere?"

"Everyone is in port at this time in the spring. The merchant ships wait until the shore ice totally melts before they begin their trading season. That will happen in a week or so, I imagine. Until then, everyone in Ardenia is still icebound. Costair's climate is completely different. They don't get cold enough to freeze that far seaward and their ports stay open all winter. Not that they capitalize on that blessing and do anything industrious with it. Then again, without a winter to worry about, I guess they've never needed to think too far ahead. As for finding Deacon, I guarantee he will be in a tavern either drunk or on his way to being drunk, likely in the company of a lady with questionable morals." More thumping against the wall, as if Colt was bracing himself against it as he stood. "I'm ready, how are you doing?"

Tess straightened and ran her palms over her skirts. "I've been ready for a while."

"So, we've both been leaning against this pathetic excuse for a wall talking to each other when we could have been on our way?"

"I guess we have." She took one last look in the mirror and pinched her cheeks, not that they needed any additional color. Good enough. She flounced to the door and flung it open.

The captain waited in the hall, one shoulder propped against the wall. When she stepped out of her room, he pushed away from it and gazed at her. For a moment, neither of them spoke. Then Tess cleared her throat. "Good evening, Captain." She looked up into his eyes.

Colt's eyes, soft and deep, were fixed on hers. When she spoke, he swallowed hard and blinked, as though returning from somewhere far away. "Good evening, my lady. You, um, you look beautiful tonight… in that dress. The dress is really beautiful, and you in it, tonight." Colt shook his head and laughed, nearly displacing the bow and quiver he'd slung over his arm.

"Wait." She whirled around and went back into her room. When she emerged a moment later, she carried her own bow and arrows over her shoulder.

Colt shook his head. "Really?"

"I like your approach, Captain. No point trying to hide who you are. It's always best to be truthful. Besides two bows must be better than one, right?"

* * *

The Crows Nest boasted a full house. From Colt's explanation of the rhythmic economic seasons that drove Dungridge, Tess imagined every man in the room restless to get back on the water and every woman anxious to see them go. An excited tension hung in the air. An anticipation that only came when waiting for something out of your control—rains after a long drought, the first snowfall, or the spring thaw.

Grasping Tess's hand, Colt pulled her close. Did he notice the attention she had received upon entering the noisy tavern? Was this protective tendency innate or drilled-in during Bowman training?

Many of the patrons turned to watch them pick their way through the crowd to the bar. She smiled at everyone they passed. It was always best to be friendly whenever possible, especially to those of a lower station. In the Crows Nest, everyone was of a lower station.

Colt caught the attention of the barkeep, and the peg-legged man hobbled over.

Shed read countless books about pirates and had always wanted to meet someone with a peg leg. She had to concentrate very hard not to stare.

"What can I git cha, my lord and my lady, on such a fine evening as this one?" The barkeep's tone was friendly.

Placing two bladespar coins on the bar, Colt leaned close. "Some information, if you please," he replied in the same friendly manner. "We are looking for a childhood friend who sails on one of the ships that moors here. He came to Dungridge three years ago. His name is Deacon Thornby?" He spun the coins on the bar top.

The barkeep looked them both up and down and then up again. Was he taking stock? Was he trying to decide if they were a threat? More than once he glanced at their longbows.

Colt adjusted his bow. "I am a Bowman of the Realm, but Deacon isn't in any trouble, truly. We grew up together, and I have come to visit before he sails for another trading season." The noise in the room had grown steadily quieter since Colt had mentioned Deacon's name. This second mention of it silenced the room altogether.

The barkeep smiled widely. "Can I get that in writin', Bowman?" He raised his voice. "The fact that our Deac isn't in any trouble, truly?" He repeated the comment sarcastically, in a poor imitation of Colt's accent and cadence of speech. The room erupted into laughter.

She frowned. Why weren't they taking him seriously? He was a King's Bowman, for Realm's sake.

Colt seemed to expect this reaction. He even smiled in appreciation of the bartender's wit. Was this what he meant when he talked about having a tough go as half-Reyjik?

Her stomach clenched tight at the thought that racial prejudice permeated every level of her home culture.

Colt stood quietly, apparently waiting for the laughter to die out. Was there any hope of blending in now? Nope, that ship had sailed.

Leaning forward on the bar, the barkeep examined him. "'Cuz I come by good authority, *Bowman,* that our Deac is *always* in a good bit of trouble! You sure you knows him as well as you says?"

The room broke into laughter again. Bottles chimed as if men were toasting that fact.

Colt held the barkeep's stare. "Oh, trust me, I know him better than any other man in this town." He made the statement cool and even, and as loudly as the barkeep. Once again, the room went quiet.

Then a woman who looked to be a hundred years old called loudly to Colt. "But does ya know him better than any woman in this town, Bowman?"

The question received laughter and even cheers this time. Colt had to laugh, and he turned around and bowed to the elderly woman, who nodded in kind.

Tess's breathing grew shallow. They weren't getting anywhere, were they? Had this whole trip been in vain?

Another voice called out from somewhere in the back of the tavern. "If you know Deacon Thornby so well, then what did he get for his fourteenth birthday?" The man spoke in a strong sailor's drawl.

Colt didn't turn in the direction of the voice.

Tess did, but she couldn't see who'd spoken, so she looked back at Colt.

A huge smile had spread across his face. "Nothing," he called loudly to the man. "Deac didn't get anything for his birthday that year… however, he gave Mary Wilkens a hickey and he also gave Paul Smithy a black eye for saying something about it!" Colt turned to face the good-looking man who had emerged from the crowd.

Tess examined him carefully. Whoever he was, he was almost six feet tall, had blond hair and blue eyes, and was most obviously dressed like a pirate.

Colt looked him over once, laughed, and then turned to the crowd. "Ladies and gentlemen, my very best friend in the whole Realm, Deacon Thornby… the Pirate Prince!" He grabbed Deacon's hand and raised it far above both their heads.

The crowd loved it, just like the courtiers had loved the same gesture in Costair. They cheered and toasted and pounded the tabletops. Deacon pulled Colt in, and the two men gave each other a huge hug.

Tess stood back and watched. Colt had suspected they would find his old friend here. When had he realized it, when he saw the wanted poster? Why hadn't he told her? More importantly, did he plan to place their greatest hope to save the Realm in the hands of a wanted criminal?

Chapter Twelve

The Favor

Colt

DEACON TOOK TESS'S HAND, BENT FORWARD, and kissed it.

Colt clenched his fists, feeling a small satisfaction when she pulled her hand away at the first opportunity.

Deacon must have noticed too, as the raider smiled, clearly amused at her discomfort. He ran his fingers through his long hair and leaned closer to Tess the way he always did when he flirted.

He had seen this countless times before. It almost always worked which, in this moment, drove him crazy. Was Deacon trying to win Tess's affections? He'd worried about the reception he would receive from his old friend. In front of the crowd, Deac had played the part, but did he now plan to punish him, and was Tess the means of torture?

Deacon led Tess by the hand to a table at the back of the tavern, likely where he had been sitting with a few other men when he caught his name being bandied about. A fourth glass sat half full in front of an empty seat. Nodding to the three men, he guided Tess past them, to a small table in the back corner of the room. He pulled a chair out for her, then took the seat beside, and reached for her hand again.

Gritting his teeth, Colt settled on a chair on the opposite side of the table.

Shifting his seat so he was facing Tess directly, almost with his back turned to him, Deacon's intentions were perfectly clear. "So, tell me everything about yourself, Tess." Clutching her fingers, Deac sat back and studied her. "I want to hear it all, but mostly how the most beautiful girl in the entire Realm came to be traveling with this stick in the mud."

Even in the dim tavern lighting, he caught the flush spreading across Tess's cheeks. Sudden panic swept through him.

She glanced at him before leaning close to Deacon and motioning with her index finger for him to draw closer too.

He instantly complied, and Tess whispered something in his ear.

He'd been trained to read lips, but his view of Tess's was blocked by Deacon's head. She only spoke for a few seconds. Why did it feel like an eternity?

Finally, the agonizing moment passed. Deacon pulled back, a strange look on his face.

She pulled back as well, her face deadly serious.

Then the raider rose and looked at Colt. "Follow me." He jerked his head toward a doorway set in the back wall. Before either of them could respond, he strode toward it.

She stood, came around the table, and followed him.

Colt blinked. What had just happened? What had she said? He jumped to his feet and ran to catch up to them.

Deacon led them outside and into a narrow alley that opened directly onto the main wooden boardwalk. They passed three ships.

Colt read their names as they passed by. One of the names made his heart skip a beat, and he slowed to examine the ship more closely. *The Dancing Girl*, written in elegant emerald cursive graced the hull of the last in line.

Pushing ahead, not appearing to notice his interest, Deacon led them to the largest slip, one that ran adjacent to an enormous, three-masted galleon named *The Bishop's Bride*. The ship—which boasted the pirate's flag, hung from its central mast—was dirty—rigging lay everywhere, barrels were stored haphazardly, and the deck was filthy.

"Yours?" He flashed his old friend a knowing smile.

Deacon didn't reply, only jumped the three feet from the slip to the gunwale and then hoisted himself over the main railing. Once on the deck, he turned around to set a gangplank for Tess. Colt knew better. Before Deac could get the board over the railing, she had handed him her bow, made the jump with ease, and gracefully swung both legs over the railing to slide onto the main deck, landing lightly on her feet.

Deacon stared at the girl, his blue eyes so wide his eyebrows nearly reached his hairline.

Tess ignored him and motioned for Colt to toss her bow. After catching it, she began inspecting the disorganized ship.

Colt followed effortlessly, and as he passed his friend, he patted him on the shoulder in solidarity. "You should see her shoot."

"My quarters are up here. We can talk freely there." He motioned to a narrow door behind the main bridge.

Tess and Colt followed him through the opening that led to a small room as messy as the rest of the ship. A narrow bed built into the wall and a set of drawers standing next to it comprised most of the furnishings. A small table against an inner wall, a chair and two barrels pulled up to it, completed the decor. Playing cards lay on the table. Colt pulled the chair out for Tess this time, and all three sat facing each other around the circular table. Would either of them let him know what Tess had said to Deacon in the pub?

Deacon crossed his arms. "Okay, we are totally alone. No one is on board. Apparently, the fate of the Realm is at stake. So, what is this about, Colt?"

Ah. So that's what she had told him. Obviously, Tess had cut right to the quick. Colt attempted to assess the tone of his friend's voice. Was Deacon angry at him? Was he sober? He seemed completely coherent, but as Colt well knew, his childhood companion could hold his liquor.

He shot a look at Tess, who simply nodded and waited. He swallowed. He had a lot to say to his friend, but not now. "Deac, there are many things I want to say to you, one in particular, but I don't have the time. For now, I need a favor."

"Go on." Picking up the deck of cards, he pulled off the top two and balanced them into an A-frame. Repeating the process, he made a second and then set a card across like a roof. How many times had they built card-towers together?

"The Reyjik have attacked Costair. They took the castle in just over an hour, which means they likely had help from the inside. A delegation from Ardenia, including Lucius' daughter Sasha, was swept up in the onslaught. I figure that King Salmon's top security officer, General Gerhert, betrayed them. He used the royal visit as an excuse to cut all military presence, insisting the officers attend the ball instead of standing guard. The occasion proved the perfect cover."

Deacon rubbed his bristled face and set another card. "What do you need from me?"

Tess folded her hands on the table. "We need intelligence. We have to know exactly what you or any of your men might know about the situation—number of ships, troop capacity, weaponry, location, all of it. And we need an airship to conduct an aerial reconnaissance of Costair to ascertain the invaders' true strength. Then we need a ride up the coast to the Ridley so we can inform the king at Fairgates. He will launch a counterattack." She matched the cold, even tone both men had assumed.

Leaning back from his tower, he looked Tess over yet again before smiling and shaking his head. "Full of surprises, this one."

Colt exhaled. "You have no idea."

She made a face at him but didn't respond to the patronizing comments.

The pirate scratched his unshaven face and then ran his hand through his shoulder-length blond hair, gestures Colt remembered him always making when he was attempting to come to a decision. After a moment, Deacon stood abruptly and walked over to a small cupboard above his unmade bed. "I need a drink." Grabbing a bottle and three glasses, he returned to the table, sliding easily onto the barrel. After pouring his own drink and one for Tess, he slid the bottle in front of Colt. The slight was unmistakable—the old Deac would have poured it for him.

Sipping his brandy, he shifted his attention from Colt to Tess before settling on Tess. "Explain to me how a *princess* like you learned to talk like that."

She straightened but didn't reply, so Deacon continued. "I mean, honestly, 'troop capacity, weaponry, aerial reconnaissance, counterattack,' where did a priss like you learn that?" He took another sip from his glass, not taking his eyes off her.

"I read a lot." She gave him a sly smile.

Deac chuckled and lifted his glass in her direction before draining the contents.

Colt shifted on the barrel. "Tess is a lady-in-waiting to Princess Sasha. She was part of the delegation." When Deacon didn't respond to that, Colt pressed his hands to the top of the table. "Are you going to help us or not?"

Deacon tore his gaze from Tess, finally, and sighed. "I know I owe you for what you did there at the end. And I know we have history, but I'm also mad. You chose the corps over me and I'm mad, Colt!"

Well, there it was. At least it was out in the open. *Don't get distracted with the past.* Colt leaned forward. "I know you are, and I don't blame you. But is there any chance we can set that aside temporarily, for the sake of the Realm? We need intelligence. Is there anything you can tell us? Anything you've seen?"

Deacon grunted. "Wasn't sure you thought that intelligence and me went together." He grabbed the bottle and tossed another slug of brandy into his glass. "How would I know anything if I were icebound all winter?"

He spotted the trap a mile away, but he didn't care. This ended now. "Yes, Deac, the ship on which you chose to bring us hasn't seen open water since last fall. Judging by the condition of the deck and the ice that still binds the ropes to their tie-offs, it hasn't left this slip in months. But two of the three interceptor class schooners we passed have recently returned to their slips. Given the conditions of their hulls, one went north, needing to crash its way through ice, and one went south, where the Idernia current has already thawed the coastline. I'm guessing you commissioned both trips. That, coupled with the fact we saw *The Dancing Girl* airborne, two hundred yards seaward of Ardenia's precipice, casing the hoist and struggling with a nasty downdraft, I'm also guessing that you are well aware of the Reyjik's presence in Costair, and that you are as worried about it as we are."

"Thinks he's pretty smart, doesn't he, *princess*?" Deacon's remark dripped with contempt, but Colt dared to hope he caught a hint of respect as well. His friend stared into his crystal brandy glass a few seconds before throwing back his head to empty the contents. Then he set the glass on the table with a thud. The tower of cards crumpled flat to the table.

Had Deacon made a decision? Colt's heart pounded.

His friend ran a finger around the rim of the glass. "Information, I can give you, but we'll need to talk about the ride north to the Ridley." He splashed more brandy into his glass. "I've been making patrols for the last month. Most ships are icebound, but the two interceptors have reinforced hulls shaped to handle a little ice. And, of course, I've been testing *The Girl's* new blimpoon and fins for the hoistments. A businessman needs to diversify, you know. I only went seaward at first, wanting to get the jump on the first of the Ardenian hoistments after our thaw. Those first hoistments are chock full of everything everyone's been waiting to hoist for the last four months of freeze. Which means that pirating is always best right after thaw." He grinned, clearly unashamed of his *business practices*.

Colt shook his head. He'd suspected it from Bowman intelligence reports coming out of Dungridge. He had known it since first seeing the wanted poster in the clothing shop. Hearing the shopkeeper's tale of the pirate prince working there had been the final confirmation. Although Colt had declared it dramatically in the tavern, Deacon had never owned the title. Now he was clearly proud to call himself a criminal. His throat tightened. Had he lost his friend forever?

Deacon shrugged. "I sighted your Reyjik fleet three weeks ago, when I was casing the sluice and the lochs. They were staging to advance. I stayed hidden in the mist, so they wouldn't have sighted me, but I got a good look at their numbers. I would say they could carry up to eight hundred men in the ships that waited to head down the Sislay." He took another sip.

A wave of relief flooded through Colt. "That's what I counted in the siege force. At least seven hundred fifty men, maybe more, holding the castle and neighbouring village." He slapped his old friend on the arm. "That is helpful, Deacon. That lets the king know what he is walking—"

Deacon raised his hand. "That's not all. I also sighted two more Reyjik ships. They passed Dungridge and carried on northward… and they were flying."

Nausea gripped his stomach. The Reyjik were using lighter than airships in the tier of Ardenia in violation of the Sacramance Accord? All his life, he'd faced a mild bigotry for being different, but he rarely let it bother him. The Reyjik spoke differently and looked different, but they valued honor and perseverance and resourcefulness, and he had always been proud of his mother's people. Until now.

Deacon looked grim. "They were small schooners, like *The Dancing Girl*. Still, that's the biggest type of ship that can fly. I wouldn't have spotted them from the port. I had an interceptor a half mile out from shore, and I sighted them when the mist blew out suddenly."

Colt tapped his fingers on the rough side of the barrel. "Could those be the same ships that brought the troops to Marduke, empty now and not wanting to stay in the Sislay River drawing attention?"

"Nope. The ones I saw in the sluice were too big to fly." Deacon swirled his brandy again.

Pursing his lips, another concern hit him. "Deac, who knows about this, about the Reyjik at Costair?"

He shook his head. "Just me. Fifteen men crewed *The Dancing Girl* with me, but I was the only one up in the crow's nest, and I haven't said anything to anyone. The Reyjik spook these sailors. I want my men itching to get raiding, not citing superstitious nonsense and dredging up old ghost stories about the Reyjik. These men fear what they're not used to, plain and simple. They fear the unknown. And there isn't much more foreign to these waters than the Reyjik." He shot Colt a look. "Sorry."

Colt's thoughts flashed back to the revelation of only an hour previous, that Tess hadn't even noticed he was Reyjik. And nothing about their time together since revealed that she cared about his mixed parentage one way or another. She wasn't bigoted like almost everyone else in Colt's life. He couldn't help but steal a glance in her direction.

She watched Deacon carefully, as though considering everything he had said. She hadn't touched her brandy, which didn't surprise him. As though she sensed him looking at her, she glanced over.

He lifted one hand. "Well, my lady, what do you think?"

Tess planted her palms on the table the way he had earlier. "I think we must sail north and get this information to the king. He needs to know about Costair. Captain Thornby has confirmed what we saw from the lookout, so there shouldn't be any surprises."

Deacon almost choked on his last sip. "*Captain* Thornby? I ain't never been called that before." He snapped his fingers and pointed at her. "Ah, I see what you're doing. You are payin' me back for callin' you *princess*. That's it, isn't it? Well, it won't work. I won't quit. *Princess* suits you too well."

Tess rolled her eyes but didn't appear too upset.

He wasn't surprised. Deacon had always had the gift of charm, especially with girls. Clearly, he'd won Tess over already. He shifted on the barrel again. *Focus on the task at hand.* Why had those ships travelled skyward to Ardenia? Were they connected to the invasion in Costair or was there a second threat?

"Captain." Tess touched his arm gently to rouse his attention. "If you're worried about the ships that flew north, we can send word to the king when we pass the Ridley, and then we can sail on to investigate them for ourselves."

Colt nodded slowly. How could she read his mind like that? "That's a sound plan." When he met her eyes, they shimmered, as though she was as grateful for his praise as he was for her counsel. He couldn't look away.

"Well, that's the trick of it, isn't it, *Captain*?" Deac smirked at the title. "Going north is a lot harder than going south right about now. I tried to follow those ships a week ago, just for my own interest, and it wasn't easy. Now, I could have flown like they did, but that is the fastest way to get yourself shot down by those blasted Bowmen."

Colt didn't dignify the comment.

"With so much invested in this old *Girl*, I couldn't risk it, so I tried to sail up the shore. There is a lot of ice left to thaw. If you want to get down the Ridley right now, you'll need a ship with an experienced crew who can avoid the ice as you go or break it if they must."

Colt frowned. "Don't you have an experienced crew who could handle that?"

"Yes, I do, but you are going to have to get them to agree to sail north." Deacon flashed a mischievous grin.

He took the bait. "Aren't you the *Pirate Prince*? Can't you just make them sail north and get us up the coast? Deacon, this is important." His whole body felt warm, and his chest had tightened.

Deacon leaned back and clasped his hands behind his head. "Well, *Pirate Prince* may have been a bit of a misnomer." He flashed his sly grin again.

Colt's jaw tightened. "In what way?"

"I got the job about six months ago, after a mutiny. See, the old prince was killed by his first mate, literally stabbed in the back. I wasn't part of the mutiny." He leaned towards Tess and whispered as though explaining something important. "They save a special place in Gehenna for mutineers, Princess." He sat back up straight. "But after the dust settled, here I was." Bowing, he smiled at Tess, clearly happy to take full credit.

"Of course you were." She rolled her eyes again.

"Now, I really didn't feel right about Old Belt-notch getting it in the back like that. Felt so bad that I lost three good nights of sleep. Then it occurred to me."

Tess gasped dramatically. "Not a pang of conscience? Not a shred of morality. Surely not guilt?"

Deacon only smiled. "No, of course none of those. Don't worry, *Princess*. It was merely self preservation." He waved a hand through the air. "I realized, in a great moment of clarity, that if you take power from your men, you are always at risk of having them try to take it back… and by whatever means they see fit."

"Say, like stabbing someone in the back?" Tess raised both hands palms up.

"Exactly." Deacon offered her a smug look, clearly impervious to her judgmental tone, "I reckoned that if I wanted to keep the position for any length of time, I couldn't take power from my men, so I instituted a bonafide democracy. We vote on just about everything. They even voted me into power. More of a Pirate Prime Minister, really, although Pirate Prince has a nicer ring to it."

Deacon smacked the top of the table. "See, Colt, that was the problem with the Bowmen, with the regulars too, for that matter. It was always orders. Always rules, imposed by someone higher up. Meaningless rules and orders."

"Meaningless?" Colt's forehead wrinkled. The Bowmen held to the highest code of morality. Those rules were based on the Sacreds. Colt knew for a fact that the rules were what kept Ardenia secure. They were the very foundation that had made her great.

Deacon pounced on the word like a wolf on a rabbit. "Yes, Colt, meaningless. They *mean* nothing because they *mean* nothing to me. See, that was the problem all along. Men with more stripes barking orders at men with less. Maybe if the men with less had the chance to weigh in on decisions, cast votes, considering their fates are also on the line, maybe that would make those orders *mean* a little more."

He studied his friend. He'd never seen Deacon so passionate about anything. When he glanced over at Tess, for the first time since she'd met Deacon her face betrayed a hint of respect for the pirate, which tightened his stomach.

She leaned forward, her eyes on Deacon. "What about the Sacreds, or the All-Father, or the Bowman Code? Do any of those mean anything to you?" She spoke with sincerity, all sarcasm missing from her tone.

Deacon regarded her seriously for a moment. "You know, Princess, that's a funny thing. Maybe the captain hasn't mentioned it, but we grew up together in Thornton." Deacon sprang forward and grabbed his wrist before he could pull it back. Blast! Deac held his arm tight to the table. He knew exactly where Deacon planned to take this. If he resisted, it would only throw fuel on the fire, so he forced himself to lean back and relax. Deacon pushed his sleeve back, and then did the same to his own shirt. "See these scars? These are the forearms of a thorn farmer, the very poorest wretch in the tier of Ardenia." Deacon sat back and let him go. He didn't pull down his sleeve, wouldn't give Deac the satisfaction.

"Want to know why we grew thorns, Princess? I mean, seriously, who in their right mind would want thorns? Well, I can tell you, when you have no money for barbed bladespar to keep your fields and pens, or even wood to corral your animals or hedge your gardens, you are mighty pleased to buy thorns. Oh, we were the poorest, all right. Not a winter went by without a family losing absolutely everything, and they would have starved to death, every time. Didn't matter the circumstance or the reason, we were all just poor, that was the reason, and we all would have starved at some point if it weren't for each other. Year after year, we would share and help and take kids in and nurse the sick for each other. Blast, Colt's mother took the lion's share of it, and that was after his pa died. You want to know what I remember most about all that?"

Tess, her features grave, nodded ever so slightly.

"I remember all those rich seaward Ardenians walking through Thronton in all their finery, passing right by our young'uns in their rags and bare feet and headin' straight for our precious shrine. They came back every year, praying for help and blessings and citing compassion and generosity, and yet it never crossed their pious minds to share a little of that generosity with their needy tiermen, did it?"

Tess held her jaw tight. She sat perfectly still, her ears pink.

Colt's jaw cramped with pain, witnessing how this stung for her. He shifted to face his old friend. "Oh, come on, Deac, I seem to remember you doing quite well with your little side hustle during pilgrimage. You used to say those dumb seaward well-to-dos padded our pockets twice each year. And you made merry with quite a few well-to-do daughters too, didn't you?"

Deacon's face flushed, his comments clearly catching him off guard. He recovered quickly, though, heat blazing in the eyes fixed on him. "I did what I had to do to survive, yes. Still do."

Tess's shoulders relaxed ever so slightly. "I am very sorry for their indifference, Captain Thornby. There's no excuse for it."

Deac tore his gaze from Colt to look at her, his mouth dropping open slightly. Clearly, he hadn't expected an apology. "Thank you." The customary cockiness had faded from his voice.

She nodded. "We address your men in the morning, and they can put it to a vote. Just know this, the Captain and I will recon those ships and reach the Ridley."

"How can you be so sure of that?"

She rose, tucked in her chair, and curtsied, her eyes dancing. "They are pirates, after all." Turning she slipped out the door.

He and Deacon sat staring at each other, neither of them blinking. After a moment, Deacon broke the tension. "Well, she's the prettiest handful, I'll give you that. But what a handful. Right?" He leaned forward and slapped him hard on the shoulder, a wide smile breaking across his face.

Colt laughed. He couldn't help it. Still grinning, he rose and returned a strong slap to Deacon's back, a lifelong custom between them. "You have no idea!"

Chapter Thirteen

The Democracy

Tess

A LONG MOAN ROSE FROM SOMEWHERE outside the door. The wind? The stairs creaked again. Did someone slowly climb them, intent on foul play? Tess pulled the woolen blanket up to her chin. Maybe if she covered her ears, drowned out the constant squeaks and creaks, she could fall asleep. She raised both hands to her head to do just that when a gunshot sounded from somewhere on the streets below. And then another creak. *That's it.* She couldn't go on like this. She had to know what was happening. If someone was creeping up the rickety stairs to her room, she would rather face them than wait in her bed to be stabbed in her sleep.

She rose, grabbed her bow from the mattress beside her, and strung it without a sound. Silently, she nocked an arrow and then tiptoed to the door. She clasped the latch, her left index finger curling around the nocked arrow to hold it in place and leaned in to listen. A creak and another squeak. It must be the building, shifting in the wind, the wooden planks rubbing against each other, rather than someone advancing up the stairs.

Still, she needed to make sure. Tess pressed down on the door latch ever so gently with her right hand, the cuper cold to the touch. Her left hand closed tightly around the handgrip of her bow. A sword would be better for close combat like this, and she liked fencing. She was proficient with a sword, at least as good as her older brother Fredrick, though no match for Derek. She needed to get a sword as soon as possible.

Tess attempted to ease the door open inch by inch until she could survey the stairwell, but as soon as she released the latch, the door swung inward. She stumbled backward as down onto her bare feet fell one Bowman of the Realm. He had obviously been sitting on her threshold, leaning into a pillow propped against her door.

She gasped and pressed a hand to her chest, barely maintaining her balance.

Colt lay on his back looking up at her, no trace of shock on his face. He simply smiled. "Can't sleep?"

"What are you doing out there?" Her breaths came in ragged gasps.

"What? I like sleeping sitting up in stairwells—beds are totally overrated." He made no attempt to rise off her bare feet, where he had landed, only continued to lie there smirking at her.

She couldn't repress the giggle.

Colt's smile faded. "What are you doing up? Did you hear me out here? Did I wake you?"

The staircase creaked as it shifted again, and the wind whistled through an unknown crack in the walls, causing a haunting moan. "No, I couldn't sleep, thanks to that." She paused for emphasis, listening to the noises. "I kept imagining someone climbing the stairs to kill us in our sleep."

His eyes darted to her bow and the nocked arrow she still held to the handgrip with her finger, ready to fire. A wide smile spread across his face again. "Swords are better for close combat, Tess. We should get you one." He winked before sitting up. How did he read her mind like that? And that blasted wink!

"Truly, what were you doing out there?"

He swallowed and his neck and cheeks reddened ever so slightly. "I just… your door seems more exposed than mine, and with all the shifting and creaking, I wasn't sure I'd be able to hear someone approach. I wanted to make sure you were safe… my lady." The red wave crept farther up his face. "I wouldn't have gotten any sleep in my bed for worry, so I figured sitting out here, at least I had a chance of drifting off. I had just managed it when I had this strange dream where the hoist fell out from under me and I woke with a start." He winked again.

Butterflies filled Tess's stomach. He'd sat out there to protect her. If she hadn't found him like that, would he even have mentioned it? Now what? She couldn't leave him to sit out there while she slept comfortably in her bed, in safety, benefitting from his sacrifice. Still, it seemed totally inappropriate to suggest they share a room.

Colt edged out the door and readjusted his place on the threshold. Then he looked at her and nodded in the direction of the door, gesturing for her to close it so he could resume his post.

She returned to her bed, grabbed the pillow and wool blanket, and walked though the door, closing it behind her. Then she eased herself down next to him and leaned against the door. The captain was right—his door was tucked around an awkward corner in the makeshift design of the building, and hers was more exposed to the stairs. She arranged her pillow behind her head and covered her legs and feet with her blanket.

Colt stared at her, his eyes wide. "What are you doing?"

"I'm sitting out here." Her cheeks warmed. Obviously, that was what she was doing.

"No, you're not." Colt laughed. "*I'm* sitting out here."

She crossed her arms over her chest. "Well, I'm sitting out here too." Was that the best she could do, seriously?

"No, you're not." The amusement was gone from his voice. "The entire reason I'm out here, not sleeping, is so you can get some rest, safe in the bed I paid for."

Heat rushed into Tess's chest. "Why should you be the one to sacrifice, Captain? Shouldn't I sacrifice in solidarity?" There. She had regained her stride.

He stared at her, his eyes flickering. "Because I'm the Bowman. It's in the code. *Help the helpless.*"

She whipped around to face him. "Helpless? Seriously? Did you not see me shoot the night of the ball?" She fluffed her pillow and let out an irritated sigh as she flopped against it. After all they had been through together, how could he possibly say she was helpless? A minute passed with only the wind and creaking wood daring to speak.

Drumming his fingers on the floorboards, he cleared his throat. "So, what's the plan for the morning, play to the crew's greed and offer to overpay?" His tone had softened, but somewhere deep inside her, that little flame still flickered.

"You're the all-knowing Bowman, and I'm just the helpless maid. There isn't a problem in the Realm you can't think your way out of, so I'm sure you'll figure it out. I only hope you'll be able to concentrate in spite of my snoring!" Tess pretended to sleep for a long time before she actually drifted off. All that time, the Bowman sat upright, vigilant.

* * *

Tess shifted on the barrel. The sun hadn't yet crested the precipice, and darkness shrouded the misty predawn harbour. The ship swayed ever so slightly, but Tess's entire body craved the novel sensation, as though she was born to it and had finally returned home. Dungridge certainly proved worthy of its popularity, the natural harbour shielding the rows of docked ships from the rough weather that blew in from the Endless Sea. She breathed deeply, drinking down the salty air that clung to the morning fog.

Colt strode to the railing at the base of the stairs leading to the bridge and leaned casually against it. She tried to catch his eye, but he was focused on the crew.

Looking him over as they loafed past, sizing him up, he matched every stare with a resolve stronger than bladespar.

Why had she been so cold when he'd tried to discuss this moment with her? What could he say to convince this motley crew to help them?

Deacon strode to the bridge and grasped the railing, leaning well over until each man returned his gaze. "Men of Dungridge, Men of the mist, Men of our precious *Dancing Girl*." Cheers erupted from the crew. They stamped their feet and pounded barrels with their fists. Then, all at once, they grew silent, removed their hats, and looked to the central mast, as if making the sign of descent itself.

She didn't blame them. Unlike the huge galleon where they had met with Deacon the night previous, *The Dancing Girl* was immaculate and deserved this reverence. She was magnificent. Her lines elegant and true, obviously worshiped through constant attention, continual maintenance and cleaning. Every rope hung perfectly coiled, every crate squared to the gunwale, rigging stowed, wood oiled, and brass polished.

Deacon held his hand over his heart a moment before returning it to the railing. He looked to Colt, who stood only paces from where she sat, and winked before continuing. "Men, you know the very beat of my heart. It beats for your suffrage."

The large man standing to her left cocked his head to the side. Two other men turned to each other. Both shrugged.

"Your political franchise." Deacon tried again. More wrinkled foreheads, more shrugging and shifting.

Tess finally caught Colt's eye. He bit the inside of his cheek and pressed his lips together. She focused on her toes. *Whatever you do, do not laugh, Aratess!*

"Come on men, your right to vote, to choose, to have your say." The crew straightened, stood tall. "The right to claim personal agency over your own fate!" Men shifted and cleared their throats.

Tess's eyes flashed to Deacon's. He stood staring at her, as though waiting for her attention. When he raised his eyes skyward, she couldn't help but allow the smile that threated to breach creep to the corners of her mouth.

The pirate lifted his arms to the sky. "I feel it deep in my bones, men—my sole calling in this world is to make sure that you are the masters of your own destiny… and, of course, that your destiny includes as much d'orite and baldespar and brandy as *The Dancing Girl* can hold." Cheers erupted from his men. How could forty-five men make that much noise? Deacon had explained he only needed twenty-five men to sail the ship under normal circumstances, but that twenty extra men were required when ice was involved.

Raising his hand, silence fell at last. "I suppose you are wondering why I have roused you at the un-fatherly hour."

"Aye, Captain!" Their voices rang out as one.

"Well, men, you can blame the Bowman." He lowered his arms and pointed at Colt, who didn't so much as twitch. "The Bowman has asked a favor of you. Do you feel like you *owe* this Bowman something?"

Grunts and whistles rose from every corner of the deck.

"We owes him nothin', Captain!" a tall, thin man bellowed.

"Owes him a little payback for shooting down our friends," a short, one-eyed man yelled.

"That's right, it's not like we've forsaken the All-Father and flown through the Dark Mist, have we?"

"No, Captain!" Their shouts rose to the crow's nest.

"Never committed a sacred sin, never descended to the Forbidden, even though we can. So, do you feel like you owe him?"

"No, nothing, captain." They shouted even louder.

Deacon stared at Colt, looking like the cat who'd just eaten the canary. "Well, men, I owe him. Just a little, but a debt all the same. I owe him your votes. I'll lay out the request and you can decide for yourselves, chart your own course, choose your own fate."

"Aye-aye!" echoed off the masts and deck as the members of the crew pumped their fists in the air.

Deacon raised both hands, palms down, lowering them along with the noise from the crowd. "The Bowman wants you to serve your king." Boos rang out. "He wants you to sail straight past the Ridley, king's waters." Jeers and curses were exchanged.

Her eyes widened. Was every single man present a wanted criminal? She shifted her attention to Colt, who hadn't taken his eyes off the *pirate prince*, who clearly loved to play the part of their champion in the quest for personal agency.

"He wants you to risk serious ice resistance, all to pursue mysterious ships holding unknown cargo."

More booing.

Interesting. Colt had asked Deacon not to disclose the Reyjik's tierality, and Deacon had complied.

"Better still, you aren't allowed to raid these ships. Whatever booty lies sound in their holds must there remain. No spoils for your efforts. No prize for your work. No reward for your risk."

The complaints reached a peak. The men stomped and yelled even louder than before, the wood thudding beneath their feet until Tess feared it might drop out beneath them. Did they hate the thought of loosing out on the booty more than that of serving her father? A flutter of hope stirred her heart. That was the angle they needed.

"Lastly, men, we might very well take fire, sink, and drown in freezing water for this *favor*. But now that I have laid out all the details for your information… vote your conscience, men."

Vote your conscience? Was he being serious? He had all but brainwashed every one of the forty-five pirates against Colt before the Bowman had even been given a chance to defend himself.

Deacon bowed low to his men and then waved his right arm to the floor, stepping back as he did to give Colt a chance to speak.

Colt nodded at his old friend, mounted the stairs to the bridge two at a time in even stride, and strode to the exact place where Deacon had addressed the disgruntled crew of raiders. Men booed and jeered at the sight of him.

A nauseous wave crashed through her. Her fingers trembled, and she clenched them into fists to regain control of them. Closing her eyes, she whispered a prayer. *Please, All-Father, please.*

Colt raised his hand, and an eerie silence fell over the crew. For all their dramatics, were they curious? They leaned in as though anticipating what he had to say, which was a hopeful sign. Wasn't it? Perhaps they were only waiting for an opportunity to pounce on him, toss him overboard. She pressed a palm to her stomach.

Clearing his throat, he glanced down at her for a split second and then looked past her at the crowd. "Men of the *glorious Girl*… if you do this, King Lucius will pay you two months' wages for two days' work." Colt tipped his head to the men before striding back down the stairs to the place he'd been standing while Deacon addressed his crew.

Time slowed as if Tess's heart beat at half speed and her lungs couldn't fill fast enough. One second of silence, two, three, and then all at once the men cheered. They whooped, and laughed, and slapped each other on the back.

A huge grin spread across Colt's face.

Her eyes met his and she nodded. *Well played, Bowman.*

Chapter Fourteen

The Stone

Colt

COLT LEANED AGAINST THE AFT CABIN unnoticed, a perfect vantage point. Tess stood at the stern of the ship, practicing with the longbow that dwarfed her. She perfectly repeated the technique he had shown her only the day before.

His stomach twisted as he approached her. The nerves felt completely foreign. Normally, girls threw themselves at him. He had learned quickly after entering the Ardenian regulars that country girls didn't seem to look past his uniform. That had proved true with the Ardenian green-coat and even more so with his Bowman uniform. He only needed to flash a smile to enjoy company at a pub. Girls loved his confidence and made their interest clear with blatant proposals for company. As yet, he had never traded in on his popularity, not the way Deacon had, who appeared to treat his interactions with women as a sport.

Even so, he had never wanted for conversation or even harmless flirtation when off-duty. Now this girl seemed to resent the very things that usually won him favor. He swallowed hard. *Please don't say anything stupid, Hawthorne. Try for at least one conversation without offending her.*

"I'm impressed you didn't dry-shoot the bow. You've obviously been properly trained with the weapon." He strode to her side. "Are you ever going to tell me who taught you to shoot?" He flashed a smile.

She smiled but didn't reply, simply checked her arrow, drew again, and repeated the whole process. Was this the secret she kept? How could it matter?

"Well, are you at least going to take a shot?"

She turned to him immediately. "Take a shot? I thought ... I thought it would be imprudent to waste my arrows." Letting go of the bow with one hand, she twisted her hair with her index finger.

He grinned as he produced two dozen arrows from behind his back.

Her eyes wide, she examined them carefully. Would she notice they didn't match the standard-issue Bowman arrows they carried in their quivers? "What are these? Where did they come from?" She ran her finger down the beige feathered flight.

"Deac says he raided a Lindsor hoistment to Ardenia last fall. Somehow, he's convinced himself that stealing from Lindsor isn't really stealing. These were in the cargo. They're not military grade, but the quality is decent enough. He has hundreds of them." He couldn't restrain the smile that spread across his face.

Tess smiled back in kind. Victory. A wave of relief flooded over him, one that he couldn't explain. Maybe being on board the ship with no possible way to do anything else productive until they reached the Ridley explained the exultation he felt at being able to offer Tess this gift—the opportunity to hone her skills.

Not that he hadn't tried to be productive. He'd spent from mid-morning until past-peak poring over Deacon's detailed maps of the coastal seas, trying to deduce where the converted Reyjik airships might take up position and what those positions might reveal to him of their military significance. If he could determine the Reyjiks' motivations, perhaps they could predict their next move. Some critical piece of the puzzle was still missing, though, and he had completely converted Deacon's quarters into a chart room. Tess had visited the small quarters and tried to talk the plan through, but they'd made little progress.

He had a knack for figuring out people's intentions based on their motivations. Or he could figure out their mindset by analyzing what they had done, but he could not reconcile the Reyjiks' motivations. Breaking the Sacramance and the trade peace that had lasted for generations simply didn't make sense, so he couldn't guess their next play. He didn't know enough about what they had done, or were in position to do, so he couldn't yet discern why they'd done it.

Although desperate to at least get eyes on the ships that had flown north, he was at the mercy of the wind, something else out of his control. The wind, impervious to his skills of reasoning, or deduction, blew as it willed, and no matter how well he understood the sea charts, he could not cross the distances marked on them any faster.

He'd given up trying to fabricate sound intelligence out of thin air and resigned himself to the fact that he wouldn't be able to learn more until they reached the Ridley or sighted the Reyjik airships. Until then, a feeling of triumph swept over him as Tess took an arrow from his outstretched hand, her green eyes shining.

She nocked the arrow to her bowstring and made full draw. She sighted a small ice floe about two hundred fifty yards away and let fly. Her arrow struck the very back of it, and from the smile on her face she'd satisfied herself with this for a first attempt.

"Nice shot," he remarked as he nocked his own arrow. Drawing effortlessly, he raised his arm until his trajectory was exactly forty-five degrees and then let it go. The arrow arced high in the sky and then landed about three hundred seventy yards away in completely open water. That felt good. When he looked at Tess, though, a smirk had crossed her face. Did she think he had missed?

He shrugged. "Sometimes I like to see how far I can get them to go." He grinned, and she smiled back. Blood pulsed through his veins. He loved to shoot. He knocked and released, knocked and released as fast as he could. The rest of the world faded away as he drifted into that blissful place of focus that only came with a bow and a full quiver. He shot flawlessly, fiercely, and fast. When Deacon's quiver was empty, he shifted his attention to Tess. From the look of wonder on her face, he might have actually impressed her.

At that moment, joy washed over him, and Tess seemed happy too. She even laughed at times. Maybe he had bought her a few minutes of distraction from worrying about her princess. That idea made him even happier.

Then, as he lowered his bow after making a particularly difficult shot, she reached for it, wrapping her fingers around the handgrip just above his. Colt's stomach flipped as he lifted his gaze to meet hers.

She bit her lower lip. "Captain, I know you've thought through every possible scenario for those ships and the Reyjik invasion, but have you considered using the stone in your bow? I mean, that's what it's there for."

No. Did she have to bring that up? Colt rested the end of the bow on the toe of his boot, but she didn't let go. He sighed and gripped the railing with his free hand. How could he answer her? If she knew the truth, he wouldn't be able to face her. "I don't need the stone. My superiors worked very hard to train me in all strategy tactics, interrogation techniques, counterintelligence, how to read non-verbal signals, and facial tells. I read people, my lady. I don't need to ask some tiny emerald pebble to tell me anything." Tearing his eyes from hers, he passed his thumb over the inlaid jewel.

She regarded him thoughtfully. "You graduated two years ago?"

He nodded.

"I happen to know that the year before last, the king traded a full hoist of bladespar and the hand of his daughter to Lindsor for only a pocketful of emeralds. Each truth stone had one final destination—the sacred bow of a graduating Bowman. That stone you don't *need* came at a very high price to the Realm, meant to aid you in your undaunted efforts for truth." She spoke just above a whisper.

Sighing, he shifted his attention from the stone to her. "I—" Something she'd said struck him and he stopped. "Lindsor? What would Lindsor have to do with Sasha's hand? I've never even heard Lindsor mentioned when their betrothal is discussed."

She swallowed hard, her eyes darting out over the sea. "Not Sasha. The prince of Lindsor was given first right of refusal for Sasha's younger sister when she comes of age." She shook her head ever so slightly and gripped the bow tighter still. "That doesn't really matter. What matters is that Bowmen are expected to use their truth stone when they need it. Are you doing your duty if you don't?" Still holding fast to the handgrip of his bow, her slender fingers rested only inches from his.

"What if I don't have my bow with me? I hate the idea of being dependent on something like that. I will always have my wits, my skills. I don't want that stone to become a crutch."

"Right, there isn't a problem in the realm that you can't figure out. You know, Captain, at some point you might need to accept help. It isn't weakness."

Closing his eyes, he rubbed them with his fingers. Of course, accepting help didn't equate to weakness. Bowmen were trained to commandeer and delegate and make the most of their resources. He was good at that. Did that include his truth stone? A rising sense of defeat caught him off guard. "I don't think it works for me, anyway. I've never made it glow." As he whispered the confession, he opened his eyes to see Tess staring at him.

Her entire countenance changed. She seemed to melt somehow. And then she slid her hand down his bow, laying it over his own.

His heart leapt into his throat.

"May I try to help you with it?" Her hand, cool and soft, instantly made his warm, and a strange sensation passed up his wrist through his elbow and to his shoulder, as if lightning coursed through him, originating at her touch.

His heartrate quickened. "Sure. I mean, yes, all right, my lady."

Tess took a deep breath. Her brow creased as though she was concentrating deeply. "Say something true, something you have been thinking about recently, very recently, that you know for certain is true… and it has to matter, Captain, not like an empirical fact, but something that matters to you that you know to be true."

Her hand still covered his. Did she feel what he felt or was she immune to the pulsing surge that radiated from their touch? *Focus on what she said, Hawthorne. Don't waste this. Don't mess this up.*

He closed his eyes and thought deeply. Tess, Tess mattered to him. At this moment, and every moment since he'd met her, she had dominated his thoughts one way or another. Of course, the Reyjik mattered. His entire identity felt jeopardized by their attack. He had never before felt ashamed of his mother's heritage, but now he felt lost in that regard. Deacon mattered. Blood or not, Deacon was his brother, and now they were completely at odds with each other, standing on opposite sides of the line drawn by the Sacreds themselves.

He opened his mouth ever so slightly. Did he dare? He snapped it shut. Forget it. He didn't need this. He didn't need help. He'd managed just fine until now without help. In fact, he'd managed better than fine. He was the youngest captain in the corps. His family and lineage a disadvantage, he still outshot and outranked men twice his standing, and he would gladly tell her that.

Before he could, Tess squeezed his hand gently. Then she placed her thumb over his and pushed it across the smooth surface of the emerald.

He didn't resist.

"Captain Colt Hawthorne loves Deacon Thornby like a brother," she whispered. The emerald blazed just above the handgrip. Colt inhaled so sharply that Tess jumped. She gently pulled her hand from his and slid it behind her back. The stone still shone–not quite so bright, but it glowed just the same.

Colt's eyes locked with hers. Bright and kind, they reminded him of the emerald she had just set aglow.

"How did you do that? How did you know what to say?" Colt felt shaky all over.

"You did it, Captain. I just helped a little. Anyone can see that you love Deacon. I didn't need training in counterintelligence for that one." She grinned, reached for another arrow, and then resumed shooting as if nothing had happened. As if nothing had changed… but everything had changed.

Chapter Fifteen

The Rematch

Tess

TESS TRIED TO CONTROL HER BREATHING. Her hand, her entire arm, still felt warm from his touch, as though tiny sparks flooded up to her neck and risked spilling down into her heart. She felt shaky, but it was worth it. The look on his face. He believed, even if only for that moment, he believed in the power of his truth stone.

She smiled as she thought about him and Deacon. Yes, they were brothers, through and through, blood or not.

Her thoughts flashed back to MaryLee, her nurse, her surrogate mother in all respects. MaryLee wasn't blood either, but she had never felt more connected to anyone. MaryLee was intelligent, kind, funny, and well-bred, yet when her oldest brother Derek had asked for permission to marry her the king had sent her seaward to Reyjik without warning. She woke the next morning to find MaryLee's bed empty, only a note in her place. She shot another arrow, and another, watching them fly and hit the targeted ice floes.

Her heart ached. How could she miss someone after ten long years? Only eight, when MaryLee left, what did she even really remember? Laughter, kindness, and the feeling that she mattered most to someone, something she hadn't known since. Maybe she embellished her memories. If she were honest with herself, she wouldn't even be able to recognize MaryLee now, so what did she really know of this Reyjik girl? Was she as wonderful as Tess remembered?

And why did these feelings surface around Colt? She had laid them to rest years ago, and suddenly, Colt made her feel that profound loss again. Why? Was it because of his mixed parentage? She shot again and again, forcing herself not to look at Colt.

Blast! Her thoughts jumped to her careless mention of her impending possible betrothal to the prince of Lindsor. Why had she brought that up? Why did being around Colt cause her to think of it so often? Or maybe timing played the greatest factor, with her eighteenth birthday only a month away. *Am I really that terrified of Prince Jestin's decision?* She had managed to ignore that feeling for the last two years, but Sasha's upcoming marriage dredged up the fear that had crippled her when she first learned of her father's contract with Lindsor's king. Her hand, her very future, traded for emeralds.

She shoved the fear deep down. None of that mattered. None of it. Not MaryLee, not her betrothal, not the Bowman, none of it. She shot again and again. Sasha mattered, and Ardenia mattered, and the unity of the Realm mattered. Finding the truth behind it all mattered. None of this was about her. Tess reached for another arrow, but the case Colt had brought for her was empty. She sucked back the cool air, her chest heaving.

"I think she just might be the better shot, big, strong Bowman."

Tess whirled around.

A smirk on his face, Deacon jumped to the deck right behind them, the boards rattling beneath his feet. Tess startled. Had he been sitting on a barrel watching them and she hadn't noticed?

"It wouldn't be the first time." Colt smiled, seemingly unphased by the jeer.

"Really?" Deacon stepped towards Tess, leaned close, picked an official Bowman arrow from her quiver, and twirled it through his fingers. "Then I think we should have a bonafide competition right now. The Bowman versus the princess, if only to settle my curiosity. And as official sponsor of this little event—after all, I am supplying the venue and arrows—I name the terms, rewards, and reprisals." He switched the arrow to his other hand and repeated the twirl pattern with ease.

Nerves gripped Tess's stomach and she glanced at Colt. He was smiling widely. Had it always been like this? Two competitive friends trying to best each other, never letting it affect their bond? Yes, it had, she could see it in their eyes. Somehow, Tess sensed all this meant more for Deacon.

"What do you have in mind, Your Highness?" Colt bowed dramatically.

Deacon rubbed the scruff on his chin. "Moving targets, what say you both?" He flicked his wrist, catapulting the arrow a few inches skyward, grabbed it mid-twirl and tossed it into Colt's quiver. Colt didn't flinch, only reached out his hand and they shook on it. Deacon snapped his heels together and stepped away towards the main hatch.

Colt turned to face her. "I'm sorry, Tess, but I've already bragged about your shooting, and I know he needs to see for himself. He won't let it go. It's just as well we get it over with." He rolled his left shoulder and stretched his neck.

Warmth flooded her cheeks. Had Colt actually spoken well of her shooting ability? Did the pirate care? She bit her lower lip. A moving target? Could she manage that? Even though she practiced every day at home, she hadn't shot at moving targets in ten years. What if she disappointed them both?

In under ten minutes, Deacon had finalized the details of the competition. Every man on the ship sat ready to watch. They had literally come out of the woodwork as word of the match spread. Raiders crawled out of trap doors in the deck, others slid down ropes, and she could have sworn that two popped out of barrels. The crew was scattered across the stern of the ship, and Colt and Tess had been instructed by Deacon to shoot towards the bow. Two men stood in the crow's nest—one they called Shifty and the other Clubber. Shifty held a basket of wood shingles, and Clubber, the oldest man Tess had ever seen, held one in his right hand, ready to throw.

Deacon stood tall and cleared his throat. "Gentlemen, un-gentlemen, raiders, friends, and our most enchanting… *princess*." He feigned a traditional pirate accent, and his men cheered and whistled in response. His inflection of the word *princess* simultaneously dripped with triumph and sarcasm. Every time Deacon used her proper title, it made Tess nervous. One of these times, the coin might drop for Colt.

"We have today a most exciting event. Both our Bowman and our resident miss-priss have agreed to test their proficiency with a match." His men cheered.

She studied their weathered faces. Did Deacon's crew genuinely like following him? Did they want him in charge? It seemed so, and she liked that.

"Our competition today will take the form of the best of five arrows, arrr… The winner enjoys dinner with the captain, and the loser must match me drink for drink. May the best archer win!" He ended with a flourished bow.

Deacon had already given Clubber instructions on how to toss the wooden shingles. Clubber had practiced a few, and her muscles tightened at the thought of trying to hit them successfully in front of an audience. Worst still, the thought of attempting to best the Bowman who stood casually beside her seemed impossible. All the times she had shot at the stern, she'd watched him out of the corner of her eye, and he was the most gifted archer she had ever seen. His accuracy was unmatched, his speed almost superhuman, and somehow he made it all seem effortless.

Her stomach churned. *Please don't let me embarrass myself in front of the entire crew.*

Colt touched her shoulder. "Have you ever done this before?" The kindness in his eyes eased a little of her apprehension.

She shook her head, her mouth dry. "I practiced this twice with my brothers as a child. But girls of my age and standing don't shoot, so target practice is a solitary exercise, conducted alone, deep in the woods. I never have anyone to throw for me."

Colt smiled and squeezed her shoulder before letting her go. "Okay, it's not hard when you think it through." And then, as if Deacon and the forty-five crewmen did not exist, he leaned close. "Clubber will toss it like a disk. At first it will move fast, but then it will slow down. It should follow an arc shape. Draw first and then call for Clubber to throw. While it will prove strenuous to hold the draw, it's critical you don't lose time when you want to release. Track the shingle with your arrow tip as it climbs. You want to shoot right before it reaches the top of the arc, when it nearly comes to a stop before it starts to fall. After that, it will pick up speed and you will lose your chance. The arrow moves so fast, you only need to release it a second before you think the shingle will reach that point. Does that make sense?"

It did make sense. It made perfect sense. She felt decidedly better, even excited to try what he had just described. She wanted to thank him, but her dry mouth wouldn't let her. She just nodded again and forced a weak smile.

"I'll go first so you can use my turns almost like practice to get a feel for the timing. All right?" When she nodded again, he positioned himself facing the crow's nest and drew.

"Toss it, Clubber!"

The old man whipped a shingle as Colt had described. In fact, everything transpired as he had said it would. The shingle moved quickly at first, in an arc, then slowed. Her heart pounded in her chest. This was the moment. The sound of Colt's arrow release sent a lightning bolt through her body. A profound sense of satisfaction washed over her as the arrow lodged perfectly into the heavy shingle, altering its trajectory and pushing it out over the water at the bow. The crew cheered and she let out a squeal of delight. Deacon held a straight face, and Colt only smiled. He had made a dead shot without even a practice throw. Amazing.

Unable to restrain herself, she grabbed his right arm and squeezed it. Colt's smile warmed, although it turned into a slight grimace as he rolled his left shoulder again. His arm must still hurt.

"Your aim is great, Tess. You're a natural. You just need to get used to the timing. Watch me each time, track it yourself, internalize when I release. You have this."

With each shingle thrown, and each opportunity to judge the angle and timing of release, Tess grew more confident. No longer dreading her turn, she tapped her foot on the deck, anxious for the chance to try. Colt shot perfectly. Not one miss. All five singles lay floating in the cold water, each with an arrow shaft sticking straight up in triumph. She should have felt threatened, but she didn't, only happy.

Deacon sighed and faked a yawn, patting his open mouth for emphasis. "Not bad, and totally expected, Bowman." He spoke to Colt but looked straight at her, a smirk on his face. "You're up now, Princess."

What did the pirate hope for, for her to fail? Or did he want her to succeed and best Colt? She couldn't tell. She reached for her first arrow but stopped when Colt rested his hand gently on her arm.

"I meant it. You have this. Just relax. Feel the timing. Breathe," he coached.

She obeyed immediately, taking in a deep breath. She planted her feet. Raised her bow to an angle that matched the one Colt had just used and drew. "Yep," was all she could manage to say under the intense strain of holding full draw. Thankfully, it was enough to give Clubber the message, and he threw a shingle almost exactly the way he had for Colt. Tess's heart beat wildly as she tracked the spinning square of wood. Then, as the makeshift target followed its path upward, everything went quiet. She could no longer feel her heartbeat. Oblivious to everything around her, she felt the timing somewhere deep within, aimed, and released.

The arrow shot so fast, and the target was so close, relatively speaking, that it pierced the wood before Tess had even recovered from the effort required to make full draw. She had done it. She had hit it. First try and she had hit it! Instinctively, she whirled to look at Colt.

He was laughing. Pure delight shone in his eyes. He didn't try to hide his joy. Infinitely more pleased with her success than with his own. He leaned close. "How tired are you? We've been shooting for a while now. Do you have four more left in you?"

Tess shook her head. She didn't. She hated that fact, but she was spent.

"Want to call it?" he asked in a whisper.

Tess nodded. Might as well quit while she was ahead. Holding the draw had taken an immense amount of effort, and she doubted she could manage it even once more.

"Well, Your *Pirateness*, there you have it. Equals." Colt turned to the crew, grabbed Tess's hand, and raised it high in the air in triumph—Colt's signature gesture, to be sure. The men hooted and hollered, all the while stomping on the wooden deck. Clearly the crew wanted her to do well, which sent warmth drifting through her. She felt endeared to each and every one of them, accepted by them. Her face ached from the wide smile she couldn't restrain.

She peered over her shoulder, checking for Deacon's reaction. He leaned against the mast, clapping slow and easy. Their eyes met, and she saw something in the pirate she hadn't before, not surprise, or scrutiny, or desire, but respect. Warmth crept into her cheeks, and she turned to face the crew again. The men continued to cheer as Colt pumped her hand in victory a few times before lowering it.

"Captain, can you even believe I hit it? Honestly, I can't. I tried that twice as a little girl and failed miserably both times. My brothers never had the patience to show me how it was done. Thank you for helping me the way you did. You explained it so well, and it all made sense, and you were so kind not to just trounce me the way I know you can, and to call the draw like that." Tess caught her breath. She had said too much.

Colt smiled so wide his entire face lit up. And those eyes. "You really are a natural, Tess." He bit his lip and looked down at their hands.

Was she still holding his hand? What? Tess tugged hers free. "Sorry." She couldn't look at him. She turned and slipped through the lingering crew, desperate for her quarters. Was her heart beating faster than it had during the competition? Why did she feel so sick?

Chapter Sixteen

The Ice

Colt

COLT TIED THE NECKERCHIEF LEAVING THE knot left of center, just how his mother had shown him. His injured arm ached. He'd pushed too hard shooting that afternoon. Why was he dressing for dinner? Who dressed for a formal dinner aboard a pirate ship? The idea was absurd. But Deacon had insisted on it and seeing as no clear winner or loser had resulted from the competition that afternoon, Deacon insisted both he and Tess make good on the dinner. He had no intention of attempting to match his friend at drinking and he had made that clear, but how could he refuse dinner? Maybe spending some time together would help thaw the icy new dynamic to their relationship.

He retied his neckerchief. Why did he feel so bothered? He knew why. Deacon had kept his relationship with him ice cold, yet he could not help but notice Tess warming to the raider. Late this afternoon, Colt had found Tess and Clubber practicing her shooting. Clubber tossed from the stern railing, just as he had done from the crow's nest, and Tess shot out over the water. The range, much closer now, decreased the level of difficulty, but it still made a great set-up for practicing her timing and aim. She shot true almost every time. He had grabbed his bow to join her, but Deacon beat him to it. The raider came with his own bow and shared her arrows. Deacon was still a great shot, and Tess had appeared impressed.

He'd spent the better part of an hour trying to busy himself on the ship and not overhear them as they talked and laughed. Why did it bother him? He had a mission. The fate of the Realm rested in his hands.

Leaving the dark quarters where the crew slept, he made his way above deck. Deacon had given Tess the quarters of his first mate, Reynolds, so she would have some privacy.

He was equally grateful and leery for her private cabin. He didn't like the fact that she slept alone and worried about her safety on board a ship full of raiders. When he'd mentioned his concerns that afternoon, Tess had simply pointed out that, as every man on board had witnessed her proficiency with a bow, he didn't need to worry. She made a good point.

Should he stop by the small cabin and escort her to Deacon's quarters for dinner? He quickly shook free from the idea. The memory of how she had pulled back her hand that afternoon still made him cringe—a sting he did not want to repeat.

He rapped quietly on Deacon's door. Two quick taps, a pause, two more quick taps another pause, and a single tap. Had he just naturally tapped out their secret knock from childhood? He immediately regretted it. How would Deacon react? Maybe Deac hadn't heard it. Maybe he didn't remember it. The solid oak door did seem to dampen the sound, totally the opposite of the barrel lid they'd used for their tree fort hatch, which made the knock resonate. The door swung open wide.

"Seriously? How did you remember that? I had totally forgotten about that knock." Deacon's eyes were wide.

He laughed. "I don't know. I just went to knock and that's what came out. Strange how the mind works, right?"

Both men smiled, and Deacon gestured for Colt to enter. The room seemed smaller than the quarters on the big galleon, and far cleaner. Had the entire space been recently tidied and dusted? A bed built against the interior wall was neatly made. A desk and chair, made of fine maple, held only a blank sheet of parchment and a d'orite-plated quill pen. A small round table, set with three chairs, sat in the middle of the room. And, of course, there was a beautiful maple liquor cabinet, stocked full of brandy.

The table was set and dinner had already been served. It waited under bladespar-domed warming covers. The table boasted cloth napkins, crystal glasses, real silverware, and three lit candles. Despite himself, he was genuinely impressed. Deacon held out a hand for him to sit down and then did the same. Only a few seconds after they had pulled in their chairs, they heard a quiet knock at the door.

Deacon sprang up and practically leapt to the door.

He stood as well, in expectation of the third dinner guest. When Deacon swung the door open, there stood Tess. She had changed out of the boy's clothing she had worn all day and donned the green dress he had bought her the night before. She looked beautiful, luminescent. He had to convince himself that she couldn't possibly be shimmering, even though that was how it seemed.

She smiled warmly at Deacon, curtsied, and then turned to face him. He swallowed hard, not sure what to expect after she had bolted from him only hours earlier.

"Evening, Captain." She smiled sweetly but didn't quite meet his eyes. He felt a tightening around his heart. Were they all right? *No, Colt, focus on Deacon. You've waited three years for this. Don't mess it up.*

The dinner went far better than he expected. He asked question after question about the last three years in Dungridge, and Deacon answered them eagerly, acting like his old self again.

He had to check his moral judgment and indignation over the sea-raiding exploits, or the entire evening would have ended before it began.

Flaunting his success, Deacon made no apologies for his actions based on one overarching justification—he only raided hoistments from Lindsor. Deacon believed, unequivocally, that the Sacramance Accord—and every other law pertaining to property and ownership— fell null and void when it came to Lindsor. The rules simply didn't apply to the skyward tier that had attacked Thornton in greedy ambition and left their village in mourning for the last decade.

Everything Deacon described pointed in a direction he felt compelled to follow. He knew he took a risk, asking, but he simply needed to know. "Deac, I mean no offense, it's just curiosity, but when did you shift into…" He had a hard time saying the word out loud.

"Raiding, piracy, utter lawlessness?" Deacon, obviously fairly drunk at this point, laughed at his hesitation.

"Well, I probably would have said something like, moral ambiguity, but yes."

Pouring yet another glass of brandy, Deac offered the bottle to his two dinner guests. He clearly didn't notice that Tess hadn't so much as touched her first drink, and his still sat three quarters full.

"Well, it's a funny thing. I served as first mate on *The Bonnie Lass*, my second schooner, for over two years. Her captain ran a legitimate shipping business. Oh, he dabbled in smuggling when the right opportunity presented itself, but he never had the nerve to raid outright. He was a brutal man, and he could be ruthless at times, but in some ways, he proved a coward. Too blasted scared to take what was ripe for the pickin'. I worked hard—you would have laughed at how hard—and the men loved me. So, I got promoted, but the pay wasn't worth it all, you know? I was already thinking of movin' on when the mutiny happened."

He nodded, as did Tess.

"The men I served with really did love me, thankfully, 'cause when they mutinied, they didn't kill me alongside old Beltnotch." Deacon propped an elbow on the table and leaned sideways to whisper loudly to Tess, "I had no part in that, don't worry. I know there is a special place in Gehenna reserved for mutineers. What do they say? Utter darkness for all eternity?"

She nodded again.

Relief coursed through him at the revelation that Deacon hadn't been complicit in the mutiny, as truly, mutiny was a heinous crime.

"And then what?" Tess slid the bottle of brandy back to Deacon. She sat at attention, the most perfect posture he'd ever seen.

Deacon propped his chin on his hand. "Then I convinced the lads that I should be their captain, promising only a fair say in their own fate and all the booty we could raid." He contemplated her as though waiting for a reaction.

"And when did the mutiny happen?"

He repressed a smile. *Nice, Tess. He never did answer my question about how all this began, did he?*

"Hmm, I suppose it happened about a half year back. Yep, sometime during the seaward tarragon migration last fall. I remember, cuz old Beltnotch was trying to shoot himself a tarragon at the bow of the ship when he got the knife in his back."

His head jerked. How could Deacon have chosen this life? "But why, Deac? Why raid, why steal? You could have used your ship in a hundred other ways to earn a living. I'm not trying to judge. I'm just trying to understand it. You never stole like this when we were kids." Blast, that sounded like judgment, to be sure. Saying he wasn't trying to judge probably made it worse.

Thankfully, Deacon didn't flinch, only sat back, totally relaxed, raised his arms off the table, and locked his fingers behind his head. "That's a funny thing too. You know, I've thought about it, but no one has ever actually asked me that. I guess I have two answers for ya. In general, every pirate out here raids because there's a demand for our precious bladespar. If it weren't for the king and his monopoly on it, the black market mightn' even have sprung up. Don't even think he realizes that the tighter he shuts that fist, the harder he strangles the progress of the other tiers."

He shot a glance to Tess. She closed her eyes, her face twisted as though she'd just taken a shot to the gut. The king's policy was somehow personal for her.

Deacon yawned. "In the second place, I just felt a sort of moral apathy… no, more like moral release. As if great shackles fell loose and I was free to reach out and take anything I could figure out how to steal. I mean, honestly, if I can figure out how to get it better than you and your men can figure out how to keep it, I reckon I've earned it fair and square. What is even more amazing is that I do feel bad, but not because I'm breaking King's Law or Sacramance. Wanna know why I feel so bad sometimes?"

He swallowed hard and nodded, his heart in a vise that twisted tighter with every word Deacon spoke.

"I feel terrible that I wasted all that time trying to be honest. Look at the spoils." He waved a shaky hand around the room, gesturing to the many luxurious stolen goods on display. His words slurred slightly as he made this grand declaration.

Colt frowned. Did his old friend really mean it? How could he? This moral shift had happened a half year back; why did that feel so significant?

Before he could reply, Tess touched Deacon's arm. "Thank you for your candor, Captain Thornby."

Deacon leaned forward, grabbing the table to steady himself. "Oh,

I will always be candid with you, Princess. You can count on my honesty, that is for certain. Unless, of course, dishonesty is required to get something I want. Speaking of candor, has the good Bowman told you about any of the stunts we pulled when we were young?" A sly smile spread across his face, and he turned and winked at him.

No, no, please don't tell Tess all we did. "Oh, Tess isn't interested in our stories from when we were kids, Deac." He tried in vain to sound casual.

"Actually, Captain Thornby, I'd love to hear about your childhood exploits with the Bowman." Tess turned to him, smiled, and then winked.

Warmth crept up his neck. She had him and she knew it. Blast. What would Deacon say? Would he purposely embarrass him? He certainly had tons of ammunition.

Deacon opened a second bottle of brandy and then the stories began. Every childhood story of note came out of the vault. They were funny, and cited almost infinite examples of recklessness, but whatever embarrassment he suffered, Deacon suffered alongside, and Deac loved it all. Colt's guarded heart began to thaw a little. The men laughed until their sides hurt. It had been a very long time since he'd laughed that hard, since Deacon had quit the corps, to be exact.

Tess laughed right along with them. Was this the first time he'd truly heard her laugh? She seemed to love those exaggerated childhood retellings as much as the two friends who'd lived them. She needed to be included in the fun, so he related to Deacon the story of their meeting and the shooting competition at the ball. Deacon seemed fascinated. He then regaled him with the bear story. Tess blushed and covered her face each time. How could someone so confident also feel genuinely shy?

Deacon loved all three stories. Now decidedly drunk, his head resting on his right hand, and his elbow propped up on the tabletop, he stared at Tess in disbelief. "The bear? You were worried about Colt killing the bear?" He laughed so hard he had to hold a hand to his stomach. "Honestly, Princess, who are you? I can say with great certainty that I have *never* met a girl like you. And trust me, I have known a lot of girls!"

His skin grew hot with embarrassment over the innuendo and the way Deacon slurred a few of his words. Still, if he were honest, he wanted to learn the answer to the question and couldn't resist taking the opportunity to press her on it.

"Yes, Lady Tess of Ardenia, for the third time now, who are you and where did you learn to shoot?"

Tess's gaze shifted from him to Deacon and back to him. In silence, she twisted a loose piece of hair at the nape of her neck and wrinkled her eyes and nose. Was she debating with herself as to what to tell them? What was she hiding?

Finally, she sighed deeply and opened her mouth. Before she could say a word, a horrible scraping noise broke the silence, followed by a terrible crash.

"Ice! The yell came from somewhere outside.

Colt grabbed the table, with one hand to brace himself and reached out with his other hand to grab hold of Tess. She already held onto the table with both hands. Thankfully, the table was screwed to the floorboards for rough weather like on most ships this size.

Deacon hadn't fared as well. He had tumbled to the floor at the first impact, tangled up in his chair, groaning as he rolled into the table's heavy oak pedestal. The ship heaved and listed under the force.

After a few moments, Colt felt stable enough to stand. He ran for the door and made his way to the bow of the ship. Deacon and Tess followed right behind him, and the rest of the crew joined them on deck.

He stared at the amazing scene that stretched out before him. The sea no longer dark and no longer liquid, was comprised of white and turquoise shifting floes of ice, like scales on the haunches of a giant frost dragon. They slid over and under each other, moving in organic patterns as they floated on the frigid water beneath.

Deacon shouted orders to his men. "I want fifteen polemen on the port side and five on starboard. Get those ice poles above deck and start pulling those floes out of the way!" He yelled the commands as if chunks of ice slamming into the ship were a regular occurrence. "Throw up the main sail, our *Girl* will need a little extra umph if she hopes to dance over this."

His men stood mesmerized by the surreal seascape before them. It took Deacon bellowing a second time to press them into action.

"Well, are you waiting for us to get cut to ribbons? Let's go! We only have an hour and a half before pitch and we drop anchor."

"What can I do?" Feeling like a fish out of water, Colt grabbed his old friend by the arm.

"What can *we* do?" Tess echoed.

Deacon scrutinized them both. "You ever man an ice pole?" He crossed his arms and pursed his lips, clearly enjoying the moment. He alone excelled in this arena, and he knew it. They shook their heads. "Then just sit back and enjoy the show." Turning his back on them dismissively, he strode to the bow.

The entire crew sprang into action. The standard crew manned the rigging, hoisted up the main sail, and adjusted the jib, which gave *The Dancing Girl* more speed. The concept seemed counter intuitive for him, but out of pride, he didn't question Deacon about this course of action.

Deacon stood by the prow surveying the ice ahead and keeping his eye on his men and their progress.

Deac kept his eye on the water, a spyglass in one hand and a mug of coffee someone had handed him in the other, as Tess approached him. "Captain Thornby?"

"Just Deac, Princess," he replied.

Colt joined Tess at the railing.

"Okay, Deac, why are we speeding up? How does it all work? How do you negotiate the ice?" She stared up at him in earnest.

"Never read about this one, eh?" He flashed her a sly smile. She laughed and shook her head. "Well, Princess, it works like this. *The Dancing Girl* is special. Her hull is shaped just shallow enough to slip up onto the ice, if she's going fast enough."

"Onto the ice?" Her nose wrinkled and she cocked her head.

Deac chuckled. "Yeah, she needs to get up and onto the ice so her weight can break it. That's how it works. She slides up and then cracks through. I had her hull reinforced so she doesn't get cut to pieces. My polemen then use the sticks to shove the broken pieces behind us. If they get piled up ahead of us, we can really be in trouble."

The whole experience seemed surreal. As Deacon had described, the ship lunged up and forward, and the scraping noise of ice against the hull was deafening. At the moment of climax, when *The Dancing Girl* had enough of its mass over the floe to break through, the whole ship dropped. The thunderous sound reverberated to his core.

Tess smiled with every lurch and every drop, and Colt couldn't help but watch her. When his eyes met, she grinned from ear to ear before turning back to Deacon. "Why do you have so many more men on the port side?"

Deacon flashed him a look. Obviously, he liked Tess's curiosity. "Well, the real question, is *where is this ice coming from?* If you figure that out, your question will answer itself, really." Deac called out more instructions to his men. They were doing well, but ice was beginning to build up on the port side. He ordered two more men from the starboard to give those on the port side a hand. Once that was sorted, he contemplated Tess, obviously waiting for her to come up with an answer.

Tess refused to ask for help, she bit her lip and then climbed up on the railing, dress and all.

His heart in his throat, Colt moved closer, prepared to grab her if the boat lurched suddenly and she lost her balance.

Snatching the spyglass from Deacon's hand, she surveyed the coast ahead. After a moment, she pointed. "The Ridley!" She gasped. "It's coming from the Ridley River. Of course! The river is fed by a whole freshwater system of headwaters. The ice and snow from Lindsor melt and fall and feed the entire watershed. The river's shallow, maybe five yards deep, it practically freezes solid during the winter. Freshwater has a higher freezing point than salt water, and the river flows down to the sea, so, during the spring break up, the ice flows right out here, into the delta. The freshwater ice floats on the seawater. I mean, ice of any kind would float, because it's less dense than water, but even when it's liquid, the freshwater floats out on the seawater, making the brackish estuary. So, of course you need more men on the port side, because the river comes out right there from the coast." Tess sounded practically giddy as she pointed.

Deac laughed. "Well, Princess, I think you must have read a few books to come up with all that." He shook his head.

Colt's chest swelled a little at Tess's intelligence. Leaning back against the railing, he peered over his shoulder and watched the men as they heaved the ice out of the way and shoved it along the port side of the ship. The operation, as smooth as it could be under the circumstances, successfully saw them sail to the Ridley. And then, all at once, a polemen jerked up against the railing, pulled off balance as his pick lodged in the ice. Frantic thoughts raced through his mind. *Let go! Let go and accept the loss of the pole. Don't hang on! Don't try to dislodge it!* Then, suddenly, the man vanished. Just like that.

Colt sprang from the railing, yelling, "Man overboard." He ran to the port side and peered over but couldn't see the lost seaman for all the ice floating alongside the ship. He grabbed a length of rope and followed it to the main mast, about twenty yards long. He tested it with a sharp tug, tied it around his waist in seconds, and secured it with a lock-knot. Then he jumped over the railing, landing feet first on a large floe. The force of his impact started to flip the chunk of ice over on itself, so he scrambled on all fours to another floe. His hands and knees screamed in pain. He searched the black water, desperately looking for any sign of the crewman. The ice was freezing, and the water that flooded over it, a result of his added weight, was equally cold. Already his hands and knees were going numb. Suddenly, he heard a cry from above him.

"Colt, Colt, there, in front of you!"

When he looked up, Tess was pointing to a place only a few yards ahead of him, to a small dark break in the shifting surface. He swallowed hard. He could feel himself hyperventilating, and he tried to control his panicked breathing. The cold, unbearable in its own right, made his next move unthinkable. So, he didn't think, only dove headlong into the freezing black water.

He couldn't even process what he felt. Not cold, but pain, searing pain, bit into every surface of his body. His brain shut down. He gasped for air and searched wildly for the ship. He managed to make out Tess wrestling with a rope at the side of the davit arms. She yelled something to him. *Think, Colt. Concentrate.*

"Colt, he is right there! Grab him and we'll pull you out!"

His forehead wrinkled in confusion. *Who* was in front of him?

Tess screamed his name again. The panic in her voice roused him from his foggy agony, and he swung his gaze in the direction she was pointing. The crewman thrashed in the water. He found new strength somewhere deep inside and forced himself forward, until he reached the crewman. It was Shifty. He had stopped thrashing but was somehow managing to keep his head above water. Colt grasped Shifty's sodden shirt at the back of his neck and lifted his free hand into the air. He shot a look back at Tess. She released the winch on the davit arm. A large fishing net crashed onto the frozen, fractured surface of the sea, but with the forward momentum of the ship, he had no hope in reaching it. When he shot a hopeless glance at Tess, the rest of the world faded; all he saw was the torture in her eyes.

Before he could think what to do, Tess leapt over the railing and landed on the shifting ice beside the net. Panic shot through his entire body. *No, Tess, no!* She lunged forward into the water, grabbing hold of the net and letting out a yelp just before her head disappeared beneath the waves. When she reemerged, she paddled desperately towards him.

Colt's arms and legs were numb. The unconscious crewman shook violently. How could Tess survive this? What if she didn't survive this?

When she reached him, he shoved both arms through the net, as though he were giving the crewman a bearhug, and tangled himself in the twisted rope as best he could. Tess did the same from behind the crewman's back. All at once, they were heaved from the water. He struggled to hold onto the crewman with arms so numb he could no longer feel the constant ache in his injured left one that had plagued him since Costair.

Tess had locked her arms around Shifty's waist and was somehow managing to hold fast. Her entire body shook as she turned to him and their eyes locked. Her lips blue, she forced a pained smile. Colt feared his heart would burst.

It took less than a minute to hoist their three freezing bodies up and swing them over the deck. Free from the water, pain racked his entire body and he couldn't stop trembling.

Shifty lay next to him on the deck. Colt turned his head the other way and saw Tess, Deacon at her side. Then everything went black.

Chapter Seventeen

The Impossible

Deacon

"GET THEM TO MY QUARTERS--AND get Clubber and Thomas!" Deacon shouted orders at the top of his lungs. He heard the fear in his voice, and it sounded foreign to him. If his throat wasn't growing sore under the effort, he would swear the orders were coming from someone else.

"Blankets!" he shrieked. "I want every blanket on board brought to my cabin. Reynolds, you have the ship. Get us past the Ridley and then drop anchor!" The group of stunned crewmen gathered around him as he worked desperately to try and save three lives. He signaled to four of his yeomen to help him carry the trembling victims. The men managed Colt and Shifty. Deacon carried Tess. Once inside his cabin, he set to work.

"Lay them down and find Clubber and Thomas, now!" Deacon took a deep breath, willing himself to regain his composure. Time was their greatest enemy. Shifty had been in the water the longest, and the effects of hypothermia were already wracking his lean frame. Deacon stripped Shifty himself and threw the freezing clothes to the corner of the room. He then covered him with two blankets. Clubber appeared, out of breath, in the doorway, eyes wide. The man looked ancient at the best of times, but tonight the great-grandfather also looked terrified. He had been on the sea all his life and still insisted on climbing up into the crow's nest at least once a day. No coward himself, Clubber knew just how critical the next few minutes would be.

"Clubb, I need you to strip her down to her skivvies. Take off your shirt, and then lie on top of her, now!" Clubber stared at him, eyes wide. Deacon gritted his teeth. They didn't have time for this. "Clubb, she's gonna die if she don't get warm. You said she reminded you of your granddaughter. Well, get to savin' her."

Clubber obeyed immediately. Thomas appeared in the doorway next.

"Thomas, you need to get that coat and shirt off and warm your brother. Under those blankets, now!"

Deacon had no time to check to see if Thomas had obeyed and helped Shifty. He had to undress Colt. His friend lay unconscious, still shaking violently. Deac fumbled with the wet buttons of Cot's dress shirt, finally ripping it down the middle, popping them off in the process. His own dry shirt slipped off easily. He pulled two blankets over him and Colt, trying to hold the shivering man tightly enough to quell the tremors that wracked his frigid body.

What if Colt died? What if this was it, and Colt died right here on the floor of his cabin? Deacon tightened his grip. No, Colt couldn't die, not like this, not now. He was too good for that. Blast, why hadn't Deacon written him back? Month after month he ignored the letters, punishing Colt. And for what? For not quitting the Bowmen, the corps he idolized, the only place he'd ever felt valuable? Even after that, when Colt needed help, who did he come to? His best friend, the one who had given him the silent treatment over nothing. No, his brother who'd given him the silent treatment over nothing. *Despite everything, he still trusts me, counts on me, even though he knows I don't deserve it. Under no circumstance are you dying, Colt. I need another chance to make good on that trust, and you are NOT robbing me of that!*

Tears filled Deacon's eyes just as Colt's opened.

Colt inhaled sharply, and turned to Deac, fear flashing in his eyes. "Is she okay? Where is she? Is she all right, Deac?" He pushed against Deacon's hold, trying to sit up and look for Tess.

Deacon held him down to keep him under the warmth of the blankets. "Hold on, Colt. Club, how's she doing?"

Colt planted his palms on Deacon's chest and pushed him away so he could sit up. Blast! He was so strong.

"She's all right, Bowman. She's warmed up some and she's stopped shakin.' She's tougher than she looks, that's fer certain!" Clubber held Tess tight. Her eyes were closed, and she looked peaceful in his arms.

Colt edged closer to see for himself, a look of desperation in his eyes. "She's breathing? Is she okay?"

"I'm okay, Captain. And you sound okay. How's Shifty?" Her voice barely above a whisper, Tess didn't open her eyes, but she remembered Shifty's name. She'd recognized him from the match that afternoon and remembered his name. Deacon shook his head. Without a second's hesitation, she'd dove into freezing water and almost died for a pirate she had only just met. Who *was* this girl? Deacon felt a strange sensation deep in his gut, something he had never felt before.

Colt breathed a huge sigh of relief and glanced over at Shifty.

"Thomas, how's yer brother?" Deacon tried to sound casual, not like he felt, which was overwhelmed by a completely foreign ache in his heart.

"Well, Capn', he certainly smells a lot better. The water did him some good in that department, at least." A mischievous grin crossed Thomas's face. Shifty was fine.

With a small sigh, Colt sank onto his back next to him, staring up at the ceiling. He took another measured breath.

Deacon rolled onto his side and rubbed his friend's arm to try and warm him.

Colt turned slowly and contemplated him through drooping lids. "Deac, I'm not one of your girls. It takes more than dinner and a midnight swim to get me into your arms."

Deacon laughed, but he felt like crying. Why did he feel like crying?

Colt smiled, closed his eyes, and exhaled.

In about an hour, all three patients were sleeping peacefully. Reynolds had come to check on Deacon, and he had filled and stoked the woodstove. The room was warm and cozy, and Deacon nodded, satisfied that all three would be all right. Deacon had lifted Tess to his bed. Colt and Shifty rested on a makeshift mattress of blankets on the floor.

Doc Manfred had given them a once-over without waking them, satisfied with Deacon's work. "You saved their lives, Captain. Quick thinking!"

All three would be exhausted, so Deacon ordered Clubber and

Thomas to leave them to sleep. Then he dressed and made his way back to the bow to check on their position and status. Pleased to see that the *Dancing Girl* had cleared the ice flowing out of the thawing Ridley River and now floated, neatly anchored, just south of Gilbet's point, he sighed in relief.

Gilbet's, the port that serviced any vessels not able, or not wanting, to sail up the Ridley to the castle, lay quiet.. Warm yellow lights glowed from the windows of the houses, but the shops and transport offices were dark. Behind the small port town, the cliffs of Ardenia stretched high into the night sky. They glowed an eerie gray, the moon reflecting off the variegated slate.

Lights still shimmered at the hoist, and he pictured the hoistmen counting down the minutes until their shift ended. Then, all at once, the lanternlight rose directly skyward. Seven lamps, all set at the same height, rose in the distance at a smooth, even pace, no jerking motion at all. The hoistmen of Ardenia prided themselves on being the best on the spire. One last hoistment before they would dismiss for the day. A full hour of hauling straight skyward, and then seaward again.

He knew the exact window of opportunity for raiding a hoistment on its way seaward from Lindsor. He had spent the last three months casing the operation and finally felt ready to apply the recently retrofitted *Dancing Girl* to the task. If Colt hadn't arrived in the tavern the night before, he would have raided this very hoistment on its return trip seaward. Deacon smiled to himself at the irony, that he now felt sorry for the men and their two hours of remaining toil before resting for the night.

Gilbet's also had a sophisticated overland haulage system as well as couriers who worked out of the port, so merchants could still do business with Fairgates and the surrounding village and yet not *get their keels dirty* as the old expression went.

An intense sense of gratitude swept over the raider. No one had died. They had crossed the Ridley 's estuary and, despite the near tragic excitement, they made it in one piece, thanks to a following wind and a faithful crew.

The black sky told Deacon that somewhere south over Reyjik the sun had decidedly set. He had never seen a true sunset, and he longed to. The clear sky boasted a million bright stars. He thought of the three friends recovering in his quarters. They were all fine. Truly, they would be fine. He knew that, so why did his heart continue to race? Why did he still battle waves of nausea? This reaction didn't make sense. He held his hand out, palm down. It shuddered uncontrollably, despite his best efforts to hold it still.

"It's called shock."

Deacon turned to see Colt walking up to join him at the bow. "Blast, Colt, what are you doing out here? You should be resting inside where it's warm!" Again, Deacon did not recognize the voice that now chastised his old friend.

"Then let's find someplace warm." Colt gestured for Deacon to lead.

He nodded and led Colt to his first mate's cabin, the one he'd given to Tess. He entered, stoked the fire in her stove, and then sat down at the small table pushed against the wall. Colt lowered himself to the chair opposite him and sat back, his fists clenched on the table, his jaw tight.

For a moment, they only stared at each other. The look in Colt's eyes could break bladespar. What did he need to say? Obviously, something important plagued him. Nerves gripped Deacon's stomach, and he decided to break the tension.

"Thank you for going in after Shifty. He would have been a goner, otherwise. Seriously, Colt, you saved his life."

Colt unclenched his fingers, lunged forward, and grasped Deacon's wrists, tightly enough he winced. "What were you thinking, letting her go in the water after us like that?" Colt growled his voice as cold as the waters below. His eyes narrowed, focused on him as though he were a target.

He had never seen his friend this angry before.

Colt continued before he had a chance to defend himself. "She is just a girl, Deac. Honestly! She is so tiny, and she could have died tonight. I mean it. She literally almost died… because of me. How could you? How could you be so reckless?"

Colt didn't raise his voice, but fury dripped from his words, searing drops of contempt and disappointment and blame.

Deacon pressed his lips together. Better to let the rage run its course.

"You literally had forty-four other men who could have helped us. Or you, you could have come after us. How could you let her risk herself like that? She should have been the very last person to try that, the very last, Deac. How could you?"

At last, he let go of his wrists and lowered his face to his hands.

Deacon gave him a full minute before responding to the accusations. "You've spent, what, three and a half days with her now?" He kept his tone calm and easy.

Colt lowered his hands to the table and nodded.

"Well, even after knowing her for that small amount of time, how much chance do you think I had of keeping her in the ship"

When Colt's eyes met Deacon's, they held defeat. "Not much, I suppose."

"Exactly. She was over the side before I even noticed." His conscience was totally clear on that. He knew exactly what had taken place, and there was no way he could have expected Tess's reaction or prevented it.

Both men took a deep breath and then sat quietly for a few minutes.

Colt looked broken. His lip quivered, and he closed his eyes. What troubled him? Could Colt read his thoughts? He sure hoped not. The pirate had never been so confused. His hand still trembled slightly. He had just lived through the greatest scare of his life, which seemed impossible, as he hadn't even been in danger. Deacon had been in countless naval skirmishes. He had overrun numerous armed merchant ships and even some light military vessels, and not once had he been scared. On several of those occasions, he could easily have lost his life. But tonight, though never once at risk himself, he'd experienced the most acute fear ever.

Sitting in solidarity with his lifelong friend, it dawned on him. Did he fear losing Colt? The concept, though foreign and truly daunting, made sense, even if it felt as though it was more than that. His forehead wrinkled. Wait, was he equally terrified of losing Tess? That didn't make any sense at all. He had just met this girl the day before. His eyes widened. The only thing that would explain such a reaction proved unthinkable. His pirate heart wasn't falling for her, was it?

He shook his head, trying to free himself from the thoughts that confounded him. He took another deep breath.

Colt slumped in his chair. He looked exactly like Deac felt.

Deac searched his friend's face. "Sweet descent to Gehenna, Colt. You're in love with her."

Colt just closed his eyes and exhaled.

Again, Deacon couldn't read his friend. The man might simply be too tired to do anything else. Was it only exhaustion weighing him down? No, he had never seen Colt like this, in all the years he'd known him. From the moment he had encountered Colt in the tavern, something seemed completely different about him. It must be Tess. Colt had absolutely fallen for this girl. "Colt, all the years we've known each other, all the girls who have thrown themselves at you, never once did you let one turn your head. Never did you let one steer you from your responsibility. You barely gave a girl a second look. You've been so focused on doing your duty to the king, being the best. You are so true to your moral code. I didn't even think you had it in you to—"

Colt slammed his hand down on the table. "Not one thing has changed. Everything you just described stands. Deac, we're undoubtedly standing on the precipice of war. I don't care what you think you know. Let me be crystal clear. I have a job to do. I have a duty to my king. I am a Bowman of the Realm. I'm a King's Bowman, and I will see this through whatever it takes. The only thing you need to worry about is this—if it is in your power, I don't ever want her in harm's way again, do you understand?" He shoved back his chair, stood, and stalked from the room without another word.

Deac sat alone for what felt like hours, playing it all over in his mind, losing track of time. Was he truly falling for this girl? Was Colt? What would that mean for their friendship? When he finally resolved to act, taking all the strength his spent heart could muster, he walked to his first mate's cabinet and poured himself a drink.

Chapter Eighteen

The Cliffs

Tess

Tess looked to the north. Dawn broke over the inland Sea of Ardenia, leaving the vast stretch of water edging the narrow precipice in golden oranges and pinks. It took her breath away. She glanced over her shoulder at the soaring gray and orange slate, the sun illuminating the veins of cuper and emerald.

It felt strange to be standing on solid ground again. Gilbet's Point lay quiet, as she had expected. It would be at least another hour before shopkeepers, dockworkers, or transport men emerged from the sleepy village. But Colt had insisted they take the skiff and go ashore as early as possible. *And* he had insisted that she accompany him. Why did he want her company? He had been so cold that morning. Had she done something wrong? He seemed angry even as he thanked her for jumping in to save them. Since that short conversation, he hadn't spoken to her. He'd asked Clubber to tell her she needed to come to the Couriers office with him.

Clubber had come with them and presently slept on the front porch of the King's Couriers' office. Colt sat beside him, writing. She had peered over his shoulder for most of this endeavour. He had been writing nonstop for the last twenty minutes, crafting the letter he would send to her father, detailing the situation at hand and his plan to travel north to investigate the two Reyjik lighter than airships that had flown past Dungridge. He would return to Gilbet's before dark, by Deacon's best estimation, and await further orders.

Colt, so consumed with his task, had not once looked at her. She was terrified to interrupt him, afraid to receive another icy response.

She wracked her mind. What had she done to upset him? In her mind, she began to slide over the edge and down the dark slippery slope of rejection and self-doubt. Colt was the same as her father and sister, using her if she proved helpful and otherwise sweeping her aside. *No! Stop it, Tess. Absolutely none of this is about you!* The captain was doing his best. Under intense stress and nearly insurmountable odds he was attempting to do his duty. She resolved to give him the benefit of the doubt.

Upon finishing the letter, Colt stood abruptly and walked off the south side of the porch. She followed while Clubber remained sleeping on the bench.

"Where are you going, Captain?"

"These couriers usually live on site. I am going to wake one." He placed his hand on the horse stall and hopped up to the back porch. He strode to a rear window and began to pound on it. It only took a few seconds for the curtains to part. Colt flashed the man his Bowman crest and signaled for him to meet him in the front office. The man scanned the crest and then nodded. Colt passed her on his way back to the office, not bothering to look at her as he did.

Her heart sank as she followed him around the building again.

Inside the office, the small stove pumped out warm, dry air. The courier produced himself in his proper uniform, his hair a little disheveled but otherwise leaving no obvious sign that he had just been sleeping.

"Yes, Captain, sir." He stood at attention. "What can I do for you?" This was the respect a King's Bowman deserved, and Tess couldn't help but smile.

Colt placed his communique on the counter. "I need you to courier this to King Lucius at Castle Fairgates. It's of the utmost importance to tieral security. He needs to be made aware of its contents at the very earliest opportunity. I would take it myself, but I'm needed on another task. Do you understand the importance of this?" He placed both hands on the counter and sized up the young man who stood before him.

The courier nodded soberly. "Yes, Bowman, I will see it done immediately."

Colt relaxed his hands on the counter as though reassured the man was competent. "I will need to secure your services for the entire day. Is that clear?"

The man nodded and leaned forward as though listening intently for the orders that were sure to come.

"I'm heading up the coast but will return to this office four hours past peak. I will expect to find you here with orders from the king. I need you to disregard any other requests or tasks today. You are busy with Bowman business; do you understand that?" Colt held his stare.

"Yes, sir!" Standing perfectly straight, the man saluted sharply.

The edge of Colt's eye crinkled. The salute was endearing, and the Bowman must have thought so as well. He looked satisfied, even encouraged by this keen public servant. Colt sealed the pouch and imprinted it with his crest. As a Bowman, this service cost nothing, but he needed to seal and sign the message and place it in the official pouch himself.

"This is Lady Tess. She lives at the castle. You will escort her and my associate as well and see them safely into the king's care. Do you understand?" Colt narrowed his eyes and focused straight ahead, refusing to look at her.

The warmth drained from Tess's face, and the room spun around her. What had he just said? Of course, he wanted her to come ashore. Of course, he wanted to get rid of her. Her heart began to pound and her breathing shallowed. The young courier smiled at her and nodded in acknowledgement. She had to stop this from happening.

"Excuse me, Captain, may I have a word with you, please?" She barely managed to grind the words out between clenched teeth.

"No, my lady." Still, Colt did not look at her. He signed the documents that finalized the transaction with the king's courier.

An intense heat gripped Tess from her head to her toes. Before she said anything to undermine Colt's authority in front of the courier, she spun on her heel and stalked from the office. Slamming the door behind her, she crossed the porch and jumped the three steps that led to the walk.

She sprinted down the main boardwalk of Gilbet's Point at full speed, heading for the skiff that had brought her here. Footsteps pounded behind her, but she didn't slow until two strong arms circled her waist.

"For Realm's sake, Tess!" He lifted her clean off the ground.

Tess didn't care that she had made him angry. He'd made her angry. Enraged, even. When he let her go, she whipped around to face him.

"I will run, Colt. I will run and I won't stop! You think that courier is going to be able to both catch me and deliver that pouch on time? Not a chance. There is nothing you can say to persuade me otherwise. I will swim back to *The Dancing Girl* if I must. You know I'm not afraid of that water. You will not send me away. There is no version of this where I don't see this through with you." Tears filled her eyes, which made her angrier still. She took in a deep breath in a vain attempt to steady herself.

Colt said nothing. For the first time that morning, he looked her straight in the eyes. She wanted to break down and sob, but she refused to give him the satisfaction. Why didn't he understand what this mission meant to her? Why did everyone find it so easy to dismiss her?

She could pull rank. She could. As princess she outranked him, and he would have to obey her and let her help. No, that would make everything worse. The code would demand he forego everything else to ensure her safety. He wouldn't be able to run the reconnaissance he needed. The Realm would suffer.

All she wanted was to help him. She frowned. What? No, she wanted to save the Realm. She wanted her life to matter, to make a difference. She wanted to serve Ardenia. *I am their princess, and it's my job to fight for them. That's what matters most, not some Bowman.*

It proved useless. What mattered most stared back into her eyes, silently searching her. What mattered most was helping this arrogant, overconfident, cocky, honorable, brave, selfless, brilliant Bowman. Blast, why did she need to help him so badly?

"I thought we were a team, Captain." She tried to keep the hurt from her voice without much success. Lifting her chin, she waited for him to reject her like everyone else.

Moments passed. Sighing, he turned back down the boardwalk. "All right." Striding towards the courier's office he didn't look back.

He said nothing as he rowed them to *The Dancing Girl*. Tess's heart was heavy. She'd made a royal nuisance of herself to the Bowman. Still, she wouldn't change a thing. Deep inside, she knew that greater things were at work. Her heart simply told her that taking this stand was necessary.

Deacon helped his men haul the skiff aboard.

Colt jumped to the deck first.

The pirate then offered a hand to Tess. "Well, that went about how I expected."

Reluctantly, she took his hand.

Colt didn't acknowledge the comment. He didn't look at either of them. He only strode to the room he had commandeered for his charts and closed the door behind him.

* * *

The sun had just fallen past peak when Tess climbed out of the skiff again. For the second time that day, she felt the strange sensation of solid ground under her feet. Did she like the feeling or did she already prefer the sway of the sea? Holding her hand above her eyes, she blocked the bright sunshine that still breached the edges of Lindor's highest peak, the vertical horizon, and surveyed the towering cliff they were about to climb. Not for the first time, she was grateful for the boy's trousers and tunic she wore.

Colt, already yards ahead, had insisted that none of the crew come. Keeping the invasion and the Reyjik's presence a secret for as long as possible was a top priority for the Bowman. Nothing could interfere with gathering their intelligence and then reporting back to Gilbet's by dark. The captain had convinced himself that the fewer people who knew about the Reyjik, the better.

Deacon had agreed to this secrecy and Colt had insisted he accompany them. His on-the-spot assessment of the ships and their carrying capacity, firepower, and range were an asset. To whatever degree Colt grew cold towards her, he had proportionately warmed to

Deacon. Had the old friends overcome their earlier issues? She hoped so, but her heart still ached over her own loss.

Deacon skipped a step to match her stride. "Don't take it so hard, Princess." He nudged her elbow with his own. Did he speak quietly so Colt wouldn't overhear?

She walked in step beside him without speaking.

"He is full to the brim and spilling over with his allegiance, responsibility, and duty. Whatever scruples I lack in those areas, Colt has enough for both of us. He truly believes to the very bottom of that big heart that it's his job to save everything and everyone. Protecting you falls directly dead center of all that duty and valor." Deac nudged her again.

She had to smile. When, exactly, had she come to like the pirate that now walked with her in solidarity? Somewhere between his saving her life and advocating she come on this reconnaissance mission. Whenever her heart had shifted, she now understood Colt's loyalty to him. She glanced sideways. When she caught his eye, she couldn't help but smile again.

Deacon slid an arm around her shoulders, pulling her in close as they walked.

Her stomach tightened as she shot a look at Colt's back. Straightening, she tried to swallow, but her mouth felt too dry to manage it.

"Now, valor and duty are great, and the Realm needs men like Colt, but here's the problem. See, Colt there will always need to clip your wings. You'd never be free to fly. And Princess, from what I've seen, you were born to fly." He raised his hand and swept it dramatically through the air, as if tracking her trail through the sky.

Nerves wracked her entire body. Why did she feel so nervous being close to Deacon? His touch was friendly, not threatening. Still, what if Colt saw them together? She curled her fingers into tight fists.

"But me? Well, I have no problem watching you soar, none whatsoever." He squeezed her shoulder.

There is no way this raider gets the last word, Tess! She was about to respond when Colt turned around.

He glanced at her and then glared at Deacon.

Deacon flinched and, for a split second, loosened his hold on her shoulder. Then, as if he'd regained his composure, he tightened it again. He turned from Colt, ignoring the look of warning, stared down at her, and smiled.

Her stomach knotted as Colt inhaled sharply, turned, and began to scale the cliff. Was this a game for Deacon? Was she a piece on some imaginary chessboard? "Captain Thornby, why would you ever think I wanted to fly? Obviously, swimming is my thing." She lurched forward a step, pivoted her shoulder, and slipped free from his grip. She then skipped two steps to walk a full pace in front of the raider. He said nothing, for which she was grateful, as her mouth, completely dry, couldn't offer another response.

They climbed for the better part of two hours. She didn't tire. Deacon even remarked on her unnatural stamina. The back side of the cliff that they were ascending was rugged but easily passable. A path, cut into the rock in many places, made it little more than a grueling hike. They truly climbed at only five points, where the path could not ascend the sheer rock. Even those places had crevices and grips where she still managed a good foothold.

A breathtaking view greeted them at the top of the ledge. This northern section of Ardenia's sheer cliff was slightly less sheer. First ascended by a Thornton man named Arsten Cooper, it had kept the name. The ledge at the top overlooked the small section of the sea that hooked around to the freefall, directly seaward from the town of Thornton. Peering skyward, she imagined the two young men with whom she climbed growing up together on the small half-tier that soared just overhead. She heard a noise above and sighted three tarragons roosting in the crags only twenty yards above. She smiled. The migration had reached Ardenia—spring had truly begun.

They crested the edge of the landing and perched on a barren rock ledge. Only a little low grass, moss, and lichen clung to its sandy surface. Stretching twenty yards across and thirty yards long, this sizeable ledge provided a perfect vantage point of the sea *around the bend,* as its locals called it. The sun shone down brilliantly, and Tess lifted her face to allow the warmth to fall across it. The cliff below them dropped over three hundred yards straight down, a sheer face with no other such landings. The rock at the bottom disappeared into the sea. Waves struck against it, creating an ethereal spray. At least, that was how it appeared from three hundred yards up. Violence often appeared peaceful from a great enough distance. Tess thought back to how peaceful Castle Costiar looked during the invasion as she dangled so far above it.

The Dancing Girl, anchored on the southwest side of this geological feature, floated calmly, waiting for its captain to return. Deacon had refused to sail around Cooper's Cliffs, knowing full well that, once they did, they would be exposed to whatever lay in the western waters. Remaining unseen would prove impossible, so *The Girl* had no recourse but to hide herself. Deacon was simply not willing to take the risk that the Reyjik didn't wait west of the cliffs.

Tess marveled at the young sailor's instincts. Lying on her stomach halfway up the towering wall of rock, she sighted the first of the Reyjik ships in her spyglass. About one nautical mile from where the three unlikely companions lay watching, five ships drifted on the water. Five!

Colt had sighted them first and immediately launched a barrage of questions at Deacon. Deacon did his best, obviously straining to apply everything he had learned from his father, from the last three years on the sea, and from his time in the military, to this new situation.

She contemplated Deacon. Every situation prior had seen the raider dismiss Colt's authority with a joke or condescending comment, but now he spoke earnestly. Had Deacon decided that Colt was worthy of his respect? Coupled with Colt's natural leadership, had the seriousness of the situation forced him to rise to what Colt needed? Maybe. However, despite his best efforts and intentions, he was still Deacon. She suppressed a laugh as she listened to the two men.

"What do you think, Deac? How many men could those ships hold?" Colt didn't take his eye from the spyglass. He waited.

She looked over at him.

"Deac?" he asked again.

"I don't know, Colt. I was never good at math. I am working it out." Deac's brow furrowed, and he closed his eyes.

Colt sighed. "Seriously, Deac? In one ship. How many men could one ship hold? You should know that without doing math." He tapped the spyglass impatiently.

"Right. Of course. One ship could probably hold four hundred men, at least. They would need a crew of fifty to man it, so I guess that would leave room for more than three hundred fifty soldiers." Deacon opened his eyes, a triumphant look on his face.

"And those cannons, what would their range be?"

"They can shoot about sixteen hundred yards. But honestly, their accuracy falls to tarragon dung after five hundred yards."

"Tess, can you try and count the men you see on that ship, second from the left?"

As Colt hadn't spoken to her since the morning in Gilbet's, she immediately endeavored to comply. The sailors didn't move much, which made it easy. She counted as quickly as she could, noticing something odd on the deck of the ship Colt had chosen as she did. Should she mention it?

"I count forty-eight men, Captain... I also see three large pieces of equipment on deck. They are covered by a tarp, so I can't make out what they are, but they're lashed to the deck so they don't roll."

"Thank you, I see them. It looks like some sort of field gun or cannon. But we're more worried about their numbers right now. Can you watch just that ship and try to see if the men rotate?" He spared her a glance, more than he had done for hours. "I know it might be hard to tell, but look for men coming up from below deck, and other men going back down."

"Got it, Captain." Tess set to work.

"Deac, how long could a ship of four hundred men last on the supplies it could carry on board?"

Deacon shifted uncomfortably. "Seriously? I was never good at logistics. You know that." He ran his hands through his hair with a sigh.

Tess bit her lip. Should she help? Did she dare speak up? Colt had been so cold, but she had to. "Deac, if you were taking *The Bishop's Bride* out, with a crew of fifty, how much hard tack would you bring for a month-long run?"

"Easy, a barrel for each man." Deac slapped the dry rock with his hand.

"So, they would need four hundred barrels of hard tack if they were out for a month without resupplying?"

"Yep."

Colt nodded. "Could that ship carry four hundred barrels in its hold along with fresh water and the four hundred men?"

"Just. Well actually, those galleons look bigger than *The Bishop's Bride* by a stretch, so they might carry even more."

She dared to look at Colt. He'd been watching her, the hint of a smile on his face, but when she turned to him, he quickly looked away. Her stomach tightened.

"Deac, is there any way for you to determine if those two small schooners were the same ships you saw flying?" Colt propped himself on his left arm.

"They're about the same size, but I can't be sure. It was dark and misty that night. But clearly that can't matter. Your problem isn't with those two, it's the three galleons you should be worried about." Deacon acknowledged what none of them had. Indeed, they had climbed up here expecting to find two ships.

Colt crawled back from the edge of the cliff and sat up.

Tess still watched the galleon Colt had asked her to observe. At this distance, it was hard to distinguish individual sailors. She had only counted three possible rotations, and she couldn't even be sure of those. Choosing another galleon, she attempted the same thing. She counted the visible crew and then watched to see if any of the men went below deck while others emerged. It proved futile at her range—the ships were simply too far away for her to trust what she saw. She crawled back and kneeled in front of Colt.

"We've got a problem, don't we?" she asked quietly. The captain simply nodded.

Deac crawled back and joined them as well.

Colt cleared his throat. "We have five ships with a possible carrying capacity of two thousand soldiers, including crew. They are up here, waiting for something." He closed his eyes in concentration.

Tess touched his arm. "They may be waiting, but they are running out of supplies. Whatever they're here to do, they'll need to do it soon. Deac saw those two ships three weeks ago. Which means they likely met the other three around that time."

Colt inhaled sharply and pressed both hands to the back of his head. "Deac, where in the Realm did those three galleons come from? I've been off tier for over six months, so I'm out of touch. Do you recognize them? Where would they have moored?"

"I don't know. Not at Dungridge, I can vouch for that, but they might hail from a smaller out of the way port."

Colt rubbed his eyes hard. "It's sedition. The Reyjik came up here, and I don't know how they managed it, but they convinced Ardenian sailors to sell them, or stole them, or commissioned three enormous ships to unseat our king. I mean, it's treason against the Spire. It stomps all over Sacramance. How could..." Colt closed his eyes again and rubbed them even harder. "Wait, Deac. They can't possibly, fly right?" Colt's eyes shot open and he sat at attention.

Her heart cinched tight.

Deac wagged his head back and forth as if attempting to shake something loose within his mind. "No, they're too big. They couldn't possibly fly."

Was he completely convinced?

Colt breathed a sigh of relief. "We need to talk to King Lucius. There's an imminent threat to Castle Fairgates and the capital. Our refineries and bladespar production are at risk. We must get down there and report what is going on." He pushed to his feet. Clearly, he had made his decision, and the conversation was now over.

Tess wanted to say something to comfort him, but she had no idea what she could offer. *You will him do his duty for Ardenia, whatever the cost.*

They ran across the top of the cliff to the narrow path they had just climbed. It only took them half an hour to descend the steep route that had brought them to their vantage point. Rowing the skiff as if it were sinking, the men raced back to *The Girl*. Obviously desperate to get to the king with this new information, Colt's sense of urgency was contagious.

Once on board, Deacon and the crew made short work of turning *The Dancing Girl* east and running under full sail back down the coast. Colt wanted to fly, but Deacon refused. If they were spotted and shot down by Bowmen, the ship wouldn't survive crashing into the surface of the water, and the entire mission would be jeopardized.

Colt paced the bow of the ship. Tess wanted to speak to him and offer encouragement, but she suspected he wouldn't be able to hear it. He carried a great burden, and he carried it on his own.

They were so different. She brought her burdens, all of them, to the All-Father. Colt stood alone, relying on his own ability to solve his problems, believing his duty demanded it. He was so talented, so capable, so smart, and skilled, and he had been responsible for himself and his mother since the age of ten. He excelled at everything he tried. No wonder he depended on himself.

Tess's heart ached for him. How did he manage to carry the load alone? She desperately wanted to help him, but she abandoned the idea. He had been brutally cold to her simply for refusing to leave his side. He didn't want help. Colt had built a wall around himself, and even though he stood so close, the young captain felt out of reach.

Chapter Nineteen

The Bait

Colt

FISHING? HOW COULD DEACON BE FISHING? Colt had replaced his pacing with a less frantic walk the length of the entire ship. Now at the stern, he was shocked to see Deacon casually holding his rod out over the ocean. Heat crawled up the back of his neck. Why did Deacon's indifference bother him so much? Why did it rouse such frustration and disappointment? He exhaled. On the clifftop, he'd felt Deacon's support, as though the pirate was taking something seriously for a change. But Deacon had dashed those hopes when he set bait on a hook, as if he didn't have a concern in the world. How could Deac care so little for his tier?

"Sit down, Colt. Want to fish?" Deacon placed his rod in its cradle and set a second for Colt.

Colt's anger boiled over. "Are you serious right now?" Throwing his hands in the air, he stomped his right foot. "How can you fish at a time like this?"

Deacon jigged the line. "I'll tell you, if you answer a question first." He fiddled with the second rod.

"What?" Colt snapped.

"Are you walking so quickly so that you're creating enough wind to push *The Dancing Girl* faster down the coast?" The pirate crossed his arms and stared at him, clearly waiting for an answer.

He was beat. Sitting down on the deck beside his friend, he dangled his legs over the edge and snatched the rod from its cradle.

Deacon reached for the first trolling rod he'd set.

"Remember when we used to fish with your dad?" Colt asked quietly.

His friend nodded.

"I think he would be proud of you, Deac." He couldn't explain why he believed that. Deacon was a mist raider. It felt strange to think that his father could be proud of that. But over the last two days, he'd also come to see Deacon as a loyal, strong leader who genuinely cared for his men. Any father would be proud of those things.

"Thanks, Colt." Deacon bumped Colt's shoulder with his own.

Contemplating the wake of *The Dancing Girl*, he rested his free hand on his knee. "Do you actually think you're going to catch something?"

"Remember what my dad used to say? *You can catch anything when you have the right bait!*" Reeling in his line, he showed Colt the sizable fish he was using as bait. The pirate smiled widely.

He laughed, remembering well the expression on Harrison Thornby's face as he said this to the delinquent friends. The two boys were usually catching a beating for some prank or mischief. Deac's dad always asked them why they *baited* him to punish them. The man had a point, one which they never quite learned.

"I miss your dad, Deac." He swallowed back the choking feeling in his throat.

"He would have been so proud of you, his second son who always got it right. I miss yours too."

A sense of peace and nostalgia swept over him.

It lasted about three seconds before Deacon nudged him again. "I don't want to wreck our little moment here, but I'm pretty sure I have to come clean about something, so we don't end up hating each other for all time."

He repressed a sigh. What now? What law had Deacon broken? What unthinkable line had he crossed? He felt certain he'd heard the worst and, ironically, simultaneously the best of Deacon's exploits the night before at dinner. What could he possibly have left to confess?

"You worried I'm not going to like it?" He finished reeling in his line and cast again.

Deacon just held his line, letting it troll. "I'm absolutely certain you're gonna hate it!"

Great. Better get it over with. "Well, out with it. What could you have possibly done that is so heinous it could threaten our friendship?"

"It's not what I've done, Colt. It's what I'm planning on doing. I'm takin' my shot with Tess."

Every bit of warmth drained from Colt's body. "What are you talking about?"

Toying with the handle of the reel, Deac looked out over the wake. "You made it clear last night that you weren't letting anything—or anyone—distract you from your duty, same as always. Tess is one in a Realm, so if you're not gonna do anything about those feelings you won't admit, I'm gonna. If she were just another girl, I'd stay out of it, but she's too remarkable not to make the attempt. I'd regret it, and I'd always wonder. So, I'm takin' my best shot. And I mean, my very best shot, and I just thought tellin' you was the honorable thing to do."

Colt pressed a hand to his stomach, pretty sure he was about to throw up. Deacon's *very best shot* with a girl had never missed, not so long as he'd known him.

Deacon cast his line again.

Colt stared at the spot where it had landed, watching the bait fish pull along at the speed the schooner sailed, just under the surface of the water. Suddenly, a huge coastal clipper half-flipped out of the water and smashed down on the line.

Deac sprang to his feet, rod in hand, and braced himself against the railing. He shot a look at Colt, his eyes alight with triumph over the fish.

His stomach twisted. *This isn't betrayal, Colt. It seems like it, but it's not... even though it feels that way. Focus. You don't have the luxury of chasing girls. The Realm is at stake. You need to stay focused.*

Rising quickly, he didn't acknowledge Deacon's declaration or the fish. Gilbet's Point approached, and he needed to be ready in the skiff as soon as they dropped anchor. Desperate to meet the king's courier, he would then need to make his way to Fairgates as quickly as possible. Without another word for Deacon, he left his old friend to wrestle with the fish alone.

As he approached the davit arms, he noticed Tess waiting for him. Swallowing hard, he didn't break stride. A wave of guilt crashed over him for how he'd treated her all day. He'd justified his cold behavior with that same need to focus. Still, she didn't deserve his severe reaction to her brave act of self-sacrifice. She should have been applauded for risking her life to save his, but the whole thing had rattled him. She could have died, and she was so good, so brave, so precious to him. What could he say to make it right?

"Captain, I'm sorry." Tess twisted her hair with her finger. "I'm so very sorry about this morning. I acted like a spoiled child."

He frowned. What? Why was *she* the one apologizing?

"It's just, I'm not making excuses, but I wanted to explain. I have lived my whole life inside Fairgates. Those walls are so thick and strong and high. For everyone in the kingdom they are a symbol of strength and security. But for me, for me they might as well be prison walls. Life at court is shallow, superficial, and devoid of everything meaningful. I hate it. I've never admitted that to anyone, but I do, I hate it. I know I should be grateful for my position. I get to serve Ardenia in some measure, my own sort of measure, I guess, but all I have ever wanted to do is what you do." She inhaled sharply, her jaw set tight. Then all at once she exhaled and offered him a half smile. "I love my home, but these last few days, out here, out with you… I just, I just wanted to see it through."

His chest ached. She thought he was angry with her.

She spun around and strode to the bridge.

A sick, nervous feeling ran through his entire body. It was painful, impossible, agonizing to admit what he now forced himself to acknowledge. He cared for her, for exactly the reasons she believed him to be angry with her. Except that he couldn't tell her that. Blast!

At that moment, he spotted the young courier waiting at the end of the dock. His eyes widened when the man stepped into one of the skiffs and began to row toward *The Dancing Girl*. What was he doing? The strange gesture piqued his interest, and he watched until the courier reached the ship and climbed aboard. The man's hands trembled, and he shifted from foot to foot.

Colt faced him, his hands on his hips. "What's your name?"

"Sam, sir." The keen courier stood at attention, although he continued to gasp for breath.

"Come with me, Sam." Turning, he walked to the chart room. The courier followed. When he entered the commandeered quarters, Deacon and Tess were studying a map of the coast. Deacon leaned over Tess as he tapped a finger on the map laid out on the desk. He cleared his throat and they both looked up, surprise flashing across their faces at the sight of the king's courier.

Colt turned to the young man. "All right, what is it, Sam? I was planning to row in, as I need to go to the castle immediately to speak to the king in person. Did he send back orders for me?"

Sam held out the courier case.

Taking it from him, he thrust it open. When he pulled out the message, it was his own, the one he had sent to the king. and the seal wasn't broken. Why wasn't the seal broken? Hadn't the message been read? He whirled toward the courier. "What is this? Why didn't you deliver it?"

The courier wrung his hands. "Sir, Bowman, the king isn't there."

He shoved back his shoulders as Tess rose and moved to stand beside him. "Explain everything, Sam," he ordered.

The courier nodded and took a deep breath. "I arrived at the castle and asked for the king, and the guards informed me he was gone. I told them I had a top priority message from a King's Bowman, and one of the men, a porter, I think, told me that the king had left three days ago. Both his sons have gone with him. I was shocked, sir. So, I kept asking around as to what happened. It was a lady from the kitchen that knew. Imagine that. The kitchen help knew what was going on because she had prepared and loaded the food for the men." The courier threw his hands up in disbelief.

He forced himself to remain calm as he placed a hand on Sam's shoulder. "What men, Sam?"

"The soldiers, sir. King Lucius has descended to Costair to fight the Reyjik. They are holding his daughters hostage, so he left three days ago."

The room began to spin around Colt. Three days ago? How was that even possible? He needed more answers. "How did the king know about the attack? Why did he descend? Who told him?"

Sam swayed slightly, and Colt placed a hand on his back to guide him to an empty chair. "Now that, I learned from the blacksmith." Sam puffed his chest out. "Apparently, a man ran into the castle four nights ago screaming about the Reyjik and how they had attacked Costair's capital, and he was the only one to escape. He insisted on speaking to the king. He told the king all about how his daughters were being held captive and that four hundred men now occupied the castle. The blacksmith knew because he was the one who shoed the auxiliary horses so that Lucius and the princes could descend with a thousand fighting men. The blacksmith said that with those numbers, and our bladespar weaponry and shields and Bowmen and the like, Lucius should make quick work of four hundred men. The king left one hundred militia men to guard the castle in case of trouble. But the blacksmith said Lucius and the princes were Gehenna-bent to get to the girls."

Colt braced himself with a palm against the top of the desk. Every single piece of information he had heard in the last three days flooded his mind. All at once they rushed past his consciousness, and they all fit, everything fit perfectly. He sat down at the desk and peered up at Deacon and Tess. They both took seats beside him. He tried to take in a deep breath and steady the sick feeling that overwhelmed him.

Tess touched his arm. "Captain, what is it?" she asked softly.

"Bait, Tess. You can catch anything with the right bait." For some reason, he could only manage a whisper. "It makes sense, all of it. It fits now. I had it wrong about the delegation. I thought Gerhert was using the royal visit solely as an excuse to reduce military presence and leave the castle defenseless. But that wasn't all. Sasha was bait." He drove his fingers into his dark hair.

"Bait?" Deacon leaned forward.

"Yes, bait. The Reyjik couldn't be sure Lucius would hoist seaward to defend Costair. It was possible, since they are trade partners, but there was no guarantee. Costair and Ardenia have no mutual defence treaty. Lucius might have been advised to accept the loss of the fruit and wine and d'orite. Coming to Costair's aid may simply have not been worth it, not worth war. So, Gerhert planned it during the Ardenian delegation's visit. Then they had Sasha and the other

Ardenian nationals. There was no way Lucius would leave that act of aggression unanswered. You said it yourself that night in the lookout, Tess. You said he would answer." Colt glanced at Tess.

Her face had gone ashen. Was she trembling?

"But, sir," Sam gripped Colt's forearm, "why would they want to get Ardenia involved in an invasion of Costair? Why would they want another whole tier to fight?"

"Because they don't want Costair, Sam. They want Ardenia. They want Fairgates. They want the secret to our bladespar production. They want our carbonite mines and our graphite refinement and our ferrite. They want the manufacturing. They want the capital. They want it all. And they have five ships holding two thousand men waiting north of Cooper's Cliffs who are going to come in and take it all, but they needed the army gone. They needed to ensure that the castle was undefended to accomplish that. With the elevation from Reyjik and a nonexistent supply chain, they couldn't pitch a conventional battle. They needed Lucius's forces to vacate the capital, to leave it essentially undefended." He turned to Deacon. "Those ships you saw flying past Dungridge no doubt dropped off the Costair man who was clearly complicit in the plan. There's no other way to explain how that man arrived at Fairgates the very same night as the battle. And it worked. Lucius descended with over a thousand men, right, Sam?"

Sam nodded.

Colt clasped his hands behind his head. "That's his entire complement of mounted knights, men at arms, and archers. He took them all, but he's operating on false intelligence. You said the blacksmith thought they were facing four hundred Reyjik at Costair, right?"

Sam nodded again.

He drew in a shaky breath. "We know they have double that force, already dug in and with the strength of the castle. Those five ships will sweep down the coast in a matter of hours once they're given the order. They will bombard Fairgates and take her without opposition. Then the two schooners will fly back seaward to Costair and help rout Lucius. He will be hopelessly outnumbered, and they will get Costair and Ardenia in one fell swoop."

Deacon's mouth hung open.

Tess twisted her hair around one finger. Was she reasoning, calculating in her own right? She bit her lower lip. Then her eyes narrowed. "But they haven't taken Fairgates, have they, Captain?" She let go of her hair and pressed both palms to the desk. "They haven't and they won't because you insisted on heading to Dungridge—because you insisted on getting more information. You confirmed the existence of five more ships. Now you have figured out their entire plan." She grabbed his arm. "The king can handle the force at Costair with a thousand men, Captain. All we need to do is defend the capital and keep the schooners from flying seaward."

Colt studied her. How could she be so certain in this moment? So certain of him? So certain of victory.

Resolve formed in him, so deep it almost scared him… almost. He lifted his chin. He would save the whole sun-forsaken Realm, and, if he had to, he would do it all by himself.

Chapter Twenty

The Plan

Tess

HEAT COURSED THROUGH TESS. HER TIERDOM was under attack? Her fingers closed into fists. She wanted to fight that very moment.

Colt rubbed his eyes and then stood. He slid the piles of charts off the table and spread one map—of the Ridley River—across the center. It clearly showed every jetty, every curve from the castle to the sea. Colt studied it intently for several minutes. Was he memorizing it? Was he just staring at it while contemplating something else? She glanced over at Deacon.

He was already staring at her, concern on his face.

The room waited in silence. Even Sam, the courier, knew better than to break the Bowman's concentration.

Finally, Colt straightened, pressing a hand to his lower back as though it ached. "Our objective is two-fold. We can't let them take the castle, and we can't let them get away. It doesn't matter so much about the galleons, but if the schooners inflate, fly seaward, and reinforce Costair, the king is done for. If they take Fairgates, the tier is done for. We can't let them disembark either—there are too many of them. We must destroy them completely while they are still on the river."

Colt smacked Deacon lightly on the arm with the back of his hand. "We don't have a lot going for us in terms of assets, Deac. We need your men and *The Dancing Girl* to have even the slightest hope." He clasped Deacon's shoulder. "I have a plan, but I need you. And I know how you feel about your men having a say. If they don't want to stand and fight, I understand that. I just need to know before we go any further.".

Deacon rose and walked to the door. "Well, let's put it to them." He flung the door open and strolled out.

When Deacon rang the dinner bell, every man on board appeared within minutes.

Tess studied them. They were eerily quiet. Not a hint of the usual joking and cussing. Did they sense something in the air? Each man quickly found a place to lean or sit. The chattering died away when Deacon held up a hand.

"Men, you have a choice to make. Our borders have been breached by the Reyjik." No one reacted to the statement Deacon had uttered without emotion. They remained silent, gaze fixed on their captain as he continued. "They have taken our countrymen hostage in Costair, including our princess. Our king hoists seaward to defend his people, but this was a clever trap. More Reyjik, many more, wait around Cooper's Cliffs to attack Castle Fairgates and then fly seaward and kill our king."

Deacon smacked a fist into his palm. "Yes, I said our borders and our tiermen and our princess and our king! I know we make our living thieving, but we raid only Lindsor. These are *our* tiermen the Reyjik have taken. It is our bladespar they want, our prosperity. Their plan is to march in and grab it. They'll do it, just like that, save for our Bowman's plan. The Bowman needs us. No doubt his plan risks all your lives and our beautiful *Dancing Girl*." He patted the main mast. "Know this, whatever you choose, I choose to stand with our Bowman. I choose to fight for Ardenia."

Colt stood just behind his friend, his arms crossed over his chest. His face held no emotion, as though he was reserving it, waiting to see how the men would respond.

Tess clasped her hands in her lap. *Please. Please. Please.*

"For Ardenia then." Shifty stood and crossed the deck to Colt. He stood at attention and saluted before the man who had saved his life.

"For Ardenia, then." Tess recognized Clubber's gruff tone. He smiled warmly at her, and she waved.

Then each man answered in kind.

Colt stepped forward. Were his eyes misty?

"I will do my very best to save Ardenia." Colt paused, and then, as Deacon had done, he lovingly patted the mast of the ship every man on board held dear. "And I'll do my best to save your *Girl* as well."

The men nodded before slowly returning to their posts. They didn't ask questions. They didn't raise concerns or make demands. They didn't mention payment. Maybe there was something to Deacon's unorthodox form of pirate leadership after all. Could she even think of them as pirates after this?

* * *

The map of the Ridley lay littered with the oddest collection of knick-knacks and small objects. Riley, Shifty, and Reynolds, Deacon's top officers, had joined Tess, Deacon, Sam, and Colt for this unconventional briefing. About to explain his plan, Colt waited for Deacon to pour himself a glass of brandy. Tess had to smile. Since his stirring speech, Deacon had grown progressively more nervous. Tess felt certain his anxiety centered around a deep concern for the role *The Dancing Girl* would play in Colt's desperate plan. Was it the crew that had him so anxious or the ship herself? Regardless, he clearly needed to steady himself with a full glass of brandy before Colt could begin. After drinking the entire glass in one long gulp, he sat and grabbed a deck of cards.

"I figure everything depends on us sinking those five ships before they reach the castle. We can't let them reach the docks, and we can't let them get away." Colt rubbed his chin.

"How on earth are we going to do that, Colt?" Deac had already erected twelve cards into four A-frames with roofs.

Colt remained as cool as ever. "Our plan has four critical components. Four things must happen, or it all falls apart." He walked to the liquor cabinet. "First, we need all five ships to enter the river." Taking two trips from the cabinet to the desk, he carried five crystal brandy glasses over so he could slide them down the river on the map in a neat line, allowing everyone to visualize what he had described.

Tess contemplated the glasses. Was it possible?

"I don't think this part will be all that difficult, considering that's what I'm betting they are coming to do anyway. They need to use the castle docks to efficiently disembark the troops."

Shifty cocked his head. "Why's that, Bowman? Why couldn't they use Gilbet's and march to the castle, save 'emselves the trouble?"

She took a step closer to the desk. "Gilbet's is too shallow, Shifty." She shot a look at Colt, who nodded for her to continue. Her cheeks warming, she touched the map with one finger. "The king has the Ridley dredged every year to allow for the giant keels of his merchant ships. They can pull up to the dock so crew members can disembark. A shallow underwater rock shelf runs right along the coast at Gilbet's, like an unseen, underwater tier too shallow for the keels. They would need to disembark men in skiffs. It would take forever and leave those men vulnerable. The Reyjik would never risk that." She returned to her seat, her fingers trembling slightly. Hopefully Colt wouldn't mind her offering her opinion so strongly.

"The second piece is *The Dancing Girl*." Colt plucked a small ship in a bottle from Deacon's narrow shelf.

Deacon and the crew straightened, careening their necks as though keeping an eye on their beloved ship.

"*The Girl* will be waiting south of the Ridley's delta and out of sight around Blind Man's Curve. She has one main job—to keep those galleons from leaving the river."

Reynolds leaned so far forward he nearly toppled from his chair and had to grab the edges of it to steady himself. "Shouldn't we be in the river, Bowman? To keep them from getting in range of the castle?"

None of the crew of *The Dancing Girl* referred to Colt by his rank. They seemed to intuitively reserve the title *Captain* for Deacon. Tess couldn't help but smile.

"No, just the opposite. *The Girl's* job isn't to keep them *out of range* of Fairgates. The *Girl* needs to keep them *in range* of Samson and Serena."

Her heart skipped a beat at the mention of her cannon. Samson, the enormous cannon mounted to the top of the easternmost wall of the castle, had truly been the place of dreams for Tess.

"Who in blazes are Samson and Serena?" Shifty slapped his hand down on his knee.

"Not who, Shifty, what," She corrected gently. "Samson is a huge cannon with a rifled barrel and a range of three miles. Serena boasts two and a half. They can sink a ship all the way out in the Ridley's estuary with the right trajectory." She bit her lip. She had promised herself she wouldn't interject.

Colt smiled, easing her concerns. "That's exactly what we are going to do. We are going to keep those five ships between this point here, at Tapper's Elbow, and the delta." He tapped a finger on both locations on the map and the men gazed at the spots as though reviewing the plan carefully. "So, once they've entered the Ridley, *The Dancing Girl*, with a crew of twenty-five, will fire on them to keep them from coming back out again. I'm not looking for you to sink them, Samson and Serena will take care of that. We just don't want them changing their minds and making a run for it once we start to fire on them." Colt slid the old ship in a bottle into position at the delta of the river to represent *The Dancing Girl*.

"How are we going to keep them from coming straight up the river and firing on the castle with their guns?" Deacon rested the last card on his third tier, then placed his finger on the first crystal brandy glass and slid it to a point in front of the castle docks.

Everyone looked up at Colt, doubt reflecting on several faces.

Deacon rested a finger on the rim of the glass. "I mean, they can get to within nine hundred yards easy from this point. I know I said their cannons were not that accurate after five hundred yards, but in this case, they won't need to be accurate. The castle won't be moving like a ship would. They will figure out the range to the wall, and they will pummel us! How will we hold them back if you've got *The Dancing Girl* in the delta?" His tone riddled with doubt, Deacon crossed his arms and waited for an answer.

Again, every eye turned to look at Colt.

She bit her lip. Did Colt have an answer that would satisfy them?

The tall captain nodded his understanding of Deac's concern. "We aren't going to hold them back. The ice will." Colt laid a white cloth napkin from the docks to Tapper's Elbow. "This section of the river, the narrow part closest to the castle, is always the last to thaw. Tess told us that Sasha's delegation had to come overland from the castle to the hoist because it was still frozen solid. My guess is that it will provide the best barrier we could ask for. And the Reyjik live so far seaward, they will have no experience with a frozen freshwater river like this. Their ships are certainly not designed with the hulls required to handle it, right?"

Deacon uncrossed his arms. "Yes, that should work. I would bet *The Girl* herself they won't be able to get through the ice. At any rate, it will slow them down so much that we'll have time to sight and sink them with your Samson." A smile formed on the raider's lips.

"The cannons are the third critical part of the plan. Deacon, I will need you to take twenty of your men to operate them. Samson is mounted on the northeast rampart of the castle's top wall. It's a beast! Serena is on the west wall. The shot should be ready and waiting. We will need a few kegs of gray powder, at least." Colt gave Deacon a sly look. "Based on previous… let's say… occupational demands, I imagine you have experience operating a cannon and firing on unsuspecting vessels."

Deacon smiled proudly and crossed his arms over his puffed chest.

Reynolds leaned over the map. "What's the fourth part, Bowman?"

She frowned. Colt's plan already seemed complete. What more could there be?

All eyes settled on the young captain again.

Reaching across the map, Colt placed a small compass in the treeline twenty yards from the northern bank of the river, one hundred yards east of Tapper's Elbow.

"Me," he answered simply.

Everyone looked from the compass to the Bowman. "You?" Deacon and Shifty asked in unison.

Colt smiled widely. "I will dig in right here with my bow and pick off the crew, specifically anyone who is doing anything useful, like making headway with the ice or attempting to fire on the castle. More importantly, I'll fire as many flaming arrows as possible onto the decks of the ships. From here I figure I will have the first two ships in range, maybe even three. Flaming arrows are not going to be very effective, but they will cause a lot of confusion, and I might get lucky and hit something flammable. Fallman knows you have the arrows for it."

Everyone regarded Colt with wide eyes and slightly open mouths. Truly, he commanded total respect from every man in the room. Deacon reached over and shook his hand. Reynolds began discussing with Deacon who would man Samson and who would captain *The Dancing Girl*.

Tess studied the map. Was it because the conversation in the room now focused on *The Dancing Girl* that she noticed the wrinkle? She thought it over and through. Within moments she had convinced herself that what she rolled around in her mind was mission critical. She stepped closer to Colt, who spoke with Sam.

They discussed the best route for Deacon's men to take to the enormous cannons that sat atop the castle.

Tess edged closer. Her heart raced, still stinging from Colt's cold treatment from earlier. She twisted her hair with her right hand. "Captain?"

Colt kept speaking with Sam. Had he not heard her?

"Captain, um, can I speak with you about the plan?"

He held up a finger to Sam before turning to her. "Yes?"

Tess took a deep breath. "I am worried about *The Dancing Girl*." Deacon, Shifty, and Reynolds stopped their conversations. Was it the mention of their beloved *Girl*? Of course, it was.

Colt straightened. "Go on."

"Well, *The Dancing Girl* sits here, right at the estuary." She reached out and touched the ship in a bottle with her index finger. "I'm worried about this last ship, sir." As she touched the fifth crystal glass in the line of pretend Reyjik ships, she could visualize the problem. As she pictured the crew she had come to care for under fire, she pushed back her shoulders. "I'm worried that this last galleon will be in lethal range of *The Girl*. Because of the width of the Ridley, they will no doubt struggle to cross the T and use their main cannons against *The Girl*, but they're armed with numerous other guns, isn't that right?" She looked to Deacon, who nodded his agreement. "If I were commanding that ship, and my progress down the river was impeded, and then I was bombarded by cannon fire, I would focus all available firepower, all resolve, all effort, at sinking the ship that prevented my escape."

Tess decided to go for broke and propose the solution she had conceived. "Captain, I think you need a second Bowman here." She gently placed a brass candle snuffer shaped like an anchor at a point on the north side of the river, one hundred yards from where the Ridley opened into the sea. "If you had a Bowman dug in here, they would be able to harass the last ship. They could pick off any Reyjik who tried to operate a gun or, as you put it, anyone who tried to do anything useful. They could lob flaming arrows from this point as well. She could ensure the crew of *The Girl* was protected."

Colt's eyebrows arched. What had she said?

"*She*? *She* could ensure the crew of *The Girl* was protected?" He shoved a fist onto his hip. "Did you have anyone specific in mind?"

Tess lifted her chin at the sarcasm in his voice. "Yes. You know I can do it. You know I can shoot that far. I have proven I can hit a moving target. I've been practicing. I can do this!"

Colt's face softened. "I don't doubt your ability, Tess. But I can't let you put yourself in harm's way like that."

She gritted her teeth. Was he patronizing her? It seemed as if the notion of her helping sounded so absurd that he found it endearing, which was maddening.

Shifty cleared his throat. "She's really good with a bow. I don't want Miss Tess in danger any more than you do, but she does have a point about that last ship, doesn't she? We might be sittin' ducks for their eight- and ten-pound guns, Bowman." Shifty didn't look at Colt as he finished, only scuffed the wooden floor with the toe of his boot.

Sam took a step forward. "I could go with her, Captain. I know that side of the river like the back of my hand. I'd make sure she found good cover the entire time. I could make sure the Reyjik never know where her arrows are coming from." Sam met Colt's heated gaze steadily.

She couldn't pass up this moment of support. "Captain, please let me help. This is my tier too. Fairgates is my home. I won't do anything risky. I'll stay hidden. I promise I won't be reckless."

Colt surveyed the river again. He said nothing.

She peered at Deacon. He smirked and then nodded at the map, as if he knew what Colt would decide.

Colt still said nothing. After a moment, he contemplated Tess, shook his head, and then slowly picked up the compass. Grabbing the candle snuffer with his other hand, he switched their locations and placed them back down on the map.

"You're right about *The Dancing Girl*, but I'll handle their suppressing fire. You'll harass the first ship."

Without another word, he turned back to Sam and began discussing the best place for Tess to take cover near Tapper's Elbow.

She couldn't believe it. Her heart felt as though it would burst. It took all her resolve to keep herself from hugging Colt. She glanced at Deacon, who stood watching her, smiling wide.

The pirate playfully used his middle finger and thumb to flick the candle snuffer. It slid a few inches and stopped, its wide hollow base preventing him from knocking it over.

Shifty then flicked the bottom corner card of Deacon's tower and in a moment, razed it to the tabletop.

Throwing his hands in the air, Deac strode across the room and left the cabin.

Tess walked over to the other side of the map and carefully returned the candle snuffer to its proper strategic position. How could being allowed to fight bring such relief? She desperately wanted to serve her people, and now she would. Tess looked up from the map. She caught Colt watching her, and for the first time that day, he smiled at her. Her cheeks flushed. Was her feeling of relief rooted in the fact that she would be helping Colt? Yes, it absolutely was.

Chapter Twenty-One

The Secret

Colt

COLT AND DEACON HEAVED THE THIRD case of arrows up through the main deck hatch. Deacon then signaled for two of his men to load the three cases onto the waiting skiff.

Shifty and Clubber waited at the davit arms, along with Sam and Tess.

Colt couldn't help but smile over Deacon's recommendations. Shifty seemed unwavering in his loyalty and Clubber would take an arrow for the accomplished girl he had come to adore. They were the natural choices to assist the two archers during the impending battle. He'd decided to make the most of the little time they had left. He'd insisted the party of six supply the archers' ambush sites along the river and then head to the castle where he would brief the militia men and ready the two massive cannons.

He tried to ignore Tess, but it proved impossible. She fidgeted and shifted back and forth from one foot to another. Most noticeably, she twisted the strands of hair that had come loose from the ponytail she'd tied with a length of ribbon. He'd observed her doing this before, always when she felt nervous. Was she concerned about the battle? Of course, that must be it. Tess had shown such uncommon bravery in the short time he'd known her, that he sometimes forgot she had never experienced combat or true conflict of any kind. He promised himself he would check on her later.

Satisfied with the two sites he had chosen to ambush the Reyjik— high ground with good natural cover and well within range of the river but far enough back they'd be difficult to sight—He moved on to the castle. Sam had been very helpful in the selection of the archers' spots. He hadn't exaggerated when he said he knew the routes like the back of his hand, and Colt decided that during the battle Sam would help Tess and Clubber. Having the competent courier with Tess would ensure she stayed as safe as possible under the circumstances.

She walked a few paces ahead of him. Probably a good time for that conversation. He lengthened his stride until they walked in step. "Um, Tess, you're clear on the plan, right?"

She turned and looked up at him with a warm smile. "For the third time, yes, Captain." She twirled her hair again. "Try not to worry. It's a very good plan."

His stomach churned. Tess didn't really know of what she spoke.

She cocked her head. "What's wrong? You look worried. Aren't you happy with the plan?"

How she could do that, read his thoughts like that? He didn't answer, only kept walking until she touched his arm. Compelled to face her, he stopped and turned.

Deacon, Sam, Clubber, and Shifty had been walking behind them, and they all stopped and focused on Tess.

"What is it? What's wrong? Is there something wrong with the plan? Can we help?" She squeezed his arm gently.

Colt sighed. He didn't want to worry any of them, especially Tess, but there were always so many potential variables in battle that it was impossible to devise the perfect plan. "There are at least five things that could potentially go wrong." He took a deep breath. "First, the Reyjik could break the ice. I know I made that part sound foolproof, but truthfully, they could shoot the ice with their cannons, or maybe the ice isn't even that thick any longer. I mean, the tarragon are here, which means the nights are warmer, so who knows how solid it sits?" He paused. "And second, if the ice holds them back, what's to stop them from simply running their ships onto one of the banks of the river and disembarking there? It wouldn't be pretty, but it would be possible if they got it just right."

Tess's fingers still rested on his arm. "That's why you are going to speak to the militia now. You're already ahead of that one." She was so sweet.

He didn't even want to continue, as he hated to disappoint her. "Yes. I hope giving them time to prepare for a possible attack will make a difference, but there are other problems. Samson and Serena may not sink even one ship. They have the range, but those galleons are enormous and extremely tough. They can take quite a pounding before sinking. Deac will have to hit them square below the water line for a chance at it. Then there's the risk to *The Dancing Girl*. The more I think about it, the more I worry about her. And what if the ships get away?" Colt stopped. Judging by the men's faces, this speculation wasn't helpful. He wanted to salvage the moment but couldn't think of what to say.

Tess stepped closer. "Your concerns are totally valid and show you have considered this from every angle. But, with the time and resources we have, we are just going to have to do our best and hope. It's a good plan, Captain."

She sounded so sure, Colt found himself nodding and smiling until fear swept through him again. He couldn't need her assurance like this. Afraid his eyes would betray his feelings for her, he avoided her gaze, then turned and quickened his pace toward the castle.

The first time Colt saw Castle Fairgates, he was ten years old. His father had taken him to visit the capital, and he remembered feeling dwarfed by the massive limestone walls. Nothing had changed.

The castle, built on top of an impressive hill that rose from the west bank of the Ridley River, soared up from the hillside. The gray limestone walls—towering over a hundred yards to the clear blue sky—shone peach in the late glow of past-peak. Bladespar roofing glistened an industrial silver. Behind these regal walls, the Ardenian cliffs reached straight up to the Lindsor precipice. The manufacturing district tucked between the castle and the cliffs lay adjacent to Ardenia's main hoist. Stone stairs wove their way up the hill from the Ridley docks, stopping at a huge, bladespar portcullis. The green ivy that covered the central keep hinted at the age of the beautiful building. And swooping down over the forest that surrounded the majestic castle, the tarragon chased spring flies. Standing there, at the foot of his king's castle, he could hear the Bowman's Code echo off its walls. How he longed to keep his oath, do his duty, and serve his tier.

As they approached Fairgates, he peered over his shoulder. Tess had fallen to the end of the single file line. When had she slipped from his side? When he checked again, she had stopped walking altogether. Colt stopped as well. He asked Deacon and his men to wait for him before jogging back to where Tess was standing, fidgeting with her bow.

"What's wrong, Tess? Are you all right?" He tried not to sound too concerned, but she had been acting strangely all morning. Was she not up to the role for which she had volunteered?

For a moment, she didn't answer, only stood holding her bow at the handgrip and fidgeting with the draw string. Finally, she inhaled. "I'm fine. I was just thinking that I should get more familiar with my position in the woods. I thought I could look for alternate ambush points nearby and a good escape path in case I need to retreat?" This last statement sounded more like a question, and she twisted her ponytail again. She was definitely worried about something.

His stomach tightened. Did she want to back out? He would like nothing more than to remove her from the fray. "Tess, if you're nervous, if you're even a little scared, you don't need to fight. I don't even want you there, and you know that. We'll manage without you. You don't have to do this." He reached out and grabbed her bow.

She straightened. "I'm not scared. Not at all. I want to fight more than anything. I only thought that I should prepare as much as I can while I have the chance. I will double back to my position, and you can pick me up on your return."

The uncertainty was gone from her voice. Was she trying to sound as tough as possible? Was his cold manner towards her and the fact that he had tried to have her escorted to the castle the day before the cause? A lump rose in Colt's throat. He'd decided not to apologize to Tess until the battle was over, as he didn't want to wake the feelings he was trying so hard to bury, but seeing her like this proved too much.

"Tess, I'm sorry," he said softly. "You apologized to me on deck yesterday, but I was the one in the wrong."

Tess glanced up at him, her eyes wide. She didn't look away this time.

Colt exhaled. "I've been cold to you, and I wanted more than anything to send you to Fairgates." His stomach tightened. "See, when you jumped in after Shifty I... I just felt so guilty. I'm supposed to protect you, and I put you in danger. This whole time you've been in danger. I know that. If I'm honest, I allow it because..." He had no idea how to finish that sentence. Tess was so smart, so brave, so genuine. Having her with him made anything seem possible, but he couldn't tell her that. He couldn't say any of those things, not now.

Suddenly, he realized he had been holding onto her bow the entire time they'd been standing together. She still grasped the hand grip, and he must have reached out to rest his hand on the top. Unable to look at her, he stared at their hands, not wanting to let her go.

"Captain, I need to tell you something." She stepped closer.

"Colt! Everything all right? We gotta go!" Deacon's tone betrayed annoyance.

Relief and regret warred inside him. He didn't have time to say any more. He would have to take Tess's word on how she felt about the battle, since he couldn't press her any further right now. He needed to speak with the militia leader as soon as possible. The man would need time to prepare, raise arms, and potentially conscript more troops from the villagers and castle staff, and he had to interrogate the accomplice from Costair.

"Sam," He called the eager courier. "Take Lady Tess back to her position and acquaint her with it. We'll pick you up on our return to *The Dancing Girl*." He whirled around and, leaving her behind, focused on the task at hand.

* * *

Standing beside the stables, the pungent stench of manure filled Colt's nostrils. How could empty stables smell so bad? Sargent Privit had ducked inside to retrieve his spyglass left in his saddle bag, and Colt took a minute reprieve to survey the open space that might soon host combat. An eerie, hallow feeling filled him as his eyes swept across the empty castle courtyard. Everything felt wrong. The jarring ring of bladespar striking ferrite echoed off the limestone walls as a blacksmith worked on a set of horseshoes. Each strike cut through to his heart, driving home the reality that everything in front of him, Fairgates itself, the very heart of Ardenia was at risk, and his to lose.

The gray sky loomed overhead, and he shivered, then shook his head. No, he was satisfied with the condition of both cannons. Colt felt a small measure of relief. His inspection indicated they were both in working order and had been well serviced. He confirmed their range with the militia leader—both could cover the stretch of river they were using to engage the Reyjik and Samson could fire just past the edge of the Estuary. Privit, the militia leader, seemed competent. Colt also got the distinct impression that the man was no coward. Obviously enraged that King Lucius had been tricked and the capital itself sat in jeopardy, he wanted only to serve his tierdom.

Colt advised on strategy, arms, and the best defensive positions. All of this had proven encouraging, but the information he most needed concerned the man who had brought the message of the capture of Costair. Indeed, this man must have been an accomplice, a traitor, an actor, or one of Gerhert's men, and he needed critical answers from him. The interrogation of this man could prove the most fruitful of everything he had done so far.

Privit crossed the cobblestone square twirling the spyglass in his palm.

Colt closed the distance between them. "Tell me, Sergeant, where is the man who brought you the news of the attack on Costair?"

The unshaven farmer shifted uncomfortably but didn't speak.

"Where is he staying, Privit?"

"I'm sorry, Captain. That man left Fairgates right after King Lucius dropped. The king thought he was injured. King Lucius wanted to bring the man with him to the battle, but he said he was in too much pain to go. Then, the morning after His Majesty and his sons descended, he was gone. He must have left in the night. We didn't have him under guard because there didn't appear to be any reason not to trust him. He was a Costair officer, after all, a lieutenant in their tieral guard."

His mind raced. "Sergeant, how long would it take to travel from here to Cooper's Cliffs on foot?"

Privit thought a moment. "Maybe five days."

Colt contemplated the blacksmith across the courtyard of the village, who pounded a horseshoe flat. "And on horseback?"

"Probably two days, Captain," he answered easily.

"And have you had any horses go missing?"

"No, sir. All the horses went with the king." His forehead wrinkled. "Now that you mention it, though, a mule did go missing. You think this man took it?"

He tracked back the timing. The traitor who brought the bogus report to Lucius had escaped from Fairgates two days ago. That meant that at this very moment the galleons waiting at Cooper's Cliff could be receiving the signal to attack. Indeed, that man had undoubtedly left to do just that. The Reyjik would need to be certain that the king and his force had left before they came up the river. Once that was confirmed, they could mount an attack as early as dawn the next day. His stomach tightened. "I do."

The sergeant swiped at a bead of sweat trickling down his temple. "We didn't really think much of him until your courier started asking questions yesterday. I worried all last night. I had this feeling deep in my gut that something was seriously wrong. It feels so off here without the king's regiment, and the place feels empty without the men at arms. We've been on edge since that man turned up gone, and we haven't really known why. You coming and explaining things has at least straightened out what's gone on. You bring bad news for sure, Captain, but at least now we have a chance to defend ourselves."

Colt had to take stock of all possible assets. If there was any possibility for help, he needed to know. Why would the king leave the castle so poorly defended?

"Sergeant, did the king have a plan for reinforcing your men? Did he send word to other provinces to send troops to backfill the men he dropped to Costair?"

"I can't say as I know, Captain. But I did hear the king was in a terrible state over the princesses. He was beside himself with worry. Felt guilty for letting them both go without a larger complement of guards."

Colt's eyes narrowed. Princesses? Plural? Sam's report, that the King's daughters had been taken hostage, fully registered for the first time, *daughters*, plural. He tried to remember what he knew of the royal family. There was Derek, the crown prince, and his younger brother,

Fredrick, and then Sasha. All born of Queen Enda. And then a fourth child born of Beatrice, a girl.

"Princesses, Sergeant? Sasha was in Costair. I saw her myself. There was no other princess." A wave of nausea flooded over him, revelation hitting just as Privit spoke.

"Yes, Captain, Aratess went with her sister. She's the wee one. The last one, born of Beatrice. The one that's always out in the woods. She and Sasha were both part of the delegation. Can't imagine how the king feels with both his daughters in danger like that. It's no wonder he descended in such haste."

Colt couldn't breathe. *Of course.* That was Tess's secret. What she'd been hiding from him. No wonder she'd been nervous all day, and why she didn't want to come to the castle.

How could I have been so blind?

Chapter Twenty-Two

The Reckoning

Tess

TESS PRESSED HER HANDS TO HER heart as Colt paced in front of the map table and Deacon leaned against the wood cabinet. Something was wrong. Colt had run the entire way back to Gilbet's, forcing Tess, Sam, Deacon, and his men to keep up the quick pace. He hadn't said anything to her. He hadn't so much as looked at her. Deacon had explained that Colt had been rattled after he'd spoken with the militia sergeant and realized that the Reyjik ships could attack as early as dawn.

Colt had insisted that she and Deacon report to Deacon's quarters immediately. They had been waiting several minutes now. Colt just paced. Deacon simply watched him. Tess just worried. Colt wouldn't look at her and nausea churned in her stomach.

Deacon finally pushed away from the cabinet. "Whatever it is, can't be that bad, Colt. We'll figure it out. Heck, there doesn't seem to be anything you two can't figure out together."

Colt stopped and turned. Looking straight at her, he inhaled sharp, pain flashing across his face. "Were you ever going to tell me?"

She lost her breath. He knew. Tears welled in her eyes and she looked away, unable to meet his gaze. She didn't make a sound, but somehow hot tears ran down her face. Wiping them away with her hands, she tried to steady herself by breathing deeply.

"What in the name of the Fallman is going on?" Deacon scowled. "Colt, why is she crying? What didn't she tell you?"

The breathing worked, and she regained her composure. She hated to look weak in front of the two men she desperately wanted to impress. She couldn't speak yet, not without crying.

Colt waved a hand in her direction. "Deacon, meet Princess Aratess, Lucius' daughter."

"What?! Princess Aratess?" Deacon whirled toward her. "Why would you pretend to be a lady in waiting? Why wouldn't you tell us who you were? How are you able to shoot like that?"

"I have no idea, Deac. Want to explain, your highness?"

Despite Colt's cold tone, heat crept up Tess's neck. She wanted to explain. She desperately wanted to explain all of it, but it was taking all her effort to keep breathing.

When she didn't reply, Colt released a hiss of disgust. "I don't have time for this. We're facing an invasion in the morning and the men aren't ready. Deacon, you need to get your force into position tonight. You'll have to lead them back to Fairgates and sleep at the castle. If I were leading the Reyjik, I would sail under the cover of the early morning mist and come up the river at dawn. We'll need to let Reynolds and the crew of *The Girl* know. Shifty too." He stalked to the table.

Before bending over the map, he shot Tess one more glance. He may have spoken without emotion, but the pain in his eyes betrayed his feelings. He met her gaze for only a moment before grabbing the candle snuffer that represented Tess's position from the table and tossed it to her.

She caught it instinctively.

"And you're out, Princess." Colt strode across the room, flung open the door, and slammed it behind him.

Tess's throat was so tight she could barely draw air. More tears slid down her cheeks.

Deacon crossed the floor of the cabin and grasped her arms. "Tess, stop. It's all right. Please don't cry. Everything will be all right." His voice was soft, his hands warm. When she sniffled, he wrapped his arms around her and embraced her gently. "Please stop crying, Tess," he begged, his voice barely more than a whisper.

She stepped back. "You called me Tess."

A devilish grin spread across his lips. "There she is." He winked. "Well, Tess, I can hardly go around calling you *princess* now. It's not really teasing when it's your official title, is it?" He held her arms again. "I figure I will just have to go ahead and break protocol and call you by your first name, now that it's inappropriate."

She wiped the tears off her cheeks with her fingers. "Go right ahead." His grin was contagious and she managed a weak smile.

Taking a step back, Deacon narrowed his eyes, studying her. "You know, they make this big deal about how beautiful Princess Aratess is. Way prettier than her older sister. I guess I just don't see it." He let her go and shoved both hands in his pockets, rocking from his heels to the balls of his feet.

Despite her shattered heart, she laughed.

Deacon smiled at her before reaching for the hand that gripped the brass candle snuffer. "What are you going to about this?"

Her thoughts leapt to Colt. "Oh, Deacon, I've hurt him so badly." A surge of panic shot from her heart. No matter how angry he was, she needed to apologize and explain and convince him to let her fight. She had to make things right.

* * *

Tess couldn't find Colt below deck, at the bow, the stern, by the skiff, or in the storeroom. She even checked Deacon's quarters again, but she found only the pirate prince sitting and drinking alone. Where *was* he? Alone on the deck, she rubbed her hands up and down her arms. Her Bowman's cloak. She could retrieve her Bowman's cloak and then keep searching. As she made her way down the narrow passage that ran under the stairs to the bridge, her heart skipped a beat.

Colt leaned against the door, waiting for her. He seemed to meld with the shadows.

Both hands flew to her chest. "Colt, oh my goodness. You scared me."

He didn't say anything.

"I've been looking all over for you. I…" When she dared to look at him, his face was solemn, his eyes sad. "Can I talk to you?" She kept both hands pressed against her heart.

He just nodded and unlatched the door before backing out of her way and motioning for her to enter first.

A wave of nerves cascaded over her. What could she say? Where would she start? She turned and backed against the tall cabinet that stood against one wall.

Colt didn't close the door to her room. He remained in the entrance, leaning against the frame closest to the cabinet where she stood, only inches away. "I don't want anyone to know who you are, Your Highness." The words were barely audible. It felt surreal to hear Colt address her so formally. "Not yet. Not until I can properly secure your safety."

She tensed her jaw. "That is exactly why I didn't tell you, Colt." She summoned her nerve and gently clasped his forearm. "I know the oath you swore. I know that your first duty as a Bowman, above every other pledge, is to protect the king and his family. I know that. And I was convinced that you were the only Bowman, the only person for that matter, who could do anything about all this. You needed to get to the coast. You had to get answers. You couldn't not, Colt. I knew that. You didn't have time to worry about getting me to the castle. If I had told you, you would have been hamstrung by your duty to me as the king's daughter." She stopped to take a breath and tried to read Colt's face. Her room was dark. She hadn't lit the lamp, and the fire from earlier in the day had burned down to embers. She could barely make out his features.

He said nothing.

"It was a good thing too. Had I told you, you never would have found those five ships. We would be totally unprepared for what faces us tomorrow, and Fairgates would be lost. Ardenia would be lost. You must understand, Colt. As a princess of the Realm, I have a duty as well. My duty is to my people. I am responsible to do everything in my power to protect them, and you are their best hope. I am confident the All-Father is going to use you. Making sure you could do your job without having to stop and escort a spoiled brat back to her daddy was my responsibility."

She searched his shadowed face. What was he thinking?

Silently, he inched toward her. She backed up instinctively, dropping her hand from his arm, the solid wooden doors of the cabinet pressing against her back.

He froze and stood there staring down at her. As her eyes slowly adjusted to the light, his face became clear. He was so handsome. Her throat felt tight for a moment.

Exhaling, he inched closer, ever so slightly. "I'm sorry about your sister, Your Highness, and I am sorry that your father and brothers have descended into a trap."

"I'm sorry too. I'm sorry for not telling you. So very sorry, Colt." Her hand pressed against her heart. The eyes searching hers were sad and kind and deep.

"Why were you pretending to be Sasha's maid in the first place?" He tilted his head.

Tess's cheeks warmed. The whole thing seemed truly ridiculous. "I didn't know she was going to introduce me that way. She explained after the introductions that she wanted me to investigate Durbink's character. She thought his servants might be honest with another servant. And I hate court anyway." She wrinkled her nose.

Colt's eyes flashed with just the slightest sparkle.

Suddenly, she became aware that her hand was cramping. She still gripped the brass candle snuffer that had come to represent her role in the battle. Raising her clenched hand to her waist, she slowly opened her fingers to reveal what she held.

He glanced down and then met her gaze again.

"I need to help, Colt. You need my bow," she whispered.

He slowly shook his head.

Her heart wrenched with fear.

"Absolutely not, Princess. I can't. You can't. There is absolutely no way now." He lowered his head ever so slightly as he spoke.

Reaching out with her free hand, she touched his chest. "Please, Colt. I thought we were past all this. I can help, I need to help."

He wiped a tear from her cheek with his thumb. His touch sent a thousand tiny shocks of lightning through her entire body. "Aratess, I am a Bowman and you are the princess. I've sworn an oath. There is no version of this where I let you fight, where I put you in danger." His tender tone didn't match the finality of the statement.

A burning feeling sparked deep inside her. "That doesn't make sense, and it's not fair. Aren't I the same person you entrusted with the task? I have the same abilities, the same convictions, the same desire to serve my tier that I had before you learned of my royal birth. How is the life of Tess the lady's maid worth less than that of Tess the princess?" She pressed her hand more firmly against his chest.

He wiped away another tear, and she melted at his touch. He leaned in closer, and she rested her head against the cabinet, frozen, mesmerized by how close he was, holding her breath.

"Tess, please, never doubt how much you're worth to me." His eyes misted over. Then, without another word, he turned and left the room. A large shadow swept behind him as he closed the door. His footsteps faded as he walked away.

Tess stood alone in the darkness, holding tight to the candle snuffer.

Chapter Twenty-Three

The Rank

Deacon

DEACON CONTEMPLATED THE LIQUOR CABINET, TRYING to decide which bottle of brandy to open next. Every bottle held a story. He remembered each ship he'd raided, each captain's cabinet or hold where they'd been stored before he *liberated* them. This cabinet proved the only place in his quarters that never needed dusting. He laughed. Then a flash of concern flooded him. His reliance on the liquor had doubled since he'd started raiding a half-year previous.

He was reaching for a thirty-year-old selection housed in a crystal bottle, one he'd been saving, when Colt stormed into the room.

His old friend dropped into the chair he'd habitually assumed since embarking two days ago and leaned his head against the wall.

He couldn't help but smile a little. If saving the Realm wasn't enough, Colt had to deal with his first case of girl troubles, and judging by the slump in his shoulders, he'd taken a beating.

"She can do it, you know. And she wants to do it." He grabbed a crystal glass from the map and slid it in front of his friend. He then poured him a generous glass of brandy.

Colt looked up and sighed. "I know she can do it. She's remarkable. And she's as brave as any Bowman I've met. But it's not just that she wants to. She needs to, Deac. I know exactly how she feels. There's this call, this pull, this unstoppable hoist to duty, and this certainty that you know you can answer, you *must* answer the call. Like it hurts not to act, to answer, because you are certain you can help. You must help. And she has that, I can tell. All her life she's been forced to curtsy and smile, all the while desperately wanting to answer that call."

Colt closed his eyes.

Deacon sipped his brandy. He'd never once felt that call, not to duty, anyhow. Maybe to making his way in the world, maybe to vengeance on Lindsor. He definitely felt a call to his men, to Colt, but never to duty. "Never felt that call to duty, Colt. And I never understood why you wouldn't quit the Bowmen with me, make our way like we planned, get rich… not until now."

How had he never realized that his friend was made of totally different material than him? Guilt over punishing Colt flooded through him. Like the spire, whose strata varied so dramatically from tier to tier, Colt was different from him. So was Tess. Colt and Tess were made of the exact same stuff—pure, strong, and rare, nothing like himself. Funny, then, that he felt so drawn to both of them. As the magnetists said, opposites attract.

Deacon took another sip of brandy. "So, if you understand her need to answer that call of duty, and you believe in her ability to answer, why don't you put her back into play?"

"I'm bound by my oath, Deac. As a lady in waiting, I could justify it, but how can I put the king's daughter at risk? How can I do that without trampling on the very first line of the blasted code?"

Deacon thought hard, trying to remember the line. The effort hurt. He didn't have Colt's aptitude for this stuff. "That is a pickle, Colt, but you're a smart guy. I'm certain you'll figure it out."

"*I am a King's Bowman, my lady. I assure you that there isn't a problem in the Realm that I can't think my way out of.*" Colt mumbled the words under his breath.

"Pardon me? That is possibly the most arrogant thing I've ever heard you say! Did you tell her that?" He laughed.

Colt nodded and laughed as well. "Yeah, during our very first conversation, correction, our first argument. And she has skillfully teased me about it at every opportunity since."

Deacon's chest squeezed tight. His friend obviously cared for this girl and understood her on a deep level. Still, Colt had taken himself out of the running for her affection. And Deacon had been honest about his intentions—that went way above and beyond in terms of friendship, didn't it?

"Serve king and tier with all thy strength… king *and* tier… " Colt inhaled deeply and then straightened on the chair. A smile spread across his face. He was on to something.

"That was quick. That's the code, right? You figured it out?" He swirled his brandy as Colt rose slowly to his feet. His friend's eyes narrowed as he worked out the details, following the line of reasoning he'd clearly latched onto. Deacon had seen this countless times before as kids.

"Yes, my duty is to the king *and* the tier. If Ardenia falls, there is no king, and it's my first responsibility to ensure that never happens!" Colt's eyes danced.

The door to Deacon's quarters flew open. Tess stood in the doorway, standing as tall as her five feet and maybe eight inches would stretch. She crossed both arms in front of her chest and raised her chin, eyes fixed on Colt.

Deacon rose out of respect for her.

Colt stepped toward her. "Tess, Your Highness, I was just, I was about to come talk to you. I…"

"Well, I came to talk to you first, Captain, so you can just hear me out."

Oh, this should be good. Deacon masked a smile with his hand as he sat back down.

Tess stalked to the table, looked Colt directly in the eyes, and placed the brass candle snuffer at Tappers elbow with considerable force. She then stepped back and recrossed her arms. "I am the ranking senior Captain. Like it or not, I'm in charge!"

Colt's eyebrows rose nearly to his hairline. "Ranking senior?"

Deacon spat his brandy across the table in a mist propelled by uncontrolled shock and laughter. How would Colt handle this one?

"That's right, as princess and member of the royal family, I am the commander and chief of Ardenia's forces in the absence of my father and brother. That means I outrank everyone, including Bowmen, maybe especially Bowmen, *Captain.*" She uncrossed her arms and shoved her hands onto her hips.

Colt stood frozen, his mouth hanging slightly open.

Deacon couldn't help himself. "You know, Colt, I don't

remember much from the academy, but that one was so basic they taught it during first week when I was still paying attention. She's right. She's ranking senior in her father's absence."

Colt's face turned red, which didn't deter him in the slightest.

"Can't believe you didn't immediately think of it, you being so smart and the resident Bowman and all."

Colt spun toward him, his eyes narrowed. Deacon felt the warning shots his friend had just fired over the imaginary bow of his ship. He laughed outright, unable to stop himself.

Then Colt whirled back to Tess.

She held up a hand before he could speak. "Your plan is sound, more than sound, brilliant. Miraculous really, Captain. I only have one objection."

"Let me guess, I need a second archer at Tapper's elbow?"

She nodded, raising her chin even higher and looking absolutely adorable as she did. Deacon's heart swelled.

Colt stared at her. They passed a minute in silence, neither of them moving, giving ground. What could his old friend be thinking?

Deacon stood, crossed the room, and clapped him on the shoulder. "Colt, weren't you on your way to tell the Princess about some grand revelation that reconciled her fighting within the Bowman code? Something that wouldn't require you to break your oath but that would acknowledge you understood her need to answer the call of duty?"

"Captain?" Tess stepped forward and cocked her head to the side, her entire demeanour changing, softening towards Colt.

You're welcome, buddy.

"Yes, well, I just agree that strategically we need you, and I know you are more than capable, and you've made your desire to fight clear. Above all, I understand your need to help, to serve, I share that and so I…"

"You what, Captain?" She took another step towards him.

Colt sighed. "I've sworn to serve king and tier with all my strength. I don't only serve my king but the tier. That tier needs a miracle, and you are part of my strength, Princess." When her cheeks reddened, he rushed to add, "You're an asset. I mean, your ability is an asset, and I need to utilize every resource to saving the tier for my king.

That's all. I was about to come tell you that I had figured out a way to use your bow, which we need, as well as to reconcile my conscience."

The way Tess gazed at Colt suggested to Deacon that he might have made a terrible mistake. Yes, if winning her heart was his end game, then he had just made a horrific tactical error. Why had he done it? Maybe he *had* heard that same call to duty, faint, drowning, submerged inside a bottle of brandy at the back of his liquor cabinet, but there after all. Regardless, he would need to make a grand gesture if he stood a chance with the princess.

* * *

Deacon couldn't sleep. The entire castle seemed awake along with him, and he had nothing to ease his nerves. Colt had dropped the brandy Deacon craved overboard only hours before. Every last bottle sat somewhere on the seafloor off Gilbet's. Every single drop! He had tried to persuade Colt against it, but it was futile.

Giving up on rest, he clambered out of bed and made his way to the side of the enormous cannon nicknamed Samson. He rechecked the powder, the shot, the rammer. Everything lay ready, as he had left it. Riley would command Serena, and Deacon had the responsibility of commanding Samson. In truth, he looked forward to seeing this massive example of modern engineering in action. He had operated many cannons in the last three years, but none anywhere close to the size of Samson or with nearly the range. He couldn't even conceive of a weapon firing as far as three miles. Was the anticipation the reason he couldn't sleep?

The air smelled of spring, budding trees, blackflies, and Tarragon. The thought had barely crossed his mind when two tarragon swooped past him in the dark, and he ducked. Blast those creatures! Despite Colt's deep devotion to Wingblade, his pet tarragon, he still felt a measure of caution around the huge, winged reptiles. His nerves, already spent with the approaching battle, now felt completely raw.

He gazed over the river that led to the docks at the base of the large hill. This part of the river, still thick with ice, would play a key role in the morning. He tried to take deep breaths and relax. Staring down at the Ridley, he leaned against the cool stone wall and then closed his eyes, trying to imagine himself somewhere along the coast, aboard *The Dancing Girl*.

As he pictured him and Shifty, fishing off the stern, a loud crack shattered the stillness, and his eyes flashed open. The second crack—an eerie haunting sound—echoed more loudly than the first. Where had he heard that sound before?

Unpredictable, almost organic, the cracking continued, increasing in frequency. Deacon closed his eyes again, raking through his memories before he opened his eyes and lifted his head. Ice! The ice in front of the castle was succumbing to the spring thaw, and it wouldn't stop. Every hour from now until it was gone, it would only continue to break, weaken, shift, and melt. Terror ripped through his heart. The ships were coming. Would the breaking ice be strong enough to hold them back? Would he even be given the opportunity to sink them? How would this affect Tess? Tess! He shoved away from the wall.

He arrived at Tapper's Elbow sweaty and out of breath. Dawn was breaking in the north, and the sky grew progressively lighter with each passing moment. Clubber and Sam stood at the river's edge, watching the ice crack and shift. Tess worked quickly, setting up arrows behind different points of cover.

Doubt flooded his mind. At this moment, what echoed through his thoughts were Colt's words from the other night. "And if it is in your power, I don't ever want her in harm's way again, do you understand?" Colt had asked him, no, ordered him. The Bowman could not have been clearer. And now, everything had changed.

The knot in his stomach tightened. He gently grabbed Tess's right arm, tugging her aside, out of earshot of the others.

"What is it, Deac? Are you okay? Is something wrong with your team, with Samson?"

He didn't know where to begin. A lump formed in his throat as he gazed at her. He still held her arm, and when she looked down, he instinctively let go.

"No, nothing's wrong, I mean, apart from everything being wrong, you know, that we're horribly outnumbered and probably going to die and all. I came to tell you that the ice is breaking up. Things might not work how we thought." He forced a weak smile.

She smiled too. She was so pretty. "Yes, we noticed the ice down here too." She laughed a little.

Warmth crept up his neck. Of course, they'd noticed. They were standing on the blasted riverbank, for Realm's sake, yards away from the seasonal phenomenon. The cracking ice proved so loud they couldn't possibly *not* notice it. A wave of nerves rippled through him, taking him by surprise. He had never been nervous around a girl before.

"Right, yes. Well, I just wanted to make sure that you guys were settled." He winced. Definitely weak.

"I'm sure you and your men will be all right up there." She nodded to the edge of the east wall, barely visible from where they stood. "You'll take good care of your team. And I know Colt will provide the best supressing fire possible for Reynolds and your crew on *The Girl*. I'm glad it's him. They deserve the best."

Deacon contemplated her. She knew exactly what he cared about most. Did she know that she topped that list? Did he dare tell her?

"Tess… Aratess… Princess. Shoot!" What an awkward start.

She smiled at his difficulty.

He ran his hand through his hair, grabbed her right hand in his, and started again. "Listen, Tess, I literally promised my very best friend in the whole Realm that I would do whatever it took to keep you out of danger. And here you are in a heap of danger."

Worry swept across her beautiful face. Her jaw tensed, and her breathing shallowed. She gazed up at him as though waiting for him to say more.

What could he say? He didn't have time to share everything racing through his mind, and he wasn't even sure what he wanted her to know, so now what? "I don't know, Tess, honestly. Just don't die, all right? Colt will never recover from the guilt of letting you fight, and I'll, well, I will never recover, period, so don't be reckless, Princess." He gently squeezed her hand.

Her eyes widened.

Did she understand what he was trying to tell her? Pink tinged her cheeks as she lowered her gaze. Yes, she understood enough.

Instinctively, he leaned forward and kissed the top of her head. Neither spoke as he turned away.

Deacon ran the entire route back to the castle. Grand gesture indeed.

Chapter Twenty-Four

The Resistance

Colt

COLT HELD HIS BREATH AS THE first Reyjik ship entered the Ridley's delta. Its enormous hull—decidedly more massive than he had envisioned when he had looked at it through the spyglass on Cooper's Cliffs—took over a minute to glide past his position. All the while, it scraped and crashed through the ice floes. The towering masts reached higher than the trees on the other side of the river. His heart seized with fear and self-doubt, his plan crumbling into pieces. As the second ship, a schooner, entered the river, he questioned everything he had reasoned, decided, ordered, and executed over the last few days. He knew with certainty that everyone in Fairgates, every sailor on *The Dancing Girl*, and the militia, was in grave danger.

He watched silently as the third galleon passed him, tortured to have to wait like this without knowing what would happen farther down the river. He desperately wanted to know if the ice would hold. Had the first ship passed Tapper's Elbow? How did Tess feel when she saw it up close? Was she scared? He glanced at Shifty. The young man's face held trepidation.

Their only hope lay with the ice that would hold back the giant ships. Now the galleons made easy work of the same ice that would have given *The Dancing Girl* a run for her money. Despair gripped him.

At that moment, he remembered a wise word the Bowman chief had spoken countless times during his training. "You can only do the good you can do," Commander Laidlaw would say. He had taken it to mean that sometimes even Bowmen were limited as to what they could do. He had done his very best and now, here he stood.

His duty made him responsible to the sailors on *The Dancing Girl*. Those men, whom he had come to trust and respect, had in turn put their trust in him. Somehow, he needed to protect them from the second schooner that rounded the estuary and entered the river. The battle was imminent. All five Reyjik ships sailed to Fairgates, completely unaware of the hopelessly underpowered resistance that waited for them. In only a matter of minutes, Reynolds would sail *The Girl* into the River delta to play her part in this madness, and then his part would begin.

He nodded to Shifty, who stood waiting with a tar-dipped arrow in his hand. He'd decided that the first shot would be a flaming arrow, for good measure. He shot faster with standard arrows and figured he could take out five or six crew members a minute if they were in the open. He would attempt to do exactly that, and then, during the confusion that followed, he would search for the most effective targets for his flaming arrows.

A resounding boom filled the river valley. It echoed off the banks, bouncing off the huge hull that glided in front of him. The deep boom had come from Samson. Their fate was sealed, it had begun. The men on board the fifth ship ran across the deck in a panic. They all crowded at the bow, attempting to catch a glimpse of the source of the noise. He couldn't let this opportunity go to waste, and shot the flaming arrow Shifty had ignited for him square into a man's chest. The man hit the deck, and then the shouting began. Colt launched five more arrows, killing five more Reyjik before the men on board the galleon extinguished the first arrow. Another boom echoed off the riverbanks, followed by more shouts. Truly, the Battle for Fairgates had begun.

* * *

Deacon called out orders continually. The massive cannon took a team of ten men to operate, but by their third shot, they finally found a rhythm. Their fourth attempt marked their first hit—a shot onto the deck of the first schooner. He had aimed for the first galleon, but he couldn't dwell on that. He took the win and quickly sent a message to Riley with the exact trajectory of the successful shot. He relished the fact that he could sink the schooner and prevent it from flying to reinforce the

Reyjik in Costair. Hopefully, both cannons could bombard one ship until they filled it so full of holes it had no choice but to sink.

Indeed, when the first ship came into view, he had cursed out loud. The ship looked enormous, far larger than he had expected, and he doubted the shot they were loading would be anything more than a mild nuisance to this monster. His thoughts went immediately to Tess. He could picture her waiting behind the large rock at Tapper's Elbow. She would begin to fire on the massive ship, exposing herself to its secondary movable guns. Colt should never have let her fight!

* * *

Tess's heart pounded in her chest, so loudly she worried the Reyjik could hear it as well. She tried to breathe to steady herself, but to no avail. She was drowning in her fear. How could she fire on such an enormous vessel? How could she even make a dent in a crew of so many?

Her attempt to breathe deeply failed—all she could manage were shallow gasps. The world began to spin around her—and then it happened. The massive galleon crashed into the solid ice that lay between Tapper's Elbow and the Castle. An enormous crashing sound initiated the chain of events—the huge ship lurched, the tall masts pitched forward and to starboard, and then it stopped dead.

She laughed out loud. Since Deacon had visited her position at dawn, she had been praying the ice would play its part, and it had. She made the sign of descent before signaling to Sam to light the first flaming arrow.

Clubber passed the tar-dipped arrow to the young courier, and Sam held it above the small oil lamp they'd brought. Sam's hand shook, and he was clearly struggling to hold it in place long enough for the tar to catch. He glanced at her, white as a sail, and mouthed the word *sorry*. Regret, shame, and fear shimmered in his eyes.

Somewhere deep inside, her own flame of determination sparked and flared. She smiled from ear to ear and held out her hand. It trembled as well, but she slowly, dramatically, curled each finger into a fist, narrowed her eyes, and then pumped the fist in the air, mastering her fear.

Sam watched her, drinking down the message. He nodded, took a deep breath, and held the arrow steady. Just as it caught fire, the riverbank shook with a concussive, piercing boom. Samson!

Their concentration was so focused at that moment that not one of them jumped at the sound. Deac and the men on the ramparts had fired. The Battle for Fairgates had truly begun.

* * *

Desperation gripped Colt. He had already killed twenty-five men, yet more kept emerging from below deck. He faithfully tried to keep to his original plan, taking out as many men as he could and then lobbing flaming arrows onto the deck. It all proved futile. He didn't see smoke, let alone flames, from the effort.

He scanned *The Dancing Girl*. Reynolds had kept her both shooting and moving, as they had discussed. She fired with all starboard cannons, but they proved only a mild annoyance to the massive galleon. Between cannon fire, Reynolds yelled orders, aft, port, starboard and forward again. Truly *The Girl* was dancing today. Colt felt helpless, utterly helpless. "Come on. Think. What would mess them up the most?"

Shifty knelt beside Colt. "Can you take out their skiffs, Bowman?"

He peered around a rock. Yes, yes, that would work. Without their boats to ferry men ashore, they were rendered far less helpful. That he could accomplish.

"Shifty, you are a genius!" Aiming his flaming arrow at the rope that ran through the closest davit arm, holding the first skiff, he released a dead shot. No one noticed the flames, and the rope was allowed to burn. He quickly took another flaming arrow from Shifty, who appeared most pleased with himself.

The Bowman nodded his approval. The game was now afoot.

* * *

Deacon and his men fired with abandon. Both he and Riley pummeled the second ship in line. The deck lay riddled with holes, men ran in confusion, and, as Deacon had confirmed through his spyglass, a number of men had been killed by the cannon fire itself.

But Colt's concerns from the day before were valid. Unless they hit this ship multiple times below the water line, they had no hope of sinking her. The pirate endeavoured to do just that. He lined up his next shot, lit the fuse himself, and prayed for contact under the icy water of the Ridley. *Boom!*

A splash formed where the shot had hit even before he had processed the deafening, concussive sound the cannon made. He verified the hit with his spyglass. He wasted no time sending the trajectory to Riley, who would sight Serena to the same elevation. He ordered the reload of Samson and prayed for lightning to strike twice.

* * *

Horrified by how little she had accomplished, Tess began to panic. She had lobbed dozens of flaming arrows, downed at least ten men with her standard ammunition, and yet, she might as well have done nothing at all. To say she felt discouraged could not possibly express her level of frustration.

The first galleon had done exactly what Colt had predicted. They fired cannon shots at the ice in front of the ship. They tried to break up the ice… and they succeeded. Tess needed to think of something quickly, absolutely determined not to return empty handed. She promised to sink a ship—for Ardenia, for her sister, and for the man she so deeply wanted to help.

* * *

Sheer delight filled Deacon's heart as the upright masts of the schooner began to tilt to the starboard side. Indeed, the ship listed to starboard, and that could only mean one thing—they were taking on water— significant amounts of water. Once a ship began taking on water, nothing could undo what had been done. At the rate the ship pitched to starboard, sinking proved inevitable. As he surveyed the damaged ship through his spyglass, his chest tightened. The crew was attempting to run the ship aground on the southern bank of the river. Had the Reyjik accepted their fate? Were they trying to salvage the mission by getting as many of their men off as possible?

Deacon sent Higgits, a capable yeoman, to warn Sergeant Privit of the possibility of attack. He advised that archers should stand at the ready for Reyjik who would approach from the southwest wood that edged the docks. Then he ordered Riley to focus Serena's assault on the sinking ship making for the bank and any crew that emerged.

Seething with frustration over the fact that the first Reyjik ship had advanced to a point just around Tapper's Elbow, while attempting to make headway with the ice, he cursed that it had also unintentionally maneuvered itself to a point where he couldn't sight a proper angle of fire. He could not abide the fact that their greatest threat floated so decidedly in range and yet unreachable. Would the resourceful princess find a way to stall it?

* * *

Colt had a field day with the skiff ropes. Every rope was burning. Many of the small boats had already fallen free from their davit arms, and they floated out to sea with the small ice floes that rode the Ridley's natural current. He had ensured that no soldier would successfully disembark on a skiff.

His sense of accomplishment was short-lived. The reality—that he had not really crippled the schooner in any significant way—tormented him. True, if a soldier wanted off he would now face an icy swim, but the ship itself remained largely intact.

Most discouraging was the fact that its guns were working fine, continually demonstrated in the skirmish with *The Dancing Girl*. His free hand clenched into a fist. The cannons of this last ship were all located below deck, which was different than the other four.

He'd read about these secured guns but had never seen them. Indeed, the sides of the huge hull boasted trap doors that would flip open to allow the rows of cannons to fire, and he hadn't had a clear shot at the cannon operators. He'd killed numerous deck gunman, probably the sole reason *The Girl* still floated, but he needed more. He needed to be the one to save Fairgates. That responsibility lay with him, a King's Bowman. He wracked his brain. How could he help Reynolds and the crew? And then his ears popped with the deafening boom of a massive explosion.

* * *

To stay with the first Reyjik ship, Tess had advanced her position in the treeline three times. Sam and Clubber had dragged their arrow cases to her new position, and she had managed to continue firing. When the galleon rounded the corner of Tapper's Elbow, Tess set up behind a rock and nocked another arrow.

Sam stood right behind her with a basket of pitch tipped arrows. She swiped her fingers across her forehead. Why had Deacon and Riley stopped firing on the ship? Didn't they understand the strategic significance of this first ship? Didn't they know it must not be allowed to break the ice and dock?

Wait, if the ship had advanced out of their targeting window, they might not be able to get a true firing angle. Cold chills swept over her. She alone stood in position to stop the beast that relentlessly attacked the ice before it.

Tess used her spyglass to survey the deck. There must be something she could do. The ship turned slightly to port, set her cannons, and then fired a mere two-hundred yards down the river, shattering the ice on impact. They had used this same tactic twice before, enabling them to advance around Tapper's Elbow. She checked the deck again. This time, she caught a glimpse of something next to the aft cannon. A Reyjik ram-rodder had left a powder keg open.

Hope flooded her mind. She signaled to Sam, and he lit an arrow as he had done countless times before. She closed her eyes and said a quick prayer. If she missed this shot, it would alert the Reyjik to the potential danger, and they would surely close the hazardous keg. No, she couldn't miss. She thought through everything Colt had taught her, and even though it took all her waning strength, she managed one last full draw. She held the flight to her cheek, sighting the top lip of the barrel. Holding her breath, she released it.

The arrow cut through the air at a menacing speed. She had only just recovered from her draw when the powder ignited, causing a devastating explosion that engulfed the entire stern in flames. Every soldier abandoned their post and jumped headlong into the river.

The heat set off two other kegs at the stern of the ship, and more explosions followed in quick succession.

Water rushed into the ship, flooding all aft compartments. The bow pitched up with the weight and pull of the water. Reyjik soldiers still left on board screamed and slid, then hit the icy water. The ship sank at an alarming rate.

Then a fourth keg of powder from the bow rolled down to midship and exploded from the heat and flame. With no possibility for recovery, the vessel was doomed. Its crew swam to the banks. She had done it. The consecutive explosions created such concussive force that she hurtled backwards through the air, hitting a tree before landing on the ground. Hard. She managed to keep her wits, her ears ringing, the entire woods spinning.

Her vision filled with flames. Sam? Clubber? They had been behind her. Where were they now? She managed to turn her head. Sam lay unconscious at the foot of a tree, and Clubber lay on his back behind the large rock.

A final explosion shook the earth beneath her. A wave of heat and pressure crashed over her, and then everything went black.

* * *

Colt dropped his bow and covered his ears at the first explosion. He had never heard anything so loud in his entire life. The constant cannon fire paled in comparison. Before he could lower his hands, a second and third explosion sounded and then a fourth. Huge clouds of smoke filled the sky upriver. One of the first two ships must be burning. BURNING!

"How could it be burning?" Could a cannon ball ignite something on impact? No, that couldn't be it. Had a deck hand been careless? Maybe a lit cannon fuse gone wrong. And then a sick feeling gripped the young captain's heart. That explosion was the ideal outcome for a flaming arrow. A one-in-a-million shot, to be sure, but the very reason he was where he was doing what he was doing. His mind raced. Tess!

Had Tess blown up a galleon off Tapper's Elbow? How close was she? Was she all right? What if men made for the shore? What if soldiers found her? Blast! BLAST! *Focus, Colt. She's smart and she's resourceful. She can handle herself, focus.*

"Think. Concentrate on your ship and *The Dancing Girl*. Reynolds and the boys need you. Focus!" He spoke the words out loud to help hone his attention, then peered at Shifty, who stood on tiptoes, clearly trying in vain to see more from the direction of the explosion.

He stared at the beloved schooner. Did she ever need him. In the short time since the explosion, *The Girl* had taken the most intense fire of the entire battle. Splinters of shrapnel exploded with each shot. Reynolds was trying to dance around the onslaught of five-and ten-pound shot, but the galleon had simply too many guns and too many men to man them.

If he didn't think of something quick, the Reyjik schooner would soon be sailing out of the Ridley and over the wreck of *The Dancing Girl* as it escaped.

"Shifty, take the spyglass and act as my spotter. Search for any powder kegs on deck." He continued shooting as he gave the orders.

Shifty immediately complied. After forty-five seconds of concerted effort, he reported in. "Nothing, sir. I think the powder is all below deck."

Colt thought quickly. What were the two objectives of this battle? What had he stated so clearly at the briefing?

"We can't let them reach the castle, and we can't let them get away." He quoted his own words back to himself. He thought of the king. He could picture him on the battlefield seaward in Costair, already taking significant casualties and then being overrun with the reinforcements from this ship. Desperate to stop that from happening, he gazed up at the towering masts of the ship attempting to escape. He followed them down to the deflated blimpoon waiting on the deck, scanned the billows of folded Reyjik silk. In that moment, he knew exactly what to do.

* * *

Deacon cursed incessantly. Since the massive explosion, he had adopted a new routine. He checked his spyglass, stood on the wall, looked without the spyglass, checked the spyglass again, and then cursed for at least a solid minute. He repeated the entire ridiculous routine over and over again. Checking his spyglass was pointless because of the thick plume of black smoke. Unable to sight the third, fourth, and fifth ships undoubtedly trying to escape the river, helplessness swept over him. "What good is a blasted cannon that shoots three blasted miles if you can't see the blasted delta?" he muttered to himself. He paced the wall in a pointless attempt to sight any of the three ships he so desperately wanted to sink.

Left with no real choice, he reasoned that the ships had made at least some progress up the river, so he adjusted his trajectory by a few degrees and then fired blind. He could only hope the shots would find their marks through the thick smoke. He resigned himself to the fact that his part in the battle had been played. Samson had taken one of their ships from them, which was something, at least.

Wait, what about the force of survivors attacking the castle? He leapt from the wall and ordered a yeoman to continue covering the river but not the delta.

When he arrived at the castle, Sergeant Privit had lifted his arm, about to call the order to fire on the advancing foot soldiers. Deac estimated more than three hundred men threatened the castle and the village. As he surveyed them through his spyglass, he noticed they were almost entirely unarmed and dripping wet.

He focused in on one soldier who brandished a long, curved sabre. Indeed, this man, potentially a leader, was the only soldier holding a sword. His jaw dropping, Deacon watched as the wet soldier tied a white shirt to the blade of his sword and waved it high over his head. These Reyjik were surrendering. Surrendering!

Privit nudged him in the side with his elbow. "They're probably so cold from their unplanned swim that they are in no shape to fight. And, in the confusion and panic of escaping a sinking ship, they mustn't have grabbed weapons. Those who had, probably dropped them in favor of using two hands to get out of the icy water as quickly as possible."

He laughed, the relief a welcome change from the numbing panic of the last two hours.

"You know, Captain, I've spent the last twenty-four hours raising recruits, readying defensive positions, and briefing my militia. In that time, I did not secure one woolen blanket, which, as it turned out, is what I need."

Deacon slapped Privit on the back and laughed. "To be accurate, you're gonna need about three hundred woolen blankets." He slapped him on the back again. And then his thoughts leapt to Tess.

* * *

Colt shot his arrows almost straight up. The ship towered over him as it attempted to sail into the estuary, and its massive sails shaded him from the bright sunshine of pre-peak. It was those sails for which he aimed. He shot arrow after arrow into the huge billows of stretched fabric, hitting true every single time. He needed to be thorough. He shot the mainsail, the jib, and the second sail. He shot the silk blimpoon that lay waiting to be unfurled. All were now burning. All were compromised. None would function to sail to their escape or fly off the precipice and seaward to Costair. He had done it, the ship was truly crippled. No soldier could disembark, they were without wind power. And they couldn't fly.

He stopped firing, not wanting to waste ammunition. The schooner fired furiously at *The Dancing Girl*, then pushed past her and out into open water. He could do nothing to help *The Girl*, as both ships were out of range. Focussing his attention on the two remaining Reyjik ships clearly attempting to escape the river of death, he planned to use the same tactic on these and burn out their sails, rendering them useless as well.

Turning to Shifty for another lit arrow, he was surprised the sailor—who had proven to be most efficient and helpful throughout the battle—didn't have an arrow at the ready. Not once had he needed to turn or wait for ammunition, until now. He peered over his shoulder.

Scrambling from tree to tree, Shifty searched behind rocks and checked the two baskets. He then looked at Colt with the most apologetic expression plastered across his face. "We're out of arrows, Bowman… flaming and otherwise." Pulling at his hair with both hands, his face twisted.

Colt scowled. "Out of arrows? But we brought four hundred of them. Two full cases."

"Yes, sir. You fired them all, sir." Shifty still tugged on his hair.

Colt spun toward the river. The third ship sailed past, and the fourth ship had already sailed out in the estuary, completely unscathed. Both galleons, now decidedly out of range, furled every sail. What? Why were they furling their sails? Surely, they'd need them to return to wherever they moored. A sick feeling knotted in Colt's stomach. He ran to the riverbank and stood on tiptoes. Shifty joined him immediately and handed him the spyglass.

Raising the lens to his right eye, he closed his left. He twisted the telescopic joint to the right by degrees until the deck of the huge galleon came into focus. His stomach roiled as the giant masts lowered to the deck, horizontal to the sea. Massive billows of cream-colored silk fluttered and filled. No. How?

Horror gripped his heart as a black blimpoon more enormous than he could ever imagine inflated over the galleon. He lowered the spyglass. A second black blimpoon grew above the other galleon. Neither looked compromised in any way. And they filled at an alarming rate.

Colt turned and screamed at *The Dancing Girl*. He jumped and waved his arms until they ached. Shifty joined in his vain attempt to alert the crew of *The Girl* to the massive lighter-than-air galleons. They were out of earshot. They weren't watching.

A sick helpless feeling took root in the innermost part of his heart. One after the other, the galleons lurched out of the sea. Streams of water fell to the waves beneath, until they rose to a height where only mist wafted into the waves. How could they do that? How could they fly?

They rose continually in elevation but never wavered in their trajectory. They headed straight south down the coast, not attempting to conceal their intentions. They didn't need to. They were heading for the precipice where they would fly over the seawall, and seaward to Costair.

In one day, they would reach their destination and deliver the crushing final blow to King Lucius. Colt stared at *The Dancing Girl*. Still afloat, she didn't appear to be listing, and her sails were intact. She would do. They could pursue the two ships that escaped, which left a glimmer of hope for the Realm.

Chapter Twenty-Five

The Aftermath

Colt

COLT HAD A COMPLETE PICTURE. HE had returned to *The Dancing Girl* and had received a thorough briefing from Reynolds. *The Girl* would make it to Dungridge, and she could fly… most likely. He received word from Sergeant Privit of the surrender of three hundred and ninety-six Reyjik soldiers, now being served hot soup in the castle's dungeons. The king could worry about the diplomacy of what to do with these men, if Lucius survived this invasion. In the meantime, Colt ordered the sergeant to be merciful, vigilant, but not overly generous.

He sent two of Privit's most reliable men to take word to the neighboring provinces of Jeness and Lostrov. He had written and sealed official Bowman requests for two hundred troops from each, to secure the capital in the king's absence. He'd also sent word to Deacon and Riley to return to *The Girl* immediately.

Tess, Clubber, and Sam were with Deacon's crew from the cannons, and he waited for the skiff containing Deacon's team to board the ship.

As the crew hauled the skiff up the side of the ship, he searched for Tess's face. When he couldn't find her, he searched for Deacon. He had heard that both friends had fared well during the battle, but he longed to see them with his own eyes.

Peering over the side of *The Girl*, he stared down into the rowboat. There, that must be the back of Deacon's head, but the blond-haired man on whom he fixated was seated, looking down. Strange, since every other man on the skiff peered up at the davit arms.

They all watched as their crewmates hoisted the huge ropes over the pulleys and pulled them on deck. Yet, Deacon continued to gaze down at his lap. Where was Tess? His stomach tightened. Had he trusted the status reports too easily? Where was she, and what was wrong with Deacon?

Jumping from the railing to the deck, he sidestepped three holes that still contained shot and arrived directly in front of the skiff. Why weren't the men pouring off the tiny boat to greet their crewmates triumphantly? Not one member of *The Dancing Girl* had been killed in the battle—shouldn't this be a time of celebration and reunion? Yet, no one climbed off the skiff.

Finally, Deacon swung his leg over the side of the small boat and jumped to the deck. He stepped forward to embrace his friend, but the look on Deacon's face stopped him dead. Deacon turned back to the skiff. Sam's head appeared before the courier carefully handed Deacon something. The pirate's broad shoulders blocked his view of the rowboat and he couldn't see beyond.

Then he caught a glimpse of two laced boots flopping limply over Deacon's right arm. Colt lost his breath completely. He had purchased those boots himself. The ship whirled around him as Deacon turned, carrying Tess in his arms. The pirate would not look at him, his gaze fixed on the lifeless face of the princess.

Colt rushed forward. "No, please no."

"She's alive, she's breathing." Deacon's tone was cold and broken.

A wave of temporary relief quelled the nausea that had almost overwhelmed him.

Holding his hands out, he attempted to take Tess from Deacon. "What happened, Deac?"

Deac refused to look at him. "I've got her." He picked his way past to her quarters.

Colt froze and a second wave of nausea crashed over him. This was his fault! Crashing from the battle rush that had carried him through the day, he struggled to jog ahead of Deacon. He opened the door to Tess's cabin and scrambled to her bed to arrange the pillow.

He tried to drive the image of Tess, pale and unmoving, from his mind. For a moment he believed Tess had been killed, and that moment proved an eternity to his heart. Seeing her limp like that haunted him.

He couldn't speak to his old friend as tears were too close to the surface. He only listened as the broken man briefed him on Tess's involvement and its outcome.

Doc Manfred arrived minutes later. He pressed two fingers to Tess's throat, checking her heartrate, while Colt stood helplessly and watched, his own heart thumping dully in his chest.

Deacon continued to ramble on about the battle and what Sam had relayed of Tess's part in it as Doc Manfred completed his work.

Manfred turned away from Tess, and Colt gave Deacon a look that silenced the pirate before nodding for the doctor to speak. "She's all right, Bowman. According to your courier friend, they were both thrown back by the blast of the explosion. Sam woke first, but she came to a minute or so afterwards. He thinks she may have hit her head when she was thrown, but he's not sure. There doesn't appear to be any real injury to her head at any rate, just cuts and scrapes from the blast. He said she was awake, but shaky. Apparently, she was yards closer to the explosion, as she had run to the edge of the bank to make the shot and got thrown a good spell. When the captain here took her on board the skiff—" Manfred gestured to Deacon "—well, she just collapsed in his arms."

Colt whirled on Deacon. "Did you talk to her? Was she awake? Was she herself?"

Deacon held up a hand. "Yes, Colt, she was awake, only a little shaky. Then she just sort of fell asleep on my lap."

"Bowman, I think she's just exhausted." Doc Manfred stroked his gray beard with a thumb and forefinger. "She has undergone an immense amount of stress, both physical and mental, and her body is trying to help itself recover, is all." He paused and bit his lower lip. "Or maybe she did hit her head. In that case, we need to wake her. I'll check her eyes and let ya know. In one case we let her get as much rest as she can, and in the other we make sure she stays awake until her mind settles. That is the best I can tell ya for right now." The medic sighed and fished through his case with both hands before pulling out a thin vial. He carefully removed the cork and then gently passed the open end under Tess's nose.

Every nerve in Colt's body tensed. It only took a few seconds for the smelling salts to take effect. Tess gasped, jerked her head away, and then slowly opened her eyes.

He dropped to his knees at her bedside. Doc Manfred sat on the edge of her bed, Deacon just behind him.

Tess met his gaze and smiled weakly. She closed her eyes again and mouthed the words, *I'm sorry.*

Doc wasn't satisfied. "Oh, no you don't, little miss 'I'm gonna sink me a big bad ship and render myself senseless while I'm at it.' Old Doc gets a onceover before you close them pretty eyes of yours, Princess." He waved the smelling salt beneath her nose again.

Tess's eyes flew open. "Sorry, I'm sorry, I'm awake," she said quietly. She focused on Colt, this time without a smile, before shifting her attention to Deacon. "The castle? Is the castle still ours? What about *The Girl*? Are you both all right?" Her eyelids fluttered slightly.

Colt's heart ached. Her thoughts were of the kingdom and her friends. She didn't even ask about her own condition.

"Not a chance, Princess," Doc interrupted. "I'm the one who gets to ask the questions right now. You look at the light for a second, and then I'll be out of yer way." Doc held a candle about twelve inches from Tess's face. Both pupils constricted instantly before Tess squinted and turned away. Doc lowered the candle. "Yep, Bowman, I think she's fine. Just exhausted, is all. I says she needs to sleep until she wakes up on her own. Then she should take it easy for a few days." Doc replaced items in his case as he gave his opinion. "I would normally stay with her, Captain." Grasping the handles of his bag, Doc stood and faced Deacon. "But I've got fifteen men down below who need me more than the princess. I'll check on her later, if that's all right?"

Deacon nodded.

Colt planted his hands on the edge of the mattress and pushed to his feet. "We should send her to Fairgates. She would get better medical attention there. I mean, they must have a proper doctor at the castle. No offense, Doc, but she could rest better."

Deacon wrung his hands. "The king took the three doctors and two herbalists with him. I checked with Sergeant Privit. Our old Doc is the closest healer for miles."

"Well, if I can't be the best, I best be the closest, right, Captain?" Doc gave Deacon a slap on the arm, and Deac offered him a smile that was clearly forced. Doc Manfred exited the small quarters, leaving the three friends alone.

Colt struggled to grasp the situation. For the first time since seeing Tess nearly lifeless, he let himself think. Had he made the wrong decision? She insisted it was her call as ranking senior, but could he have stopped her from endangering herself? *Should* he have stopped her? No. No, how could he rob her of being who she was? She was a fighter, a warrior, to her very core. She had the heart of a Bowman. But as he looked at her soot-covered face and examined the scrapes on her elbows, his heart ached.

Too tired, too brittle, he wanted to bolt out the door and begin unraveling the web of problems facing him, but he simply couldn't leave yet.

Tess reached out and gently touched his knee. "How did we do, Captain?" She searched his eyes.

Crouching next to the bed, he exhaled. He would answer this one question and then find a way to leave.

"We did okay. You did outstanding!"

She appeared to be straining to keep her eyes open and hold his gaze.

"The castle is secured. You sank the first ship and Deac sank the second. I disabled the fifth and two galleons got away clean. They took flight, on their way to Costair. You're on *The Dancing Girl* right now, and the crew is fine."

"You mean schooners, Captain, not galleons." She closed her eyes, allowing her head to sink deep into the pillow.

His hand began to tremble. A release from battle rush. He hated to admit what he was about to say. "No, Tess, two galleons escaped the river unscathed, inflated their blimpoons and flew down the coast." Failure pressed down on his chest like an anvil.

She pushed off the thin mattress with her elbows, raising her head, eyes wide. "How in the Realm could they fly. You saw them. Those were the largest ships I've ever seen. Ships that large can't fly!" Indignation echoed in the small room.

He turned to Deacon. "How could they do it, Deac? How could they heat the air efficiently enough in blimpoons that size? You saw them. They were enormous. Blast, Deac, they breached our borders with enough troops to unseat the king. For Realm's sake, how is that possible?"

Deacon fidgeted with his spyglass. He collapsed the sections, extended them, and then collapsed them again, clenching his jaw tight.

He slapped Deacon's arm with the back of his hand. "What is it? What aren't you telling me?"

Deacon sighed and shut the spyglass tight between his thumb and index finger. "The Reyjik, Colt. They suddenly have a form of gray powder that is stable enough to burn without exploding, and it can superheat air faster than anything we've ever had." He ran both hands through his hair and squinted his eyes shut in agony. "Up until about six months ago, all lighter than airships were small, big enough to raid hoists but light and not a real threat in terms of firepower. *The Dancing Girl* is really pushing the limits of the old fuel needed to heat her blimpoon. With this new gray powder, I've heard you can inflate and heat bigger blimpoons, but I never thought that big."

All warmth drained from Colt's face.

Deac stared down at his knees.

Tess cocked her head. "What's the matter, Captain. That information is helpful, isn't it?"

Colt turned in her direction, but he couldn't bear to look her in the eye. His people were traitors. They had trampled over Sacramance. They'd done it repeatedly.

Deacon sank beside him, sitting cross legged. He fidgeted with the spyglass. "See, Princess, Colt's had it harder than most, growing up half-Reyjik. That's one of the reasons he fights so well, and did he ever need to fight. He had to fight for respect in Thornton and then again in the regulars and then again in the Bowman corps, and he managed to win them all over." Deacon grabbed his knee, but Colt couldn't look up.

Deac's hand trembled. "I think the only reason he could stand so tall was because deep down he was proud to be Reyjik. I've never once heard him apologize for it because he believed they were honorable. As strong as bladespar itself was his resolve that his mother's people were tough, ingenious, and principled, so he didn't care that he looked like them or that he was tall like them because he wasn't ashamed of anything they'd ever done."

His heart splintered. Touched by Deacon's insight, he couldn't take any more. He needed to leave.

Deacon's grip on his knee intensified. "Listen, Colt, I don't know how the Reyjik got the fuel, but it hit the black market."

Heat rushed back into Colt's face. "Why didn't you say anything on Cooper's Cliffs? I asked you outright and you said they were too big to fly. If you knew all this, why didn't you say something?"

Releasing his knee, Deac's hand pressed to his heart. "I only heard rumours. You know how raiders talk. I didn't believe half of what they said about the stuff. They were only rumours, Colt."

He forced his tone to remain even and calm. "Well, those rumours have flown seaward to kill our king and his men."

Tess reached down and grabbed Colt's hand, still clenched tight. Her soot covered fingers were cool, and soft, and smooth. "But you didn't know. You can't always know everything. You did an outstanding job, Captain. You saved Ardenia, just like you promised." She whispered the words.

Overwhelmed with a sense of failure, inadequacy, and shame, he knew with total certainty that he had not truly done well. Two ships threated the very sovereignty of their tier. Once they had routed the king in Costair, they would fly skyward and finish what they had started. They would send for reinforcements. They could not have embarked on this venture without a means to finish it all.

He rose and walked to the door. Ahead of him lay a night of endless planning and briefing. When he glanced back, Deacon had taken his place at Tess's bedside.

Colt longed to sit there. He ached to sit with her as she rested and recovered, but he couldn't. Duty called him straight back to the fight. "Get some sleep, Princess." He eased the door closed behind him and headed for the recently commandeered HQ.

* * *

Scanning the room, Colt studied the exhausted men that sat before him. He wanted nothing more than to order them to their hammocks, but they couldn't afford the luxury of rest. They desperately needed to plan. Shifty, Sam, Reynolds, Riley, and Deacon all stared back at him. Colt reminded himself to begin at the beginning.

"Okay, let's put what we know on the table. First, let's talk about the problem. We have at least eight hundred Reyjik ready and waiting on the plains north of Castle Costair. They have the strength of the castle and all the arms and supplies that come with it. We have our king, who will arrive tomorrow with a thousand men. They traveled light and fast, no doubt, and will be expecting a force of four hundred, not eight hundred. We have two ships bringing at least eight hundred fresh troops to reinforce the enemy. They will arrive tomorrow night if they fly straight for the precipice and then on to Marduke."

The men's faces were grave. They understood the bleak situation, he didn't need to spell it out for them.

He was about to list their assets when the door slowly creaked open. Every man in the room turned to see the princess.

Holding tight to a blanket wrapped around her shoulders, Tess offered them a small smile before walking slowly to the bed. She had cleaned the smoke and soot from her face and had let down her hair and combed it. Carefully climbing up, she propped herself against the wall, then tucked the blanket around her legs and rested her head against the wall for support. "I only want to hear what's happening, Captain. I'll sit here with my eyes closed and listen."

This seemed irresponsible. Tess should rest. Colt could only shake his head and smile as he tried to refocus on an honest assessment of their assets. "All right, what can we do about all this? Let's think. We know *The Girl* can make it to Dungridge by dawn, if we sail straight without stopping. She doesn't need to fight again, we only need her to fly. Is she airworthy? How long to ready the blimpoon, raise more men, and take off for Costair?"

Deacon narrowed his eyes and cocked his head to one side. "She's a mess, Colt, but we can have her ready in about an hour. Maybe two. That's with all hands-on deck, about forty more men."

Crushed by a wave of guilt, he stood and walked to Deacon's side. He had just assumed that Deac and his men were at his disposal, along with the already crippled ship? He couldn't continue without addressing that. "I apologize, Deacon."

The pirate's eyes widened. "For what?"

"I forget you're not military. You and your crew have given the most. I have risked all your lives and totally compromised *The Girl*. Now I am assuming you will give more, risk your lives again. I'm sorry for being so arrogant. I just get so focused sometimes. You aren't obligated to give any more. You can wash your hands of all this at Dungridge."

Leaning back, Deacon clasped his hands behind his head and looked up at him. "Oh, we're finishing this, Colt, be sure of that. You keep scheming away. Whatever I can give you, you'll get."

Brittle and exhausted, he swallowed hard and nodded.

Tess raised her hand like a girl in primer school. "Captain Thornby, my father will compensate you for any losses you incur. You and your men will be paid handsomely for your service. You have my word."

Deacon nodded and smiled warmly at her.

Regaining a solid grip on his composure, he swallowed hard and took his seat. "All right, so two hours at the most puts us in the Sislay River sometime in the middle of the night. We might make it in time to be of help. The question is, how much help can we give them? Our guns won't reach the battlefield from the river, and we'll be shot out of the sky if we fly within range. Ninety men aren't going to make much of a difference, although we do have three strong archers." Colt nodded at Deacon to show that he was including him in that tally.

When he risked a look at her, Tess smiled at him through drooping eyelids.

"That's if you're up to it, Your Highness. Fallman knows we could use another one-in-a-million shot like that."

She blushed.

"But three archers won't make a dent in sixteen hundred men

either. We need to think of some way to help the king. Blast! We simply need more men.”

He couldn't hide his frustration over the situation. “I'm going to get some fresh air.” He rose and crossed the floor to the door without making eye contact with anyone in the room. He was letting them down. He should have the answers, but he didn't.

He strode to the bow of the ship. The sky was clear, the stars brilliant overhead. He had to walk carefully to make sure he didn't turn his ankle in one of the craters left from the battle, the deck of *The Dancing Girl* now littered with holes left from ten-pound shot. Leaning against the railing, he closed his eyes. If he could just clear his mind completely.

Someone touched his right arm. Tess stood at the railing, wrapped in the blanket. Her feet were bare, explaining how she'd approached without a sound. She gazed out over the sea, not looking at him or speaking. She just leaned on the railing and watched the cliffs pass by.

Colt contemplated the slate cliffs and the emerald star, the very symbol of their tier, sparkling in the moonlight. It had never looked so brilliant to him before. The Tarragon had taken up roost in the crags, and they dropped and swooped over the forest, feeding on the swarms of blackflies that plagued the woods in spring. For a moment, standing there on the deck with her, he felt the way he had in the Bowman lookout back in Costair. He remembered being desperate to say something that would impress the girl who could shoot so well. The moment seemed a lifetime ago.

“Captain, remember being up in the lookout in Costair, before all this happened?” How could she do that, read his mind?

“I was thinking about that just now, Princess.” He turned to lean against the railing and face the stern. “Will you finally tell me who taught you to shoot?”

The most mischievous smirk crossed her lips. “Colonel Merriweather taught me to shoot when he trained my brothers.”

Colt's mouth dropped open. Colonel Merriweather, chief superintendent of the Bowmen, a legend, and the best archer in the history of the corps, had trained her. “Colonel Merriweather? Are you serious? He is the very best! I haven't even met the man.”

"He's a friend of my father's." Tess placed her hand on his arm. "And I think you're the better shot."

He wanted to say something to compliment her, but she looked down and tilted her head as she gently ran her finger along his scarred forearm. He forgot that he had rolled up his sleeves to accommodate his archer arm guards and hadn't yet unrolled them. He made a habit of keeping them cuffed, and for good reason—his arms were horribly scarred from his fingers to his elbows. His instincts told him to pull his arm away and cover his marred skin, but her touch felt so soft, he couldn't bring himself to do it. He swallowed hard. "We all have them, anyone who's ever spent a summer harvesting in Thornton."

"You hide them on purpose, don't you?"

His breathing shallowed. "Yes, I think we all do. It marks us, you know, as the poorest wretches of the entire tier. Not even enough money for the gloves that prevent them." He faked a laugh. Would she see through it?

She only smiled, and he relaxed against the railing, watching her.

Pulling her finger away, she began tracing the woodgrain of the railing. "I remember when you leaned on the railing up in the lookout, exactly like that. I couldn't believe how comfortable you were up so high. It was so high up there, remember?"

"This coming from the girl who spends her time on top of the castle wall? I was up there yesterday, Princess. That is a formidable drop."

Her face softened and looked even sweeter. "Did you name your tarragon?"

His heartrate quickened. He'd wanted to bring up the strange connection he'd felt since discovering they had both nursed the same wild creature. "Maybe, did you?"

"Yes, Berkely. I called him Berkley."

Colt laughed. Under no circumstance would he admit his name for their pet —Wingblade had never seemed so juvenile.

She giggled as well, and then her face softened again. "You mentioned finding him the spring your father died?" When he nodded, she looked back to the cliffs. "That's so strange because I lost someone as well, my nurse, and Berkely needed my help the same month she was sent home. When I look back on it, nursing Berkely did me a lot of good, took my mind off my loss, you know?"

He did know, he knew exactly. But why was her nurse sent away? Where was home? He reached over and gently rested his hand on her arm.

"Why did your nurse need to leave?"

She folded a splinter of wood, no doubt broken and bent from an explosion, flat on the railing where it belonged. "MaryLee was only thirteen when my mother died. She visited on a language exchange, but when my mother passed, my father was desperate for help. She was good with me, and she stayed. She lived with us for eight years, and I loved her. The problem was that everyone loved her, including my oldest brother. Derek wanted to marry her, and he asked my father's permission. Instead, my father sent her seaward." Tess's eyes misted over.

His heart ached for her. Why would the king do that? "But she was your nurse. Didn't he care that it would hurt you? Didn't he see that you had already lost your mother and that losing this girl would devastate you at that age? What could be so bad that he would do that to you?" Grabbing the railing, he gripped his fingers around the smooth wood.

She fixed another ragged railing edge, pushing it into place with her nimble fingers. "Nothing, there was absolutely nothing wrong with her, but she wasn't royal, and she wasn't Ardenian, she was Reyjik."

A knife twisted in Colt's side, pure agony, and not because of the blatant bigotry from the very man he'd sworn to protect. He grieved for Tess. She had already lost so much, he couldn't bear the thought of her losing this girl, a surrogate mother, because of her father's selfish notions regarding societal pretense.

He touched her arm gently, and she turned to him. "I am so sorry, Tess. He should never have sent her away, if only for your sake." Looking deep into her sad eyes, his heart melted.

"It's all right. Our lives aren't supposed to be about us. We're supposed to give, help, and serve, I just learned that younger than most, maybe. But it's better than the alternative, never learning it at all. Sometimes, I just need to be alone. That's why I ran to the lookout that night. If I hadn't, we would have been swept up in the onslaught."

Tess's eyes grew wide. "Colt. We saw everything from up there, remember? After we heard that first cannon shot, you peered through your spyglass and called out all sorts of information about the attack. And then we ran to the grove, and you confirmed it all. Maybe some of that information could be useful. What did you tell me? The number of men on the wall. The number of men who took up position on the plains. The number of men who had surrounded the ballroom and the barracks?"

His heart pounded. "The soldiers," he whispered. "There must be hundreds of men at arms and archers and knights locked in those barracks."

She nodded, her eyes dancing. "Besides the barracks, there were about a hundred officers locked in the ballroom. Do you think we could get to them? Do you think we could free them all and arm them?" She squeezed his arm.

He gazed into her eyes and a strange sensation overwhelmed him—something he couldn't really control.

"Let's go, Captain. We need to plan." She squeezed his arm again and pushed off the railing.

Colt nodded, but he didn't want to go back yet. He wanted to stay at the bow, just as they were. As she turned to the bridge and he watched her walk away, a terrible doubt crashed through his mind. Would he have thought of the Costair soldiers on his own? So much of everything he'd managed during the last few days involved Tess, her help. His stomach churned. No. He didn't need her or anyone else. He'd never needed anyone, but somewhere in the deepest recesses of his heart, that doubt wouldn't drown, it whispered and echoed through his soul. He needed her. *No, it couldn't be true. How could it be true, she was just a girl? This had to stop.* He couldn't abide continually placing her in danger because he needed her. He wouldn't let it be true!

Chapter Twenty-Six

The Impossible

Tess

THE SAME TIRED MEN FILLED DEACON'S quarters, but this time things were different. This time, instead of staring into a bleak future, they stared into the downright impossible. Tess tried to read the men as she and Colt laid out their plans. One idea birthed another, a rapid succession of hopeful *what-ifs*, nothing concrete or based in fact. Everything they hashed out rooted in one common foundation—hope. Three times, one of the men had interrupted her and Colt with some version of, *and how do you know that?* To which they immediately and unapologetically answered, *we don't.*

They were almost halfway through, and the men were confounded, none of them truly grasped their plan, it was written on every face. Even Deacon struggled to keep up. Tess herself was exhausted, cold, and still shaky, but she was determined to help. Colt needed her. The look on his face had shouted it when he learned of the new gray powder, and the Reyjik's hand in it all. She shook herself. She would best this weakness. In the meantime, she still needed the blanket's extra warmth and she needed to sit with her back propped against the wall beside the bed for support. Talking tired her, but she'd read the room and knew the men needed to truly grasp the plan or they would never trust it.

Examining the rough drawing of Castle Costair that Colt had rendered, a bird's-eye-view of the wall, she noted the gate and every building. He had used one of Deacon's graphite sketching sticks. The discovery of Deacon's hobby had caused a great deal of interest amongst the pirate's officers, and even Colt had laughed as he flipped through Deac's sketch pad.

As she looked over the castle drawing for the hundredth time, she tried to focus on the most critical parts of their plan and everything that was necessary if it were to unfold as they hoped.

Colt argued with Deacon over the merits of his men wearing Ardenian regular uniforms. When Colt rubbed his eyes for the tenth time, she found a strength deep inside.

After clearing her throat, she spoke. "Sorry, Captain." She would have raised her hand to speak, but her sore arm convinced her not to make the effort. "I'd like to lay it all out at once for everyone. Captain Thornby, I know you're having a hard time with the plan, but I think it will come together if you can hear it all at once." She met his gaze, silently pleading for his attention for just a little longer.

He smiled warmly at her, and her stomach wrenched tight. His strange profession before the battle, which wasn't entirely clear, made her feel a little nauseated.

She took a shallow breath.

Deacon crossed his arms. "I'll go over it again, Princess, but I'm pretty sure it isn't gonna sound any more possible this time through. The whole thing would take a miracle."

For the first time, she noticed his scars, same as Colt's from his wrists to his elbows.

"That's right, Deac, a miracle. Every detail depends on the detail before. I agree, we have no way to be sure of any of it, not until we are in the thick of it. But we are not going to quit. I mean, that's not an option. We are just going to have to hope." She shot a look at Colt, who smiled at her and nodded his solidarity. Why did his approval mean so much to her?

"We hit Dungridge in about an hour and a half. Deac, the Captain and I will go to Old Ebeneezer's and try to get an Ardenian regulars' uniform for every man that flies with us. I know you all hate this idea, but I hate something even more. I hate the idea of burying one of you because you were killed by friendly fire. So, you are all wearing the uniforms."

She shifted her gaze towards the first mate. "Reynolds, you'll ready *The Dancing Girl*. Focus on shot, powder, and arms. If you have arrows, swords, anything, stow it. You'll need to ditch everything else on board. We have to lighten her as much as possible to compensate for the weight of more men. We don't need food as badly as we need weapons. If things go well, we'll have the provisions in the castle. If things go badly, well, you don't feel hungry when you're dead." This last statement might have been too dramatic, but the men seemed to be with her. "Time in Dungridge is critical. We want to lift off as soon as we possibly can. We'll need the cover of night when we try and sneak into the castle." She nodded at Colt. He was the expert on what came next. "Captain, do you want to continue?"

Colt rose and walked over to the drawing of the castle. "Thanks, Princess. All right, we haven't been through this part. We are going to disembark a team of four to infiltrate here, the very north side of the castle. Castle Costair sits right on the edge of the precipice. The sheer cliff drops straight down to the Dark Sea, and it's impassible… at least, it was when it was built, before lighter than aircraft were invented."

She pointed to the location on the map, and every man in the room smiled from ear to ear, even Colt.

"Deac, how good are you at keeping the girl steady when she flies? She'll need to be steady enough to let a small team of four climb to the castle wall. There's a window on the back wall that leads to a passage that's been closed off. I can get us in here as long as we can get close enough."

Rubbing his chin, Deac examined the rendering and squinted at the location Colt had indicated. "I don't know, Colt. What are the downdrafts like? We ran into trouble with downdrafts that night you saw us. If we get that close, I'm afraid the same thing will happen, that the wind will push a fin or the blimpoon itself straight down. We survived it last time, but we might not be that lucky, which is a big risk considering we haven't even got to the really miraculous part." Uncrossing his arms, he began bouncing his right leg up and down at an alarming rate. "How on earth are you going to get through the castle, to the barracks, and free the men without being seen and shot?"

Colt took the pirate's concerns in stride. They both knew this was the part most reliant on hope. "We are going to count on the darkness and the late hour for some help. I figure most of the Reyjik will have taken up position on the battlefield on the south side. They may even be engaged with the king if the battle has started. We are hoping that most of the men guarding the barracks will have been called out to join the ranks. Then, we'll cause a distraction on the river. We'll take a page from the princess's book and blow a powder keg or two. *The Girl* will float over the Sislay and conduct an aerial attack on the ships moored there."

Colt tapped the Marduke docks jutting out into the Sislay River. "We'll need to time everything perfectly. We will be relying on stealth and shadows and a miracle, really. But I know the castle layout perfectly. I will supply covering fire from a location on the wall, here." He pointed out a place on the inner wall, up against a low tower that marked a corner. From this position, he could cover the entire courtyard and successfully sharpshoot any guard who noticed their presence. "If Princess Aratess positions here"—he tapped another point on the map—"we should be in good shape to stop anyone from raising an alarm."

Deacon rubbed his head with both hands before letting out a long, dramatic sigh. "Let's say that you manage to get into position on the wall. Then let's say you manage to be all stealthy like and don't rouse an alarm. My real problem with all this hangs on the fact that everything depends on the very bleak hope that the troops inside the barracks are alive and have been fed for the last four days."

Silence swept the room. No one dared move. Tess glanced at Colt, but he held Deacon's gaze. Both men looked grave.

"Colt, I hate to be the one to bring this up, but it needs to be said. Those men could all be dead. Why would the Reyjik spare and feed hundreds of soldiers? Men who could revolt and unseat them? They wouldn't! They would kill them at the first opportunity to stomp out the threat they pose. There is absolutely no reason they should be alive, and you are hanging the entire plan on the fact that they are. You both charged in here with this miraculous plan, which is absolutely reckless, and the riskiest thing I have ever heard. Bear in mind that I'm a pirate and have conceived terrible plans in the past. Even so, I could get behind it if the entire thing didn't hinge on those men being alive. Colt, why in the Realm would the Reyjik have spared and fed them?"

Tess's heart swelled, and she pushed off the wall and sat at attention. "Because of the Sacramance Accord, Deacon. It breaks the Sacramance Accord to kill prisoners in times of war. Those men have been held prisoner, unarmed since the very first moment of the invasion. They never had a chance to revolt or pose a threat, Gerhert made sure of that, so it would break Sacramance to kill them."

Deac wagged his head from side to side. "Nope, Tess, that doesn't fit. The Reyjik have attacked their trade partners. They have invaded sovereign soil, and they have used lighter-than-air craft to do it. All three of those break Sacramance. Their emperor has thrown Sacramance right off Freefall and watched it plummet all the way to the mist below. They've proven they don't give a rip about Sacramance, and we need to assume the worst of them."

"No!" Colt smacked a hand on the table and all heads swiveled in his direction. "No, Deac, they wouldn't, they couldn't do that, not that. They are an honorable people, and they wouldn't kill unarmed prisoners, I know it!"

Deacon shifted to the edge of his chair and placed both hands firmly on his knees. "Colt, I'm with you on this. I want to help you. I will do almost anything you ask of me, but I can't fly *The Girl,* full of men who trust me to lead them, into a warzone, risking all their lives, based on your faith that the Reyjik are honorable. Those men are dead. Nothing else makes sense, and you said it yourself—without those men we have nothing."

Colt's eyes revealed pain. He sat perfectly still, focused on Deacon, but somewhere deep inside his mind, he was slowly unraveling, Tess was sure of it. She needed to do something to help him. "The Emerald Star! The captain could confirm it with the Emerald Star."

Every man shifted their attention from Colt to her. She lifted her chin. "Don't look at me like that. Every last one of you knows that the Emerald Star confirms truth. My father consults it at least once a year. You've seen it glow; everyone has seen it glow."

Deacon and Colt shared a look before Deac leaned forward and ran his hands slowly through his hair. "Princess, none of us is allowed anywhere near the Emerald Star. Only the king can use it. Not to mention the fact we don't have the time to climb up there. The return climb takes a day."

Her spirits soared. "No, Captain Thornby, that's not the rule. The truth of the star is for the use of the ranking monarch to bestow as they choose. With my father and brothers and Sasha off tier, that's me. I am the ranking monarch, and I bestow it on our Bowman. We don't need to waste a day on the climb. You're going to fly us up there immediately. The captain will make his statement, that the Reyjik have shown mercy and kept the Costairs alive. The star will glow, and then we won't waste another second. We'll fly down there and start fighting for our tierdom."

She pressed her hands together, studying Colt. Deacon wasn't the real problem, it was Colt. He had already confessed he didn't believe in the power of the star. Would he even entertain her idea? Did he have a choice?

After a moment, Colt met her gaze. His eyes softened, and the smallest smile touched the corner of his mouth.

Chapter Twenty-Seven

The Emerald Star

Tess

TESS STOOD DIRECTLY UNDER THE WOODEN frame. Shaped like an octagon, the frame attached to billows of Reyjik silk that lay piled on the deck around her. Deacon walked straight to her, lamp in hand. Without a word, he took her hand in his and led her under the central hole of the frame, ducking so he would clear the funnel point and could stand dead center. She followed him and Deacon removed the glass hurricane globe from the lamp and handed it to her. He winked and jerked his head towards the fuel source.

Grasping the handle of the small lamp, she touched the open flame to the burner. Instantly, the fuel ignited. Heat emanated from the burner, and the air above appeared watery. Instinctively, she leaned back. The sheets of silk surrounding her began to shift, ruffle, and rise. A bead of sweat trickled down her forehead, and she suddenly felt lightheaded. Deacon grabbed her hand and pulled her down through the circular access ring, the air below fresh and cool. How could it heat the air so quickly?

"Well, Princess, there she is. You asked how it all works. That's all there is to it. The fuel burns super hot, as I'm sure you felt. It heats the air, and the light air rises. The silk is a new Reyjik weave, or so I've been told. It traps the hot air, and we all rise with it." He tugged on her hand and pulled her to the port side of the ship. "Our fins help direct us, and *The Girl's* original keel gives a little stability, but truly, if you don't know how to ride the wind, you're at its mercy."

Every mast, hinged just above the deck, lay horizontal, and the blimpoon continued to stretch to its full size. Tess ran to the bowsprit so she could see as much of it as possible. It looked enormous, dwarfing the schooner that hung suspended below. She couldn't wipe the smile off her face. *The Girl* began to rise out of the water. The bladespar cables that connected the blimpoon to the ship creaked under the strain, but she continued to rise. Straight up and then towards the slate cliffs of Ardenia.

Colt crossed the deck and leaned against the bowsprit beside her, his face pinched with worry. "So, Princess, you said I need to make a statement, not ask a question?"

She smiled at him. Despite his skepticism, he seemed to be trying. "Yes, you say something like, 'The soldiers of Costair are alive and well and able to fight,' and the stone will glow to confirm it. Don't worry, Captain, I know the stone will confirm it. I can feel it. The plan will work, I just know it will."

He smiled, but the worry in his eyes didn't melt away.

Smiling back, she pointed to the breathtaking view that stretched out beneath them. She watched a pair of tarragon as they glided near the surface of the inland sea. Colt stepped closer, and together they watched as the sea gave way to the shoreline, then Gilbet's, then Tapper's Elbow, all passing beneath them. After a few minutes, they soared slowly over Fairgates, her wall, and beloved Samson. Tess felt free.

* * *

Colt drew his bowstring and took aim three yards above the largest vein of emerald. Pitch black, the night enveloped *The Dancing Girl*. If not for the deck lanterns, he wouldn't be able to see the massive cliff that loomed only fifteen yards away, as the clouds and mist had completely blocked the moon. Inhaling, he steadied his arm and then jumped as Tess rested her hand on his left forearm and eased his bow seaward. He returned his bowstring to a resting position. The princess's face glowed in the lamp light, her eyes filled with concern.

"Shoot, Princess, I nearly fired. What is it, are you all right?"

"Yes, no, I don't know. Captain, this is important. This is sacred. It's real. You need to know that, to believe that. This stone has helped lead our people for generations. I'm not sure it will work if you don't believe. I know what you think about it…"

Colt raised his finger and gently rested it on her lips. Her eyes widened.

"I don't actually know what I think, Princess."

Her face softened.

"I will give it my very best shot, I promise."

Her lower lip quivered ever so slightly.

"I promise I will try to believe. I won't waste the opportunity. You have my word." Gently, he passed his finger over her lower lip. It felt so soft. *Breathe, Colt.* He lowered his right hand to his bowstring.

Her eyes misted over. She nodded and stepped back.

He took another deep breath, sighted the open slate between the veins, and fired. The specialized bladespar anchor tip bit deep into the cliff face, cleaving the stone as designed. He tugged the rope twice, testing the hold of the ingenious arrowhead, as solid as he could hope for. His heart pounded as he walked to the edge of the deck and peered over the starboard side of the schooner that floated five hundred yards above the castle woods. After retrieving the second rope from his rucksack, he tied off one end to the railing. Using a lock knot, he attached the free end of the safety rope to his Bowman belt. A few twists of standard rope would hold his very fate and the fate of the realm, so he checked them twice.

The winds were light for the moment, and the downdraft hadn't caused any problems yet. Glancing over his shoulder, he caught the entire crew of expectant raiders and one very concerned princess watching his every move. He nodded to Deacon, grabbed hold of the rope with both hands, planted his foot on the railing, and jumped.

Swinging directly to the face of the cliff, he raised his feet in anticipation of the impact, absorbing it with his legs and knees accordingly, a perfect landing. Now for the tricky part. He walked up the side of the cliff, hauling himself skyward hand over hand, wishing he could have rigged his harness and pulley system. Choosing each foothold with the utmost care, he tried not to over tense his grip on the rough rope. It took only a minute to reach the stone. His heartrate quickened. Would this work? Would the stone sense his skepticism?

Did the fact that he even worried about that possibility betray that part of him might actually believe?

Shaking his head, Colt focused on the stone. It appeared rough and dull, no facets or shimmer or sparkle at all. Letting go of the rope with his right hand, he traced a tiny vein of the kimberlite with his index finger. At his touch, the entire web of emerald began to glow in slow, rhythmic pulses. he nearly let go of the rope with his left hand. When he shot a look over his shoulder, his gaze locked with Tess's.

She leaned way over the railing, smiling at him.

His heart pounded harder, and he forced himself to focus on the central stone as he raised his right hand over it. Just as his palm made contact with the pulsing jewel, green runes began to glow in the slate above. Two lines, written in Old-Realmish carved into the slate, flashed above the sacred jewel. How was that possible? His stomach tightened as he whispered the words to himself.

"If truth ye seek, ye may speak, and my light shall shine for those words most right. But know ye this, thy chance do not miss. For only at the deepest truth that thy soul seeks shall my light shine bright. True to your heart or no truth at all shall shine for thee this night." What? What in the Realm did that mean? Colt read the warning twice more. His arms ached, and perspiration formed on his forehead, despite the white clouds of breath puffing from his lips. Blast!

He looked over his shoulder at Tess again, biting his lip.

She clung to the railing, leaning as far towards him as possible. "What is it, Colt, what's wrong?"

What's wrong? Only everything, Tess! He knew exactly what the words meant. He felt them in the very core of his being. The stone would confirm the truth he spoke, but only if it was the truth for which his soul longed the most.

Closing his eyes, Colt couldn't even pretend to care most about the reality that waited for them in Reyjik. His soul longed for one truth, one far above every other. Did he need Tess? Did he truly need her to finish all this? He knew for certain he'd never relied on anyone's help before. He also knew he'd never felt like this before, simultaneously lost and found, as if he could accomplish anything with her at his side yet paralyzed by the guilt of needing her with him. After all, being with him placed her in constant danger, which was the very thing he'd sworn to prevent at all costs. But could he still perform his duty, all that the Realm needed, without her? Blast! He'd failed. Not only had he let himself rely on Tess, he'd failed to remain focused. Now the mission would suffer.

What should he do? Should he make the statement he had planned to make and hope the stone didn't know? What a ridiculous concept. How could the stone know anything at all? It was only an emerald, and yet, legend told that the magic of the stone came from the All-Father. He had placed the four stones in the four tiers to guide men to truth and restrain evil. Did Colt believe that? His arm ached.

"Wind is picking up, Colt. You think we could get a move on?" Deacon spoke slow and easy, but Colt caught the edge in his voice. He had run out of time. He had run out of time and excuses. Deacon seemed sure that Colt and Tess could overcome absolutely any obstacle together. When Colt thought about it through that lens, it seemed a strength, not a weakness. Unless it meant that Deacon believed Colt couldn't manage on his own.

Closing his eyes, he tried to clear his mind. Doubts swirled and fears crashed against the break wall of his heart. He opened his eyes, cleared his throat, and pressed his hand firmly against the dull, domed jewel. Instantly, everything went quiet. His eyes closed involuntarily, and his mind focused to a razor's edge, as though every thought was being sifted, refined in the fire, and only one remained critical, pure enough to warrant every ounce of his focus.

Did he need her?

"I... I need Princess Aratess." The words, barely a whisper, passed his lips with the greatest effort. No sooner had he spoken them, than he heard screams and cheers from the schooner hanging in the air behind him. Colt opened his eyes, only to close them instantly, for a blinding green light flashed inches from his face. Forcing himself to try again, he squinted, only allowing his lashes to part by the slightest degree. Even then, his vision filled with brilliant green light.

The safety line pulled hard on his belt, and he fell backwards. Apparently, Deacon had come to the end of his patience. Keeping his wits as he plunged through the air, past the hovering ship, Colt managed to hold onto the rope anchored to his specialized arrowhead, letting it slip slowly through his loose grip. He couldn't let go of that rope. He only had one arrowhead, and he might need it again. When he reached the end of it with a jerk, he hung suspended in the air, doubled at the waist, dangling under *The Dancing Girl* on his safety line and prevented from plummeting to the ground only by the lock knot he had tied to his Bowman belt minutes before swinging to the cliff.

Obviously, Deacon didn't want to wait for him to swing back to the ship of his own accord, or maybe he enjoyed seeing Colt in the helpless position in which he now found himself. As the men hoisted him onboard, he considered his situation. He still had no idea if the Costairs locked in the barracks were alive, and he couldn't lie about it, his oath would not allow him. He also couldn't let anyone know what he'd declared and why the emerald star shone.

Colt swung around and took it all in. The entire cliff face shone, sparkled, and glowed. At the center, the emerald star pulsed a blinding green light. It reminded him of a heartbeat, his heart. Since he was a child, he'd overcome any challenge alone, and as he reached for the ship's railing, a deep aching, one he'd never known, cascaded through him, setting off a chain reaction of fear and doubt.

Once on the solid deck, he looped his lead line around his arm and pulled straight back, attempting to retrieve his anchor arrow. The anchor tip didn't budge, but he needed to busy himself with something. He couldn't face them. What could he say?

"Well, I guess them Costairs must be all right, Bowman. The Princess says the star has never shone so bright in all recorded history, whatever that means." Shifty slapped him on the back, as did every other man on the deck, each slap pounding the reality of his situation deeper into his soul.

A crowd formed around him. *I better get it over with.*

Lowering the line still connected to the cliff, Colt looped the end of the rope around the railing. Then he walked to the middle of the deck. The anchor arrow would have to wait, he needed to confess. He raised his hand up to get the attention of all present.

"Stop, everyone, please. I didn't ask about the Costairs in the barracks. I couldn't. I…" The deck of the schooner fell silent, and he stopped, caught off guard by their reaction to his confession. The wind whistled as it circumvented the huge blimpoon. Bladespar cables creaked and wood shifted.

"Sweet Eve of Descent, Colt, what are you talking about? Why didn't you ask about the Costairs?" Stepping out from the crowd, Deacon faced him, eyes narrowed.

Heat pulsed through Colt's entire body. How could he explain? Every pair of eyes locked onto him, waiting for an answer, including Tess's. He turned from her slightly and directed his attention to the men. "I couldn't, Deac. There is a condition, a caveat, that comes with using the stone. You can only ask what your heart longs to know most or it won't answer and I... I..." He couldn't force the words out.. He rubbed his eyes, hard, with both hands. If only he could rub it all away. The guilt over his failure in this regard weighed too heavily, pushed down on him to the point of crushing. How did the ship remain airborne under the weight of this guilt? What could he possibly do to fix it now?

"Captain, she's jumped!" Shifty's scream broke the tense silence. Every man whirled in his direction, and they all gasped at the sight of Tess swinging to the cliff face.

Colt ran back to the railing, cold shuddering through him.

She had used his anchor line, but she didn't have a safety rope. What if she let go? What if the wind picked up? She had wrapped the rope around her left arm, as he had done, and placed her right hand over the stone.

The men were silent again, every pirate clearly holding his breath for worry over the girl they'd come to love.

In a clear, strong voice, she made her declaration. "The soldiers trapped in Costair are alive and well and will help us."

More gasps echoed around the deck as the emerald star that had dimmed after his return to the ship glowed bright again. Not nearly as blinding as the flash Colt's statement had produced, but enough to confirm her truth all the same. She had done it. Like a true Bowman, she cared about the mission most.

His mind sprang into action. "Deac, drop us below her."

Waving his understanding, Deacon leapt to the burner.

Colt leaned as far over the railing as he could, cupping his hands to his mouth. "Princess, wait for us to get underneath you, and then kick off with both feet, swing out as far as you can, drop, and I'll catch you!"

"Understood, Captain!" She waited, watching over her shoulder until *The Girl* slowly sank seaward. Then she pushed, swung, and released the rope without hesitation. At exactly the same moment, a strong downdraft caught the starboard fin, and *The Girl* dipped seaward and to port. Colt braced himself against the sudden movement, watching in horror as Tess passed just beyond his reach. Without thinking, he launched himself over the railing and after her.

He plunged into the night, only falling for a few seconds before his arms clasped her slender waist. A moment later, the safety rope still attached to his Bowman belt jerked tight. Their momentum carried them all the way under the ship, a shower of seawater soaking them as they swung.

Tess held tight to his shoulders, her face buried in his chest. Slowly, she inched back far enough to look him in the eye.

His heart beat so fast he thought it might burst. Everything outside of the two of them stopped, faded. The drop, the ship, the raining seawater, all of it seemed to blur into the background.

Her long eyelashes dripped with water. "Nice catch."

He smiled. "Yeah."

"Thanks, Captain." Her lashes fluttered, but she held his gaze. *Say something, Colt. Tell her.*

The rope jerked skyward, and he grasped her tighter still. The closer to the hull, the worse the dripping water soaked them.

"Well, I guess we were due for a bath anyway." She tightened her grip around his neck and rested her face against his chest again. Could she hear his heart? Could she tell it needed her?

Deacon's face looked paler than Colt had ever seen. Even before Tess had cleared the railing, he pulled her from Colt and into his arms, holding her tight the entire time it took to undo the lock-knot that connected Colt's belt to the safety line.

Tess rested her head on Deacon's shoulder and laughed occasionally at whatever he said.

Colt's stomach cinched tight, as if it needed any more strain.

Finally, he released her, and she made her way clear of him.

Deacon walked over to Colt. "That was some catch!" He slapped him on the back the way he always did. "Reynolds will fly us to Dungridge. You better get back to briefing us on this great plan you and the princess cooked up."

Deacon threw his arm across Colt's back and pulled him in tight, then steered him towards his quarters.

Colt nodded as he peered around the pirate, searching the deck crew for Tess. Finally, he located her. She knelt at the railing, facing the star, praying. She had done it. What he couldn't get right, she'd managed. The star was right. Never in his entire life had Colt felt like such a failure.

Chapter Twenty-Eight

The Hitch

Deacon

DEACON'S HAND STILL TREMBLED. HE HADN'T expected the shocking display of magic he'd just witnessed. Never in his life did he think he would even consider believing in the stone, yet he couldn't deny what he had seen. He shifted in his chair, stared down at the drawing, and tried to focus on the rest of the plan, but flashes of green still edged the corners of his vision. *Concentrate, Deacon!*

He cleared his throat. "All right, Colt, who is going to spring them if you are up on the wall? No one knows the layout of the castle." Despite the effort it took to muster the thought, he managed to make his point.

Sam raised his hand. "I do, Captain. I was born and raised in Costair and have delivered half a dozen courier pouches to the Castle. I know exactly what this looks like. I can stick to the walls and shadows and get over there." Sam raised his chin and threw his shoulders back.

He barely resisted the urge to roll his eyes. This kid really did try too hard. He forced himself to pay attention when the courier continued.

"I will need something to open the doors. I mean, I'm sure they have them chained or braced somehow. But as long as you and Princess Aratess can keep the guards off my back, I can get the men out."

Colt smiled. "Thanks, Sam, but I need you to be a courier and get word to the king. Lucius needs to know he has help from the inside. You'll run from the riverbank to the king's command tent with a Bowman message. Shifty will have to free the men in the barracks. Don't worry, Shift, I will go over it with you before you do." Colt slapped Shifty on the back, and the lean raider laughed. Shifty admired Colt, Deacon could tell.

"The men will know where the armory is, so we won't need to direct them. When they're armed, there is no more need for stealth. The archers will make their way to the wall, and the regulars will come out this door here and this door here." Colt pointed to two small doors that opened onto the east and west sides of the castle. "I will split the regulars and they can come from either side and enfilade the Reyjik."

The men watching Colt all reacted when he said the word *enfilade*. Sam wrinkled his nose, and Shifty glanced at Deacon, who merely shrugged.

Tess leaned forward off the wall. "To enfilade means to shoot or attack down the ranks. You are attacking from the side, not head on the way they expect. It is very effective and causes great confusion and casualties."

The men nodded their understanding, but Deacon shook his head. How did she know so much?

"The captain will lead the archers here." Tess pointed to a central place on the north wall. "They will shoot down on the Reyjik from above."

"We'll have them hemmed in on four sides, practically speaking." Colt rubbed his eyes again.

"If it all works as you hope." He crossed his arms and stared at Colt.

"If it all works as we hope," Colt repeated, acknowledging the fact that his reservations were warranted. He leaned back against the wall, obviously tired.

Tess let out a huge yawn. One by one, every man in the room yawned in response. Deacon tried to suppress the urge but lost the brief battle. The tired team couldn't help but laugh.

"I guess that is a pretty good sign we should quit for tonight." Colt pushed off the wall. "If you can manage it, get some sleep. We have a lot of work ahead us." The men filed out of the room one at a time, obviously more than happy to be dismissed.

Tess rose from the bed, wincing as she did, then slipped through the men to the door where she stopped and slowly lifted her right hand. She lowered her hand to her side and raised her left, then pulled open the door and disappeared into the darkness.

Deacon frowned, but Colt hadn't noticed as he was speaking to Sam.

Sam asked question after question and then made three suggestions.

Colt stretched, yawned, and rolled his left shoulder. That's right, he'd been wounded escaping Costair, but he never mentioned it.

Catching his eye, Colt raised both eyebrows. Deacon knew when he was needed.

"All right, Sam, that's good for tonight. We're probably all gonna die tomorrow anyway, so why don't we make sure we're good and rested for our date with destiny, what do ya say?"

Sam spun around, but he must have caught the smile on Deac's face, as he laughed.

After Deacon gently pushed him out of his quarters and closed the door, he walked straight to the liquor cabinet in search of a bottle of brandy.

The cabinet lay completely bare. Right. "Blast you, Coltrik Hawthorne. You and your blasted temperance There is absolutely nothing in the Bowman's Code about drinking brandy. Even I know that much."

Colt had left a single carton of peach juice on the center shelf of the cabinet, and Deacon snatched it up. *Blasted juice. What am I, five?*

Before Colt could say anything, Deacon pulled out a chair and poured him a glass.

Colt sat, slumped forward, and flopped his head on his arms, staring sideways at the glass of juice.

Pouring his own, he took a cautious sip. It tasted sweet and peachy, and altogether nothing like brandy. "It's awful!" He winced for dramatic effect.

His friend didn't respond. only lay with his head on his arms. "Deac, I have a problem, and I need to talk to you about it."

"I've been keeping track, and I'd say you have about thirty-seven problems. Which one do you want to discuss?" He chuckled to himself. Not a bad joke under the circumstances.

Colt winced, his eyes tortured.

Deacon sobered. "What's wrong? I mean, besides the certain doom of this insane plan of yours?"

Colt lifted his head. "I failed, Deac. I totally failed. I needed to ask that stone about the men, and I couldn't, not if I were being honest with myself." He let out a shallow breath.

What in the world did that mean? The strange, nervous sensation returned as he remembered the display of magic, and his hand began to tremble. "So, you need to ask the stone what matters most to you?"

"Declare."

"Right, so you need to declare what matters most?"

Colt nodded. "There was this warning carved into the cliff that if you asked anything other than what your soul longed most to know, the stone wouldn't work. It's a truth stone, and half of it centers on being true to yourself, I guess, so I couldn't ask about the Costairs in the barracks, because…" Colt lowered his head to his fists again.

Deacon studied him. What had Colt declared. Something about Tess? Or the Reyjik and their honor? "Are you telling me that you set that entire mountain ablaze like a Reyjik firework display by declaring your love for Tess?"

Colt's head remained firmly planted on his fists, but he shook it slowly where he lay. "Worse."

"What then?"

"I lit the stone by declaring that I need Tess."

His mouth fell open. When Colt looked up and met his gaze, his friend's eyes showed a mix of agony and hope. Deacon choked back the sudden need to vomit.

"Well, what in the Realm did you say?" Did he really want to hear the answer?

"Just that I need her."

No! No, Colt. His heart plummeted. Why? Why did Colt have to need the only girl Deacon had ever fallen for? The sting hurt, but why? He already figured on Colt's feelings for Tess. Why did this revelation devastate him so? Deacon forced himself to face the truth—did he need Tess? Did he share the depth of connection she shared with Colt? Then he dared ask the most terrifying question of all. *Would the star have shone that bright if I had made that declaration?* Somewhere deep within he knew the answer. It lay drowning beside his call to duty, in a brandy bottle resting on the seafloor somewhere off Gilbet's point.

"That's good, right? I mean, isn't that the answer you wanted?" *Stay cool, Deac.*

"No, I wanted to do my duty. I wanted to care about what I'm supposed to care about. Instead, I failed, and she had to fix it for me. The declaration I made, and more importantly the one I couldn't make, proved how weak my commitment to the mission is. Pathetic What kind of a Bowman am I?"

Frustration and anger flared inside Deacon. "The ungrateful kind, you whiny wretch!"

Colt stared at him, eyes wide.

"What?" Deacon scowled. "Why are you looking at me like that? You expect me to feel sorry for you? To sympathize? Well, sorry, Colt, you're not getting even an ounce of sympathy from me. I get it, the timing stinks. I get it, she's a handful, and you haven't figured out how to manage it all, protecting her and letting her be who she is. But we both know that you have never so much as given a girl a second glance before. No matter how pretty, flirty, or sweet, not one was ever smart enough or good enough for you. Now finally, because of fate, destiny, or stupid luck, you and the most remarkable girl in the tierdom are forced together. The only girl who will ever prove your equal, who, under normal circumstances, you would never even have met, I might remind you, and you're too blind to see that for what it is, a miracle. Well, I think that should be enough to help you get over this failure bit. If not, you don't deserve her!"

Deacon took a giant swig and swished the liquid around to savor it, and then for dramatic effect, he slammed the glass on the table. *Sweet Descent, that wasn't brandy!* He spat it out across the table, soaking the diagram of Costair and their notes.

Colt broke up laughing. "Forgot it was peach juice?" He barely managed the question amidst his peals of laughter.

Deacon's anger melted. "Yes, I forgot it was peach juice." Laughter took hold, and soon his entire body shook. They both sat back and laughed until it hurt. Maybe it was release from the stress of the day. Whatever the reason, he figured no one needed it more than Colt.

Chapter Twenty-Nine

The Truth

Tess

TESS STILL COULDN'T SLEEP. BEYOND EXHAUSTION, her body longed to rest, but her conscience wouldn't allow it. She stood at the stern of the ship. They had embarked from Dungridge rearmed and *The Dancing Girl* floated steadily seaward. Old Eb hadn't let them down, giving them one hundred pristine Ardenian uniforms, along with four Reyjik uniforms they'd never dreamed of finding. They could use these uniforms as disguises to infiltrate. Deacon insisted on riding the mist under the plane of the precipice, not wanting to be sighted by Reyjik sentinels.

Colt had ordered every man not critical to the piloting of the ship to sleep until they reached the back of Castle Costair. Deacon had gladly obeyed this order, as had most of the ninety-five men who now sailed south. More scared than she had ever been in her life, Tess simply couldn't sleep. Fighting in the battle towards which she flew didn't bother her at all, but the fear that she would not be able to fight crushed her.

The effort it took to raise her bow with her left hand was daunting. Even more terrifying, she couldn't raise her right arm to nock her arrow. She tried to roll her shoulder and then to stretch and ease her aching back muscles, but it was no use. She set the arrow down and attempted only to draw the bowstring, which proved totally impossible. *Why am I so completely useless?*

Tess paced back and forth at the stern. Her sister needed her. Her father and brothers needed her. Ardenia needed her. She stopped quickly, raised the bow as if to fire, and then attempted to draw back on the bowstring. Barely able to raise her hand to grasp it, her arm fell limply to her side. It was impossible.

Panic gripped her. She paced outside Deacon's cabin, which contained all their plans, the Reyjik uniforms, and one tenacious Bowman. Tess pictured her position on the wall of Castle Costair. She needed to supply covering fire for Shifty. Colt had trusted her with that task. How could she let him down? She wanted to knock but lost her nerve. Would she be stronger in a few hours when needed?

Before she could decide, the door swung open. Colt stopped in the doorway and thumbed in the direction of the chart table. "Are you going to come in, Princess, or do you want to pace some more?" Placing both hands on the lintel, he leaned forward, his eyes gleaming. Blasted brilliant Bowman! He'd been aware of her presence for the last two minutes, while she second guessed her decision to come clean.

She sighed in defeat and walked into the briefing room, not sure what to say.

Deacon lay fast asleep on his bed. He snored lightly, totally unbothered by the oil lamp that burned brightly just two feet from his head.

She turned to face Colt, now leaning against the closed door. Biting her lip, she promised herself she wouldn't cry in front of him, not again.

"What is it you came for, Princess. Are you all right?" He stuck his hands into his trouser pockets.

Desperate to be honest, she shook her head. "I can't shoot, Captain, truly. I can't even nock an arrow, let alone draw or shoot. I don't understand it. I shot fine the whole time at the Ridley. I didn't even feel my arm get tired. Now I can't raise my arm above my waist." Her voice shook. *Don't you dare cry, Tess.* "I can't help you cover Shifty and the others from the castle wall. I'm useless. Totally useless, and I don't even understand why."

Colt smiled warmly at her, which simultaneously melted her heart and filled her with deep frustration.

"Don't do that, Colt. Don't look at me like that. I want to help. I need to help. You understand that, right?" She tried again to raise her right arm in a draw motion. Pure agony. "No matter how badly I want it, I just can't do it. Why? Colt, help me, why?" She could hear the desperation in her own voice. Had Colt heard it too?

He stepped towards her, grabbed her right wrist, and gently lowered her right arm to a resting position at her side. Then he pulled out a chair for her to sit.

She did so reluctantly, her arm falling limp again.

Lowering himself to his knees in front of her chair, he stared deep into her eyes.

Tess's heart raced, her stomach threatening to burst from butterflies. Why did he make her feel this way? She couldn't feel this way. Could she? No, she wasn't allowed to feel this way, not until Lindor's prince refused her hand. Her future was still uncertain. Her course had been charted two years before, and though she had done her very best to miss the mark where Prince Jestin was concerned, he could still decide to confirm their contracted betrothal. Ironic that the very pursuits that effectively dissuaded Jestin were exactly what she relied on to help Colt.

Colt reached out and touched the back of her limp arm. "Princess, you have badly strained every muscle in the right side of your back and your right arm. These muscles are torn and damaged. I did the same thing when I first began Bowman training. I wanted to win this competition my very first week at the academy, and I practiced for two hours straight. I must have fired two hundred arrows in a row. Then, when I woke up the next day, my whole right side was totally useless. I couldn't even shoot in the competition." He chuckled to himself. "Oh, you should have heard the ribbing I got from Deacon. He couldn't let me live that one down."

Tess couldn't accept that this was merely overuse or muscle strain. "But I didn't feel that bad this morning. I just kept firing."

"That was battle-rush, Princess. Your body is capable of amazing things when it believes it has no other choice. I was shocked when I got your case of arrows back. Judging by what was left, you fired one hundred and sixty-five arrows consecutively. That would have been an immense strain on your back. I mean, face it, there really isn't much to ya." He leaned back on his heels and smirked.

She sighed. "Well, how can I fix it? I need to help."

Still smirking, Colt shifted until he was sitting cross legged on the floor. "I can't say I didn't anticipate this." He ran his fingers through his dark hair. "Maybe I hoped that you could play a totally different role when we got to Costair."

A small spark of anger flickered inside at his tone.

"I may have already worked out an alternative plan where you go straight to the ballroom, free your sister, King Salmon, Prince Durbink, and all the courtiers, then lead them to safety down the back stairs you took the other night and out to the Bowman lookout."

Heat rushed through her.

"You would still be doing a great service, and you would be safe." He said that as if he were doing her a favor. Indeed, Colt seemed most pleased with himself. He had already analyzed her capabilities, made an assessment, and adapted the plan accordingly. Was she merely a cog in his machine? She had performed the way he had expected, and it pleased him to be right in his estimation. Rage burned in her belly. Hot, helpless, rage.

"I'm glad that I didn't disappoint you so I could play my pathetic part in your grand plan." Tess may have been whispering, but in her heart, she screamed. Utterly disappointed in herself, failure consumed her. She gritted her teeth at the idea that Colt had such low expectations of her, and, worse, that she had proven him right. Shoving back her chair, she rose and stalked toward the door.

When she'd learned that Colt had included her as one of the three archers to help in the mission, she'd been so proud. Had that all been for show? Had he never intended to use her bow in his plan?

"Please, Captain, do me the courtesy of telling me the truth. If you didn't want my bow, you should have said so. I thought you saw me as a legitimate archer." Tess threw the words over her shoulder as she yanked open the door with her left hand. That hurt.

Colt scrambled to his feet, but before he could reach the door, she slammed it shut in his face.

Chapter Thirty

The Infiltration

Deacon

DEACON LOOKED UP FOR THE TWENTIETH time. *Blast that full moon! Blast that stupid cloudless sky! You want to know how many times I prayed for a clear, bright sky like that, so I could raid past dark? Know how many times my prayers were answered? Never, not once. But tonight, the one night I need it to be dark and misty so we don't immediately die, it is as bright as blasted past peak.* Complaining didn't help his nerves.

Everything felt off. His two friends hadn't said a word to each other since their argument. Tess stood at the bow and Colt the starboard side where they would disembark into the window of the castle.

He couldn't truly hate the full moon, as it was the moonlight that allowed him to sail by hand signals, affording *The Girl* a silent passage through the clear sky. He had chosen to drop below the Costair precipice and fly under the tier edge their entire approach, so the Reyjik wouldn't sight them. Flying exposed like this was dangerous, as updrafts off the Dark Sea were notoriously unpredictable and deadly, but the winds had proven manageable thus far.

Checking his charts, he reasoned they should be directly under the north side of Castle Costair. Pressing the spyglass to his eye, he confirmed their location, sighting lights just above, the warm glow from two windows looming against the clear sky. He motioned for Reynolds to stop their forward progress and begin the slow ascent. Deac leaned in close to Reynolds to give final instructions.

Both Colt and Tess noticed their change in trajectory and joined him at the bridge.

"Reynolds, you know what to do. Wait exactly half an hour after we're in and then light up that keg of powder and drop it right on their deck. You know the plan. Use a flare as a fuse, light it, and drop it. Should be four galleons docked at Marduke in the Sislay River right now. Take your pick and light one up. Feel free to repeat if you survive the first one." He slapped Reynolds on the shoulder.

Reynold's face broke into a wide smile and then, as that smile began to fade, the middle-aged man cleared his throat. "Honestly, Captain." He shifted from foot to foot. "These last six months have been the best of my life. Never felt as I had a say in anything 'til you gave it to me. And even a skipper me-self sometimes. Best time of my life." He coughed and gazed up at the moon.

A lump formed in his throat. He had never considered what his leadership might mean to a man like Reynolds. He patted the man on the arm and then made it official. "*The Dancing Girl* is yours. Do your worst!" Deacon peered past the older pirate. Tess watched them intently. She smiled at him. She loved his crew, truly loved each and every man, and they all loved her. She had won their undying respect and devotion. She was perfect…and Colt cared for her too. His tortured heart could break the forced silence with a soul-splitting scream. Instead, he only smiled back at the princess and watched her take position.

This was it. The infiltration team would disembark, Reynolds would wait half an hour, and then, after bombing the galleons, land in the Sislay and unload the rest of the men.

Colt led Shifty, Tess, and himself to the starboard railing, where his bow and modified arrow lay waiting. The glossy, black granite reflected the moonlight, and Deacon could make out the shadow of the ship's hull silhouetted by the large, lunar circle. Tess appeared to be studying the eerie effect, avoiding Colt altogether. He thought back to the argument he had overheard in his quarters a few hours before. He had been woken by their whispers, which had soon escalated to a slamming door.

He couldn't blame Tess for her reaction. At the same time, on a deep level, he now understood Colt's need to protect her. Indeed, he had to side with the Bowman on this one. Having Tess provide covering fire, exposed on the wall like that, proved too risky. Deacon's admission of this last reality still caused him heartache. He swallowed hard and shifted his attention to Colt.

"That window leads to a passageway that isn't used anymore. We'll climb over and then set to work immediately. Deac and I will make straight for the top of the inner courtyard wall. Deac will cover Shifty as he heads to the barracks. I will cover the princess as she makes for the ballroom. Shifty has the steel pry-pole and he knows how to use it." Colt winked at Shifty.

Deacon thought back to the hour of training Colt had given Shifty with this tool. The Bowman had laughed out loud over Shifty's aptitude, although Colt had seemed enormously impressed with Shifty's weight-to-power ratio.

Shifty mimed levering a heavy object up off the deck. "Like you said, Bowman, it's all 'bout the leverage."

Tess smiled at the exchange, and Deacon's heart split open. He couldn't believe that she could still look so pretty, even with her face smudged with bootblack and her hair tied up under her helmet. *Focus, Deac!*

Colt grasped Shifty's arm. "Wait for Reynold's distraction from the river. Don't make your move until the explosion. As soon as you get those doors open, tell the men you are Ardenian, that you fight with King Lucius, and that they are to get to the armory. Tell them that Captain Colt Hawthorne, Bowman of the Realm, will direct them. They've all met me. They'll remember me. But bear in mind, they might be confused. We don't know their condition. I know we've been over all this—you are just going to have to do your best." Colt patted the man on the arm before pulling back and turning to Tess.

"That brings us to you, Princess." This was the first time he had spoken to her in hours.

She straightened, her expression serious and determined.

"Princess Aratess, you are going to head straight for the ballroom. Don't run. Walk with a purpose, but don't run."

The concern in Colt's eyes betrayed that he regretted involving the princess at all.

"I know, you told me twice already, Captain." Tess rocked to her toes and back again.

Colt swallowed. "Try not to engage anyone. If someone asks you something, bluff your way through. You speak Reyjik, use that."

Although she wasn't looking at him, Tess nodded. "Yes, Captain, you've already instructed me to do that, as well."

The hot, humid air pressed down on them, but ice dripped from her every word.

Colt winced but didn't respond, only touched Shifty's arm again. "Shifty, once you're done at the barracks and have sent the men my way, I want you to help the princess. As you know, she is going to lead all the royalty, civilians, and servants down the back stairs, across the west courtyard, and out to the Bowman lookout in the orchards. She's been there before, and she knows the way. Just go with her and help. All right?"

Shifty nodded.

Colt faced Deacon. "After we regroup, we will attempt to enfilade the Reyjik dug in against the walls. We will shoot their archers atop the wall and take over their position, which will let us shoot down on them from above. Hopefully, Sam will have reached King Lucius by then, and he will know what we are up to. And remember, Deac, once the men are out and you join the fight, take off that blasted Reyjik uniform. I have two greencoat uniforms with me. For Realm's sake, don't forget to change into one!"

Despite the urgency in his friend's voice, Deacon was distracted by Tess. She'd been fidgeting, but now she had grown still. Her eyes were closed, and, as he watched, she made the sign of descent.

Clearly, she was ready.

Chapter Thirty-One

The Battle for Costair

Colt

COLT HELD HIS BREATH. TESS HUNG from the rope suspended between *The Dancing Girl* and the castle, thousands of yards above the Endless Sea, and she made it look easy. Even though her right arm was strained, she climbed hand over hand with her legs wrapped around the rope for extra hold and security. His entire body tensed. Why had he let her do this? She leaned her head back, looked at him upside down, and smiled. Was she even breaking a sweat?

Colt had fired the grappling arrow, and it took hold on the first shot. He didn't tie off the other end to *The Dancing Girl* but left it in the hands of three strong crewmen. Indeed, if the Girl, caught in an updraft, needed to rise or shift with the wind, a tied rope could pull tight and snap. By trusting the crewmen to hold it, he allowed some flexibility in terms of the distance of the span. He had shimmied across first, then Shifty, and then Deacon, who cursed during the entire crossing.

The winds were light, and it hadn't been difficult. He watched from the window as Tess began the dangerous task of climbing to the castle window, hanging from the taut rope and making good progress.

At the halfway point, Colt began to breathe more naturally, replacing the short gasps he was drawing in when she first set off with longer, more relaxed breaths.

Then, without warning, a strong updraft buffeted *The Girl*. Her starboard fin caught the wind, and she listed heavily to port, rising all the while. Colt's heart hammered in his chest. He watched helplessly as the three crewmen at the railing allowed the rope to slide through their grip, giving the span slack to accommodate the greater distance.

His eyes darted to Tess, who held tightly to the rope. Suddenly, she let go with her right hand, her injured arm. Her left held fast, as did her coiled legs, but she did something strange with her right hand. What was she doing?

"Hold on with both hands, Tess," he called, as quietly as he could. "The wind isn't done with her yet."

She didn't grab the rope. What was she doing with her hand? Why had she stopped climbing across?

His heartrate soared as *The Girl* caught another strong updraft and rose thirty yards above the window. No! What if the men on board let go? What if Tess shook free?

The thought had barely crossed his mind when the rope suddenly fell. *Tess!* Colt lunged over the windowsill. The rope had dropped to the castle wall, but Tess had somehow managed to hold on, and she dangled against the smooth, black stone. Colt grasped the rope and began hauling her skyward.

"Tess, are you all right? Hold on!"

She didn't answer. Why didn't she answer? What had happened? Had the men let go? *The Girl* slowly backed away from the castle and descended again. No, the crewmen all still held tight to the end of the rope, but only five yards of rope dangled in the wind. What had happened? He hauled on his end of the rope secured to the windowsill.

Shifty and Deacon grabbed hold too, and the three of them managed to hoist her into the open window only moments after the harrowing fall.

Colt reached down, grabbed her under her arms, and pulled her through the window.

When her feet hit the floor, she stumbled forward. Colt grabbed her and wrapped his arms around her to hold her steady.

She rested her forehead on his chest and exhaled deeply.

Breathing in kind, he trusted that she was safe. "Are you okay? What happened?"

She didn't answer, only tilted back her head until she stared into his eyes, smiling wide. Clenched between her teeth, a bladespar knife shone in the lamplight.

Had she cut the rope? She had cut the rope behind her. She had purposefully cut the rope and swung to the wall, safe from the effect of the updraft. Brilliant!

* * *

Tess climbed silently up the rough stone wall, the path of least resistance. Even though her arm ached, this saved her walking hundreds of yards across the courtyard, up a set of stairs, and down a long walkway. At any point along that trip, she could pass a Reyjik sentry. She had seen three so far, which wasn't bad, but she didn't want to risk it. Especially not when the wall she scaled led directly to the door of the ballroom and stood concealed by the dark shadow cast by an adjacent wall. She had watched Colt do the same thing only minutes earlier to get into position, and even though this was not a part of his plan, she figured the Bowman would appreciate the economy of her decision.

Her heartrate quickened as she reached the top ledge. Colt would be watching her, arrow nocked and ready, no doubt. She swung her legs over the ledge and dropped to a standing position. She then walked purposefully towards the door, as he had instructed her. Tess contemplated the grand entrance to the ballroom. It hadn't been a full week since she'd entered through that same doorway, the nobility all watching her closely. How deeply she had cared about things which now seemed of no consequence at all.

Cold gripped her. What would she find on the other side of this door? What if she entered to find hundreds of dead bodies? No, no, the emerald star had confirmed their well-being. She had declared it herself. A strange feeling flooded over Tess. Colt had actually trusted in the star. It had shone so brightly, blazing for his declaration. She had no idea what he'd declared, something personal, was all he'd admitted. Still, she had never heard of such a brilliant display, such an obvious confirmation.

She turned to where Colt stood hidden, watching her. Although she couldn't see him like she wished, knowing he was there gave her strength. Turning to the looming door, she took a deep breath and reached out. The large oak door swung open before she could grip the d'orite handle.

A huge Reyjik soldier stood in the opening. His gaze locked on hers. Could he see the fear in her eyes?

Before either of them moved, a deafening boom broke the silence. The sky in the west lit up, and they both turned instinctively towards the glow.

Think, Tess! "They're attacking!" she cried in her best Reyjik accent. She didn't need to say anything else.

The huge soldier pushed past her and ran towards the main gate. He called over his shoulder, yelling an order to the ballroom. "Move! Move!"

Tess backed up against the wall as four more armed soldiers, huge men, sprinted past her. The last soldier turned to her. "Watch them!" he ordered.

"Yes, sir." She saluted as they disappeared down the stairs to the main courtyard. An amazing twist of fate.

Tess's mind raced. Had Shifty freed the men yet? Had Sam got word to her father? But one question quieted the rest. Was her sister all right?"

* * *

Colt strode to the edge of the southern wall of the castle, an impossibility without the Reyjik uniform he wore. Of the four Ardenians infiltrating the castle, he actually looked Reyjik, which afforded him the level of confidence required for what he was about to do. Upon reaching the smooth granite crenel, he surveyed the battlefield, an astounding sight. Colt had never taken part in a conventional pitched battle. His time in the archer trench as a boy was just that, squatting in a trench, cold and scared, devoid of any perspective on the fighting. He'd studied countless battles at the academy, but to see his countrymen in formation filled him with reverence.

King Lucius's greencoats lined up in three perfect divisions. The Reyjik employed a phalanx dead center at the base of the castle, easily outnumbering the Ardenian troops two to one. Colt refocused. He needed to spot Sam and confirm that the king knew of the Costair force being liberated from within the castle.

Raising his spyglass, he checked the treeline. A moment later, a figure sprinted from the trees, heading directly for the Ardenian troops. Colt drew his bow, nocked his arrow, and scanned the troops below him, ready to shoot any soldier that threatened Sam's safe arrival to the Ardenian force.

A Reyjik infantryman positioned against the treeline began to jog towards Sam. He carried a bow. If any other Reyjik soldiers noticed Sam, they didn't react. The Reyjik soldier began to run, raising his bow…

Colt couldn't wait for him to use his bow on Sam. He tracked his advance, marked his right thigh, and released. A dead shot. The man dropped to the long grass of the plain. No one appeared to have noticed that he had broken rank.

Taking a deep breath, he lingered only a moment, following Sam as he met a green-clad infantry man at the edge of the Ardenian force. The man escorted him through the ranks to the command tent. A flurry of activity at the king's tent indicated the monarch had received Sam's message. A wave of relief washed over Colt only to be replaced by acute worry. An impossible number of other details needed to work in their favor for them to win the day.

A deafening boom pierced the air, and a huge fireball rose above the river. Reynolds had bombed a galleon, another detail accomplished. So far, so good. Colt turned and ran down the steps, taking them two at a time. He needed to get to Tess.

* * *

Deacon watched Shifty swagger across the courtyard, and he couldn't help but laugh. He was born for this. He carried the long pry-pole at his left side as he strutted towards the barracks. With the confusion of the explosion, none of the running Reyjik soldiers questioned him. Shifty carried himself as though he were invincible. Wasn't he nervous?

A thought struck Deacon. Did Shifty feel untouchable at this moment because his captain covered him from the wall? A crushing wave of responsibility crashed down on him. No matter what it cost, he would not let Shifty down —he would earn the trust placed in him. A realization struck him where he stood hidden. That low whisper, that almost silent voice that urged him on to faithfulness at all costs, was that the call of duty?

Deacon shook his head, call of duty or not, he clenched his teeth in concentration, scanning for any soldier who seemed to take notice of the lanky pirate that sauntered through the square.

As Shifty approached the barracks, the undisciplined guards surprised Deacon with their behavior. They chattered and stood on tiptoes to see the red glow that marked the eastern sky. Shifty didn't have the princess's luxury of speaking Reyjik. He simply raised his hand.

Deacon reacted immediately. Within seconds, he'd shot an arrow through the chest of the first guard. He re-nocked and released in only a matter of seconds. The second arrow struck another guard right through the heart. Both men slumped to the cobblestones. Deacon's heart pounded in his chest. Not bad!

Now for the chains that looped around the huge iron handles. Sliding the long pole between the door and the chains, Shifty set the angle just right so he could use the handles as the pivot point.

Deacon tried to remember the word Colt had used for this point. The *funcrum*, no, the *fulcrum*. That was it.

Shifty pushed with all the might his lean wiry frame could manage, once, twice, three times.

The third attempt saw every ounce of Shifty's strength focused on the end of the long pole, and the chain gave. No, wait. Not the chain. Shifty had pried the left door handle clean out of the oak door panel, and it now dangled from the chain that still hung attached to the right handle. He had done it. He could open the door and step inside and out of sight. But what would he find beyond the thick oak door?

Deacon jumped from his position on the wall and sprinted across the courtyard. There was no time to waste. He slipped inside behind Shifty and found himself staring face to face with over three hundred men. They looked exhausted and they smelled. But they were all standing at the ready, and, Deacon decided, they would do.

* * *

Colt reached the doorway of the ballroom. He squinted as the red glow that filled the sky behind him made the unlit room appear even darker. Twelve officers approached him. He had already passed dozens of other men. Royalty, courtiers, servants, he gave them all the same instructions, to go to the armory and arm themselves. He told them that King Lucius of Ardenia fought on the plains, that he had come to liberate them.

Relief crossed their faces, soon replaced by determination. Every Costair man insisted on fighting. The Reyjik had provided for their needs. They had been fed and brought fresh water, and they were strong.

Hope surged within him. His mother's people hadn't killed these hostages, and they hadn't left them to starve. He couldn't reconcile the invasion itself, but in that moment, he swore to find out why they had attacked. If he survived this battle, he would secure peace with Reyjik once again or die in the attempt. For the first time in his life, he made the Sign of Descent to signify his conviction to this end. No one witnessed it, no one knew of the promise he made to himself. Only the All-Father, if He did exist, would have seen, but Colt didn't need a witness.

If his experience at the emerald star meant anything, it was that he needed to be honest with himself. The truth was that he didn't want a future in Ardenia if it meant war with Reyjik. But that would need to wait. His duty held fast, here and now. He first needed to defeat his mother's people, yes, a Bowman to the very core. Victory for the Realm and then a new fight for peace.

Tess stood at the other end of the ballroom, ushering the last of the women down the back staircase according to plan.

Colt ran across the room, covering the distance in only seconds, his heart pounding.

"Princess?" He gently touched her back. She whirled around at his touch, and his nerve faltered. He took a deep breath and forced himself to open his mouth.

Tess spoke before he could say anything. "I know, Captain. *Don't die.* I've had this pep talk before. Captain Thornby leaves a lasting impression." She fidgeted with her hair, obviously trying to mask her worry. "You all right? I don't think Deacon will recover if you get killed." Was that concern for him?

Colt couldn't speak, only reached out and brushed away a blackened lock of hair that had fallen in front of her eyes.

She looked up at him and forced a smile. "I'm so sorry I can't help. And I'm sorry I was angry. You didn't deserve that. You've worked a miracle. You've given us a chance, Captain. I'll be watching you from our lookout. Watching and praying."

Colt lost his breath. Before he could reply, she turned and ran down the stairs.

Had it only been a week since he had followed her down that same flight of stairs? Had so much happened in less than a week? Something deep inside him stirred. He needed to finish this. No more gathering of intelligence. No more chasing. No more planning. No more sneaking. Time to stand and fight.

* * *

Deacon had never seen this side of Colt. As his friend addressed the men of Costair, he seemed filled with a skyward fortitude. Watching the men's faces as the captain spoke, he witnessed them literally inhaling his message of hope, valor, and duty, drinking it down like an elixir of strength.

"We don't understand this act of aggression, lads, but we don't need to. They took your freedom, and that threatens everything the Realm holds dear. Now, your skyward brothers of Ardenia stand and fight for your very freedom. We will stand with them. Together we will win. The Realm wins this night!"

Deacon joined the exhausted knights of Costair in their battle cry. He would die with these men if he had to. Colt's words rang true for him. They simply couldn't let these invaders take their way of life. Not if there was even the smallest hope they could be stopped.

Helping to pass out arms, Deacon stood in the thick of the staging area. Confusion centered around who could serve as an archer. Colt wanted at least forty men to line the wall, but Deacon had to force the last five bows onto men who undoubtedly believed they were less than worthy. He then retrieved his own bow from where he'd stowed it. He approached Colt, but the Bowman was explaining to King Salmon and Prince Durbink the plan to enfilade. Colt asked that they stay in the rear and out of harm's way.

A low, haunting, eerie howl, rose from the plains—the Ardenian battle horn. King Lucius would advance, his foot soldiers no doubt in play. The battle for Costair had begun.

* * *

The howl of the battle horn echoed through the night. Tess could picture her father giving the order to charge as she reached the lookout with the civilian women from the ball. Every man, royal birth or not, had reported to the armory to stand under Colt's command. Even Durbink and King Salmon had insisted on fighting for Costair. She desperately wanted to climb the ladder and check on those allies.

When she reached for the rope and pulled, the ladder dropped immediately. As she gripped it, a hand landed on her arm. Tess whirled around. Sasha stood behind her, her face ashen. Overwhelmed with compassion for her older half sister, Tess let go of the ladder.

Sasha had never faced a trial in her life. She had never made a sacrifice. She had never been uncomfortable—and there she stood, dirty, smelly, tired, and terrified.

"Aratess, what are you doing? Where have you been? Why weren't you in the ballroom? I thought they killed you!" She broke into tears.

Tess embraced her sister, meeting Shifty's eyes over Sasha's shoulder. "Sasha. Don't cry." Tess patted her back. "Father has come. That sound is his battle horn. The Ardenian army descended all the way from Fairgates to save you, as we have. Here you are, safe and free. Please don't cry. Just pray for Father and Derek and Fredrick. Pray for our men, Sasha." She held her sister as she cried.

After a few minutes, her sobbing subsided, and Sasha let go, gently pushing Tess backwards so she could look over her younger sister. Sasha's face twisted into a frown. "What are you wearing, Aratess?" She threw her hands to her hips. "What have you done to your hair? And your face? Tess, your face is a total mess. Did you let that handsome Bowman from the ball see you like this?"

Yep, there she was. Tess grinned, proud to see that the Reyjik had not been able to break Princess Sasha of Ardenia. Tess looked over at Shifty and rolled her eyes.

"Did you just roll your eyes at me?" Sasha's mouth dropped open, and she pushed her chin out indignantly.

Shifty laughed. Tess rolled her eyes again, and then pointed to the ladder, telling her sister to stand back and allow her to begin the long climb to the lookout above.

Sasha refused to move, forcing Tess to step around her. "You won't be rolling your eyes when you're never invited to court, little sister! I know you've been trying to make Prince Jestin's mind up for him with all this tomboy nonsense, and I applauded your resolve, but you've gone too far. Mark my words, father won't be able to pay enough bladespar to put you on a royal guestlist. I don't care if you're the queen of Lindsor, they won't let you out if you don't have a bath, miss know it all!"

Tess shook her head as she hoisted herself to the bottom rung of the ladder. Not only had the Reyjik failed to break Sasha, they had failed to affect her priorities in even the slightest way—still decidedly men, fashion, and hair, in that order.

* * *

A strange measure of strength coursed through Colt's entire body. More than battle rush, something deeper. With the officers and courtiers now briefed, and the men forming ranks on either side of the castle courtyard, they were ready. He gave the order for Riley and Cage, the senior officers, to engage. The columns of troops ran single file out through the small doors in the wall and disappeared into the red glow outside. A second ear-splitting explosion echoed off the castle walls. He imagined Reynolds dropping another keg full of powder and taking out one of the galleons waiting at the docks. The glowing sky silhouetted the Reyjik archers that stood atop the southern castle wall against an ominous red backdrop. The archers were totally preoccupied as they shot down at the Ardenian soldiers charging the ground troops, apparently unaware of the small force of resistance archers that silently formed rank on the cobblestone below them.

"You run to the wall as soon as you've fired your second shot, understand? You'll be sitting ducks for those trained men on the wall. No one's a hero tonight, lads. They outnumber us two to one and we don't have the luxury for heroics, understood?" Colt had whispered this last order, but the mass of silently nodding heads that responded satisfied him. They'd heard him loud and clear.

Nocking his arrow, Colt raised his bow. His arm ached from Fairgates. The fletching of Costair-issue arrow felt soft on his cheek. The line of men acted in kind, and when the last of his men had raised their bow to the proper trajectory, he fired. His arrow landed squarely in the center of the lead enemy archer's back. The man fell forward with the force of the shot, off the wall and into the Reyjik troops below.

He nocked a second arrow as he counted how many of his men had managed the same result. Five. Five Reyjik archers had been killed in this first volley. Colt let fly two more arrows, downing two more men, before his troops had restrung their second shot. He nocked his fourth arrow and called for the second volley of arrows from his men.

As soon as they had released, he ordered his men to the wall for cover. They would be afforded a small window of grace after their first shot. The Reyjik would be confused, and it would take time to assess the origin of the threat. But after this second shot, the enemy would be certain of their location and no doubt return fire. Every man made it to the wall before the arrows rained down on the dark stone.

Colt didn't relocate with his men. He backed into a shadowed corner of the courtyard, one that allowed him a perfect sight line to the archers on the wall. He continued firing arrow after arrow as he counted. They had taken out six more men with the second volley. He had single-handily downed seven men himself, which meant the Reyjik had lost almost half their archers.

The Reyjik on either side of the line broke rank. They scuttled down the rampart and behind crenels. Colt continued to fire—eight, nine, ten. Then one of the Reyjik archers in the center called a retreat off the top of the wall.

He scowled. That was unacceptable. A trained archer was a menace on the battlefield. He needed to eradicate the threat here and now if he could manage it.

"All right men. We're not letting even one escape. We can't leave them to pick off our soldiers. Up the stairs in pursuit!"

The waiting soldiers looked all too happy to comply, leaping from the wall with his permission. Had his success inspired them? Did they want in on the action?

Colt led the men up the west stairs and ordered Deacon up the east stairs. The objective was simple, shoot as many archers as possible. When they regrouped in the center of the north wall, they had successfully killed thirty-six of the Reyjik archers. He couldn't be sure that was all of them, but he was satisfied. There could still be a threat, and his men would need to be careful of potential sharpshooters, however, the Realm now controlled the top of the wall.

Okay, what's next, Hawthorne? He surveyed the battle beneath him. A huge mass of Reyjik troops lined the castle wall. Those same troops faced a direct attack from the south. They countered this with phalanx and faced two Ardenian battalions on either flank. Now, the final assault. Riley and Cage led the Costair troops, a mix of knights, men at arms, nobility, servants, and pirates charging along the ranks from either side. The next critical task was to take out the men who manned the phalanx. Colt needed to weaken this defense and make a hole so the center attack could push through to the wall.

Ordering the range and trajectory, he called for release. The result was effective. Six Reyjik in the back row dropped to the ground. The men who weren't killed turned around, dropping their spears as they did. Their commanders ordered they hold position. He could make out every curse, every command, every desperate threat attempting to force the men to hold. He looked beyond this phalanx wall of spearmen to the Ardenian force that charged, regrouped, and charged again. They took casualties with each attempted breach. Those were his countrymen falling. Even so, Colt reached for yet another arrow, determined to do whatever it took to weaken the Reyjik defense.

Chapter Thirty-Two

The Turning Tide

Deacon

DEACON SQUINTED, STRAINING TO IDENTIFY THE men below him. Was that Buckles? Yes, there were his men. Indeed, even though the crew of *The Dancing Girl* dressed as Ardenian regulars, they couldn't hide their true pirate identities from their devoted leader. Deacon would have laughed as he recognized Higgit's peg leg, were it not for the dire situation his men faced. They made up the main force of the troops that flanked from the east, and they enfiladed the Reyjik troops. When Tess had described this tactic, she made it sound so effective and precise. As he watched it play out from above, the charge looked anything but precise. His crew formed the fist of this crushing blow. They charged at the front and center of this makeshift battalion, in the heaviest part of the fighting.

Deacon couldn't allow his men to be slaughtered by the desperate Reyjik soldiers who had been waiting a week for this fight. He redirected his bow from the back of the phalanx to the front line of Reyjik who had turned to face the flanking pirates. Was he disobeying Colt's command? Not entirely. Deacon stood on the castle wall, and he fired down at Reyjik. Even though he didn't shoot at the ordered objective, for a pirate, two out of three wasn't bad.

* * *

From atop the castle wall, Colt sighted King Lucius and the command force driving the Ardenian troops forward from the rear. He fired volley after volley, attempting to weaken the central phalanx that stalled King

Lucius' advance. The king rode out and engaged, no coward, and fought alongside his men. Colt felt a measure of pride over the man he'd sworn to serve and protect.

Colt's archers were the reason the king's men were about to break through the Reyjik force, and he knew it. He fired and fired again. Arrow after arrow. His arm ached, but a wave of satisfaction swept over him as the success of this achievement would see massive repercussions for the Reyjik. The king's central force would push through to the wall and then cut the enemy lines in half. The newly reformed, smaller Reyjik forces would be fighting a battle on all sides. He could almost taste this turn of events when he heard the order to charge called one last and definitive time.

The king's men crashed into the last of the spearmen to stand their ground. They pushed them back and then overran them completely. The greencoats did not stop running until they reached the wall. A loud yell of defiance rang out from the Costair troops, mingled with a pirate's "Arrr."

Colt continued firing. He didn't have the luxury of celebrating along with the men. Out of the corner of his eye, he saw the king raise his hand in gratitude. He stopped firing for only a moment and saluted, then resumed firing on the western flank of the battle.

Consumed with destroying the phalanx and allowing the king's men to breach the primary battle line through to the wall, Colt hadn't noticed the dire situation of the Western flank. The Ardenians fighting there struggled. Colt drew in a deep breath, but the thick, humid air was stifling. His arm ached and his fingers were numb, but his mind was razor sharp. The battle, far from over, would be decided in this western theater.

He fired and fired again. His ears rang from the clash of ferrite on bladespar, the screams of men, and the boom of cannon fire. The fighting on the western plain was so close, so tight, Colt found he was waiting too long between shots, trying to ensure an accurate hit. His position was useless now.

He scanned the western side of the castle, but no position proved close enough. The battle simply raged too far west for a sniper's roost to reach. He needed to get down there. He needed to even the odds.

Running across the wall top, Colt stopped at a full arrow case to refill his quiver. On top of the wall, he had the luxury of positioning by a full arrow case, but on the ground, he'd need to bring his ammunition with him. He grabbed a second quiver from a fallen Costair archer and filled it as well. He paused only a moment, making the sign of descent for the brave Costair soldier. He'd met this man over a dozen times, training him during the last three months. Guardili… The man's name was Guardili.

Leaping from the wall to the western stairs, Colt bounded to the battlefield. Close combat usually proved fatal for an archer. His training told him it was a last resort, only to be used when every other option failed. He burst through the door, greeted by the absolute chaos he'd watched from above. Letting out a loud cry, he called his men to his side.

"West, men, we push west!" He screamed with every ounce of effort he could muster as he ran headlong into the clashing sea of metal and men fighting desperately for their lives.

Chapter Thirty-Three

The Threat

Tess

TESS AND SHIFTY STARED THROUGH BOWMAN spyglasses, desperate to see their friends, frantic to know they were all right. Tess watched Colt and Colt alone, wincing each time he drew. He must be exhausted. She had lost count around one hundred and forty arrows. Surely, he had now doubled that number. She reminded herself of what Colt had told her of battle rush. *We are capable of incredible things when we believe we have no other choice.* But what made everything bleaker was that she saw no end in sight for the young captain. She quickly prayed for him.

Shifty stared intently through his spyglass.

"Shift, have you found the crew? Have you found Captain Thornby?"

The pirate nodded.

Tess could not steady her racing heart or quell her fears. Worse yet, she felt completely useless. Totally removed from the field of battle, she could do nothing. Even if she were standing side by side with Colt and Deacon, she wouldn't be able to help, her arm was simply too weak. Indeed, climbing across the rope and then the wall had only further damaged her strained back and arm, so much so that she had climbed the ladder to the lookout using only her left arm. How would she endeavor to fire a longbow? Impossible. She bit her lower lip.

"How do you think they are doing, Shift?" She didn't take her eyes off Colt.

"Well, Princess, I think they are holding their own. Those Reyjik must be regretting the whole nasty business by now, don't you think?"

She didn't miss the false bravado in his tone.

Shifty shifted from one foot to the other. Was that how he'd gotten his namesake?

"The captains are all right at any rate, Princess, and that's a mercy." He continued shifting from side to side.

Colt stopped firing, ran to the western side of the wall, and descended the west stairs to join the ranks on the ground. Specifically, he took up position to fire on the Reyjik who fought in the western theater of engagement.

A wave of guilt swept over her. She had not yet looked for her father or brothers. She cared desperately for their welfare. Why hadn't she checked the ranks for them? What was wrong with her? Tess scanned the men on horseback for her father. She sighted Derek first, leading the western attack. His men were badly outnumbered. Did Colt engage his archers on the ground to aid her brother's struggling flank?

Tess scanned the middle of the battle and sighted her father. He rode safely tucked in the rear of the central force, yet on the field, nonetheless. Struck in that moment by how old he appeared, his gray hair that she so often thought distinguished now only proved to set him apart as decades older than the men with whom he fought. She felt a deep sense of pride, and she knelt and prayed for both Derek and her father. Tess then scanned the eastern flank of the battlefield. She hadn't sighted Fredrick yet, and she could only hope he had not fallen.

While scanning the far eastern group of soldiers, she noticed movement along the treeline. Tess adjusted her spyglass to focus in on two Reyjik soldiers pushing what looked like a large wheelbarrow covered with a tarp. It appeared to be heavy, based on how the men struggled to move it forward. She frowned. One of the covered machines that had been lashed to the deck of the galleon. Indeed, she had spotted this same contraption from Cooper's Cliffs. Two more Reyjik emerged with the same wheeled contraption, following the first team of two. A third team trailed behind them. They maneuvered the heavy machines to the very middle of the battlefield, about two thousand yards from the castle wall and only three hundred yards from the cliffs on which the lookout perched.

What could they possibly have under those tarps? Studying the visible parts of the contraption, Tess could make out two large ferite wheels. The machines had push handles and pivoted like a wheelbarrow.

The men faced all three carts towards the castle and the main theater of combat.

Tess lowered the glass and glanced at the pirate. "What is that, Shifty?"

"What is what?" Shifty stopped shifting and looked down at her.

Grabbing the end of his spy glass, she directed it to where the carts were positioned.

Shifty's face twisted in confusion. "I don't know, Princess. Could it be some kind of siege machine?"

"But why would they position it there, so far from the castle? I mean, it looks as though they want to fire on the castle, but at two thousand yards, only a cannon would be effective."

"Two men would never be able to manage a cannon, Princess." Shifty rubbed his chin.

"I know, it doesn't make any sense." She peered through her spyglass. Three more men emerged from the trees. They carried large baskets, each of which was over a yard in length and looked like the arrow cases she had used at the Battle of Fairgates only a day ago.

The Reyjik soldier manning the center contraption pulled the tarp away and threw it behind the machine.

Gasping, she squinted to confirm what she thought she saw. Yes, mounted to the cart was a wooden block that contained approximately a hundred holes. Horror swept over her as the second team member opened the basket and began loading arrows set with paper fuses into each hole. Tess had read about this machine. It was a hwacha. The catastrophic consequences it would hold for her men on the field flooded over her.

Tess thought quickly. "Shifty, how far are those wagons from the cliff face?"

He sighted with his spyglass. "About three hundred yards, Princess."

That confirmed what she had estimated. "And how far west are we from those wagons?"

"'Bout the same, Princess, three hundred yards."

She did the math in her head. "That puts the diagonal path from the balcony of the lookout to the hwacha at about four hundred and twenty-five yards. Blast! They are out of range from here."

She ran into the lookout and began sliding open the deep drawers that held the Bowman supplies. When she found what she was looking for, she grabbed a handful of flares and a whistle. The flares—a Reyjik import, ironically—were used to signal the castle from the lookout and should burn brightly enough for her purposes. Shoving the whistle into her pocket, she prayed for a bow.

Tess flung open the cabinet from which Colt had produced her bow the week before. One bow remained, along with four loose arrows. If only she and Colt hadn't taken the other quivers of arrows with them. Finding twine, she began lashing one flare to the shaft of each of three arrows, just above the midpoint. Was that it? Was that all she needed? Her mind raced.

Shifty stood beside her, watching her.

"I need to stop them. I need to get close enough to take out that lead man. Colt will have to take out the rest, but I need to buy him enough time to get within range. Any one of those soldiers could light the fuse and set off those hwacha! I only have four arrows, so I can't completely neutralize the threat, but I need to try, Shifty. Colt can do the rest. I just need to get his attention. Think Tess, think!" She was missing something, but what?

"Hwacha, Princess?"

"Yes. Machines capable of firing a hundred arrows at a time over two thousand yards. I've read about them. They're devastating!" She tried not to lose focus as she opened a door and found exactly what she needed. She grabbed the specialized anchor arrowhead and the threaded shaft to which it screwed tight. From a hook on the wall, she grabbed the longest coil of rope she could find and a spare Bowman's belt.

"What am I missing, Shift?" She tapped the back of the hand clutching the rope against her forehead.

"You'll need to light your flares. I have no idea what you have in mind, Princess, but that combination of arrowhead and length of rope and belt tell me you are gonna need a solid lock-knot, not matter how you use them."

Right. Shifty was a sailor. He could tie the knot.

"I'll come with you and light it for you. I have the flint and bladespar I used for the Bowman at Fairgates." Shifty dipped his hand into his pocket and produced the flint kit.

Tess lowered the rope, relief washing over her. Shifty would help, but they needed to hurry. She ran out the narrow door and searched the cliff above them.

"Why are you lookin' up?"

"There's a ladder here somewhere." It must be camouflaged like the one they'd ascended to the lookout. She felt around the rock. The ladder was there, and it led to a narrow ledge. Colt had described it to her the night they met—she just needed to… Her hand hit warm bladespar. Yes! She strung the bow and slung it over her shoulder before buckling the belt around her waist and slipping her arm through the coiled length of rope. Then she threw the quiver of four arrows across her back.

Tess climbed onto the railing and then onto the roof of the lookout. From there, she could step directly onto the bottom rung of the painted ladder. Climbing as quickly as she could, with no regard for safety or caution, she ignored her arm, which screamed in agony.

Shifty climbed right behind her, a lit oil lamp dangling from a length of rope around his neck. *Good thinking, Shift!*

Climbing for what seemed like fifty yards, she stopped when the ladder ended. She reached up and ran her hand along the flat, smooth limestone. The ledge. Pushing through the pain in her arm, Tess pulled herself up onto the ledge and then ran at breakneck speed along the stone that spanned no more than a yard in width. She had exactly the amount of time it took to load one hundred arrows. After that, every man on the battlefield—Colt, her father and brothers, Deacon, the crew of *The Girl*—all of them faced a maelstrom of death. The three hwacha could fire three hundred arrows, reload, and then do it all over again, and the men on the field might never discern their origin. The topography of the orchard put the hwacha in a shallow depression, and no soldier at the castle, save for those on the wall, would be able to sight it.

She reached her destination, the point directly in line with the wagons, which would give her the closest range possible. But their height now increased the distance beyond her range. She needed to descend at least fifty feet to have a chance. But first, she removed the rope from her arm and gave it to Shifty.

He didn't waste a second, immediately tying a complicated sailor's knot.

Tess gently grabbed the twine onto which the oil lamp dangled and removed it from Shifty's neck, then hung it around her own neck and winked at the bewildered raider. She then removed the whistle from her pocket, looped the lanyard around Shifty's neck, and stuck the end of it in his mouth as he tied.

"Don't stop blowing this until it's all over, Shifty. Bowman whistles are so loud I wouldn't be surprised if Colt could hear it from here. I only have four arrows—three flare and one standard. I need to shoot that lead operator, and I need to signal the threat for Colt. I just don't have enough arrows for all those men by myself, and even one man alone can set off those machines. I need Colt's help to get them all."

Shifty nodded.

Tess nocked the anchor arrow and shot straight down into the ledge. Her arm screamed in agony, but the perfect shot buried the arrowhead deep into the rock at her feet.

"You'll help lower me down, but this will ensure I have an anchor when I'm down there, so you don't need to keep holding me. That's what a Bowman would do, right?" She attempted a smile but couldn't quite manage it.

He nodded, his face tight with worry.

"Better start blowing, Shift."

He immediately complied, the piercing sound of the whistle causing both of them to wince. How could it make so much noise?

Tess used the spyglass. Some of the men still loaded arrows, but the leader looked back at the cliff, no doubt trying to sight the origin of the sound that emanated from the massive rock. She retrieved a flare arrow and dipped the fuse into the flame. As soon as it ignited, she nocked the arrow and shot at forty-five degrees. The arrow arced high over the hwacha and slowly disintegrated into a dazzling explosion of sparks as it fell. The lead operator turned to the cliff again. Hopefully, Colt saw the flare arrow. The men loading the machine had only a few arrows left. Tess had a minute at best.

She handed Shifty the rope.

Grabbing on with both hands, he braced himself against the cliff wall, and nodded, still blowing the whistle.

Without hesitation, Tess stepped off the edge of the cliff. She rappelled downward as Shifty lowered her, using the anchor arrow almost like a pulley to absorb the forward torque of her weight.

She didn't rush, knowing Shifty couldn't handle a quick pace without gloves. The whistle's shriek was deafening, even as she moved farther and farther from it. Would Colt hear it? Was Colt all right? She steadily descended until the rope pulled tight and stopped her downward progress, the anchor now in effect, holding all her weight. Good. At least seventy-five yards straight down from the ledge. She could make a shot from this distance.

Shifty, no longer under the strain of helping to lower her to the cliff, blew even louder.

Tess dug both heels into a shallow crevice running parallel with the ground. She leaned back against the cliff and found a balance point. The Bowman belt held fast around her waist, and the rope held fast to the anchor arrow above. She retrieved the second flare arrow from her quiver, dipped the fuse into the flame of the lamp that hung from her neck, watched it ignite, nocked it, aimed at forty-five degrees again, and let fly. A hot blade sliced right through her back muscles, and she let out a hateful cry of pain.

She desperately wanted to shoot at the team of men, take at least one of them down with the flare arrow, but she couldn't risk it. If the sparks ignited the main fuse, she would be sealing the fate of her tiermen. She surveyed the scene.

The men loading the arrows appeared to be panicking at the realization they were under fire from the cliff, and they took cover under the wagon. Their leader turned to face the wall again.

Stepping to the back handle of the central wagon, the leader swiveled it, aiming it directly at the cliffs. Could he see her? The lamp. Of course he saw her, she wore a glowing beacon around her neck. Where was Colt? Had he seen the flares? She couldn't wait another second. Every man on the field—Ardenian, Costair, Reyjik, it didn't matter—was at risk of being shot by a maelstrom of arrows.

"Princess, The Bowman, he's there!" Shifty stopped blowing the whistle to yell down the cliff face.

Tess's heart soared. She looked towards the castle, and there, cresting the hill of the low vineyard, was Colt. She would recognize his height and athletic stance anywhere.

She retrieved her final flare arrow, lit the fuse, nocked it, and released, aiming a little higher than the wagons on a straight path above them. That would show Colt their exact location. The arrow whizzed overtop the wagon on the right and then buried itself in the berm just beyond. Pure agony shot through her arm and back.

The men cowering behind that wagon remained hidden, but the team on the left sprang into action. Tess could see the glowing candle they planned to use to light their main fuse. No! That wagon pointed directly towards Colt, who ran at breakneck speed towards the machines, no doubt trying to close the range so he could engage.

She caught the glow of another candle, this one in the hands of the leader. If he lit his fuse, the arrows were aimed directly at the glowing light that hung around her neck.

Tess didn't think. She grabbed the last arrow from her quiver, a standard one. She held the flight to her cheek, sighted the man holding the candle, inhaled slowly, her arm shaking with the effort. After releasing it, she couldn't track the arrow in the poor light, but the glowing light near the left wagon dropped to the damp earth and out of sight. Colt was safe. She swung her gaze to him. He was still running, rapidly closing the distance between himself and the wagons. He would finish it.

Her eyes darted back to the lead operator crouching by the center wagon. She watched in horror as he lit his fuse. The small glow climbed steadily up the fuse towards the back of the wagon. In a matter of seconds, the storm of one hundred arrows would rain against her exact position. Tess couldn't even scream.

* * *

Colt's arms and legs weighed a hundred pounds. It was infinitely more draining being on the battlefield compared with firing from the wall. He tried desperately to aid Prince Derek in his failing assault while trying to protect the prince as best he could, a King's Bowman to the last.

Colt had just sighted a charging Reyjik soldier when he heard something that did not fit amongst the cries of wounded men and the clash of ferrite on bladespar.

He downed the charging enemy soldier and then searched for the source of the sound. Allowing himself to be distracted like that could seal his death, and as a Bowman, he wore a target on his back during battle. But the noise continued, and it sounded urgent, desperately calling to him. Where did it come from? The cliffs. The sound rang out from the cliffs. The lookout? Was it Tess? No, not the lookout, dead south of the castle, hundreds of yards from the lookout.

As Colt sprinted towards the cliffs, a flash of light caught his eye. A flare. It had been attached to an arrow that arced high in the sky and fell about a thousand yards from where he fought. The screeching sound continued. A whistle. The sound came from a Bowman whistle. Tess!

He ran as fast as he could. A second flare arrow shot from about sixty yards up the cliff face. How was that possible? He tracked its course. It landed out of view, just over a slight berm in the topography of the vineyards. Colt ran faster, cresting the berm, as a third flare shot out from the same place on the cliff straight to the vineyards. The blast of light illuminated three loaded hwacha wagons—two aimed at the battle that waned in front of the castle and one that faced the shooter on the cliff.

Colt ran as fast as his burning lungs would allow. He needed to get closer. He needed to close the range to the wagons. He needed to down every single man who took cover behind them. It only took one to light the fuse. One man could kill one hundred with only a candle.

All the operator needed to do was light the main fuse and the rest would happen automatically. That fuse would light each of the individual propulsion papers. Once an arrow's gunpowder was lit, it would take off in the trajectory the cart was set and hurtle towards its target, and they flew with such force. He had read they had a range of more than two thousand yards and proved unstoppable once the ignition fuse was lit. Blast the Reyjik. Blast their brilliant inventions!

Two hundred yards to go until range, one seventy. The glowing torch on his right fell to the ground, the man who'd been holding it dropping next to it. One hundred yards then eighty yards to range.

The man in the middle lit his fuse. No! That wagon aimed at the cliff. A glowing lamp revealed the shooter's exact location. No doubt the Reyjik operator had sighted that exact spot. Was it Tess?

Colt ran faster still. The glowing flame crawled up the fuse, only seconds from the first propulsion paper, seconds from spelling certain death to the brave shooter standing on the cliff. Helpless to stop the chain of events from his current position, he dug deep, forcing himself to run faster still. He couldn't afford a long shot. He needed to be precise. He had to hit the operator. Was he close enough? The man rose from his squat position, glowing candle in hand, and moved to the right most wagon. Colt decided he was close enough.

He stopped running, dropped to one knee, sighted the man, and let fly. The arrow drove into the right shoulder of the Reyjik who had stooped to light the fuse. As Colt nocked his second arrow, the man jerked back from the force of the impact and then dropped to the ground. The candle also dropped to the damp soil.

His gaze darted to the cliff. The fuse of the center wagon had reached the first arrow, and the entire machine glowed. Sparks flew in every direction as one hundred individual ferrite tipped missiles sped towards the cliff.

"No!" he shouted at the top of his lungs. At the same instant, the tiny glowing orb, marking the shooter's location, jerked skyward by a yard, then again, and then again. Had the violent ascent been enough?

Aiming at the first operator, he released arrow after arrow. He shot all nine men who'd been scrambling in confusion amongst the deadly machines. As the last man dropped, he allowed himself to peer back to the cliffs. Somone hung, held around their middle, a glowing orb dangling from the body. The soldier looked limp, lifeless, and slight. Tess!

Racing to the base of the cliff, he barely felt the ache in his arm, or the cramp in his right leg, or the burning sensation in his lungs. He only felt heartache. He stopped just short of the limestone wall and looked up. There, above him, a shadow slowly ascended the cliff face. The body casting the shadow bobbed and jerked upwards, as though not moving of its own accord. Was it Tess? He stood motionless, breathless, waiting. And then, carried on the downdraft, a faint cry.

"All's well, Bowman."

Shifty. Shifty's sailor's drawl, undeniably the sweetest sound he'd had ever heard.

Breathing a huge sigh of relief, Colt stared into the night's sky. Peaceful and still, and as it always was, oblivious to the chaos of conflict waged beneath it. Wait…something blocked the stars. Directly above, next to the cliff face, a void of total darkness, pitch without a single pinpoint of light. How could that be? Colt squinted. Was something there? Was something black, blocking the stars? A lookout tower, a platform? He'd never noticed it before. Was it camouflaged like the Bowman lookout for daytime concealment?

Colt noticed movement on the ledge in his peripheral vision. The lantern. Someone waved the lantern back and forth. Tess? Was she trying to get his attention? Why didn't she yell, he was easily within earshot.

Something whacked into the cliff face directly in front of him. Dropping to the ground, he checked over his shoulder, was he taking fire? No, the field leading all the way to the berm lay empty save for the hwacha wagons. Rising to his feet, he crept forward. It was a rope. Tess and Shifty had tossed him a rope with a loop tied into the end, just big enough for a boot-hold. What? Did they want him to climb up? How could he climb with his foot in the loop?

A brilliant flash of light burst from the cliff face just above the ridge. Like Reyjik fireworks on Eve of Descent, sparks flew in every direction, casting a d'orite glow. The sound boom followed and then Colt saw it clearly. The brilliant cascade of sparks perfectly silhouetted a lighter-than airship.

His heartrate plummeted. A lighter-than airship? Why couldn't he see the blimpoon? What was it doing so close to the Sapphire Star? He needed to get up there. Remembering the rope, he shoved his foot into the loop and yelled. "Ready!"

Shifty and Tess didn't reply, but instantly he was hoisted skyward. How were they accomplishing it? Smooth, even skyward strokes brought him ever nearer to the ridge. Fixing his eyes on the hull of the ship, he could see it wasn't big, not a galleon, or even a schooner, but bigger than the skiffs that typically raided. What was it doing?

More sparks showered down around him, complete with a concussive boom, even louder than the first. That wasn't fireworks. That was a gray powder charge.

Only a few yards from the cliff, Shifty hoisted him hand over hand from some attachment point further skyward, but how?

The scruffy pirate leaned to the edge of the ridge. "It's a lighter-than-aircraft, Bowman. It floated only yards from us just two minutes ago, painted totally black, even black silk for the blimpoon. We could hardly see it when it was right in front of our faces. They must have left in a hurry, 'cuz their block and tackle was dragging and dangling all manner of loose, and the princess just reached out and grabbed both ends. She had me tie our rope to one end to make it long enough to reach you on the ground and then haul you up with the other end."

Colt rose to hang eye to eye with Shifty. "Where is she?" He scanned the ridge in both directions, no Tess.

Shifty's eyes slowly rose skyward to the black void waiting directly above their position. "She's already up there, Bowman, held on just above the lock knot I tied to hitch up yer rope. She's got quite a jump on ya."

Blast! "Keep hoisting me up. Shift., why didn't you stop her?" Up there all alone, she was in terrible danger.

The pirate shifted from foot to foot. "I sure tried, Bowman, but she claimed seniority, said she needed to know who they were and what they were doing. She was right, of course. I'm sorry, Bowman."

Shifty made quick work of the ascent. The block and tackle must have boasted four pulleys at least. Within minutes the hull of the ship loomed overhead, black and foreboding until a third deafening boom echoed off the rocks. Sparks showered down the cliff and the brilliant light betrayed the stealth ship for what it was, a frigate class converted to an airship. But why was it blasting the cliff and who was piloting it?

The rope ran through a five-pulley system, mounted off a single crane. He reached for the crosspiece, swung his legs over the railing, and landed behind a large barrel stowed on the starboard side.

Tess's big green eyes starred into his. She squatted next to him behind a second barrel, fear written across her face. Leaning close she whispered in his ear. "They're trying to blast the Sapphire Star right out of the cliff."

"What?" Piercing the darkness, the clang of bladespar on stone jarred him to the bone. He peered over the edge of the barrel.

Standing only yards away, totally oblivious to their presence, five men hacked and pried at the huge truth stone, sending sparks in every direction. Tess was right. They had first set charges to blast it loose, and now they were attempting to cleave it right out of the cliff that had kept it since the creation of the Spire. With every impact, the Star, and the entire web of sapphire veins emanating from it, flashed a haunting blue, as if crying out in agony. Fear cut through him. Who would do this? Why?

Gerhert's wiry frame stepped out from behind the burner. "Get that rope under the bottom. I'll slit all your throats myself if it drops."

Tess's right hand squeezed his arm. "Colt, we have to stop them. What do we do?"

Footsteps thundered across the deck. Four more men ran from the port railing to aid the other five. One carried a rope and attempted to wedge it under the stone, now partially cleaved from the wall of rock.

Glancing over his shoulder, Colt checked his quiver. Two arrows. He only had two arrows left.

She followed his focus. "I used all mine on the hwacha wagons. What can we do?"

What could they do with two arrows? Nothing. "You're getting off. Go back down the rope to Shifty."

She squeezed tighter. "No, I can help, I can fight."

"Tess, you can't stand off against even one of those men in hand-to-hand combat, they're twice your size. Plus, we don't have enough arrows." The hacking rang in his ear, over and over. Were they getting close? He was running out of time. His stomach churned with despair, but it was their only chance to stop them. "You're going back down the rope. When you're on the ridge, I'm going to shoot their blimpoon. They'll start losing altitude and won't be able to get to the Star." His heart pounded. Yes, that would work. "Now go."

She placed her other hand on his. "You come too. You can shoot the blimpoon from the ridge."

Shaking his head from side to side, he flipped his hand and squeezed hers gently. "It's jet black and I can't see it from the ridge. Go, I'll come as soon as I make the shot."

Her lip quivered and she bit it with her front teeth. Tears misted in her eyes.

"I can't do it with you on board. Tess, please." He swallowed back the lump in his throat.

Another slash, more sparks, followed by an eerie blue glow. Nodding, she turned to the railing and slipped up and over without a sound.

Suddenly, a massive updraft hurled the ship twenty yards straight skyward.

Men screamed, Gerhert fell to the deck and a deafening crack split the night sky. All at once, the entire cliff face faded into utter darkness.

Gerhert's voice rose above the cries for help. "Have you got it?"

"Yes, two men lost, but I have it." The thick voice grunted the status of the stone.

Leaning over the railing, Colt checked for Tess.

She clung to the rope with both hands, legs coiled tight around it. "Shoot the blimpoon. We can't let them take it." Her whispers carried on the updraft that continued to buffet the ship. She was right.

"Get seaward to the ridge as fast as possible. I'll stall." Spinning, he stood, took aim, and drew.

"That won't do you any good, Captain." Gerhert's cold voice, calm and sure, cut to his heart.

He'd seen him first. It didn't matter. "It will do me a Realm of good to bring you down in splinters, Gerhert." *Stall Hawthorne.* "The battle's over. We won. And when they find this wreckage, they'll find the Sapphire Star right as rain and just put it back."

Grunts and gasps sounded from the soldiers. Colt listened for footsteps. Nothing, no one dared provoke him. Just a little more time. "What do you want with it anyway? Truth seems the last thing you care about, besides the fact your heart needs to be pure when you make a declaration. It wouldn't confirm so much as your name if you declared it." The emerald in Colt's bow glowed a brilliant green. A fire deep within forged the slightest measure of faith—he wasn't really alone.

Gerhert laughed, an icy, hollow laugh. It bounced off the deck and echoed against the blimpoon, sending a chill down Colt's spine.

Why was he laughing. Colt had him. Did he question his resolve to shoot at the cost of his own life? He shouldn't, he knew Bowman loyalty.

His laughter hissed to a stop. "You think the power of this stone ends with simple party tricks? You pathetic ingrate. A century of squander when we rotted down there, the only ones worthy of their power, the only ones who remembered." Unbridled hatred dripped from every word.

Something about his tone struck fear to Colt's core. *End this while you can, Hawthorne.* "Tess, you clear?"

"That's right, you and the princess were both unaccounted for."

How did he know who she was? Colt pivoted his stance to face Gerhert and shifted his focus to the man's empty gray eyes.

"Oh please, Captain. Of course, your little lady in waiting was Aratess, Lucious' youngest. You see, this is exactly why I chose you above the other Bowman candidates. When I read your application, saw that you were a half-blood thorn farmer, I knew you'd be no match for me."

Boiling rage churned within him. "No match for you? We've thwarted your attacks in both capitals. You've lost everything. It's over."

Gerhert threw back his head and laughed, the icy cackle ripping through Colt's confidence. "Oh Captain, it's too bad you won't live to see that it's only beginning." Gerhert stepped clear of the burner, nothing to block a shot. He was baiting Colt. Low and slow, in the most sour, taunting moan, he began to sing. "Forbidden is hidden, crumble makes you stumble, turn and burn, for the star so far."

What? Why would he sing the song to a children's game? He couldn't wait another moment. Something about Gerhert's tone terrified Colt. "Tess, Clear?"

"She's clear, Bowman." Shifty's voice rose faint but sure.

The fletching soft on his cheek, the ache of his arm, roiling in pain, he was keenly aware he'd never feel these sensations again, never feel anything again. He released, drew a second arrow, nocked and fired again.

Two hits side by side. The blimpoon puckered at the strike-point and split under the tension. Air whistled out of the hole, and the airship listed seaward.

The Star. Could he get to the truth stone? He had to try.

Lunging for the railing, he grasped smooth wood, and hauled himself against gravity, toward the soldier holding the stone.

The huge man buckled at the knees with the sudden loss of altitude and fell to all fours, dropping the Star to the deck, where it skidded to the stern.

Releasing the handrail, Colt slid directly to stern, the stone only yards from his grasp, when a sudden updraft buffeted the ship straight skyward. He hit the stern railing, launched up and over, just managing to grasp some rigging with one hand before he cartwheeled into the abyss.

The ship fell seaward, spinning slowly as it plummeted.

Reaching up, Colt clutched the rope with both hands, his legs carried by the centripetal force of the spiraling aircraft, spinning him horizontal.

A huge, gray man appeared above him. With one hand he clung to the railing, in the other he raised a sabre over his head, the moonlight reflecting off the wide blade. He stopped as if frozen and hissed something to Colt in a totally foreign tongue. Guttural, and sharp, and completely unintelligible. Throwing his head back, he laughed.

The ship spun to port.

The soldier leaned his entire torso over the railing. "Two stones ours, let's see how you like the dark." He brought his blade down in one smooth stroke and slashed the rope through.

Hold on! Colt fell for only a moment before smashing into the cliffs, and everything faded to darkness.

Chapter Thirty-Four

The Kings

Colt

COLT GRIPPED THE OAK ARM OF his chair. It felt smooth, sanded to a perfect finish, oiled to a rich luster under his sweaty palms. He couldn't squeeze it hard enough. He scanned the room again. For three days he'd been staring at the luxurious board room, a true meeting room for monarchs.

Reyjik silk, dyed a rich emerald green, lined the walls. Four huge tapestries, woven from Reyjik linen, were displayed along the interior wall. The tapestries hung one on top of the other, each depicting a tier of the Spire—Reyjik, Costair, Ardenia, and Lindsor, each woven with the intricate goods native to their tier.

Beautiful dishes, fashioned of hammered Costair d'orite, spread down the center of the board table, each boasting imported fruit and cheese from the seaward tier.

Colt's hands, hidden from view under the matching oak board table, avoided the king's scrutiny. He could squeeze all he wanted. King Salmon was speaking and gripping the chair arm proved his only recourse in managing his reaction.

"We must strike them now! We must raise a force, sail down the sluice, and hit them as hard as we can. I will not wait for a second strike. I will not allow their aggression to go unchecked. They took the Sapphire star. Our sacred truth stone, for Realm's sake. My people are terrified. They are looking to me. I want vengeance and I want it now!" King Salmon slapped the tabletop with his right hand and cringed slightly. The slap must have hurt.

Colt glanced at Colonel Merriweather, but he sat fixated on King Salmon, nodding.

"I agree, Salmon." Tess's father, King Lucius, spoke with more control, but not much. "What the Realm needs now is stability. We must secure our tierdoms. We should attack Reyjik right away and hit them before they have a chance to reorganize and rearm."

Colt had heard enough. It had been an entire day of exactly the same sentiments, and his colonel had only listened and nodded. Not once had Merriweather offered strategic counsel. He appeared afraid to speak up to the kings. Colt couldn't stand another longwinded speech spouting revenge and reprisal and strength.

The sun streamed through the window, leaving the boardroom uncomfortably warm. He pegged the time as a quarter to past peak. The last three days had been beautiful, the best Ardenian spring had to offer, though he only observed the sunshine from behind the stained-glass window. Both kings and Merriweather had requested his participation in the meetings and had grilled him for the first two days on every detail that had transpired.

He had told them everything, but as they spoke now, it seemed they'd only heard what they wanted. The debriefing had digressed into speech after speech about the evils of Reyjik and the need to seek revenge.

He longed to loosen the top button of his collar and breathe deeply. He needed to address the king's plan. He had to make them listen. If Merriweather wouldn't, Colt must.

Releasing his grip on his chair arm, he raised his hand slowly above the table and then stretched it high in the air the way he used to in primer school or classes at the Bowman Academy.

All three men turned to look at him. Merriweather raised a questioning eyebrow.

He ignored his superior and stayed the course.

"Excuse me, Your Majesties, Colonel, but I have been sitting and listening intently for a full day, and I feel I must speak."

King Lucius flashed a look at Merriweather and then shifted his attention to Colt.

"Of course, Commander, we welcome your counsel. That's why we requested your presence here." He gestured for Colt to speak.

Nerves twisted his stomach. "Well, Your Majesties, you have

spent considerable time indicating your desire to seek reprisal, revenge even, on Reyjik, but we haven't yet discussed the inconsistencies with the attacks."

All three men studied him. King Salmon's brow creased into a deep furrow. Merriweather only nodded again.

Lucius stroked his white sideburn. "What inconsistencies, Commander?"

What inconsistencies? I don't know, take your pick. "Well, Your Majesty, to begin with, the Reyjik have been at peace with the Realm for generations, a welcomed trade partner and a trusted ally."

Both kings scoffed at his declaration.

Colt frowned. What? That was a well-known fact. Why did they challenge it? "Your Majesties, I must insist that we all acknowledge the facts, that Reyjik has not once shown aggression towards the Realm in any manner in more than a hundred years." He couldn't back down on this. He met their stares and refused to flinch.

They looked away, not able to raise a true challenge.

"As I said, they have been peaceful, and this aggression is totally uncharacteristic, specifically in light of the fact that they gained nothing and could gain nothing from the attacks."

"Thanks to you, Commander. Without your response, they would have taken both tiers and all our resources." Lucius threw his hands in the air.

Colt's frown deepened. Did the man know nothing of supply chain and logistics? "I'm sorry, Your Majesty, but I've had a chance to asses their provisions and they could never have taken both tiers with the men and arms they brought. With no supply chain, they couldn't feed those few soldiers. They couldn't hold the castles for long with their numbers, let alone secure our bladespar production. No, nothing about the attacks makes sense, especially the fact that all they truly managed to accomplish was to make you both angry."

"They succeeded in that to be sure!" Lucius wagged his index finger and the other two men nodded.

Colt needed to continue, before he lost them for good. "We never found General Gerhert's body amidst the wreckage. We know that he, and at least two of his men, escaped with the Star." No matter how warm the room, saying his name out loud sent a chill along Colt's spine. "And none of the Reyjik prisoners of war we questioned have any idea why they were ordered to attack or anything about the strategic end game. Some thought they were taking part in training exercises. Training exercises, Your Majesties!" He tried to meet their gazes one at a time, but Lucius peered down at the table and Salmon gazed out the window.

He repressed a sigh. Was he getting through to them at all? "And then there is the soldier I met on the airship, he stated that two stones had been taken… Which makes me wonder whether the Diamond Star has also been stolen from Reyjik's cliffs."

Both kings snapped their attention to Colt with this statement. Finally. He needed to press further.

"I have intelligence that something happened in Reyjik a half year past, some sort of political intrigue that resulted in a super potent gray powder hitting the black market. This powder can superheat the air inside a blimpoon and turn very large vessels into lighter than aircraft."

"Which is why we are making our own lighter than aircraft fleet." His colonel spoke up for the first time all day.

Colt studied him. Like the kings, he looked old, tired, and afraid. "Of course, sir, but that presents another problem. We are now arming ourselves with weapons to match their increased capacity for destruction, which renders peace increasingly less likely."

King Salmon leaned way forward and narrowed his eyes, studying him. "Peace? Who said anything about peace?" He almost hissed the question.

Lucius, motionless, didn't say a word.

Hot waves rose within him, his left hand still gripping the arm of his chair threatening to crush the oak into pulp. "I did, Your Majesty. The Realm, all three tiers, has been at peace with Reyjik for generations. It was a Reyjik emperor who first conceived and authored the Sacramance Accord, for Realm's sake. We need their gray powder for our mines and their cotton for our clothing, and we use their bamber. Our entire trade system will crumble without those things. We all want peace, Your Majesty!"

The kings both raised their chins in response and Merriweather glared at him.

Had he gone too far? Why were they so afraid? Why wouldn't they at least try to figure out what happened? Didn't they want to know the truth? Wait, the truth! Yes, that might work!

"Your Majesties, I have an idea. Should we consult the Emerald Star on the matter? King Lucius, could you not make a declaration regarding the Reyjik's intentions, at least try to understand what transpired?"

Lucius began shaking his head before Colt finished the question. "No, Commander, absolutely not. We know what we must do. The security of our tiers demands we strike back. The truth can be confusing, and I fear being spun around when what is required is already so clear."

A sick feeling swept over him. The kings no longer sought truth. Indeed, fear, not the pursuit of truth, clearly governed their decisions. He was alone, as though pinned under the main hoist, invisible to the hoistmen, and they continued to lower the crushing load despite his silent screams.

Two stones ours, let's see how you like the dark. Darkness closed in around him. Did that foreign man know something? Had the Diamond Star been taken? Was that the catalyst, the inciting event that had forced every other action into motion? How could he find out? What could he do about it when his superiors wanted only war and revenge?

Serve king and tier with all thy strength...In all things, trust the truth. Words from the oath he had taken drifted through his mind. *Well, my king might not want truth, but my tier needs it.* Colt pushed back his shoulders. He knew exactly how to work it out.

"You are right, of course, Your Majesty. We need to secure Ardenia and Costair, and to accomplish that we need to strike hard and ensure victory."

Both men leaned back in their chairs, smiles forming at the corners of their mouths.

He jumped on their obvious approval. "And victory is guaranteed through good intelligence. We need to know their numbers, their strengths and weaknesses. We must infiltrate their military leadership and learn their plan. If they have ulterior motives, we need to discover them. If they have goals, we must find out what they are so we can respond with force. We need to find the chink in their armor so we can exploit it to the greatest degree possible!"

Both kings smiled and nodded.

"What do you propose, Commander?" Colonel Merriweather crossed both arms and stared at Colt.

"A spy, sir. I propose we send a spy into Reyjik. He needs to hold military rank, an officer's rank if possible, and he must speak and understand Reyjik. If he looks Reyjik, understands cultural nuances, and passes for Reyjik in every way, he can earn their trust, learn their plan, and turn around and advise you on how to deliver a precision hit so devastating, they will never again invade the Realm."

The three men stroked their chins thoughtfully, almost in unison.

He would have chuckled at the sight were he not so terrified they would refuse their consent.

"And how do you suggest we manage all that, Commander?" His colonel's tone was rife with doubt.

Colt swallowed hard. "We release the prisoners, sir. We repair their last galleon, the one I disabled in the Ridley. We round up the survivors from both the Battle of Fairgates and Costair, and we plant one man amongst the soldiers. We have Reyjik uniforms to spare. With all the different platoons and all the different ships, men will not necessarily know each other. So, we embed him with the shuffled prisoners, and we let them all sail back to Reyjik, citing diplomacy and good will. This man infiltrates, learns their weaknesses, and advises on the most devastating way to exploit those weaknesses. And then you strike, sir. Only when we are assured victory through sound intelligence do we wage war."

Sitting back in his chair, he studied the effect of his efforts. It had to work. All three men seemed mentally paralyzed, unable to entertain any thought besides war and revenge. Thankfully, they also appeared to be carefully considering his plan. It had to work. He had pandered to their desire for vengeance. They would take the bait.

They must.

Finally, King Salmon slapped the table hard. "I like the idea, Merriweather, how about you?"

"Well, Commander Hawthorne is one of our best and brightest. I would expect nothing less than a brilliant piece of strategy and subterfuge. How long do you think you'll need, Commander?"

You'll? Colt's eyebrows rose. Maybe he wouldn't have to convince them he was the perfect man for the job.

"Two months, sir. Three at the most. I speak and read the language fluently, so I am ready to leave immediately. The voyage will take time, and I'll need to work my way to their capital, which might require a promotion. It could be a month before I learn everything I need to properly inform our invasion."

"Three months?" Salmon slapped the table so hard this time he had to shake out his hand. "What if they invade us first?"

Think, Colt. "Well, Your Majesty, I will be privy to military goings-on, so if they are preparing to invade, I'll surely know, and I will inform you. You will have your ear to the ground, so to speak, an inside man. I am confident it will take time for the Reyjik to reorganize as it is, but if they remount a second attack, you'll be ready for it."

Lucius stroked his beard, his gaze fixed somewhere on the back wall of the room. "Why don't we strike now, while they are reorganizing?"

Because I need time to figure out what is going on and how to restore peace to this sun-forsaken spire, if that's even possible. And I need time to find two truth stones and the people behind their theft. He took a deep breath. He had played on their vulnerability and desire to get back at the invaders. They had to give him time to figure out what happened, time to understand if peace was possible, or if it had vanished into the mist that rose from the dark sea. *Say something, Colt, make them listen.*

"Striking back immediately might be just what they are hoping for. We could descend into a trap. Or accidentally attack their most defended fortification or strike their strongest division and needlessly sacrifice more good men. We need to assess their weaknesses and strike there."

The elderly man nodded slowly and then swung his gaze to Merriweather. "You and the commander will see to it immediately then?"

Colt tried to suppress a deep sigh of relief. He would go. They were giving him a chance to do his very best to save the spire.

A strange sensation washed over him, flooded with a vivid memory of standing in the lookout with Tess. She had spoken with such passion about the delicate balance of trade that connected each tier. He had taken that balance for granted, scoffed at the greed of men which proved a mild nuisance to his duty. Only a few weeks later, he was fighting for the chance to save that balance, that delicate peace, an endeavor so rife with risk he wondered if he would even live to appreciate its beauty.

A strong knock on the heavy wooden door startled every man in the room. A porter entered and stood at attention. King Lucius nodded his consent for the man to speak.

"Your Majesty, you asked me to inform you when the delegation from Lindsor had arrived for the ceremony, and they have." The slight man bowed, exited, and closed the door behind himself.

Tess's father rose from his chair and stood straight and tall. "Salmon, Colonel, Commander, we've done good work here. We'll expect regular reports as to the commander's progress and findings. He must be sworn to the utmost secrecy. No one, not a living soul outside of this room, may know of the plan. We can make the arrangements for him to join the prisoners tomorrow, but for tonight, we celebrate." He bowed to Salmon, who bowed in kind.

"Yes, we celebrate. With our tiers united, and the force of two Realm militaries, we will prove victorious!" Salmon puffed his chest as he rose.

Colt barely resisted the urge to scowl. What a fool! What did he really know of war?

Lucius paused at the doorpost and turned to face the men in the room. "With Aratess's marriage to Jestin, we'll soon have three militaries, I'm sure. His decision to pursue the first right of refusal we gave years ago could not be timelier. I can't imagine Lindsor wanting to sit out with so much at stake, and a mutual defence policy will be included during the negotiations for her hand." With a final nod, Lucius disappeared into the hallway.

Aratess's marriage? The warm room spun around Colt. She was to marry Jestin, the prince of Lindsor? He sat abruptly and gripped the arms of his chair again as Tess's words flashed through his mind. *"Well, Captain, I happen to know that the year before last, the king traded a full hoist of bladespar and the hand of his daughter to Lindsor for only a pocket full of emeralds…That stone you disregard came at a very high price to the Realm."*

Somewhere deep inside, Colt's very soul began to crumble. He couldn't stand. He couldn't force himself off the oak chair. His legs had melted to water. Yet, he must. The ceremony. He needed to see it through, for her sake. She had earned it, he owed it to her, so he needed to rise.

Chapter Thirty-Five

The Ceremony

Tess

TESS COULDN'T FOCUS ON HER FATHER'S words. The speech was no doubt rousing, sincere, and patriotic, as evident by the multiple times he needed to wait and allow the applause to die down, but Tess wasn't listening. Choosing a shield on the back wall to cast her attention upon had worked. She had successfully made it through the entire opening remarks of the ceremony without sighting the prince, or the Bowman, and falling into a mist of despair.

The program shifted to the awards. They had been through all this the day before. The two kings would read the words of commendation. Sasha and Durbink would award the various medals. Tess, not required to do anything but stand to the left of her father and clap at the appropriate times, felt relieved when the ceremony drew to completion. Her abdomen, bruised black and blue from when Shifty had yanked her out of the path of one hundred arrows, still made standing for long stretches difficult.

The kings commended Sam first. He received the award of valor, never before given to a king's courier. The crowd cheered. While Sasha and Durbink did the honors, Tess allowed herself to look at Sam. He caught her eye and smiled widely. He looked so proud. She forced herself to smile in kind, as she knew Sam longed for approval.

Next, they honored Derek and Fredrik for bravery in battle, and then they called forward the officers of *The Dancing Girl*. Both kings took turns reading out the list of service, sacrifice, and accomplishment of these most unlikely heroes, Shifty, Reynolds, Riley, and Deacon.

Deacon winked at her twice. She couldn't help but laugh that, even in the finest of men's fashion, all four still managed to look like pirates. The crowd absolutely loved the way they kissed Sasha and slapped Durbink on the back as they received their awards.

Tess had located Jestin out of the corner of her eye, beside his father in the front row. He stood tall, a subtle lean to his right. He wore a military dress uniform, though she knew for a fact he'd never served a day in Lindsor's military. He stared at her, but she refused to meet his gaze. Her father had made his wishes crystal clear. She wasn't to leave Jestin's side at the gala. She was to play the part of the perfect princess, hanging off his arm and giving him her full attention for the sake of Ardenia. The Realm must unite, he had declared. They needed Lindsor's strength of arms. Her marriage would accomplish that. Tess felt like vomiting.

In all this time, Tess hadn't seen Colt. He'd been there three days already. Why hadn't he come to see her? She sighed. Colt's reaction to her made perfect sense. He only behaved how everyone else in her life had ever behaved. When she proved helpful, he tolerated her company, but now she placed so far down his list of importance that he hadn't even bothered to see her. Why did she want to see him? To what possible end? With her future set, literally in stone, his indifference made everything that much easier. No, Captain Colt Hawthorne, Bowman of the Realm, was just that, a soldier in her father's army. He loved that calling, and it would always place decidedly first in his life, as it should. He barely managed to allow people to help him, and that proved better, easier, safer for her.

The announcement of the final award came. Her father introduced Colonel Merriweather, who had been standing on the far right of the stage. Merriweather walked to his place beside her father. He cleared his throat and addressed the expectant crowd.

"As you know, the Bowmen of the Realm exist to protect your fair tierdom and your king." The crowd erupted into applause with the colonel's opening statement. Word of Colt's achievements had spread like wildfire. His role in the two battles were now stories of legend. She had heard the maids speak of him as they changed the flowers in her room and stoked her fire. He had fired five hundred, no six hundred, no one thousand arrows that night in Costair.

Jestin did not clap.

A seasoned orator, Merriweather paused and let the crowd show their support. "I would like to call forward Commander Colt Hawthorne, King's Bowman."

She bit her lip. Commander. He'd been promoted.

Again, cheers filled the ballroom. A solid minute passed before the applause and appreciation from the audience died down. Colt strode forward from the far right side of the stage. He took his place at Merriweather's side and stood at attention. He'd cropped his hair short in Reyjik style. His chiseled features defined an undeniably handsome profile.

Colonel Merriweather cleared his throat. "Commander Hawthorne has shown uncommon bravery, unparalleled tenacity, and unprecedented resourcefulness in battle. As such, it is my great honor to present him with the Emerald Star, the highest honor available to an Ardenian soldier."

The crowd went wild. Her father handed the small d'orite star pin to King Salmon. Salmon bowed and presented the award to Colt himself. Her father stood directly between Colt and Tess, blocking him from her view, which proved a kindness.

The ceremony was all but finished. She would fulfil her obligations and wait at the gala for a half hour, laugh at a few of Jestin's jokes, and then she could plead a headache and disappear to the castle rooftop.

After the cheers had subsided, Tess startled at the sound of Colonel Merriweather's voice and not her father's closing remarks.

"As Bowman Chief Superintendent, I have never had the honor of doing what I am about to do." The crowd went silent, every eye fixed on the colonel. "Would Princess Aratess of Ardenia please step forward."

Tess inhaled sharply as the room erupted into cheers and applause once again, the display of support matching that of Colt's. Stunned, she didn't move at first. No one had mentioned this when they reviewed her role at the ceremony. What was going on?

Sasha crossed the stage and grabbed Tess's hand. She led her to center stage and positioned her directly in front of Colonel Merriweather, only a pace and a half from Colt. The colonel smiled warmly at her.

"Thanks to Commander Hawthorne, I have been well briefed on Princess Aratess's role in the saving of our fair tierdom, and I am sure the stories have reached you as well."

More applause and cheers. Heat rushed into Tess's cheeks.

"Commander Hawthorne will briefly describe them in case there are those present who are unaware of these acts of bravery."

Tess's heart stopped and her breathing shallowed. No, this was too much.

Colt stepped forward, and instinctively she looked up into his eyes, the softest, kindest, and deepest brown. He smiled before grasping her shoulders and gently turning her to face her people. He cleared his throat. "Your princess fulfilled her duty to her people at a level of highest sacrifice, bravery, and valor. If you haven't heard, she singlehandedly sank a galleon with a flaming arrow in the Battle for Fairgates. She saved hundreds of men from needlessly falling to hwacha on the plains of Costair, and she valiantly fought to save the Sapphire Star. She supported my every effort, a most faithful partner in our mission to stave off this threat. Without your princess, I would not have earned this honor." Colt placed his hand over the medal now pinned to his dress uniform. "As much as any man in the corps, she has the heart of a Bowman."

Tess's mouth dropped open slightly as he smiled down at her. Did he mean everything he'd declared in front of the nobility of all tierdoms? His eyes told her he did. Colt returned to his place.

Colonel Merriweather stepped forward. "In light of her determination, loyalty, service, and skill with a longbow, it is my honor to now induct her into the corps—Princess Aratess, an honorary King's Bowman!"

She pressed a hand to her chest. A Bowman? Had they just made her a Bowman?

The look on her face must have betrayed her confusion because Colt laughed as he placed the crest in her trembling hand. Then he grabbed her hand and, in one quick motion, raised it over her head.

The crowd cheered. Tess's heart soared. In the deepest place of her heart, she wished he would never let go.

Chapter Thirty-Six

The Proposal

Deacon

DEACON WATCHED HIS FRIEND CLOSELY. COLT hadn't taken his eyes off Tess since they arrived at the gala. Colt was an expert in observation and surveillance, so he hid it well enough no one else in the ballroom likely noticed his preoccupation. Still, Deacon caught every sideways glance, every nonchalant look in her direction. To his core, he felt Colt's pain.

The princess stood poised and perfect, lightly holding the arm of Prince Jestin. Lindsor! How in the Realm could she be marrying a Lindsite? Why didn't she mention his first right of refusal? She couldn't possibly love this man. Were her unconventional interests a distraction from this future? Were they her attempt to dissuade Jestin's intent to marry her? *She can't love him.*

Deacon crossed the floor of the ballroom to Colt's side, drink in hand. Someone had opened the doors to the terrace and a fresh, cool breeze swept through the crowded room. The decorated commander had been congratulated by every single man present from all three tierdoms, or so it seemed, and now he seemed held for ransom by Sam. Enough of that.

"All right, Sam, I need to speak with the illustrious commander for a moment, but Shifty told me he wanted to hear all about yer part in the battle for Fairgates, how you lit the princess's arrows and the like. He's waiting over by the bar." Deacon made sure to point out his second mate long enough for Sam to sight him. His chest sticking out, Sam started for the bar.

"You owe Shifty a drink for that." Colt glanced in Tess's direction, only for a moment, but Deacon caught it.

"A drink seems a bargain. I reckoned on a whole bottle." He slapped Colt hard on the back.

Colt's smile was forced, his jaw tight.

Deacon recognized the excruciating intensity of helplessness. He needed to address it. "Did you know?" He nodded in the direction of the royal couple-to-be.

Colt shook his head slowly. "She mentioned it on *The Girl*, but I didn't know she was the princess then, and I never really put it together. I found out right before the ceremony." He drew in a ragged breath.

"Well, are you gonna do something about it?" His stomach twisted. Colt clearly cared for Tess deeply. Maybe even loved her. As a rival for her affections, Deacon's greatest advantage was Colt's refusal to tell her how he felt. The last thing he wanted was for Colt to make a play for the princess. He could handle the useless Lindsite prince, but Colt was a different story altogether. Still, as a friend, somewhere deep in his gut he wished Colt would act.

The Bowman sighed deeply. "What can I do?"

"What can you do? Are you serious? Don't you know now, for certain, that you need her? The stone confirmed it. As solid as the Sacreds."

"So?" Colt shrugged, his jaw still clenched tight.

"So, tell her!" Heat coursed through him.

"I have no idea what I'd say. Not sure what it all meant, when I think about it. I was so certain in that moment, but now…" He scratched his fingers through the short hair at the back of his neck. "Now I can't need her, Deac. Not for the mission, not for anything." He sighed again, his shoulders slumping.

Deacon stepped in close and whispered between clenched teeth. "Think about what will happen to you if you don't tell her. Think about a life without her. Do you want that? You don't even have to answer because I know you don't."

Colt closed his eyes and shook his head. "None of this is about me, Deac. What I need doesn't matter. The bottom line is, it wouldn't be right to tell her." With one last, long look at Tess, he turned and walked slowly across the ballroom to the north exit. He raised his right hand to Deacon before slipping through the door.

Deacon stared at the doorway where his friend had disappeared. *Blast you, Colt. Blast your honor and blast your blasted call of duty! If you won't take a shot, I will, for both of us!*

Downing the last of his drink, he took a deep breath and headed for the princess. He wouldn't go down without a fight.

Tess appeared to track Colt as he left the ballroom. She didn't even seem to notice Deacon's approach, her attention was so focused on the hero's exit. She wore a ruby red gown. Lindsor's color. Jestin's color. Her d'orite hair shone in the candlelight, her long, dark lashes fringing sad, helpless eyes. Three long curls hung down her bare upper back. She was tragically beautiful.

The cool breeze drafting in from the open patio doors lifted her hair slightly as she continued to gaze in that direction. Did she long to be on that balcony, in the woods, anyplace but where she stood? He could give her that. He had to try.

Three kings, three princes, and a princess, no problem. This should be a hoist in the sunshine. *Stop that, Deacon, you saved their blasted tierdoms. They all owe you... all but her. Bow and make it a good one!* Deacon bowed low, hinging at the hips, extending his right arm as he did and waving it low to the floor. His arm and shoulder still ached from the battle for Costair, and his silk neckerchief felt tight.

"Your majesties, your highnesses, may I be so bold as to beseech thee for the honor of a dance with our brave princess." Rising to face the six men, he didn't dare look at Tess. If he caught her eye, he'd laugh for certain and blow it all.

Without a glance in his direction, Jestin pushed the arm to which Tess clung towards Deacon. With his other hand, he brushed Tess's slender hand off his broqued sleeve, as if he were wiping crumbs from his shirt. With a half-hearted wave of his freed right hand, he dismissed them both.

Deacon's stomached tightened. In Jestin's estimation, Deacon hadn't even warranted a word. He gave his permission to Deacon's request without so much as looking at him or Tess.

Head high, Tess stepped to Deacon's side. He smiled down at her, not able to curb his enthusiasm. She took his arm as he led her to the very center of the dance floor, placing as many couples as he could between them and the monarchs.

Almost immediately, the stringed quartet began playing "The Sapphire Sislay." Deacon had caught a break, as he was good at the waltz. The other couples blurred in his peripheral vision. He bowed low again, she curtsied, and then he slid his arm behind her back and pulled her in as close as decorum would allow.

She stiffened but didn't fight.

Breathe, Thornby. He stepped forward with his right foot and they began touring the floor in perfect time to the music. Tess looked over his shoulder, still tense, and she hadn't spoken. What should he say? What could he say?

"You can't marry that guy!" He whispered the words matter-of-factly, and Tess laughed. Her body relaxed slightly, and she leaned closer.

He held her tight.

"I can't *not* marry that guy, Captain Thornby," she whispered back. He tensed his hand, pressing even more firmly into the small of her back. When he realized how tightly he held her, he forced himself to ease his grip.

"Then run away with me." He made the statement as casually as he could, as if he were ordering a drink.

Her head snapped to the left and her wide eyes locked with his, her mouth gaping slightly.

Don't stop, Thornby, lay it all out for her, all that it could be. "I mean it, Tess. You love *The Girl* and the crew, and they love you. You love the sea. I've never seen a girl so in love with the sea, and don't get me started about flying."

She laughed again and sent another look toward the balcony doors.

He turned them in a circle. "I'd promise to make you happy, Tess, I know I could. For Realm's sake, you know you'll be happier on the sea with me than stuck in his castle up there in the shadow of the vertical horizon. Do you know how cold Lindsor gets in winter?" Deacon forced himself to chuckle, trying to mask the note of desperation that echoed as he spoke.

Tess didn't answer. He was right, and she had to know it. She loved *The Girl,* she loved the sea, and she loved the crew. She would be happier with him, even if they were on the run, even despite scandal and guilt over shirked responsibility. Anything would be better than the future towards which she hurtled.

She sighed and faced him, a mischievous grin touching the corners of her perfect mouth. "You can't abscond with the princess now, Captain, not after you've been granted a full pardon and have been given the honor of setting up our lighter-than-air division of the navy." Her voice skipped and sang, as if her very happiness wasn't hanging from the words she forced past her lips.

Nope, not good enough, Princess. "You know me better than that, Tess. You know I don't give a rip about my career or honor or reprisals. I'd run with you at the end of this blasted waltz if you so much as nodded that was what you wanted." He pulled her closer, although something in what she'd said pricked his conscience. His jaw muscle twitched with strain. This wasn't nearly as easy as he pretended.

"Yes, I know you, Deacon, and I know you love Ardenia. I know you understand how badly the navy needs your expertise. I know you would never turn your back on her, not now." She sighed again and then rested her head on his left shoulder. He dared a look down. Her eyes were closed, and she smiled the sweetest smile.

Silently, Deacon prayed the words of the waltz would prove true, that the Sapphire Sislay would last forever.

Chapter Thirty-Seven

The Parting

Colt

COLT HELD FAST TO BLIND HOPE, acting on a hunch. He hadn't slept and his soul felt raw, but he needed to speak with Tess. At the gala, she'd remained at Jestin's side, hanging off his arm while all Colt could do was pretend not to watch. He'd only managed to endure the situation until the receiving line had waned, and then he'd left, hopeless and defeated. He shook, trying to free himself from the feeling.

As he walked out onto the high rooftop, he squinted. The sun had crested the precipice. There Tess stood. He'd guessed right. Leaning on Samson with her back to the door, only paces away, could she hear his pounding heart? What would he say? He walked slowly over to the princess. "I've seen better views."

Tess jumped and then spun around to face him. "Oh, my goodness, Captain. You scared me." Her hand flew to her heart. "Sorry. Commander. Congratulations on your promotion."

He smiled. It felt good to hear her say it, *commander*, and yet he longed for her to use his name. "Sorry, Princess." He stuck his hands in his pockets. It was his turn to say something, but as he looked into her beautiful green eyes, he couldn't find the words. He swallowed hard.

She reached out and touched the medal pinned in place on his dress uniform. "I've never actually seen an emerald star medal up close. It's a real honor, Colt." She gently passed her finger over the emerald. And there it was, she had called him Colt. A newfound confidence swelled deep inside.

"How's your arm, Princess? Have you done any shooting lately?"

"I tried this morning. It's better, but I can't draw all the way." Sadness swept over her face.

"Don't worry. It'll come. Just give it time."

She smiled up at him.

He needed to say more. "It was a miracle you could fire those flare arrows. Shifty told me about how you shot the hwacha operator aiming for me instead of the one aiming for you. That was pretty reckless, Your Highness." He crossed his arms over his chest and narrowed his eyes.

Pink tinged her cheeks.

"I can only imagine how much that hurt your back. You saved my life again. You saved a lot of lives, Princess."

Her smile widened. "No, Commander, you saved a lot of lives. You saved us all." The emerald in the medal she still touched confirmed the statement with a bright flash of light. She pulled her finger back. "Have you recovered from the crash? Are you all right? I wanted to stay until you woke, but my father needed to ascend."

Colt needed to say so much to her in that moment. And yet, all he could think about was her betrothal and the fact that he was leaving within the hour. He couldn't tell her all the things he ached for her to know—his mission, his suspicions, the king's strange reaction. He was tormented by Gerhert's words and the foreign man on the ship, and he desperately wanted her counsel, yet he'd sworn an oath of secrecy. He swallowed and nodded.

Tess leaned back against Samson. "So, Commander, I guess you were right after all. You are a King's Bowman and there truly *isn't* a problem in the Realm that you can't think your way out of." She smiled, but she didn't sound as though she was teasing. She meant the statement in earnest.

Overwhelmed by guilt because he couldn't tell her of his mission, he needed to be honest about the things he could admit. He owed her that much. "No, Tess, the only thing I figured out was that I can't get very far without your help… and I hate that fact."

Her eyes grew wide.

Colt thought of the emerald star and the importance of being truly honest, especially with oneself. His mouth went dry. "I keep thinking about that night with the emerald star. I couldn't even make the declaration we needed. I couldn't, didn't care most about the mission even though that was exactly what my duty called for. You had to do it because I failed, too caught up in my own feelings... with what I cared... with something personal." *Blast! Not that honest, Hawthorne!*

Tess reached for a loose hair at the nape of her neck as she stared up at him. Her eyes locked with his, soft and sweet. The corners of her lips curled in just the hint of a smile. "Want to know why I was able to make that declaration, Colt?" She reached up and touched his medal again, fidgeting with it, passing her index fingertip slowly back and forth over the emerald.

"Sure." Mesmerized by how close they stood and how sweet she was, he answered automatically. She was different. Was she different?

She bit her lower lip. "I know how the star works, about the caveat and that the declaration must mean most to you. I should have warned you about that, but I didn't think about it in the moment, and I'm sorry. I'd never consulted the star myself before that night and I forgot." She took a deep breath. "When you swung back and you didn't... couldn't ask about the men, and I saw how torn up you were about that, I knew I could make the declaration because it would definitely mean most to me as it was what you needed right then and helping you is what means most to me."

The emerald in his medal flashed a brilliant green. Colt lost his breath. The flush on her cheeks deepened as she lowered her hand and smoothed her skirt with her palms.

His heart pounded in his chest, nausea sweeping over him.

Her hands grew still, and she sighed deeply. "You're already on mission again, aren't you?" Concern filled her eyes.

How could she be that perceptive? He managed to shake his head. "I can't talk about that, Tess. I'm sorry."

Her eyes narrowed. He knew that look. "Colt, we need to try for peace. We must try to figure out what's happened, find the stars, restore them. It seems like everyone wants a war now, but we must try for peace. How can we find the Sapphire Star? Did Gerhert say anything of importance? We need to understand why Reyjik attacked. Nothing makes sense!" Her eyes betrayed her torment. She cared. She wanted peace. Not tainted by fear or vengeance. She might prove to be the only other person in the Realm who dared hope for peace.

He couldn't speak. Her eyes misted over, and then something

inside him gave way. As though a bulwark had shattered, the flood of self-reliance and constant striving to prove himself worthy of acceptance dissipated into oblivion, released, gone. He needed her on the deepest level, now more than ever before.

He reached out and brushed a lock of hair from her tear-filled eyes. "I need your help, Tess." He barely whispered the words.

Her eyes searched his. "I'll do anything. I'll always help you, Colt. What do you need?"

Bound to his oath of secrecy, he'd need to walk a razor's edge. "Something happened on the airship. When I told Gerhert he'd been thwarted, that it was over, he gloated that all this was only the beginning."

Her eyes grew wide.

"I don't know what he meant, but it scared me, and there was something else." How could he explain this without breaking his oath? "A man on board the airship, the one who cut my rope, he spoke to me in a foreign tongue. I mean completely foreign. Then he spoke in Realmish, but with an accent I've never heard before. I need to know what language he spoke. I need to know from where he hailed. It's critical to all this, I can feel it, but I don't have time to figure it out, and with my responsibilities, I don't have the means."

She reached again for the lock of hair hanging at the nape of her slender neck and began winding it with her index finger. Was she already working the problem? "Can you describe what it sounded like? What exactly did he say?"

"Two stones ours, let's see how you like the dark." Colt mimicked the guttural accent as he quoted the dying foreigner. Then he repeated what he remembered of the strange foreign words. "That's what he said, and that's pretty much what he sounded like."

Two fingers now twisted the lock of hair fallen loose from her braid. "I have unlimited access to the royal library. What if there's a people group that we don't know of? What if there's some account in the history annals? I could check those. They go back generations." Hope seeped into her tone as she worked through her plan to tackle his request. Her face lit up, glowing in the light of early dawn, all because he'd given her the opportunity to serve her people, to help him. "Two stones ours? He must have been talking about the Sapphire Star! Do you think they have Reyjik's Diamond Star? Is that the second stone he was referring to? Does that account for the recent rise in crime? What kind of darkness? Literal darkness or some sort of moral darkness? Was he talking about the stones' power to restrain evil? Is that why everyone seems so blinded by fear?"

Tess voiced every question that had echoed through his own thoughts over the last three days. He could drown in the depth of the connection he felt to her. His heart ached, and for a moment, he forgot himself. "Are you sure you'll have time to conduct this research… with the wedding?"

Her face fell, and she lowered her gaze. "I'll make time, Commander."

He'd crossed over into forbidden territory with his question, but still he pushed forward. "The betrothal, is it binding? I mean, you said you were down in Costair investigating Durbink's character, that your sister could refuse. Do you have any say?" His heart raced. *What are you doing, Hawthorne?*

She stared at her hands and bit her lip. "I can invoke a veto through Sacramance, but my father is desperate for the alliance."

His chest felt tight, but he had to know. "Is it what you want, Tess?"

She let out a small laugh and gazed out to the sea. "I'm a princess, Commander, and the last in line. I almost never get what I want." And then she turned to face him. "Save for one glorious week, when I got to pretend I was a King's Bowman and climb cliffs and fly with raiders… and help you. I'll always help you, no matter what, Colt, always."

He needed to tell her he needed her and that he couldn't imagine leaving on mission without her at his side, that he doubted his ingenuity and resolve in her absence, but he stood frozen, their eyes locked. Blast he wanted to kiss her.

A dark shadow fell over them, and a violent sound of wind filled his ears. Whirling around, he drew his dress sword and found himself staring into the emerald eyes of a tarragon, his tarragon, *Wingblade*. Something like battle rush flooded through him, and he held his breath, frozen.

Tess grasped his hand and gently pushed his sword to his side. "Berkley!"

He replaced the rapier to its scabbard, never taking his eyes off the skittish creature.

Tess slipped past him, without hesitation, and knelt beside the crouching dragon that dwarfed her. She stroked his head and inspected his wing.

Colt squatted at Wingblade's other side. The dragon breathed hard. Its breath was warm, and its familiar smell flooded his senses. Memories of years of spring and fall migrations flashed before him. Wingblade pushed his head into Colt's armpit and nuzzled him, then, shoving him backwards onto his backside, he rested his heavy head on his lap. He laughed. He hadn't seen his friend in over a year, and yet the dragon acted as if time had stood still. He risked a look at Tess.

Smiling from ear to ear, she watched the two of them together. Edging closer, she knelt in front of him and the animal that rested peacefully. When she stroked Wingblade's slick cheek and neck, he cooed with pleasure, and they both laughed. Colt's heart ached.

"There you are!" Deacon's voice, loud and slurred—clearly still not recovered from the night before—reverberated off the tunnel ceiling. Seconds later, he and Shifty stumbled out the narrow door.

"Ahh! Sweet eve of descent!" Deacon shrieked as he surveyed Colt and Tess sitting on the limestone with a tarragon. Wingblade startled, and Tess stroked his head. Shifty stayed in the doorway, eyes wide, as Deacon edged a step closer to the nervous dragon.

"Think before you tell me that's Wingblade, Colt. Remember we agreed you'd owe me a bottle of brandy if you ever ran into him again."

Colt repressed the smile that threatened to breach his lips. "Of course, it's not Wingblade. This is Berkley."

The tarragon leapt to the cannon, spread its wings, and dropped off the wall and out of sight. Tess gazed longingly after the creature, sadness in her eyes.

Deacon sighed and then opened his arms wide, "Samson, my best best buddy!" He ran to the cannon and flung himself across it, wrapping his arms and legs around it. Everyone laughed.

Tess's hands darted to her face, and she covered her eyes.

"You want one too, Princess?" Deacon spread his arms wide.

She jumped to her feet and then backed towards the door, a smile on her face.

Deacon immediately took up the challenge. He stumbled off the cannon in a vain attempt to chase her, but the momentum brought him to his knees, laughing.

She was through the door and down the stairs before he could pick himself up off the stone roof.

Colt sighed in defeat. Their moment was over.

The three men descended the stairs. Deacon and Shifty were singing, apparently enjoying how their voices sounded in the narrow tunnel. They headed for Deacon's second interceptor, the *Bonnie Lass,* which waited at the docks below. When they arrived at the slip, Aratess waited for them.

She hugged Shifty tight. Then she made the sign of descent, warning off Deacon, but he grabbed her and pulled her in close. She let him hold her, wrapping her arms around his neck and resting her head on his shoulder. Deacon whispered into her ear for what felt like an eternity, and Colt's stomach clenched in progressively tighter waves of envy until the pirate prince released her.

Then it was his turn. Reality crashed down on him. He needed her. It wasn't a matter of wanting, and sacrificing his desire in the name of honor wasn't an option anymore, he needed her help, desperately. Admitting it to himself cleaved his heart in two, but denial didn't do him any good. He had never allowed himself to need anyone or anything, not even his truth stone, but there was no point trying to bury it or ignore it any longer.

"Tess, can I ask you to do something else for me?" He gently touched her arm, leading her a few steps from the other men. "Could you send my medal and this letter to my mother?" He unpinned his emerald star and held it out. She took it and, as she had when he was wearing it, ran a finger over the emerald set in the middle of the solid d'orite star.

He pulled the letter he'd written to his mother from his pocket and set it on her palm along with the medal. "There are important instructions in there. I mean, please don't read it, it's private I guess, but it's really important to me that she gets it."

She closed her fingers around both and pressed them to her chest. "Of course. How long do I have to find your answers? When will you be back, a few days, a week? I won't leave the library until I find what you need, I promise. If I come up short, I have another plan. I can access Costair's royal library through Sasha and Durbink. That might take longer, but I won't do anything else until I have a solid answer, I promise. A week should be long enough. Will you be back sooner than that?"

Nausea swept through him. She had no idea he was leaving for Reyjik that very minute, and he wasn't allowed to tell her. Her eyes were wide and innocent, trusting. He couldn't speak. He fought back tears.

"I will find your answer, Commander. Whoever that man was, his language, his tierality. I won't stop searching until I find an answer." The emerald in her hand flashed again.

If he opened his mouth, he would tell her everything. He needed a way out. And then it struck him. He stepped back, reached out, and slowly offered her his hand.

The sweetest look washed across her beautiful face. She took his hand, and without shifting her gaze from his, slowly slid her palm forward up his palm. Her skin was smooth and cool, yet warmth pulsed up his arm. He gripped her wrist gently, and she acted in kind. The Bowman's handshake. He tightened his grip ever so slightly, and her eyes misted again. *Go, Hawthorne, now!*

Colt's heart broke as he forced himself to let her go and board the *Bonnie Lass*. The look on her face, the connection they shared, it was real. More real than anything else, and his feet and heart were heavy as he walked away from her. He picked his way to the stern of the interceptor.

Deacon stood slightly swaying and holding onto the railing for support. "A handshake, eh? You went with a handshake?"

"It was a Bowman's handshake, Deac. She understood its meaning." Colt tried to sound casual.

"Did she understand your meaning when you kissed her?"

He could only look away.

"So, either you aren't going to tell me because you are a gentleman, or you didn't work up the nerve." Deacon crossed both arms and sighed.

He shook his head. "No kiss, Deac." He couldn't look his friend in the eye.

"Right. Well, at least tell me what she did when you told her you needed her. At least give me that." Deacon grabbed Colt's shoulders and shook him.

"I couldn't tell her that." Helplessness dripped from his words.

"Blast, Colt, why not? Why on earth can't you tell her how you feel?" Deacon threw his arms out to the sides.

"Because she's not free. She's betrothed, for Realm's sake. It's not fair to tell her how I feel if I can't follow through. It's not honorable."

Deacon's face went white before deepening to red. "Lindsor. A Lindsite wretch gets to have that… We could kill him."

Colt wasn't happy, but he couldn't help but laugh. He couldn't blame Deacon for his reaction. He had to face the reality that, in his own way, Deacon cared for Tess, more than any girl before.

"Seriously, Colt. I've never killed a man in cold blood, but for her, I'm certain I could work myself up to the task… especially seein' as he's a Lindsite." Deacon's smirk didn't mask his pain.

Colt patted him on the back. "I'm pretty sure it's called an assassination when you kill a royal."

Deacon rubbed his palms against the railing. "You said she feeds that same blasted tarragon, your tarragon. You both have been feeding that thing during migration all these years?"

He nodded.

"What are the chances of that, Colt?"

Colt shook his head. His mind spinning and his heart splintering, he didn't feel like talking.

"You should know I asked her to run away with me last night, and I made it a standing offer just now." Deacon blurted out the confession.

What? Colt's blood ran cold.

Releasing the railing, Deacon stretched both arms above his head.

"Oh yeah, she loves the sea. I've never seen a girl so comfortable on board a ship. She absolutely loves it and the crew, and they love her. I swear I could make her happy! I told you I was givin' it my best shot, Colt. And seein' as you won't, there's nothing holding me back, is there?"

All the warmth drained from Colt's face.

Deacon punched him lightly in the upper arm. "Don't worry, she didn't accept, said she couldn't take me from my duty to the navy now that I've been pardoned. I told her I didn't give a rip about all that, but she said Ardenia needed me and *The Girl* now more than ever."

Colt stared at the dock. "Sounds like her." He forced the acknowledgment past his dry lips.

Tess still stood on the slip, the wind rippling through her hair.

His heart ached. He raised his hand, and she did the same.

Then he lifted his gaze to the emerald star, glistening in the sun's first rays. He thought of Costair. No star greeted their sunrise, their cliffs lay dark. And Reyjik, when the sun was past peak in a few hours, would their fair diamond greet its light, or had it also been taken? Would the Vertical Horizon weather this loss, or would generations of peace crumble?

In that moment, Colt made a vow. Peace and truth would be restored for her, or he would die trying.

Chapter Thirty-Eight

The Note

Tess

TESS STRETCHED ON TIPTOES, HER RIGHT index finger just reaching the book. She closed her eyes. The deerskin binding, dry and rough, scratched against her callous. She pushed her fingernail under the edge of the book's spine, then pulled it towards herself ever so slowly. Her arm ached, not yet recovered from the battle. Every muscle in her back tensed as she slid the book to the edge of the shelf. How had anyone ever managed to store this book here in the first place? The library ladder didn't access this shelf, and she couldn't imagine any self-respecting librarian climbing the adjacent shelves the way she had.

The book teetered at the edge, and Tess lost her foothold. It plunged to the floor as she grasped the edge of the shelf, her fingers gripping the smooth oak with all their strength. Regaining her footing with her right toe, she shifted back to a safe position. She breathed a sigh a relief, only to cough uncontrollably, a reaction to the dust. Picking her way back down the shelving, she set the book atop the hundred other books piled haphazardly on the floor of the royal library. She was exhausted. Tears streamed down her cheeks like rivers. They cut through the dust of the countless decades, maybe even centuries, preserved on the books she'd searched that day, now caked to her dirty face.

Where was Colt? Why hadn't he returned to Fairgates yet? Two days, she thought, a week a most, to find the answers he needed, so she'd searched twelve hours a day for a fortnight. No answers. No Bowman. Why?

She wiped the tears with the back of her hand, the gray smear on her wrist a clue to how her face must look, smudged and filthy. No matter. Nothing mattered, only finding something, anything to explain the foreigner Colt had described. Tess picked up the strange journal and turned it over in her hand. She ran her finger along the spine, the faded outlines of gilded letters all that remained of its title. The blank front cover proved worn and soft, devoid of the dried glue that stiffened the binding. Prying the cover back, cracking the brittle glue as she did, she opened the book to the front page. *Personal notes, thoughts, and dreams of Emperor Dagnoon Sun.*

Dagnoon Sun! What? That was the emperor who reigned over Reyjik during tierdenation. The founder of Sacramance. *How do we have his memoir? Why would we have it?* She flipped to the first entry, Eve of Descent, exactly a hundred years prior. Her heart pounded as her eyes raced over the words. They were written in Reyjik, the most regal calligraphy she had ever seen. MaryLee had taught her to read and write Reyjik, and she'd never been so thankful for her nurse.

* * *

Tess's fingers trembled. She closed her eyes and concentrated to still them, but what she had learned in the journal seemed unreal. She squinted. Why was it so dark, the light so low? She glanced out the beautiful, stained-glass window. It must be well past-peak. How was that possible? How long had she been reading?

Blood thundered in her ears as she considered the profit of the last hours spent in study of the worn, unassuming deerskin journal. She'd done it. She had an answer. She had Colt's answer. Where was he? Why hadn't he returned? What could be more important than this?

A loud creak, stiff hinges broke the eerie silence of the library. Tess sprang to her feet. *Please don't be Jestin, not again!* Frantically, she rubbed her face on her sleeve. Could she slip out the back? She edged silently towards the servant's entrance.

"Your Highness?" A timid voice greeted her. Stepping into the waning light of the window, Sam stood at attention.

"Sam!" Tess skipped forward and threw her arms around the king's courier in his official uniform. "I'm so glad to see you. Have you come to practice? Are you finished for the day? Where's your bow?" She couldn't disclose her findings to her friend, but relief swept over her just the same.

Sam stepped back and regarded her carefully.

"What?"

He reached into his pocket and produced a neatly folded white handkerchief, bowing low as he presented it.

Tess laughed, took the small cloth, and slipped to the looking glass mounted against the north wall. She did look a mess.

"I don't have my bow because I'm on official business, Your Highness. A dispatch came in for you via carrier pigeon, and I thought you'd want it straight away."

Her breathing grew shallow. Carrier pigeons were only used by the corps, so this was a Bowman message. In the looking glass, she saw Sam search his breast pocket with his thumb and index finger and then slowly produce a curled slip of paper, no bigger than a confection's wrapper. He held it out to her.

She returned the hanky to him, unable to still her trembling fingers as she took the small scrap of paper. Her eyes locked with Sam's and he nodded. She swallowed and then lowered her gaze to the paper. *Princess Aratess* was written under the small wax seal. Colt's handwriting.

Sam cleared his throat and stepped forward. "The Commander gave me this for you as well, Your Highness. Before he left, he asked me to make sure you got it when his message arrived."

Tess's eyes dropped to the cotton pouch Sam held out. Thin cotton cords cinched the drawstring closure tight. Grasping it in her weak fingers, she shoved it under the waistband of her skirt.

Instinctively, she backed away. She needed to get higher, to the roof, though she couldn't explain why. "Thank you, Sam. We'll practice your shooting tomorrow after your shift as usual." She forced the words past trembling lips.

Taking the stairs to the roof two at a time, she burst into the ashen sky. The soft soles of her boots padded over the stone roof. She looked skyward. The clouds boasted no color at all, only gray. Leaning against Samson, she took a deep breath, and after adjusting the cotton pouch under her waistband, slowly unrolled the tightly curled note. The script, so small she needed to squint, was definitely written in Colt's handwriting.

Dearest Tess,

I'm not returning to Fairgates. I knew as much when we parted, and I'm sorry. I can't disclose where I am, or what I'm doing, but if you have successfully managed what we discussed (and knowing you, you have) it proves most critical to my present mission, and I don't have means or opportunity to manage it myself. Sorry for the limited space, but you'll need to summarize the information as concisely as possible. I sent this care of Sam, and he'll know how to get your reply to me.

Tess, there is so much I want to tell you but can't. I hate to admit that I wish you were here. Please know this, you have the heart of a Bowman.

Always, Colt

The paper shook in her hand. What? Why? Why would he…? Her hand flew to her belt, and she fumbled furiously with the cotton pouch and the tight drawstring. Blasted Bowman knots! Finally, she loosened the closure and pulled open the bag. Reaching in, her fingertips touched deerskin. A wave of emotion crashed against her heart and threatened to wash it away as she tugged free the object Colt had left for her.

In her hand, she held an original Bowman quiver strap.

Acknowledgements

I need to begin at the beginning. I am so thankful to the Lord for the gift of His only Son. His sacrifice and salvation will always be the greatest story and proves the ultimate inspiration.

Matty, thank you for your tireless support and encouragement—you have gone so far above and beyond the call of duty. Sara Davison, thank you for your continual mentorship, friendship, and editing brilliance. We both know I wouldn't have survived without it. Thanks to my mom and dad and Shondra Peters for listening when it was raw and unrefined and telling me how wonderful it was despite the fact. And to Heather, Rachel, and Ali for reading it with a smile under the same circumstances and giving praise just the same.

I am so grateful to the team at Mountain Brook Fire. Miralee Ferrell and Tim Pietz have made this journey a true joy, sharing their expertise with kindness.

I need to thank Amy Williams for her excellent feedback and story coaching; it made all the difference. Chelsea Turan, thanks for holding my hand as I jumped off the social media mountain. Your time and help were indispensable. Lincoln Koller, I couldn't ask for a better military advisor. Thanks for all the walks and talks about weaponry and strategy. I am so grateful to Abeer Al Hariri for creating such a captivating cover image, and to Lynnette Bonner for formatting the cover so beautifully to match.

If you enjoy *Heart of a Bowman*, please leave a review on Goodreads and Amazon—it makes all the difference. Their story is far from over. It gets much worse before there's a chance it can get better. Please watch for *Heart of a Spy,* and *Heart of a Warrior,* releasing in the months to come.

For updates, sneak peeks, and the inside scoop, visit my website, jilkoller.com, and subscribe to my newsletter. You can also follow me on Instagram @jil.koller or find me on Facebook, Tik Tok, or YouTube.